...SAVES NINE

LES LYNAM

ISBN-13: 978-1506111452

ISBN-10: 1506111459

Dedication:
To My Parents, Louis & Ruth
Who never got to see this side of me.
Sorry I didn't write sooner.

Acknowledgments:
Special thanks again to my Alpha Team:
My wife, Susan; my sister, Ramona; my niece, Kari.

Also to my Beta-readers for their comments:
Candi T., Mollie D., Preston F., Sarah T.

Above & Beyond award goes to:
H.S. Buddy, Bryan J. for all the technical edit assists.

Thanks to a Stranger Award: Jerry D.
Whose comments as someone not already friend or family were a great help.

Table of Contents

Prologue

"TERMINATE recording," I order, and then silently stare at the screen. "Computer: assemble best message from all four samples given. Search for clarity in sound as well as esthetically pleasing video. Compress space between words, refine opening and closing consonants, and morph any spliced video into smooth transitions."

I never am comfortable viewing myself, but I must review the content. "Computer: play completed message."

My first reaction to the face on the screen is to notice the flaws. My eyebrows are sparse, allowing my pale skin to show through the too few black hairs. I do not like the shape of my ears. They are, however, optimally functional in detecting sound and particularly well-suited for echo-location. My mouth is too small; my lips are too thin...

The sound of my voice jars me from my pointless emotional criticisms of my appearance.

My name is LX. Full designation: KLE1752-NI28-949-LX. I am a novice-level Chrono-Historian from the year 2217. My mission designation is: NA.20.MW.00042183-FM. Initial study in the year 1995 partially completed. I am about to embark on a tangential mission to the year 1969. This message is created as a fail-safe for accidental temporal corruption. Since you have received this message, assume a worst-case scenario, and intervene before September 22, 1995 in Grover's Corners, Missouri.

Probable cause of contamination: my break from standard protocol. I have revealed my true identity to my paternally linked ancestor of this era, though his knowledge of me as a time-traveler is normally hidden within his own brain. Nanites prevent his access to certain memories stored unless I unlock them with a key-code. I do not believe this particular deviation to be a risk for any contamination. He is aware of my origin only when under my direct supervision.

It was initially this ancestor's proposal to accompany me to the year 1969; the year when his father is age sixteen. Sean Kelly, his father Jonathan

1

Kelly, and I will each be the same age at that convergence. At this juncture, there is no plan to allow the senior Kelly to have any knowledge of who we are. The suggestion from Sean Kelly supposes an interesting temporal study of the interaction of a father and son at the same level of maturity. Only the son is to be aware of the relationship; thus, the object of this study. I have determined that the potential value of observations made during the study merit the violation of protocol. This message has been secured into place to rectify that decision if I prove to be in error.

I have equipped Sean Kelly with some basic tools needed to pose as a native of the target time-period. He has a rudimentary knowledge of historical facts pertinent to the decade as well as an enhanced memory of the period's popular music. We will impersonate musicians of an international origin, and that impersonation will also be used to cover any knowledge gap that Sean Kelly may demonstrate.

Assemblage of period clothing and hair extensions for Sean Kelly was necessary for physical blending since he does not have access to a pseudo-body suit.

Point of 1995 departure is from a local entertainment center known in this century as a movie theater. Sean Kelly believes he is participating in a social engagement with Nicole Townsend known as a date. Nicole Townsend is one of the impersonations I use when covertly studying Sean Kelly. Two other personae used are a twin sister, Alexis Townsend, and a maternal-figure guardian, Katherine Tuttle. I have had multiple encounters with Sean Kelly in each of these pseudo-forms.

At the completion of the tangential study, we will return to 1995 where I will continue my observations for approximately eight more months. The measure of a successful mission in 1969 is that no one ever views this message as I will erase it upon my return.

I again stare at the now blank screen. Reviewing the message did nothing to sway the internal war between my intellect and emotions. The pure scientist in me screams at the folly of this venture. My emotional side, which has recently expanded from near nothingness, urges me to continue. Immersion into this culture has required emotional interaction, and the few months I have already spent in the 20th Century have altered me to the point that I am no longer certain of who I truly am.

The cloaked S.T.E. hovers above a beverage dispensing enterprise known as *Starbucks*. I traveled 20 years into the future from 1995 to find a more ubiquitous access to networked computing. This general era is when users begin to entrust the placement of nearly all of their data in random servers they call 'the cloud'. Security for cloud-computing is still in its infancy, making it simple to manipulate with 23rd Century technology. The year 2015 is also the first year that Chrono-Historians begin real-time data collection of any and all changes to the Internet

My computer has encrypted my message by interlacing it with a video file that displays humorous actions of *Felis Catus*. Several exabytes of data are dedicated to this subject matter by 2015; most stored on a service known as *Youtube*. The computer has devised an algorithm that will, for twenty-four hours, route my file through every server that exists on Earth. If I have not intercepted it within that time-frame, the file will be posted to *Youtube* using a login commandeered from one of the current patrons of *Starbucks*. Any 21st Century viewer will only be able to view the antics of the *Felis Catus*. When the file is transferred to the future for data analysis by Chrono-Historian computers, my message will become decrypted.

I pause a few moments as my logical side again urges me to abort this folly, but I cannot. I am fully intrigued by Sean Kelly's proposal, but more than that, I desire to experience his reactions to being displaced into an era that is not his own. He sees things differently than I do. I observe, but he becomes involved in interactions with others.

I issue the command to transfer the file.

Relief? It seems to be a sensation of relief once the action is completed. Though I still harbor doubts about taking Sean Kelly to 1969, they no longer gnaw at me. The decision is made. I will continue with the preparations already in place. Now I am anxious to return to 1995. Pleased to again assume the guise of Alexis Townsend to attend Spanish Class with Sean Kelly.

Excited? Perhaps even excited to complete the day at school and join my ancestor in the guise of Nicole Townsend for one more pleasant evening before removing her from his life as he requested.

It will be an adventure.

Chapter One

"Powdered, flowered, and confettied / Bangled, tangled, spangled, and spaghettied"

September 22, 1995, Grover's Corners, Missouri

ALEX reviewed the list displayed on the front panel of the S.T.E. for a third time. For some reason it calmed him to be able to inspect the list visually, even though he'd already checked it with a direct link to the computer each time that he'd accomplished a task. The thought of Sean accompanying him to 1969 was both exciting and terrifying. He had just placed the tie-dyed T-shirts, patched jeans, underwear, and socks inside one of the backpacks and secured them into a storage area under the ship's seats where he had already placed the box containing Sean's hair extensions that had grown overnight.

In the two hours between Alexis' Spanish class and Nicole's Algebra class, he had made a (barely) subsonic trip to Kansas City where he'd purchased what he hoped was an appropriate jacket at a military surplus store, as well as the two backpacks. The sheer number of course corrections made by the collision avoidance system during the short flight amazed him. Birds. So many birds and so many kinds... and so few had survived the end of the 21st Century.

He touched the fifth item on his list to again review his own 60's guise. A doll-sized 3D replica of his design rotated just in front of the forward panel. The computer displayed dozens of 2D pictures from that era on the panel and drew dashed lines from elements in the pictures to similar features on the 3D model. The computer had validated the finished design with a 99% assurance that it would perfectly blend into 1969.

The most time-consuming task of the day had been spent on the logistics needed to segue the 'date' with Sean efficiently to the other 'date' with XL-memory Sean; smoothly transitioning from Sean & Nicole at the theater to Sean & Alex headed to 1969 in the S.T.E.

The computer had crunched through hundreds of potential scenarios with thousands of branch variations. Alex reluctantly accepted the computer's recommendation and had moved his space/time vehicle to a vacant lot located just under 500 meters from the movie theater.

The lot was strewn with rusty discarded metal, broken bottles, and other refuse; tall weeds grew in abundance. The computer had projected only a .04% chance that someone would walk onto that lot between the hours of five and ten pm that Friday, and in that unlikely event, there was only a one in 360 billion chance they would also detect the cloaked S.T.E.

Alex conceded that it was a good place to put the all-but-invisible vehicle. The lot had acceptable proximity to the theater and was unlikely to be visited by anyone. Still, it made him nervous to leave it there, even with odds of discovery greater than being struck twice by lightening. He'd been just as anxious the first few times that he had parked behind the bushes near the school, but eventually assured himself that not even the military in the 20th Century knew how to detect a cloaked vessel. In the worst case scenario, he had the option to allow the computer to stun anyone within 25 feet of the S.T.E. Even with all those assurances, he would only feel completely secure again when he and Sean were safely inside the craft and headed for the past.

Alex decided to use the Katherine Tuttle guise to get from the theater back to his home, a distance of about 4 kilometers. He timed the walk from the vacant lot to the theater at just under ten minutes, locating someone in the theater willing to phone a taxi for him took another five. It took longer than he anticipated for the cab to arrive at the theater.

Reflecting on his new experience of driving an internal combustion vehicle, he'd given some thought to purchasing one for "Aunt Katherine." The idea seemed even more relevant as he waited impatiently for the taxi to arrive. As a distraction while waiting, he queried the word origin of "taxi" and found the word came into common usage shortly after the turn of the 20th century, evolving from the taximeter, a 19th Century German invention used to measure the distance a vehicle traveled. The term "Cab" was a much older word, shortened from the French *cabriolet*, a horse-drawn conveyance.

Before he could query when those words fell into disuse, a man yelled from a vehicle that had pulled to the curb in front of him. "Hey, Lady," the driver said, "Did you call a cab?"

Katherine got into the vehicle and was soon deposited at her driveway. She was certain the driver was employing sarcasm when he said "thanks, big spender" and drove off. There was no doubt in her mind that she fully understood all of the denominations of the cash and coins of this era, but to double check, she confirmed it with the computer. There was no mistake; she had given the driver the exact amount he had requested. His surly reaction was a mystery, but she decided that perhaps he had just been having an unpleasant day.

* * *

A few blocks away, Sean ran the comb through his short hair for a fifth time. He checked his teeth again in the bathroom mirror. He studied his reflection from as many angles as he could, looking for any zits that had popped up since the last time he'd checked only moments before. He was determined to be on time... which meant he had showered, shaved the few chin hairs he had, and scraped away the peach fuzz from the rest of his face much earlier than he would have if he were merely going to hang with the guys.

It made him feel restless to have time on his hands rather than making his usual mad dash to avoid being late. Both of the Townsend twins struck him as extremely punctual, so he was determined to make a good impression on Nicole by knocking on her door at exactly five minutes before the time they'd agreed he would pick her up.

He was also more than a little nervous about the date itself. He had hoped that it would be a major step toward a closer relationship with Nicole, but their little meeting after school the day before ended with Sean walking away in a huff. He regretted how easily his temper flared. He shouldn't have allowed himself to imagine that when Nicole had asked to meet him after school that it would be anything romantic. It was likely that his anticipation was the very spark that ignited his anger when the imagined tryst had turned out to be anything but romantic. Although she hadn't *said* the exact phrase, as they parted, he felt like she was heading toward the 'let's just be friends' speech. He berated himself for hoping for a first kiss, and then reacting badly when she'd said that she 'appreciated his friendship'.

Refusing to be daunted by Thursday's bad ending, he'd been determined to make Friday a fresh start. Nicole had been friendly enough between classes, and he'd even tried to flirt with her a little on the way back from History. Still, she seemed either to miss his intent or flat out ignored it, choosing to ramble on about the boring stuff from Mr. Douglas' lecture.

At lunch, she'd made a point of asking Kevin and Raj to sit with them, and then had barely joined into any conversations... not that joining in was particularly easy when Kevin and Raj started rambling. True to form for a Friday lunch, Kevin had dominated most of the conversation as he psyched himself up for the impending football game. Sean was relieved that it was an away game so that Kevin wouldn't expect him to be there.

Nicole had seemed content simply to listen to whatever either of the guys had to say. She'd munched on her standard lunch of plain lettuce drizzled with Aunt Katherine's 'special' protein dressing but had deviated from normal by drinking a Diet Pepsi rather than water. Sean still found it beyond strange that she'd spent most of her life without even touching a soft drink.

He checked the mirror yet again, then inspected his clothes-- khakis, a light blue dress shirt, and he'd even put on his *Doc Martens* instead of his normal *Nikes*. He wondered if Nicole was also primping in front of a mirror and smiled as he thought about what she might wear. She'd worn so many great outfits to school; he hoped she had something especially hot tucked away for an evening out. He checked his watch again to find it had only moved one minute since the last time he'd checked. Only five more minutes before he would head to the car.

Dismissing the cab driver's odd reaction, Katherine entered her house. She noted that it was ten minutes before Sean had said he would be there, but based on his morning arrivals to class; she assumed she had anywhere from twelve to fifteen minutes before he would arrive at her door. Touching the controls on her neck, she shifted to Nicole's form, clad in the same clothes selected earlier for the school day.

She went into the hall bathroom to look into the mirror as she changed to the green outfit that Sean liked so well. She smiled as she added the dangling green earrings, then remembered the promise made to Sean about attempting to look less attractive. Her smile vanished as she changed to the blue jeans and blue cambric shirt worn the day the R.E.M. song had so unexpectedly tossed her into a sea of foreign emotions.

She was just beginning to experiment with different subtleties of makeup when the doorbell sounded. "House, project front door here," Nicole said calmly. The mirror became a view screen and revealed that Sean was standing at the door. "Interesting," she said softly to the screen. "He is five minutes early. It is very difficult to predict his actions when it comes to punctuality." She addressed the house again, "House, secure premises three minutes after I have stepped out of the front door. Close projection." The view screen returned to her reflection. She pulled her hair back and held it in a ponytail, crinkled her nose at the image, then shook her hair out and left it loose. She scooped up a small pink clutch purse and headed to the door.

"Hello, Sean Kelly," she said smiling warmly. "You are early."

He glanced down, taking in her blue jeans and white tennis shoes. "Ummm," he started carefully, unsure whether to continue, "Do you need some more time to get ready?"

"No," she answered brightly, "I am ready to depart."

A midnight blue Dodge Avenger convertible sat in the driveway. Nicole pointed to it. "That is not your vehicle."

"No, it's Kevin's," Sean explained. "He won't be back from the away football game until after ten. It's a two-hour bus ride back. The show should be out before then, so I thought it'd be nice to take you out in a decent car."

"There is nothing wrong with your car."

"Yeah, but this one's way cooler. I thought it'd be nicer."

"As you wish. Which film are we going to view?"

"One just came out new, today. It's called *Hackers*. I think it's about a couple of teenagers that get in trouble for hacking into Government computers. It sounded like it might be fun."

Nicole quickly checked with her computer to confirm that it was a film available to download. She mentally signaled the computer to prepare it. "Yes, that might be interesting." She assessed what Sean was wearing. "You are dressed differently than I have seen before."

"What this?" he said. "No. Just something in the closet. I felt like dressing a little different, just to get your attention."

"I had imagined that you would dress more comfortably. Are you disappointed with what I selected to wear?"

"No," Sean lied, "You always look great. And the movies are always cold, so it's probably a good idea to wear jeans." He crooked his elbow toward her. "Shall we go?" She put a hand on his arm as he guided her to the car.

Sean stepped ahead of her as they neared the car and opened the door for her. She thanked him, and he went around and got in behind the wheel. He backed out onto the street and started the short drive to the theater.

"I suppose we should have talked about this ahead of time, but... have you eaten?"

"Yes," she replied, "Did you?"

"Yeah... well, some anyway. I really wasn't that hungry. Besides, I figured we'd get popcorn and a drink. Umm, do you eat popcorn?"

"Sometimes," she said and then immediately glanced away to query nutritional information about popcorn and found it was a starchy carbohydrate. She then checked a link to movie-house popcorn. "I do not like to add salt or the artificially flavored hydrogenated oil."

"Oh... I thought maybe we could share a large popcorn, but if you don't like it salted and buttered, maybe I should just get us two separate bags."

"There is no need. I am not hungry."

"Or if you'd rather, you could get candy... but I guess you probably don't eat candy."

"Sean, it is not necessary to purchase food. We are going to view a film."

"Yeah, but... I thought everyone munched on something at the movies." He tried to picture the concession stand in his mind and mentally searched for anything that could be remotely considered health-food. The best he could come up with was chocolate covered raisins. "Well, if you see anything you like when we get there, just let me know."

When they'd driven a block with neither of them speaking, Sean slid a CD into the player. He'd brought the *Ben Folds Five* CD, thinking she might like to hear it again. Nervously tongue-tied, he wanted something to cover the silence for the few minutes that it took to get to their destination.

When he'd parked the car, and they were walking across the parking lot to the theater, he still hadn't thought of any good topics for conversation. "If there's another movie you'd rather go to, that's fine. I'm not locked in on *Hackers*," Sean said, forcing *something* out.

"No, I am sure I will enjoy your selection," Nicole replied.

"OK." They were only halfway to the door, and it seemed like miles as he struggled for something clever to say.

9

"Do you frequently attend movies?" Nicole asked.

Thank you! "It depends," Sean replied. "Like sometimes a bunch of us guys will go see an action flick, or something scary like the new *Halloween* flick that's coming out in a couple of weeks. Lots of times, though, we just get a tape from Blockbuster and a bunch of guys'll watch it at someone's home. That's most popular when it's at Kevin's house since they have a big-screen TV."

The brief topic had been enough for them to make it to the ticket window, and there were fewer than ten people ahead of them, so the wait would be short. Nicole stared at the sign behind the girl selling tickets, puzzling over the words and numbers; then it clicked that it was a list of the different movies available and the times of day that the movie started. Satisfied, she switched her gaze to the sign against the glass in front of the girl. *Adults $5.00 Children $3.50.* She was unsure of which category teenagers fell, but assumed adult. A closer look confirmed, in small print below children it read, "Under 12". She opened her clutch purse and pulled out her collection of 20th Century bills. She found one that had fives in the corners and President Abraham Lincoln in the center. Sean glanced at her hand.

"Put that away," he said in a firm, but friendly tone. "I've got this. I asked you on a date; I'll pay for it."

"That is not necessary," Nicole protested gently as she fanned out her bills. "I have sufficient currency."

Sean's eyes widened when he saw several twenties and a fifty casually being waved around. He stepped closer to her, grabbed her wrist, and pushed the money back down into her purse.

"Don't be flashing a big wad of bills like that in public," he said gruffly. "Do you want to get mugged?"

Shocked, Nicole looked up at him and saw the concern in his eyes. She quickly checked the computer for "mugged" and was horrified. "Someone would physically harm me because they wanted to steal money?" she asked as if it were unthinkable.

"Are you kidding me? Nicole, just because this is a little Midwest town doesn't mean there's no crime here. You wouldn't wave money around like that in New York, would you?"

She decided from the tone in his voice that he had expected her to say 'no'. "No, of course not," she ad-libbed.

"Well, don't do it around here, either. How much do you have? I saw at least three twenties... never mind; it's none of my business."

"May I help you?" said a mechanically amplified voice.

Sean turned to face the ticket seller. "Two for *Hackers*, please."

"Ten dollars," the voice said flatly.

Sean slid a ten into a depression under the glass barrier. The girl tapped a few keys and held a hand expectantly above a slot. Two small squares of stiff paper popped out sequentially, and the girl pushed them under the glass back to Sean.

"Enjoy the show," she said expressionlessly. "Next."

Sean held the door for Nicole to enter and noticed that her gaze flitted around the room.

"I guess by the way you are looking around that you haven't been to a movie here before," he said. "Let me give you the grand tour."

She followed him to a noisy area jammed with video screens surrounded by groups of younger boys. Two of the boys were each furiously slapping at buttons in front of a video screen with one hand, and pushing a protruding baton in various directions with the other. Nicole watched the slapping and tugging until she saw there seemed to be a pattern. On the screen, there was a very crude large-pixel representation of what appeared to be two people hitting and kicking each other. Computer generated sound loudly attempted to simulate the noise of hand-to-hand combat.

"*Mortal Kombat*," Sean shouted loud enough to be heard above the cacophony of the various machines. "It's kinda popular right now, since the movie of the same name just came out. As you can see, this is the video arcade."

"It is a rather high-decibel area," she yelled back. "Prolonged exposure could contribute to a gradual loss of hearing."

They walked away from the arcade area, across the room and up to a stand staffed by three people in maroon uniforms. The smell of fresh popcorn wafted to meet them. "Concession stand," Sean said, waving an arm in a wide arc toward the counter. "If you see anything you want, just ask for it. I'm going to get a medium combo—popcorn and Coke. Do you at least want a Diet Pepsi?"

"Yes, that would be nice. Thank you," she said deciding Sean was adamant to purchase some form of food or beverage for her. After a short wait in line, Sean requested the popcorn and two drinks.

"Eight fifty," said the girl to Sean.

Nicole ran some quick calculations with her computer. "That is approximately 1000% markup over the cost of the materials," she said, astounded.

Sean smiled at her. "Yeah, outrageous, isn't it? But I don't think it's *that* much of a markup."

"It is," she insisted.

"Now you're a mathematician?" he joked as he handed her the Diet Pepsi. "I thought math was a little tricky for you."

She frowned slightly as they walked toward the young man standing by red velvet ropes that hung from portable brass poles. Sean handed him the tickets and waited as the man tore them in half and returned half to Sean.

"Theater Five, to the right. Enjoy the show," he said evenly with a practiced smile.

They walked down a short hall and turned to go through a large wooden double door. The door on the right had been propped open. Nicole glanced up at the large stylized rendition of the number five. Below it was a black panel composed of numerous bumps in a rectangular grid pattern. Many of the bumps glowed red, spelling out the word "Hackers". Sean led the way into the dimly lit auditorium.

"We'll have to put up with a lot of commercials, but at least we're early enough to get good seats. If it's OK with you, there's some in the middle about two-thirds of the way back," Sean suggested.

"I would prefer to sit in this last row," Nicole replied.

"OK," Sean agreed amiably, while happily speculating, *Maybe she wants to make out during the movie.*

They sat in the middle of the last row. Sean munched on his popcorn and attempted to make witty remarks about the ads blasting away at them.

"If you change your mind about the popcorn..." Sean said as he rattled the bag nearer to Nicole.

"Perhaps a bite," she said, assuming it was proper dating decorum to share popcorn. She gingerly put her hand into the bag and pulled out one fluffy piece and popped it into her mouth. The taste was intriguing, she decided, then signaled her computer to activate nanites in her gastrointestinal tract to capture any carcinogenic or otherwise harmful particles. With a smile, she reached back into the bag for more.

Sean smiled back at her, "See; you can't watch a movie without munching some popcorn."

The lighting dimmed a little more, and Sean checked his watch. "And now only about 15 more minutes before the movie starts." He commented on each of the trailers shown for the coming attractions giving most a whispered "that looks lame" and a few "I'd like to see that one" remarks while Nicole watched silently, nodding slightly to each of his criticisms. Finally, the fast paced clips ended and the screen announced, "And now our feature presentation." A United Artists film company logo displayed followed by "Seattle, 1988". Nicole leaned her mouth nearer to Sean's ear.

"This is the start of the film?" she asked softly. He nodded. "Mobo Gerga retrieve LX seventeen seven," she whispered.

Sean coughed out pieces of popcorn he'd just popped into his mouth. He scowled briefly at Nicole then smiled. "I knew it! I knew you'd decide to take me!" he said, not bothering to whisper.

Someone three rows in front of them turned around to face them. "Shhhhhhhh!"

On the screen, soldiers in dark uniforms were moving in slow motion toward a house.

"I mean, I'm thrilled to go on this wild ride to 1969, but couldn't we wait until the end of the movie?" Sean whispered, keeping one eye on the guy who'd shushed him.

"We need to use the cover of the film to exit, return, and reset your normal memory," Nicole whispered back.

"I paid ten bucks and I don't even get to see the movie?" Sean hissed.

"You will have the entire movie in your memory when we return," Nicole whispered then stood.

Sean followed her but kept his eyes on the movie. On the screen, the scene had shifted to a courtroom. The judge dropped his gavel. Nicole pushed out the exit door, and Sean reluctantly followed, still looking back at the screen. He spoke in a normal tone of voice once they were in the hallway.

"Did you hear that? That judge told that poor kid he couldn't own or use a computer until he was 18. Dude, that's bogus."

"That would be impossible to enforce in my time," Nicole replied as she moved toward the exit.

"Hey, what did you mean about me having the entire movie in my memory? Are you going to download it into my brain?"

"Yes."

"So you've got this whole movie on your computer, even though it just came out?"

"Yes. I have access to all 20th Century films, though only a few hundred currently stored on my computer."

"You know I could save a lot of money if you downloaded some of them to *my* computer."

"Although they are in the public domain in my century, I believe you are governed by laws that would make it a violation of copyright for you to have them."

"You know what you are?" Sean asked.

"A 'buzzkill'?" Nicole asked.

"You got that right, Andy."

"Andy?" Nicole questioned as they navigated through the lobby.

"Just popped into my head. Alex-in-drag. A. in D. Andy."

"I will drop the Nicole disguise when we reach the S.T.E.," she said, then added, "You will also need to change."

They pushed out through the front door. Nicole took the lead and turned to the right.

"Not going to take the car?"

"No. It is less than half a kilometer this way. The car will remain safely in the parking lot until we return."

"Wait," Sean said as he pulled beside her. "You've got Steffi stashed out here somewhere?"

"Yes. There is a deserted lot not far from here."

It took them about 10 minutes to get to the empty lot, where the nearest streetlight barely lit the edge.

"You will need to watch where you step, there is much debris scattered around," Nicole warned as she reached into her clutch purse and retrieved a tiny object. Suddenly an eight-foot circle of ground lit up as brightly as if it was in full sun. Sean looked at Nicole's hand, then back to the illuminated circle. There was no visible beam from her hand to the ground, the ground somehow was as if it were full daylight.

"That is awesome!" Sean enthused. "You have got to spend a day just showing me all the cool future toys you have."

"I am surprised you are intrigued by this. You have portable illumination devices. You call them flashlights."

"They are nowhere nearly as cool as that thing! Look at it! It's tiny! And you can't even see any glow in your hand. There's no beam. It just makes the ground light up."

"I believe the principle is the same. Or at least the application. The objective is to illuminate a dark area to make it safer to see where you are going."

"Right," Sean said with an eye roll. "Gee, Mr. Lindbergh, I don't see why you're so fascinated by this 747, it's pretty much the same thing as what you flew to Paris."

"Is that one of your movie or television quotes? I do not understand the reference."

"No, but in your spare time you might want to do a technical comparison of the *Spirit of St. Louis* to a Boeing 747."

They walked into the lot, following the moving circle of daylight until they reached the S.T.E.

"Wow, Steffi is *really* cloaked in the dark," said Sean. "At least I assume that's why you stopped."

"Yes, it is directly in front of you."

Sean reached out and felt the rigid shape of the time-machine, then set his Coke cup on the top of the cloaked vessel.

"Check it out! It's like the cup is just floating in the air. That is so cool!" he said, digging into his popcorn bag and putting a handful into his mouth. "Dude, this trip is going to be so awesome!"

Nicole opened the door to the S.T.E. and reached inside to retrieve the jeans and shirt from their stowed location and handed them to Sean.

"Why don't you change first," suggested Sean. "I feel weird dropping my pants in front of a girl. Even a fake girl."

Nicole activated the pseudo-body's controls and shifted to become the long-haired oddly dressed British fellow they were going to call Peter Lindsey.

"I wish I could change that fast," Sean said as he unbuckled his belt.

14

"You know, I'll bet that if you'd stayed as Nicole, the minute I had my pants off, Megan Walsh would somehow pop up out of nowhere to suggest we were going to get it on." He laid his khakis next to his Coke and slid into the jeans. "These seem comfortable enough," he said as he unbuttoned his shirt and tossed it on top of his khakis. "Put the light on this shirt." Alex held his hand close to the T-Shirt, and it lit up as if in full sun. "Holy smokes. Those colors are so bright I'm surprised it doesn't glow on its own." Sean flipped it around from front to back, looking at all of the various web of colors before pulling it on.

Alex reached into the S.T.E. and brought out a box roughly the size of a shoe box.

"I thought you said the Doc Martens were OK," Sean said, pointing to the box.

"These are not shoes; this is your hair."

"What do we have to do to attach it?"

"Bend down and stick your head into the box."

Sean stared into the dark box, then dubiously at Alex. "Light it up first," he demanded.

Alex pointed his illuminator at the box. A nest that perfectly matched the color of Sean's hair lay in the bottom of the box. Sean stuck a hand in and touched it. It felt like hair.

"OK, so I stick my head in there, and it magically hooks onto my own hair?"

"Yes. Only it is not magic."

"So right now it kind of looks dead. Is it going to come to life and latch onto my head like that thing in *Alien?*"

"As you come into contact with it, a set of nanites on each strand will locate a strand of your hair and connect to the end, forming a bond."

"Yeah, that kind of sounds like it's going to come to life and latch onto my head like that thing in *Alien.*"

"There will be some sensation of movement as it attaches, but you will not feel it 'latch onto your head'. It will not be painful," Alex assured.

"OK, here goes nothing," Sean said as he plunged the top of his head into the box, immediately jerking it back out. "That tickles!"

Several long strands fell across his nose, and he flailed both hands over his face, pushing them back. "Yerrrgh!" he groaned. "It feels like walking into spider webs."

"Only a few hundred attached. You will need to leave your head in longer than that," Alex explained.

Sean looked at him and wrinkled his nose. "Easy for you to say," said Sean. "You're not the one sticking his head in a spider's nest."

Alex held the box patiently. Sean looked at him and frowned. "This is the only way to do this?"

"Alternatively, I could sprinkle strands over your head. I believe that would take considerably longer."

Sean took a deep breath, showed his clenched teeth to Alex and plunged his head back into the box. "Aughhgghhh," he yelled as he held his head in the box for several seconds. When he lifted his head out, a long mop of hair flopped over his face. He swept it back with both hands. "Did that get it?" he asked.

Alex pointed his illuminator into the box revealing only a few remaining strands. He examined Sean to assess the full head of shoulder-length hair. "I assume it is difficult for all of them to find a place to attach." He stepped behind Sean to look at the back of his head. "It appears that you have enough."

Sean twirled his head from side to side, and his hair swung out looking like a chimney-sweep's bristle brush. He gathered it all up in his hands and pushed it all behind his ears.

"This feels so freakin weird," Sean complained. "And it's heavy."

He fisted a handful and pulled. "Ow! It's like it's my real hair. Pulling on it pulls on my roots." He took a comb from his khakis and started trying to manage his new long mop of hair, eventually deciding that parting it in the middle worked best to keep it out of his face. Alex tied a red bandana into a headband and slipped it over Sean's head.

"How about a mirror?" Sean asked.

"Slide into the S.T.E. and I will have it project your image on the forward navigation screen."

Following instructions, Sean stared at his projected image as if it was a mirror.

"At's a bit of all right, id nit, mate?" he said in his garbled accent.

"It should be an acceptable appearance for that era."

Sean slid out and indicated for Alex to get in. "Then let's hit it!" He reached to get his clothes and folded them behind the seat, and then grabbed his Coke and popcorn and slid in. He stuffed another handful of popcorn into his mouth. "Leh ooo thith!"

"I should point out that we will be traversing more than 25 years," Alex warned. "You have only experienced relatively short jumps; this will take longer."

"I'm cool," Sean said confidently and took a long sip of his Coke.

"I do not believe you should have popcorn in your mouth as we travel. Would you like a mint instead?"

"Nah, I'm good," Sean said as he rolled up this popcorn bag and chugged his Coke. "Let's go."

Alex opened the controls on the S.T.E. and manipulated the field of boxes and icons. "I have already input your father's DNA, which will be the beacon to bring us back into this dimension. You are certain you are mentally prepared for this?"

"You bet!" Sean said, bordering on arrogance. "Hit it!"

Alex initiated the final sequence, and the S.T.E. vanished from the vacant lot with a soft pop. Sean began to feel the sensations that his brain was trying to feed him and fought them back forcing himself to focus on the console in front of him. He felt quite proud of himself, deciding he had mastered the whole time-travel thing. He waited what seemed like several minutes for the journey to end, then began to feel anxious.

"Are we there yet?" he attempted to say, but it came out slowly, and he heard a dragged out deep base tone that sounded like, "Teeeeeey Reeeeht EEEEEW Raaa?"

Something wasn't right. He looked at Alex. Alex seemed calm enough, then he realized that Alex seemed frozen in place. *Something had DEFINITELY gone wrong!!!*

"Teeeeeey Reeeeht EEEEEW Raaa?" he drawled again, louder this time. Alex still hadn't moved. He waited, hoping for some reaction.

"Teeeeeey Reeeeht EEEEEW Raaa?" he drawled again in his sluggish base tone. Still no response from Alex. Sean forced himself to remain calm and wait a few more minutes, but his stomach churned.

"Teeeeeey Reeeeht EEEEEW Raaa?" he repeated, now sick of the sound that was some parody of his own voice.

"Teeeeeey Reeeeht EEEEEW Raaa?" Was he going to spend eternity like this? Lost in the middle of nowhere, Alex out of commission, himself unable to speak intelligibly?

"Teeeeeey Reeeeht EEEEEW Raaa?" It felt like it had been an hour since he first tried to ask.

"Teeeeeey Reeeeht EEEEEW Raaa?" He had to do something, maybe he could take the controls. He tried to move his hand toward the console and watched in horror as it drifted in slow motion.

Suddenly everything was back to normal. His hand stung as it slapped against the front control panel.

"Yes!" said an exasperated Alex. "We are here! Welcome to 1969."

Sean held his right hand over his mouth and banged on his side of the S.T.E. with his left fist. Alex looked briefly confused before he understood and opened the door.

Sean leaned out and violently spewed Coke and popcorn.

Standing less than ten feet away, three half-grown calves stared at him momentarily, then turned tail and ran bawling away, kicking up their heels, sending dirt flying high in the air.

"I believe you have given the farm animals a bit of a fright," said Alex in a smooth British accent. "Feeling a bit off, are you, old sod?"

17

Chapter Two

"Me and some guys from school / Had a band and we tried real hard"

"**W**E ALMOST *died* and you're concerned about *farm animals*?" Sean exploded.

Alex flinched away from him. "I do not understand what you mean. There was no danger."

"That...that..." Sean sputtered, "That... *whatever* it was. I don't know. Did we hit a wormhole or get caught up in some kind of time-loop vortex thingy?"

"No," Alex answered calmly, "it was a completely normal transition."

"That was *normal?*" Sean continued to yell. "Everything was in slow motion and it must have taken hours to get here."

"No," Alex continued smoothly, "it was only about seven minutes travel time. Though I sometimes wonder if the chronograph functions correctly as we are moving backward in time."

"What about all the slow motion stuff?"

"There was no slow motion," insisted Alex. "Perhaps an illusion that you experienced from your own mind?"

"Bull!" Sean exploded.

"You seemed to be tolerant of the transition experience until the last few seconds, and then you grew increasingly hysterical."

"Last few seconds? Like an hour ago I decided to ask if we were there yet, and it comes out all gobbledygook and like in slow motion or something. I tried to wait it out, but about every ten minutes I asked again, since you wouldn't answer. Then I decided you were caught in some kind of time vortex and couldn't answer, so I tried to get to Steffi's controls, and my hand was moving like through a sea of molasses, then suddenly everything was back to normal and then I needed to hurl."

"Interesting"

"*Interesting?!*" Sean screamed, "I thought I was stuck in some kind of time purgatory! All you can say is interesting? How did that *not* freak you out?"

Alex manipulated some of the icons on the control screen.

"The computer monitors what happens during dimensional shifting. I will retrieve a two-dimensional representation of what it observed," Alex said, not taking his eyes from his work on the console. "I am attempting to isolate only the last thirty seconds. Here."

The screen opened and displayed a front view of both Sean and Alex. For about five seconds the images on the screen appeared to be sitting quietly. Suddenly recorded Sean looked terrified and turned toward Alex. *AreWeThereYet   AreWeThereYet   AreWeThereYet   AreWeThereYet AreWeThereYet AreWeThereYet AreWeThereYet*   Then he slapped his hand against the screen. The Alex on the screen turned toward Sean. *Yes, we are here. Welcome to 1969.* When the screen showed Sean as he started banging against the side of the S.T.E. Alex stopped the video.

"We do not need to view the next sequence," he said tactfully.

Sean stared blankly at the empty screen. Alex quietly waited several seconds.

"That's not what happened," Sean said softly, slightly shaking his head. He numbly stared at the screen eventually turning toward Alex. "How can that be what happened? That's *not* what happened to me!" He said, his voice rising.

"You know from your four short jumps that a dimensional shift alters how your brain can interpret what your senses attempt to discern," Alex explained.

"I got that part!" Sean interrupted. "I could feel that happening and I got a hold of it. Got control. Everything was fine until we hit this weird slow-motion pocket and then everything was nuts!"

"Will you become angry with me if I attempt an interpretation of the phenomenon that you experienced?" Alex asked cautiously.

"Probably," said Sean, but then with a hint of a grin rolled his eyes, "but go ahead."

"Based on what you have described, my hypothesis is that you became anxious by the length of time spent in an alternate dimension. Your own best explanation was that something had gone wrong, which triggered your consciousness to explore possibilities, and since you are an avid fan of the science fiction genre, you have many scenarios to draw upon. Since your brain can process data at a faster rate than what you perceive, those factors combined with your sensory input, which was altered by travel in the alternate dimension, made it seem as if you were moving in slow motion."

Sean stared at him for a moment. "It was a hallucination," he stated flatly.

"That is an adequate label," Alex said, "but does not explore the concept of what triggered it."

"Maybe not, but it's a lot quicker to say 'hallucination' than 'perceiving the alternate hypothesis of the dimensional triggers' you were yammering about."

"Perhaps this is another instance that you would prefer I referred to as magic?"

"Maybe," Sean sighed. "But moving on... do you have any magic that can get rid of the barf in my hair?"

"Rinsing it with water seems the logical option at this point," Alex suggested.

"Great idea," Sean said sarcastically. "Too bad Steffi doesn't have a bathroom and shower."

Alex pushed against the panel just below the front view-screen. Although not previously visible, an opening appeared and a small drawer slid out. Alex picked up a transparent cylindrical object and handed it to Sean. "It is a liter of purified water," he said as Sean gingerly took it from him.

Sean flipped it over, rotated it, then flipped and rotated it at the same time as he looked for an opening. Alex took it back from him.

"Sorry. I did not consider that you would not know how to use it," he said, and then addressed the cylinder. "Open. Three centimeters."

Dozens of arc-shaped cracks appeared, each of them meeting at the center of the top of the cylinder. They dilated like a camera shutter then angled outward, opening a funnel-shaped hole. Alex returned it to Sean, who took it and stared wide-eyed at the reshaped object.

"You can pour from it now," Alex prompted.

"I did *not* see any kind of opening. That is just crazy!" Sean grinned.

"The seal is too small to be seen without magnification. You did not miss it."

Sean pointed at the spout. "How did you know this end was the top?"

"Orientation is irrelevant," Alex said, again retrieving the cylinder. "Seal." The aperture closed until the arc shapes disappeared, forming a solid surface. He turned the bottle upside down. "Open. Three centimeters." The arcs reappeared in what was now the top of the cylinder and dilated to the same sized opening as before. Alex handed it back to Sean.

"So if both ends open, how does it know which end you want?"

Alex looked puzzled. "It was designed with the assumption that you do not wish to dump liquid into your lap when you open it."

Sean's eyes sparkled, and a smile split his face. "Seal!" He waited as the top closed; then he flipped it over. "Open. Three... no... four centimeters." A larger spout appeared. "Seal." It closed. Sean flipped it again. "Open two point five centimeters." A smaller opening appeared. "Seal." He flipped it again. "Open three point one seven nine three centimeters." It opened slightly larger than the original opening that Alex had requested.

"I thought you wished to remove the... um... residue from your hair," Alex nudged.

"Hmmm?" said Sean absently, examining his new toy. "Oh, yeah. Right." He leaned his head out the door and poured the water over the length of his hair. "You know, this is one good reason guys should *not* have hair this long." He handed the empty cylinder back to Alex. "Well, that *almost* got it all out."

Alex said *seal* as he took the bottle from Sean. He placed it back in the small drawer and said *replenish*. The cylinder disappeared for a few seconds, then reappeared full. Alex took it out and handed it to Sean. Sean was awestruck.

"Just like that, it's full again?" he said, spellbound.

"Yes."

"Where's the water come from?"

"The S.T.E. maintains four liters of potable water."

"Maintains?"

"Yes, when occupied, it retrieves exhaled water vapor from the cabin. It also can extract it from the external atmosphere. Naturally when the humidity is higher, more water can be extracted from the outside air."

Sean leaned out and poured more water over his hair. "I think that's got it," he said. He shook his head briskly like a wet dog, then took a sip to rinse his mouth and spat. "Is it always room temperature?"

"No," Alex replied, "you can change the temperature for drinking." He took the bottle and spoke to it, "Five degrees." He handed it back to Sean, who took a swig.

"That is *amazing!*" Sean gushed. "Wait a minute! Wouldn't five degrees be frozen solid?"

"It is five degrees Celsius." Alex twitched a query to the computer. "That is about forty-one degrees Fahrenheit."

"Of course it is. Celsius. Kilometers. Liters. What's the deal? When did the United States go metric?"

"Not... for... awhile," Alex said evasively.

Sean's eyes narrowed. "I'm getting better at recognizing when there's something you don't want to tell me."

"There are things about the future that are too complicated to talk about in detail."

"You've got to be kidding. Going metric is a deep dark secret of the future?"

"No," Alex said hesitantly, "but there are... complications... that precede the decision."

Sean considered pressing Alex for more details as he drank the rest of the water, then became fascinated again by the empty container. "So, could I dump a warm can of Coke in here and tell it to chill to like negative point five and get a Coke slushy?"

Alex pondered the question. "I believe it would have to be reprogrammed to accept a foreign liquid. If you could force Coke into it, I do not know whether this container would attempt to purge itself or if it would seal and refuse to allow you access to what it considered non-potable."

Sean shook his head in disappointment. "That's just sad. You've got a container that's smart enough to open only at the top, that can change the temperature at will, and it won't let you chill a Coke in it? That's just wrong."

"It is designed to assist in sustaining life. I do not believe carbonated beverages are required to sustain life."

"That's a matter of opinion," Sean said offhandedly. "But, OK, let's get back to the replenishment thing. Say you and Steffi were crashed in the middle of the Sahara Desert. No humidity. Now what?"

"That is not possible," Alex answered flatly, "The S.T.E. cannot crash."

Sean rolled his eyes. "OK, so let's say you just wanted to replenish the water fast 'cause I'm really really thirsty."

"There is a method of purifying other liquids that are mostly water, such as urine, or if you had access to sea water. Even water from a river or lake that was highly contaminated could be used as a source."

Sean scowled at the empty container, then held it at arm's length for Alex to take. "OK, science lesson over... this can't chill Coke, and I don't *even* want to think about how the water I just drank may have once been inside of you." He shivered as Alex took the container. "So, let's shift to geography. Where exactly are we?"

"Somewhere within ten kilometers of your father, and at least 500 meters from any living humans... to avoid detection when we returned to this dimension."

"Obviously we're in some pasture, because of the calves. So we might be on my Grandma's farm?"

"Very possible. You do realize that your Grandfather is also alive at this time. I am planning to collect a DNA sample from him."

Sean's eyes widened. "I hadn't thought of that. Wow! I never knew him since he died before I was born. Cool! So let's get going! How do we get closer and cleverly work our way into their lives?"

"It was my plan to do a spatial analysis of roughly three months, with this current time coordinate as the center point."

"Why's this analysis so special?"

"Not special... spatial. I will gather data points of your father's DNA stream over that three-month sample and map them to where they occur in space. We can draw many conclusions simply from the raw data, such as where he sleeps, based on finding a fixed position for several hours each day. Other location points can be examined for appropriateness of first contact."

"Did you do that kind of analysis with me?" Sean asked.

"Of course. Initially, I considered selecting your driveway as a contact location, since you were—correct me if I get this phrase wrong—'shooting hoops' every night for several weeks. In the end, though, I decided taking classes with you at your school provided a better opportunity for continued interactions."

"The reason I was out there shooting hoops every night was because I was hoping to get another chance to talk with this gorgeous blonde. Boy, turns out *that* was a waste of time," Sean complained.

"That *was* an interesting anomaly," Alex mused. "Now, I believe it would be better if you exited the S.T.E. while I do the analysis."

"Why?"

"The analysis requires multiple mini-bursts between the dimensions for spatial mapping. Given your recent distress, I thought perhaps your stomach was not yet up to such an ordeal."

Sean quickly decided anything with the word 'analysis' probably didn't include a fun factor. "OK, I'll wait here with the cattle." He swung his legs out and stood up. "Aw *crap!*"

"Did you just remember something that we have overlooked?" Alex asked.

"No. Literally...crap! You parked Steffi right next to a cow pie."

Alex twitched a query to the computer. "Since it is unlikely that there is a dessert in an open field, I will assume that you are referring to bovine fecal droppings."

"You know, using fancy words doesn't change the fact that I have cow manure all over my shoe."

"Well, if you recall, we had already planned to cake them in mud to make them more inconspicuous."

"*You* planned," Sean groused. "And this does *not* fit my definition of mud. I'm definitely holding you to your offer to replace these."

Sean moved further away, looking carefully for any other organic land mines. He wiped the side of his shoe on some taller grass. "I might need another bottle of water for this."

"I have completed a check of the local terrain and found a small stream of water forty meters to your left," said Alex. "That may provide a better way to clean your shoe, and then to cover them in mud."

Sean looked to his left and saw the far bank of a creek, then glanced up and noticed that the sun was high in the sky. "How come it's mid-day here when we left at night?" he asked.

"It was a random point selected near the middle of your father's 16th year of age. The day and hour were not specified for this materialization, purely random."

"It feels like it's probably summer, too. Don't you have some kind of display that shows you the date and time?"

"Not precisely," Alex replied. "I can calculate the longitude and latitude from the magnetic poles. From that reference, I can examine the declination of the sun." He quickly completed the calculations. "We are at approximately 41 degrees north latitude and the sun then has a declination of approximately plus 23. That suggests we are currently in early July. Since we were attempting a midpoint of your father's 16th year and his birthday is January 11th, I would estimate July 11th plus or minus five days."

"You know with all the other cool stuff you have, you should be able to invent something that would display the date and time when you arrive."

23

"As a matter of fact, it does when the S.T.E. is in an era with ubiquitous wireless connection to the internet. Then the computer can easily connect with an atomic clock for the exact time."

"So when does *that* happen, or is that another deep dark secret."

"It will work in 1995, provided one has relative proximity to a metropolitan area. By the time you finish college, your communication grid will be greatly expanded."

"Are you slipping?" Sean asked with a sly grin.

"I do not know what you mean," replied a puzzled Alex.

"You just told me I graduate from college!" Sean crowed. "You told me something from my future!"

"Hypothetically, if someone in your high school asked you what you imagined you would be doing six years hence, what would you say?"

"First, I'd wonder what was wrong with them that they said, 'hence', but I guess I'd say that I would be out of college and looking for a job... or maybe going to Grad School, depending on what I do the first four years of college."

"Since data shows that over 90% of children whose parents have college degrees also obtain college degrees, it is no great revelation that you will finish college."

Sean threw his hands up in surrender. "OK. OK. I give up. If you have to drag out data to prove you're right, I give up. Why don't you go do your special analysis, and I'll go play in the creek."

"As you wish," Alex replied.

"Hey," Sean yelled. "How long is this going to take you?"

"I would estimate that I will spend approximately three hours gathering the data, examining the outcomes, and then scouting likely locations."

"OK, I guess I'll just..." Alex had closed the door of the S.T.E., and it popped out. "...wait here until you get back," Sean finished quietly. He turned to his left to head toward the stream, but before he took two steps, the time-machine re-materialized. The door slid open. "Did you forget something?" Sean asked.

"No. I have completed the task," Alex replied.

"I thought you said it'd take three hours."

"Only two hours and forty-eight minutes, as it turned out," Alex said with just a trace of smugness.

"But you were gone only..." Sean began, but then nodded before continuing, "OK, so you *were* gone almost three hours, but you came back to a point in time just seconds after you left."

"Correct."

"You could've at least given me a couple minutes to wash my shoe," Sean complained.

"I will wait."

Sean started to walk toward the stream and shouted over his shoulder, "You *could* move Steffi closer to the creek so I don't have to walk all the way back."

Alex manipulated the controls, and the S.T.E. rose about a foot off the ground. With a tiny puff of air from the back, he began drifting toward the water at the same pace that Sean was walking. Sean looked over at him. "You look ridiculous, you know," Sean commented.

"In what way?" Alex asked.

"Well, in several ways, but I was referring to how you look from out here. With Steffi cloaked except for the open door, you look like you are floating along beside me, but in a sitting position."

"Technically, that is what I am doing."

"Well, it looks stupid from here... especially in your hippie clothes."

Sean reached the bank of the creek and found a safe place to slide down toward the gently flowing stream. Alex drifted over the center of the water and stopped, still at the same level above the ground that he had just left, which then put him above Sean's head. Sean held onto a tree root sticking out of the bank and balanced himself as he moved his foot into the stream. He swished it around until he was satisfied that he'd gotten the manure off. He next brought his foot to the very edge of the water and shifted his weight until his foot sunk into the soft mud. He reversed his position so he could sink his other foot into the mud, and then tilted his head up toward Alex. "I don't suppose you've got some kind of futuristic hair drier that can instantly dry this glop of mud stuck to my shoes," he called upward.

"No, but I believe I have an alternate solution. Climb the bank, and I will set back down upon the ground."

Alex maneuvered his craft back over land and slowly settled onto the grass while Sean climbed the bank and reached the S.T.E. just as it touched down.

"Remove your shoes and slide into the S.T.E." he instructed.

Sean did as requested then asked, "Now what?"

"Hold them outside until I get into position," Alex replied.

Sean again obeyed. Alex manipulated the controls, and the S.T.E. rose slowly. He then edged it carefully toward a tall tree near the stream. "If you hang them on a branch of that tree, they will dry in the sun," said Alex.

"That'll take hours!" Sean protested.

"Just hang them out there, and you will have them back on your feet in just a few minutes," assured Alex.

Sean reluctantly hung each shoe on a branch near the top of the tree. He turned back to Alex and raised his eyebrows expectantly. Alex was already shifting icons around in the control field. The door slid closed. Sean felt momentarily disoriented; then the door slid back open.

"You can retrieve your shoes now," Alex said, pleased with himself.

Sean reached out to grab a shoe. The mud had completely dried. He grabbed the other shoe and banged them together so that the largest clumps of dirt fell to the ground.

"Dried in the sun. OK, I get it. You don't *have* to wait for it to happen," said Sean. "So how many hours forward did you jump?"

"It was actually 2.25 days. I wanted to ensure that they dried thoroughly."

"OK, now that the shoes are done... what did you find out with your special analysis?"

Alex struggled with the urge to correct Sean about spatial again. He decided to let it pass. "Several things. Your grandparent's house is 500 meters in that direction." He pointed at an angle from where they hovered. "Today is July 12th; we had arrived on the 10th. Tonight your father is gathering with his friends in the nearby village."

"Village?" Sean mocked.

"Yes. A group of houses and associated buildings, larger than a hamlet and smaller than a town, situated in a rural area."

"I've never heard anyone call it a village. Grandma and Dad always referred to Mercer as 'going to town.' I think they call it a town."

"You refer to Grover's Corners as a town."

"Yeah, so?"

"The population of Mercer, Iowa, is about one-eighth by comparison. It seems only logical that it would fit the definition of a village," Alex explained.

"I'm just saying that they don't use that terminology around here. Hey, but it *does* kinda sound like England, though, the hamlet and village thing. I guess you could call it a village since you're supposedly British."

"Whichever term we use, your father will be in a relatively public place that we may be able to infiltrate."

"Infiltrate," Sean chuckled. "Now you sound like we're spies."

"I believe that would be a fair definition of what we are doing."

"All right, then. Let's go *infiltrate* the *village*," Sean laughed. Alex started manipulating the controls. "Hey," Sean added, "let's buzz the farm first. I want to look at it from above."

Alex nodded and started drifting toward the farmhouse like a hot air balloon. He flicked other controls, and the upper half of all the sides of the S.T.E. gave the illusion of transparency.

"That is so awesome that you can do that," Sean marveled, "I almost expect to feel wind in my face; it's so clear."

"As I have explained before, what you see on your left is the same image that would be seen by anyone to my right on the outside of this craft. It is all but an identical projection of the external projection that makes the S.T.E. appear nearly invisible."

"I know, that's the same explanation you gave me when we watched Apollo 11. I know it's super high-rez TV from the future, but it looks like there's nothing there at all."

"I assure you," Alex explained, "the structure of the craft is unchanged."

They drifted toward the barn.

"Look at those trees!" Sean exclaimed. "They're so much smaller than they are now... I mean, will be when we're back in my time. The barn looks better, too. I remember it as being a little more saggy. And the house is white with green trim! Now it's cream with a chocolate brown trim. Well, again, not *now* now... but now in my lifetime now." He paused with a frown on his face. "Terminology is kind of hard to deal with when you're just talking about stuff. I mean, I know that we're in the past... and that now is what was then... and my now is like in the future, but I still think of it as now. Does that make any sense?"

Alex blinked a few times before responding. "Yes. It is difficult to speak of one's past experiences relative to where we are. Everything in your past is from ten to twenty-six years in the future from this point in time. You also have reference points from your lifetime to compare with what you are seeing. Things are familiar, but you notice the differences, such as the color of the house and the trees that will grow taller in the next twenty years."

"Yeah, that's it," Sean agreed, "It's *familiar*... but different. That's a good way to put it. You know what would be awesome? Just kind of hang here and take a picture, and then move forward a month and take a picture and keep doing that until we are back in my time, then you'd have a time-lapse movie of the trees growing. Kind of like the videos that they showed in grade school of flowers growing and blooming in less than a minute." Alex looked perplexed. "Maybe you didn't have that in grade school?" Sean added.

Alex queried the computer for time-lapse photography of plants. He nodded. "I see what you mean. You are suggesting that you would enjoy seeing the trees grow, and the buildings sag in a short video format. I can have the computer run a simulation." He pulled open a large display screen on the panel in front of them. "I've told the computer to run a simulation of the next 100 years based on average conditions. It is compressed to one week per image. For a smooth resolution, we will view 60 frames per second, which will create less than a minute viewing time."

They watched as trees grew larger and vanished. Tiny saplings grew into huge trees. Some of the farm buildings sagged and then disappeared. When the video ended, Sean continued to stare at the blank screen. "OK, maybe 100 years isn't so cool. So many trees and some of the buildings disappeared."

"The computer simulated what would happen to some of the buildings with the assumption of little to no maintenance. The trees logically would be susceptible to disease and ice storms and wind storms in this location. Many would die. Others might grow from seed," Alex explained.

"I guess I just wanted to see the trees get bigger. I didn't want to see stuff fall down or die and just disappear," Sean lamented.

"I can rerun it and instruct the computer to not show any decay," Alex offered.

Sean forced a halfhearted smile. "That's OK. I wasn't being realistic." He reached past Alex and pointed toward the tree on their right. "See that bigger tree there? It's gone. There's nothing there since I've been around." He dropped his hand back onto his lap and turned to look to his left. "Things get old and die and disappear." He stared blankly for a few moments as they drifted over the farm.

Sean slapped his leg to snap out of his dismal mood. "OK, we've seen the farm from above," he said forcing a cheerful note to his voice. "Let's head into the village and infiltrate!"

Alex turned the craft toward the town of Mercer and accelerated in that direction. Though it was silent, and he couldn't feel any movement, Sean could see the landscape passing by beneath them at an increasing speed.

"OK, you can't be getting that kind of speed out of little puffs of air. How are you getting this thing to move like that?"

"Magic," Alex said with a smile.

"You don't have any kind of a jet engine to provide thrust, or a propeller. We're going too fast to be drifting. So what's the *magic*?"

Alex thought for a moment before answering, "It is related to the force that allows me to nullify the effect of gravity on the S.T.E. Do you know the term 'graviton'?" Sean shrugged, then shook his head. "Very well. In simple terms, I can exert an added force at angle to propel us in any direction I choose." He flipped a few icons, and they were suddenly traveling at a ninety-degree angle from their original course. The ship was still facing the same direction; their momentum had instantly altered at a sharp right angle.

"Wow! I saw what happened, but I couldn't feel it. I couldn't feel the change in direction. If I couldn't see the ground, I wouldn't have even known we changed course."

"The cabin retains inertia regardless of exterior motion. Close your eyes for a second."

Sean did as instructed. When he opened them again, the ground was whizzing past him straight overhead. He instinctively put his hands to the ceiling to brace from falling, but he didn't move from his seated position. He stared open mouthed at Alex.

"I did not previously explain to you that the gravity that you experience is wholly contained within the cabin of the S.T.E. The sensation of up and down is relative only to the interior. If you were not able to view the outside, you would not know that the earth is below your head, and your feet point toward the sky."

Sean closed his eyes. "OK, can you either flip us back or shut off the view screens? I'm getting a little queasy watching the ground scoot by over my head." He waited a few seconds then opened his eyes. To his relief, the ground was back below him where it belonged, and they'd returned to their original course toward Mercer.

"Besides the spatial analysis, I also scouted for areas near the village...town... and close to the highway that could provide a location where we could safely park the S.T.E. in a position unlikely to be disturbed."

"And what did you find, oh super-scout from the future?"

"There is a bridge over a small river near the edge of town. We will put the S.T.E. under the bridge in the shadows. With the cloak, it will not be seen. We will have easy access to the road, and be able to walk into the town as if we had been hitchhiking."

"Where will we be walking to?" Sean asked.

"There is a common green space about two kilometers from where we will leave the S.T.E."

"The park near the Courthouse? That's quite a hike."

"Roughly two kilometers, as I said," Alex replied, then did a quick computer query. "Approximately one and one-quarter miles."

"You can't find a closer place to park?"

"Nothing that is as secure. Besides, it will heighten the illusion that we have been out on the road all day and just walking into the town for the evening."

"I suppose just materializing in the park and saying, 'take me to your leader' is out of the question," Sean joked.

"Who is the leader you wish to see?" asked a perplexed Alex.

Sean rolled his eyes. "You take stuff too literally. It's like a stereotype. The aliens land their flying saucer and say, 'take me to your leader'... I guess that's kind of mostly in cartoons."

"Since you have shown that you understand the need for secrecy, might I assume that you were making a humorous remark?" Alex asked cautiously.

"Right. If a joke falls in the forest and there's no one there to get it, is humor still created?" said Sean dryly.

Alex decided not to admit to his further confusion. "We are approaching the bridge," he said and stopped right above it. He manipulated the controls to ease the craft down and under the bridge, wedging it between the underside and the embankment.

"I wish I had an inertia dampener on my car when you were trying to drive it. Then I wouldn't have had to worry about going through the windshield with your jerky starts and stops," commented Sean.

Alex opened the door, and Sean carefully stepped out onto the uneven ground where it angled down to the river. A storage panel slid out from under his side of the seat. "I have the rest of your costume," said Alex. He reached in and pulled out the Army jacket and a nondescript canvas backpack, passing them to Sean.

"Where'd you get these?" Sean asked.

"At a military surplus store in Kansas City, as you suggested," replied Alex as he reached in and pulled out a second backpack. It had a camouflage pattern but was similar in size to the first one.

"What's in them?"

"Yours has your extra clothing and a canteen. I have what the salesperson described as 'essential survival gear'. I believe there is cooking equipment, and I am unsure of the function of many of the other items."

"Essential gear, huh?" Sean said, knowingly. "Did he tell you that *before* or *after* he saw you wave a wad of twenties around?"

"I believe it was after I had taken the currency out. The remuneration for all of the items totaled less than $250.00, including the government subsidy."

Sean's eyes narrowed. "*What* government subsidy?"

"Each time a purchase is made, additional funds must be paid to the merchant who in turn pays tribute to the government."

"Is that what the Army surplus guy told you?"

"No. Surely you are aware of this. It is customary for your era. The bakery where I purchased the brownies, as well as Wall Mart, also collected the subsidy," Alex explained.

"Wait. Are you talking about sales tax?"

"Yes, that is the terminology you use in this century. However, governments have collected tribute for many centuries. It is a cornerstone of civilization, although it has also too often been an exploitation of the common man by those who reign over them."

"OK, that's a relief. I thought that guy was giving you a line of bull to get more money."

"You can check the contents. It is possible there is a line of bull in there. Is that not commonly considered part of essential survival gear?"

"I suppose my Irish ancestors would say that a line of bull was essential," Sean laughed, "but let's see what you've got here." He opened Alex's backpack and removed items. "Rope. A small tarp. Compass. This must be some kind of cook-stove; it has a little butane tank on it. Matches. Hatchet...probably don't really need that. Wow! Look at that knife! Are we planning hand-to-hand combat? Swiss Army knife...those are cool. Tin coffee pot...you can ditch that. Pan. Skillet. Metal spatula. Are we really going to need all this stuff?"

"I do not know. The merchant suggested we would. I assumed he was an authority on the subject. I believe he had survived a war. He had a prosthetic leg."

"Didn't have an eye-patch and a parrot on his shoulder, too, did he?" asked Sean.

"No," said Alex, then added, "He did have a rather large canine with him behind the counter."

"But he didn't have a guttural voice or say 'Arrrrr' every other sentence?" Alex was again puzzled. "Never mind," Sean continued, "he may have sold you some stuff that you didn't need, but I guess you can afford it." He stuffed everything back into the backpack.

"You did not locate the line of bull?" Alex asked.

"No," Sean chuckled, "but that's OK. We've got more stuff than what we should need."

They slid into the straps of the backpacks and started up the embankment toward the road. "Wait," Alex said. "The computer indicates a vehicle is approaching. We should wait until no one will see us come out from under the bridge."

They waited as two cars crossed the bridge leaving town and one coming into town. "Now," Alex announced. "There are no vehicles within visual range." The two hurried up the bank and onto the road, then started across the bridge toward Mercer. Before they reached the far side of the bridge, a car passed from behind them and honked. Alex jumped at the sound. Sean rolled his eyes and shook his head, but said nothing.

When they had walked about a third of a mile, Sean pointed to a building on their right. "That's the gas station my Dad goes to when he gets gas here. Let's check it out. I want to see how much has changed."

They walked over to the pump island. "Look at that!" Sean exclaimed. "Thirty-four cents for a gallon of gas! I paid $1.17 last time I bought gas." He rushed over to a Coke machine. "Oh, man! Twenty cents for a Coke!" Before Alex could reach him, he'd pulled a quarter from his pocket and shoved it into the machine.

"No!" shouted Alex as he rushed over to Sean. The machine clicked out a nickel as Sean pulled a bottle of Coke out.

"Check it out! Glass bottles!" Sean said enthusiastically. "What are you all in a frenzy about?"

"Give me all of your money!" Alex shouted.

"Don't lose it, dude! I'll buy you a Coke. There's a Pepsi machine right next to this one if you'd rather have a Diet Pepsi."

"No!" Alex insisted, "I need *all* of your money!"

"Dude, you said you only spent two-fifty on the surplus stuff. You should still have fifty bucks, right? Hey, if you don't have coins I'll give you a quarter."

Alex was suddenly in Sean's face. "What year is this?" he demanded.

Sean stepped back a step. "As far as I know, 1969. You're the one who landed the time-machine."

"Take the coins from your pocket and look at the dates on them!" Alex exclaimed.

"OK. 1986...1991...1978... oh crap..." Sean hissed when he'd figured out why Alex was so upset.

"There is less than a two percent chance that the coin you put into that machine is older than 1970! We must somehow retrieve it!"

Sean's mind raced as he tried to think of a way to get to his quarter. Alex was frantic. Sean decided the first step was to calm Alex down. "OK," he said in a soothing voice, "let's think this through. The machine didn't care that the quarter is from the future, so it must be the same size and weight. As far as I know, they look the same."

Alex quickly twitched a query. "The quarter dollar has the face of George Washington with an eagle on the reverse from 1931 through 1998, with the exception of 1975 and 1976 which were special bicentennial designs. In 1965, the copper-nickel clad coins replaced the previous coins made of silver."

"OK, there you go! So they should look the same. Let's keep talking this through. The machine accepted it as money. Gave me a Coke and a nickel back... that is so sweet! Twenty cents!" Sean paused as he looked at the coin. "1967...cool. Anyway... so now what happens? The Coke truck guy has his regular day to restock and take the money. He's going to dump the whole load of change into a bag or something. *He's* not going to look at it. So then he takes his big bag of money from all of his Coke machines—which is probably thousands of quarters—to the bank where they have those coin counting machines. *That* machine isn't going to see any difference, so the future quarter will get rolled up into a roll of quarters with all the other old quarters. Now where does it go? To a vault until someone needs a roll of quarters. Who's going to need a roll of quarters? Some business guy who needs to make change to customers. *He's* not going to look at the date; he's busy making change and telling the customer to have a nice day. The customer is going to put their change in a purse or in their pocket. *They're* not going to look at the date; they're more interested in whatever it was they just bought. So if it keeps cycling around like that, pretty soon several years have passed, and then the quarter's not from the future anymore."

Alex looked visibly calmer. He twitched another query. "The computer calculates a 38% chance that your hypothesis will be correct."

"There you go!" Sean said confidently.

"That means there is a 62% chance the coin will be discovered before the year reaches the coin's mint date."

"OK, so let's keep thinking. Someone might drop it, and it gets lost for decades."

"That improves the odds to 39%," Alex said glumly.

"Or someone tosses it into a wishing well."

"39.2%."

"Hmmmm... that didn't help much. OK, I've seen lots of coins that get so worn you can't tell what the date is without a magnifying glass."

"Adding that factor makes it 46%."

"See, we're getting there."

"It is unlikely you will think of enough valid scenarios that will make for more than a 50% chance of the coin's date not being discovered."

"Fifty-fifty, huh? Kinda like the same odds of a coin toss?"

"I do not believe you are grasping the magnitude of this problem," Alex said indignantly. "We should break into this machine and retrieve that coin!"

"Have you checked your computer for the odds of whether or not we go to jail for vandalism? Calm down and let's keep thinking. OK, so let's say there is a 60% chance that someone sees the date. Then what?"

"They will know the coin is from the future, and we have polluted the time-stream," Alex replied anxiously.

"I don't think so. Maybe people where you come from would make that assumption, but I don't think most people in 1995 even think time-travel is possible. And other than some sci-fi geeks, I don't think anyone in 1969 would even consider time-travel."

"We have just handed them evidence!" persisted Alex.

"Or not. If you don't believe something, what are you going to do instead? Think of a logical excuse to explain it. What's the easiest explanation to believe?"

"I am not following your current hypothesis."

"It's a fake," Sean said smugly. He tipped his bottle back and took a long drink.

"Your hypothesis is a fake?"

"No!" said Sean in exasperation. "The *coin* is a fake!" He looked at the bottle in his hand. "And maybe this Coke is, too. It tastes funny."

"You are suggesting that anyone who notices that the date on the coin is from the future would reject the true reason and therefore formulate a hypothesis that the coin is a forgery?"

"Sure," Sean replied confidently. "OK, I won't swear to it, but I don't think it was a brand new shiny quarter, so it was probably a few years old already. It's already got some wear, some scratches. Maybe it takes a couple of years more circulation here and gets more wear. Someone finally looks at the date and assumes it was messed with or flat out counterfeit."

Alex queried the latest hypothesis and breathed out a sigh. "The computer calculates a 95.8% probability that someone in this current time would assume the coin was counterfeit or altered."

"So is that good enough to stop worrying about this?" Sean asked.

Before Alex could reply, a man wearing a service station uniform stepped out from an open garage bay. His slick hair was cut short and he had a small grease smudge on his right cheek. "You guys have some kind of problem?" he asked gruffly as he wiped his hands on a towel.

Sean glanced at the man, then looked at Alex. Alex was frozen. Fear had also gripped Sean's stomach, but his adrenaline-charged brain raced for a solution.

"No, no, old boy," Sean said in his multinational accent. "My mate here is in a bit of a quandary about what drink to get. Not used to lots of these choices, yuh see. Back home it's just a lemon squeezer or a ginger fizz, id nit?"

The man stared at them coldly, then finally said, "You talk funny. Like some limey foreigner."

"Righto, old bean," Sean continued more confidently, "Spot on. Can't fool the likes of you, eh?"

"Well, we don't have any ginger fizzy so if you don't like Coke, get yourself an orange or a Grape Nehi."

"There you go, old sport," Sean said to Alex. "This here gent even comes with recommendations."

"Frightfully kind of you, my good man," said a recovered Alex, "but I believe I have decided I am not especially thirsty. Besides, Nigel, we should conserve our coins."

"As you wish, Peter, old sport," said Sean. "I guess we'll be off, then. Cheerio! Pip, Pip!"

"That's three cents deposit on the bottle if you take it with you," growled the man.

Sean reached into his pocket and pulled out some coins.

"Nigel," said Alex urgently, "we really should be hanging on to our coins. Perhaps you should drink it here."

"No worries, mate!" Sean said brightly. "It's a five cent piece I just got from the machine. Here you go, my good man." He handed the nickel to the station attendant.

The man took the nickel and plunged his right hand into his own pocket, drawing out a handful of change. He selected two pennies and handed them to Sean. "Now git out of here," he growled. "I don't need any hippies hanging around annoying my regular customers."

Alex and Sean turned and resumed their path into town. They had only taken a few steps when the man shouted at their backs, "If you want my advice, you'd better turn around and head back out of town. Mercer's got enough long-haired hippies without importing any from limey town."

Sean looked over his shoulder and called back, "Thanks for the two cents, old sod. Just the first two, though." When they'd walked another fifteen paces, Sean softly said to Alex, "I've never seen anyone that unfriendly around here before. Everyone's been really nice to us when we've visited. I'm pretty sure it was that same place where the guy gave me a free sucker when I was a little kid."

"I would suggest that our semblance might explain the difference. Visually, we represent what was referred to as 'counter-culture'. That man is from a generation that believes hard work is the key to achieving what is referred to as 'The American Dream'. Our long hair and apparel send him the message that we are opposed to his beliefs."

"I'll be the first to admit that we look pretty lame, but that's no reason to get irate," said Sean.

"Perhaps I should have covered this time-period more thoroughly with you. It is really quite fascinating. There is a lot of political and social change that takes place, as well as some very violent incidents," said Alex, gearing up for lecture mode. "There are many factors that contribute to the attitude that you just witnessed. The United States experienced considerable economic growth after the end of the Second World War. That growth was mainly in what is commonly referred to as the 'middle class'. More people who come from a lower economic family background found that they had access to

34

enough wealth to enable a better lifestyle. This new element of spending further stimulated the economic growth that, in turn, continued to raise the standard of living. In any era, when people have more resources than they need to meet their basic needs, they begin to enhance their lifestyle with luxury items."

"So why would that make old "happy days are here again" hate someone who has long hair?" Sean interrupted.

"Perhaps that can be attributed to the reaction of the next generation—those born to this growing middle class. They are historically known as 'Baby Boomers'. Some of them resented that their parents were spending more and more time working, in the quest to accumulate even more wealth. Interestingly enough, that very affluence also provided the means for a greater expansion in communication. Nearly every family had a television set, radios in their cars, and stereo record players. Some of the lyrics of the music targeted to this young generation posed questions about choices made by those in leadership. There were songs that suggested that a simpler lifestyle is better than accumulating more wealth. There were songs that opposed the war in Vietnam."

"Hold on," Sean interrupted again. "You're saying listening to the radio turned kids against their parents?"

"Your summation is overly simplistic, but I think we can at least call it a contributing factor. Besides the freedom of expression in music, there were more magazines and newspapers launched specifically to communicate to this younger generation. Many historians from my time believe that the long hair and brightly colored clothes started with musicians attempting to grasp fame with an outlandish appearance designed to draw attention to themselves. This certainly was not a new idea, musicians have employed such tactics throughout history. However, because of the affluence of their parents, the younger generation had access to enough wealth to be able to emulate the look of their favorite musicians."

"I'm sure you're getting a kick out of giving me another history lesson, but I'm still not seeing why choosing to dress stupid and not get a haircut is enough to make Mr. Gas Station Guy all hateful," said Sean.

"That is best-explained, I believe, as 'guilt by association'. The people who were very vocal against the Vietnam War as well as what they referred to as 'a lifestyle of greed' nearly always had an outward appearance similar to the way we currently look. It could be interpreted as the uniform of the enemy by people such as the gentleman we just met."

"Gentleman," sneered Sean, "that's not a term I'd use for that guy."

"Attempt to empathize with him. He has benefited from an economy that has raised his standard of living. He is able to have a better life than that of his parents. Let us also assume that he altruistically desires for his own children and their generation to also have an improved lifestyle. He perceives a movement that openly opposes the standards that he believes contribute to that improved lifestyle. The people of that movement are easily identifiable by their appearance. We currently have taken on that appearance."

"Still not getting it," said an exasperated Sean. "I'm glad you find it all fascinating and get a big history thrill, but I think it's stupid to get negative on someone just because they look different."

"You live in a time when young people question intolerance as much as the young people of this era question materialism."

"At least we don't have to dress weird just to show we're against intolerance," quipped Sean.

"You will almost certainly question your choice of dress when you look back at pictures from your high school years with your children—but not as much as your children will question your sensibilities."

"Ha!" exclaimed Sean, "Another spoiler from the future!"

"Not really," Alex answered calmly, "Fashion is nearly always questioned retrospectively. Oddly enough, it also has tendencies to be somewhat cyclical."

"OK, getting tired of history again," said Sean after taking another sip from his bottle. "You got any idea why this Coke tastes kind of weird? Is it the glass bottle? Is it old? I wish you drank Coke so you could taste it and see what you think."

Alex twitched into query mode. "I might suggest that it is merely a difference in the sweetening agent. At this time, soft drinks were sweetened with cane sugar. The beverage you regularly drink in 1995 is sweetened with high fructose corn syrup."

"Really? You think that would make a difference?"

"I cannot say, personally, but it is a change that can be documented."

"We should take some of this back with us and do a side by side comparison," Sean mused.

The rest of the trek to the park was slightly uphill, so they didn't talk much, the weight of the packs on their backs seemed to get heavier with each step. When they reached their destination, Sean let his burden slide to the ground and he sat at a picnic table, finishing the last few swallows of his Coke. Alex joined him and opened Sean's pack and took out the canteen, pouring water into a little tin cup that he pulled from his own backpack. Sean looked around. No one else was in the park.

"So when do they get here?" asked Sean.

"Your father will arrive in approximately one hour. I do not know if others will gather here before then, or if they congregate at the same time."

"What time is it here, anyway? I should set my watch."

Sean and Alex both looked at his watch. Alex queried the computer. "The local time is currently 5:37 p.m., however you do not need to set your watch. Give it to me."

Sean lifted his eyebrows expectantly as he handed his watch to Alex. "Have you got some cool way to set my watch with the computer?"

"No," Alex replied, stuffing the watch into his backpack. "I should have checked this earlier. The first digital watch did not come to market until 1972."

"That's not that far off," Sean shrugged. "We could just say I had an early prototype."

"It is very likely to be of interest since it is out of the ordinary. It will be an additional three years after the first sale before the digital watch is affordable to the mass market. The first digital watch sold for two thousand dollars. I think it is too unusual to let it be seen."

"Two thousand bucks!" Sean gasped. "For a digital watch? You gotta be kidding me!"

"Let me also calculate the inflation rate," said Alex as he twitched a connection. "That would be equivalent to over seven-thousand of your 1995 dollars."

Sean's jaw dropped. "That's insane!"

"It is not unusual for a new and very different product to initially be priced at a level only the wealthy can afford."

"Too bad we can't just sell mine. That would fix our money problems," Sean lamented.

"Yes, money... this would be a good time for me to take your money and stash it away," Alex said.

Sean emptied his pocket of change and pulled out his wallet. "I guess I should give you my driver's license, too, and my school I.D."

"Indeed. I had overlooked those items. It is unlikely that anyone would see the contents of your wallet, but it is safer to not have anything that would be suspect," Alex said as he took the items Sean handed him.

"So what *are* we going to do about our money problem?" asked Sean.

"We have just solved it," replied Alex.

"No, not the 'hide it, it's from the future' money! The 'we don't have any' money."

"Oh. My omission," said a surprised Alex. "I did not inform you that I have currency that has correct dates for this year. One hundred twenty-five dollars."

Sean studied Alex with narrowed eyes. "OK, two questions. Where'd you get it, and why only one twenty-five?"

"I brought it with me from my own time. The 1969 purchasing power of that amount is equivalent to more than $500.00 in 1995," answered Alex.

"Hold it. Time out. Let me double-check this. What year are you from?"

"2217."

"OK, I don't have any money old enough to belong in this time, but you do? Wouldn't the bills be all crumbly?"

"They are not actually that old."

"Oooohhhh," said Sean, nodding and winking. "You print your own."

"No, it is authentic. Everyone who makes trips to the past is expected to bring back large amounts of currency so that other travelers will be prepared."

Sean eyed Alex suspiciously. "What do they do, rob a bank before heading back home?"

"No. Nothing illegal," Alex retorted, then slowly added in a softer voice, "Technically."

"Now *that* sounds like a good story. Let's hear it."

"Well," Alex began slowly, "there are those who suggest the methods used are unethical..."

"Go on," prompted Sean when Alex stalled.

"The value of certain items fluctuate greatly over time..."

"Such as?" Sean prompted the reluctant Alex.

"Precious metals' values can widely fluctuate, and they can easily move from one time-period to another without detection."

"So someone hauls a load of gold into the past and changes it into cash?"

"That works better in certain time-periods than others. A lucrative exchange is the decade from 1970 to 1980."

"What's so lucrative about that?"

"The price of an ounce of gold in 1980 was over $600.00. In 1970, it was only about $35.00."

"That's a pretty good spread. What is it in my time?" asked Sean.

"A little under $400.00," replied Alex after a quick query. "To continue: ten ounces of gold brought from my era sells in 1980 for approximately six thousand dollars. It remains relatively simple in 1980 to obtain $100 bills with dates of 1970 or before. A quick trip to 1970 and six-thousand dollars purchases about 170 ounces of gold, which can then be exchanged in 1980 for $102,000.00. You can then purchase nearly three thousand ounces in 1970."

"Which you could sell for almost two million!" exclaimed an excited Sean.

"Yes. Or, you can take those three thousand ounces to 1932 and sell them there."

"How much is it worth in 1932?"

"About $20.00 per ounce."

"Well, *that's* stupid!" mocked Sean.

"Not necessarily. You would then have sixty thousand dollars in 1932."

"Big whoop! You could have had two million in 1980. That's gotta be better, even with inflation."

"That is true. The inflationary value would only be about $360,000.00."

"Since you brainy boys from the future aren't going to make a mistake like that, there must be more to the story."

"There is indeed. In 1932, shares of IBM stock sold for less than $10.00 each."

"So with six thousand shares of IBM, you come back to the future and make a bazillion dollars!"

"That is just an example of using known historical data to purchase items that will greatly inflate in value over time. Another option is in real estate. It is easy to find a date in the past when you can obtain very cheap desert land in the Phoenix or Las Vegas areas and later sell for extensive profits."

"Or you could bet on the Superbowl! Or the Kentucky Derby!" enthused Sean. "Hey, who *does* win the Superbowl next year?"

Alex checked. "The Kansas City Chiefs."

"What?" exclaimed a thrilled Sean. "No way! The Chiefs win another Superbowl?"

"I do not understand your use of the term 'another'," said Alex.

"They lost to the Packers in the first Superbowl, then won Superbowl IV and haven't been back since. Now you're saying they win next year!"

"Yes, on January 11, 1970 they defeat the Minnesota Vikings by a score of 23 to 7."

"That's Superbowl IV!" Sean yelped.

"Yes."

"I asked for *next* year's score."

"That is next year's score," replied Alex evenly.

"Come on! I don't mean next year from here! I meant next year in my future—January 1996!"

"I am not going to tell you information from your future."

"You are such a..."

"Buzzkill," both said simultaneously.

"That phrase should not be used in this time-period," Alex continued.

"What would you suggest?" Sean asked.

"Perhaps, 'you are really bringing me down, man' or 'drag' or 'bummer'."

"People in my time still sometimes say 'drag' or 'bummer'... but 'bringing me down, man' sounds like something you'd say if you were wasted."

"Wasted is also acceptable in this time-period. It seems to usually be associated with an indulgence in mood altering pharmaceuticals."

"Why don't you just say 'high on drugs'?" Sean asked.

"That does not seem as accurate."

"Whatever!" Sean huffed. "OK, so let's get back to the cash. You've got a hundred twenty-five bucks that have good dates for this year?"

"Yes."

"How about you give me half."

"I cannot."

"Come on, 'cousin'... I need to have some money so I don't look like you own me."

"I meant I cannot give you half. I have 6 twenty dollar bills and a five dollar bill. Half is $62.50. I do not have the correct currency to give you half."

"Just give me a couple of twenties and the five! You don't have to be so literal."

Alex handed Sean the three bills he requested, and Sean put them in his wallet.

"OK, so it's still at least half an hour before my dad gets here, right?"

"Forty-four minutes."

"So let's pop into that Mom & Pop cafe we passed on the way up this street. Just a block from here. I could use a little something in my stomach besides Coke."

Chapter Three

"Every little breeze seems to whisper..."

THE SMELL of fried food and cigarette smoke assaulted them even before they walked through the door they opened to "Ritchie's Cafe". Sean's nose twitched involuntarily, he'd never been in an environment with that much smoke. A heavy blue-gray haze hung over a pool table on the far side of the room. Booths framed the area on three sides and continued toward the door on the left side of the room. Several young men slouched around the table smoking and drinking beers as they watched two of their group play.

Closer to the door and on the right stood ten pedestals topped with round red vinyl seats lined up along a charcoal-gray granite bar. The wall behind the bar was mirrored above another granite shelf, reflecting the dozens of glasses stacked there. To the right of the mirrored shelf were two deep-fat frying wells and a large flattop grill. A shiny stainless steel tub stacked half full of hamburger patties, each separated by little squares of waxed paper, sat near the grill.

Sean quickly surveyed the room. Although the booths looked more comfortable, the blue haze of smoke hanging over the area made it seem less desirable. Several of the booths were already occupied, mostly by small groups of teenagers. One held a young couple struggling with a two-year-old as they tried to get in bites of their meal. Sean shuddered at the thought of exposing a toddler to so much second-hand smoke. He turned his gaze back to the bar area where only one of the ten stools was occupied. A barrel-shaped older man wearing a white t-shirt and bib overalls overwhelmed a seat farthest from the door. He had several empty beer bottles sitting in front of him. Feeling conspicuous, Sean quickly selected the two seats farthest from the man, which were also closest to the grill. Alex's head swiveled as his eyes darted around the room, taking in all the marvelous antiquities.

The man behind the counter wore black pants and a white short sleeved shirt. A white apron hung from his neck to his knees, tied behind his back in a haphazard bow at waist level. Grease and ketchup spattered the chest area of the apron. A white paper cap sat on his head, its wide white band snug over his forehead.

Alex had connected to his computer during their walk down the street and pieced together data from various sources. The owner, Ritchie Caparelli,

41

was a first generation Italian/American. His father, Riccardo, had fled Italy for America in 1937, fearing for his life after publicly speaking out against Mussolini's growing alliance with Germany. Settling his family in Chicago's near west side, he found work as a dishwasher at an Italian restaurant on Taylor Street, while his wife took a predawn shift at a bakery. They both worked hard, saving every penny they could manage, learning to speak English as best they could. Riccardo found living in the remnant of the Capone Empire to be only slightly better than fascist Italy, and after World War II had ended, he shuffled his young family to rural Iowa. In 1948, he opened his little diner, naming it for his eldest son, eventually stepping aside to let his heir succeed him in the mid-60s when his health began to fail. Ritchie had always worked for his father in some capacity from childhood and it was an easy transition to take the reins. His own children became the third generation to work in the family business.

Ritchie opened a bottle of beer and set it in front of the bulky man at the other end of the counter. He returned to the end where Sean and Alex perched on stools, their backpacks at their feet.

"What can I get for you two?" he asked with an unintentionally gruff voice.

"I'll have a cheeseburger and an order of fries," Sean said, forgetting to use his false accent.

"Regular or deluxe?" asked the cook.

Sean glanced around looking for a menu board or at least some clue to the best answer as the man stared at him impatiently. A petite girl in a pastel blue dress with white lapels came behind the counter from the booth area and dumped a tray of dirty dishes into a sink of soapy water.

"I got this, Ritchie," she said as she plopped a pad on the counter in front of Sean. "What'll it be?"

"If we could trouble you for a menu, miss?" Alex asked in his polished British accent as the cook went back to tending the grill.

The girl's face lit up. "Hey," she said, pointing her pencil at Alex. "You're British, aintcha?"

"Spot on, old girl," Sean interjected. "Good on yer. Me mate 'ere is fum Liverpool."

"Well, what are you two doin' out here in the middle of the U. S. of A.?" she asked, almost too perkily.

"As it happens, luv, we're hitchhiking across this great land of yours," Sean continued, pleased that his accent seemed to fool her.

The girl pointed her pencil at Sean and giggled. "Love. That's kinda cute. Your accent sounds different from your friend's."

"Yes," Alex said smoothly, "This is my cousin, Nigel. He hails from New Zealand."

The girl stuck out her hand. "I've never met a Nigel before. Pleased to meet you. My name is Louise." Sean took her hand gently, and she pumped his arm twice. She moved her hand to Alex, smiling brightly and lifting her eyebrows expectantly.

"Peter," Alex said as he carefully took the offered hand. "Peter Lindsey." She pumped his arm vigorously twice.

She turned her attention back to Sean. "Now, did I hear you say you wanted a cheeseburger and fries?" she asked, giving Sean her warmest smile.

"Yes, that's right. Very good ears, luv," Sean said, smiling back.

"Did you want that deluxe?"

Sean noticed that she placed the accent on the first syllable of deluxe. "I'm afraid I have to admit I don't know what deluxe is," Sean replied, accenting the second syllable.

"Oh my goodness, I'm so sorry!" Louise gushed, putting her hand on his forearm. "I wasn't thinkin' about you not bein' from around here. A regular burger comes with ketchup, mustard, and pickles. You can also get onion if you ask for it... no charge. The deluxe adds lettuce, mayo, and a big ol' slice of tomato, and costs five cents more."

"I'll just have the regular, please."

Louise wrote on her order ticket. "How 'bout to drink?"

"A Coke would be super," replied Sean.

"Ten or fifteen?" Louise asked, ready to write his request. She looked up and saw the puzzled look on Sean's face. "I'm sorry, Nigel. You're probably not real used to American, are you? I should have asked if you'd like a ten cent serving or fifteen cent." She turned to the counter behind her to grab an example of each glass. "If you're real thirsty, I'd say get the fifteen. It's almost twice as much as the ten." She smiled a big smile at him as she set each glass in front of Sean.

"Yes, the fifteen, then. Jolly good," Sean said, improvising his attempted accent.

Louise turned her cheery smile to Alex. "And how about you, Peter?"

"I believe I would still prefer to examine a menu, if it is not too much trouble," Alex replied.

Louise looked cautiously both left and right and then leaned over the counter closer to Alex's face. "I'm real sorry, Peter," she said conspiratorially using a stage whisper. "This isn't exactly a restaurant like probably what you're used to. We don't exactly have menus." She pointed to the chalkboard above the mirror. It had a few handwritten lines on it. "Pretty much everyone just gets burgers."

Alex glanced at the board, noticing that the few items listed seemed to be various forms of hamburger sandwiches. "I am afraid I do not consume meat," he said shyly.

"Really?" Louise said, then broke into her biggest smile. "Are you one of those vegetarians? Oh my goodness! I've never met a vegetarian before!" She glanced in amazement between Sean and Alex. "What are the odds? Me meetin' a vegetarian *and* a Nigel the same day!" Regaining her composure, she looked over her shoulder to the menu and chewed on her eraser. "Let's see. Do you eat fish? I don't exactly know what vegetarians eat. If you can eat fish, we've got a tuna salad sandwich." She paused again, reconsidering her suggestion. She looked both ways again and leaned closer to Alex using the same soft voice as before, this time putting a hand near her mouth on the side that faced her boss. "I don't think they made the tuna salad fresh today, though, so..." Her voice trailed off as she shrugged her shoulders and waggled her hand.

"Actually I am not very hungry," Alex said.

"Louise," barked a gruff voice from the grill, "Order up!"

She patted Alex gently on his arm. "I'll be right back. Let me do some more thinkin' about this." She turned and picked up the plates next to the grill and put them on a tray; and then moved everything down the counter and grabbed a couple of glasses from the shelf. Sean watched in fascination as she held the first glass under a spout and pumped down twice on a plunger. A red syrupy substance squirted into the bottom of the glass. She then took a second glass and pumped the plunger to the right of the first one and a brown syrup squirted into that glass. She took a scoop of ice cubes and filled each glass nearly full, then held each glass under the nozzle of the Coke dispenser as she filled them to the top. Setting the drinks on next to the plates, Louise scooped it all up and headed toward the booths.

Sean leaned toward Alex. "I don't think *she* is from around here, either," he said. "Did you notice her accent?"

"It did seem different from what I have heard in this region. I believe you are probably more qualified to determine the source than I am," Alex replied.

"Southern," Sean said authoritatively, "but I'm not sure what state. Maybe Tennessee?"

"I could have the computer alter my accent to that of 20th century Tennessee, if that would assist you in determining her origin," Alex offered.

"Nah, I can just ask her," Sean said. "Wait a minute. You can do that? You can just change accents to whatever you want just by dinging the computer?"

"I thought you understood that. Just as it modulates my voice to female when I take on the appearance of Nicole, it can also affect regional accents."

"Really? Do something weird. I know, how about speaking English with a French accent?"

Alex twitched a connection to his computer. "But of course, mon ami. Ze Fringe accent would sound some sing like zis."

Sean stifled a laugh as Louise returned carrying another tray of dishes cleared from one of the booths. "You know what I thought of?" she said triumphantly.

"What iz zat?" Alex asked.

Sean punched his shoulder. "Come on, sport, don't be talking like a frog, now, wot?"

Alex twitched another connection to his computer. "Frightfully sorry, my good man, it had slipped my mind that you were frightened by a Frenchman as a young boy."

Sean scowled at Alex, who simply ignored him and turned back to Louise. "I believe you were announcing an epiphany?"

Louise knit her brow. "I'm not real sure what that is, but if that's British for a chocolate malted, then you're right. Sometimes when I don't really want a burger, I'll just get me a chocolate malted an' it'll fill me right up. They're real good, too!" When Alex didn't respond, Louise slapped her forehead. "There I go again. Not explainin' what I'm talkin' about. A chocolate malted is three big ol' scoops of vanilla ice cream, a good ol' splash of milk, two pumps of chocolate syrup—I can put three pumps in if you really like chocolate." She glanced over to the cook before continuing, "As long as Ritchie's not watching like a hawk. A scoop of malt powder and then just spin it up as smooth as you please. It's forty cents, but it's a big ol' glass, an' it'll fill you right up."

Alex looked questioningly toward Sean.

"That would be smashing, luv!" Sean said to Louise. "That's just the ticket for old Peter here."

"Comin' right up!" Louise proclaimed. She wrote again on her pad, then tore a page off and plopped it on the counter next to the deep fryers. "One cheeseburger an' a order of fries," she hollered to the cook. He picked up the ticket and stuck it in a slot on the hood vent above the grill. In nearly one fluid motion, he plopped a burger onto the grill with his right hand and plunged a wire basket of potato strips into the deep fryer with his left hand. Louise had already grabbed one of the large glasses and was filling it with ice.

"Um, Louise?" Sean called to her. She looked up from her work. "What was that red syrup that you put in those glasses just a few moments ago?"

She carried the glass over to Sean. "Nigel, have you never had a Cherry Coke? My goodness gracious, you need to try one!" She took the glass to the pump and pushed two squirts into it. "It's the same price, and if you don't like it, I'll drink it and get you a regular." She filled the glass with Coke and set it in front of Sean, then quickly whirled to the back counter, lifted the lid on a tall glass cylinder and pulled out a straw. "Now some folks like to stir it up right away, but I always take a little sip from the bottom first. Maybe I got a little bit of a sweet tooth," she said as she plunged the straw into Sean's glass. She watched expectantly as Sean took a sip.

"Wow!" Sean said. "That's really sweet and really cherry!"

"Do you like it?" Louise asked hopefully.

"Yes, ummm... smashing!" Sean replied. "That's a bit of all right, it is!"

Louise giggled. "You have the cutest way of talkin'. I just love it!"

"And I think your accent is delightful, too, luv," Sean smiled. "Where are you from originally?"

"Well, look at you!" Louise gushed. "You can tell from listening to me that I grew up someplace else?"

"Yes," Sean said, feeling a bit smug. "I find American accents fascinating. I fancy myself as a bit of an expert, actually. I should hazard a guess that you are from Tennessee."

"That's a good guess, Nigel," Louise said perkily. "But wrong."

"Kentucky?"

"Nope."

"Texas?"

"Texas? I think you might need to adjust your expert status."

"Georgia!" Sean declared definitively.

"My goodness," Louise smiled, "you sure do know your geography... but no."

"Mississippi?"

"Now you went and jumped right over it. I was born in Alabama."

"Ah, Alabama, of course!"

"We moved here when I was twelve. My daddy grew up here in Iowa, though."

"How did you father go from here to Alabama?" Sean asked with genuine curiosity.

"He went into the Army and was stationed at Fort Rucker. It's kinda right in the middle of Enterprise, Ozark, and Daleville. Mama's from Daleville."

"I'm afraid I've never heard of any of those places."

"Not too far from Dothan," Louise added helpfully.

Sean shook his head. "I guess the only place I know in Alabama is Birmingham."

"Well, I guess that's all right," said Louise. "I don't know any of the places where you're from either."

"New Zealand has several smaller villages, too," Alex pointed out.

"So what's the name of the town you're from, Nigel?" Louise asked.

Sean shot a panicked look at Alex. He hadn't considered anyone would ask for a location more specific than simply New Zealand.

"Go ahead, Nigel," Alex prompted. "Tell Louise about Chertsey."

"Chertsey?" Louise said brightly, "That's just the *cutest* name! What's it like?"

"Well..." Sean started, looking again to Alex. "It's...um...nice... What would you say, Peter? From a visitor's point of view, I mean."

"It has a population of about 1900," Alex said.

"Well, that's about the same size as Mercer!" Louise gushed. "So you're just a small-town boy, too, Nigel!"

"That's right, luv," Sean said nervously, "Just a small-town lad, meself, wot."

"What do your folks do?" asked Louise.

Sean was completely tongue-tied. He hadn't thought of needing a family as a background story element.

"No reason to be embarrassed, cousin," Alex said, "You are in the Midwestern section of the United States. You should speak proudly of your family running a small dairy farm."

Louise put her hand on Sean's arm; her eyes widened. "That's why Daddy came back to Iowa! To help *his* daddy with the farm. They mostly grow corn, but they've got a few cows, too. I've even milked a cow a time or two." She became a little more subdued. "Gramps had an accident with a corn picker four years ago," she said solemnly, "That's why Daddy came up to help out, and then when he didn't think Gramps would be able to get back to farming the whole place himself, he decided to move the whole family up here."

Sean was anxious to steer the conversation away from life in New Zealand. He smiled his biggest smile at Louise and asked, "How did your parents meet?"

"Oh," she said with a mischievous grin, "that must have just been *somethin'!* I wasn't there of course, but to hear them tell it, it was just magical! Daddy had a day pass and he and some other soldiers went into Daleville to have a little look around. Mama and some of her friends happened to be in the malt shop after school when Daddy and the other soldiers came in to get themselves something cool to drink. Their eyes met from across the room..." Louise paused to hug herself and dreamily stare off into space. "It was love at first sight!" she sighed.

"Louise!" Ritchie barked, "Order up!"

"Oooops," she said, again putting a hand on Sean's arm. "I guess I almost forgot I was at work!" She quickly slid the plates from the grill onto a tray, pulled three more drinks and was unloading them back at one of the booths in seconds.

"She's a talker, isn't she?" Sean said to Alex.

"I find it interesting that she is willing to divulge so much information to someone she just met," Alex replied.

"Aw, she's just friendly, and happy to have someone new to talk to. And, after all, we're celebrities! You're a vegetarian, and I'm her first Nigel!"

Louise returned with an empty tray. "I'd better get goin' on your malted, Peter. Nigel's burger will be ready here pretty quick." She pulled a carton of vanilla ice cream from a freezer under the counter and placed three huge scoops into a tall, shiny metal container. She slipped the silvery cup under a spigot and pumped twice, then glanced over to Ritchie before pumping a third pump. She retrieved a carton of milk from under the counter and poured from it, eyeballing the amount needed, then dumped in a scoop of powder from a gallon-sized jar on the back shelf. She moved a step to her right to an avocado-green machine that had two long metal rods with tiny paddles at the bottom. Louise slid the shiny container up and around one of the rods, and the mixer jumped to life, whirring away. She looked over her shoulder to smile at Sean and Alex as she bounced the cup up and down for a couple of minutes.

Sean returned a warm smile as he gave Louise a closer look. She was about five foot two, dark brown hair, a fairly dark tan, hazel eyes and a cute button nose. She didn't seem to wear much makeup other than mascara, but had a pretty face without added adornment. Sean noticed she had a small faded scar under her left eye that trailed around toward her ear, and he wondered what had happened to her. Her hair was pulled back and rolled up and clipped to keep it off her shoulders. The pastel blue dress was obviously a uniform and she also wore a white apron that covered the front of her dress from the waist down. She was cute. She seemed fun. And Sean thought he wouldn't mind getting to know her better. His smile melted when he realized that back in 1995 she might very well have a daughter that was his age.

Louise set a tall slender ribbed glass in front of Alex and carefully poured from the shiny container she had just pulled off the mixer. She then stuck a long-stemmed spoon into the glass before turning back to the counter next to the machine. She whirled fluidly back to Alex and handed him a straw.

"This is a bigger straw than we use for Cokes. You're gonna need it, that malted is pretty thick!" she said proudly.

"Louise. Order up." Ritchie shouted.

She glanced his way but turned back to Sean before picking up the dish by the grill. "I'm pretty sure yours is next, Nigel," she said before quickly pulling drinks to go with the burgers. In an instant, she was gone again.

Alex assessed his large glass and straw.

"The straw goes in the malt. Your lips go around the other end of the straw, and you suck on it," Sean said with a grin.

"I understand the procedure," Alex replied, "I am not yet sure I wish to ingest this concoction."

"Now just a few days ago you were telling me that you needed to immerse yourself more into the world you were observing. You're not going to be scared off by a little ice cream and chocolate, are you?"

Alex pulled the spoon from the glass; it was coated with the viscous dairy. He handed the spoon to Sean. "Give me your impression of this... food."

Sean stuck the bowl of the spoon into his mouth. He closed his eyes as a euphoric smile sprung up behind the extracted spoon. "Wow. That is *good*," he moaned. "That is *really* good! Hands down, ten times better than a McDonald's shake."

Alex gingerly put the tip of his straw into the top of the glass and closed his mouth around the other end. His cheeks sunk in as he pulled on the straw. "It is very cold," he said as he twitched a connection to his computer. "The caloric content appears to be mostly from dairy fat and sugar."

"Don't you *dare* say that to Louise when she asks you how it is!" Sean hissed.

"What should I say?" Alex asked.

"Tell her it was smooth and creamy and yummy," Sean ordered.

"I do not believe it would be in character for Peter to speak that way," Alex protested.

Louise returned with a tray of dishes she'd cleared from one of the booths. "Well?" she asked, "How do you like it?"

Alex glanced at Sean, who returned his gaze with threatening eyes. "I can truthfully say," Alex began, "that this is the *best* chocolate malted I have ever tasted."

Louise's smile widened as she patted Alex's forearm. "I'm glad you like it," she said enthusiastically. "I think that a third squirt of chocolate just makes it all the yummier!"

Alex glanced again toward Sean. "Yes," he stumbled, "and very smooth and creamy."

"Order up," barked Ritchie.

"That should be yours, Nigel," Louise said as she turned to grab the plate from Ritchie. She spun back around and set the burger and fries in front of Sean.

Sean was amazed by the mound of fries heaped on the plate. They were much larger and browner than anything he'd ever had at Burger King or Mickey D's.

"Ketchup?" Louise said as she plopped a red plastic container next to Sean's plate. "And there's salt and pepper next to the napkin dispenser, but Ritchie usually uses plenty of salt."

Ritchie crossed behind her and set another beer in front of the man at the far end of the counter, and then stood there and talked with him. Sean glanced over to the grill and saw it was empty.

The young couple with the toddler came up behind them and stood a few feet to Alex's right. Louise glanced at Ritchie, then scooted over to face the couple. Sean hadn't yet noticed the cash register next to their end of the counter. He took a bite of his cheeseburger.

"How was everything?" Louise asked politely.

"It was good," the man said noncommittally as he handed her a couple of bills.

Louise took the money but turned her attention toward the baby. "Well, you are just the cutest thing!" she cooed. "Yes you are! You are the cutest thing!" She punched a few keys on the register, and a bell rang as the money drawer slid out. She neatly put the bills in a slot under a clip and pulled coins from two compartments.

"You can keep the change," the man offered shyly.

Louise held her hand out to the man as she closed the drawer with her left hand. "That's really sweet of you, Billy, but I know you and Janice have your hands full taking care of this one," she said, nodding toward the child. "Don't you worry, I'm doin' fine. You just keep this."

The man glanced at his wife and child as he held out his hand. Her eyes nervously flitted between her baby and the ground, and Billy turned his head slightly away as Louise dropped the coins into his hand. "Thanks, Louise," he mumbled softly, "you're a saint."

"You folks have a nice evenin' now," Louise called cheerily after them as they left.

Sean had already thought Louise was attractive; cute, vibrant, and warm. But he suddenly imagined a halo over her head and decided he was in love. Louise slid back down to face Sean and Alex. "Billy and Janice Fletcher," she said somberly. "He brings her in here about once a month for dinner, but I don't know that he can even afford that." She glanced toward the door. "She got pregnant their senior year. It's gotta be hard, but they seem to be makin' it." The smile came back to her face. "How'd you like your burger?"

"It's great, Louise," Sean said, then decided he needed to add something to maintain his guise as a foreigner. "Top-notch. Smashing! Really...ummm... popped the kipper, wot?"

"I guess those are all good things?" Louise giggled. "Anyway, I'm glad you like it."

"And these french-fries are amazing!" Sean added.

"Well, you just enjoy your dinner," Louise smiled. "I've got to get some stuff cleaned up. I'm supposed to get off in twenty minutes." She left them to bus more tables.

"Popped the kipper?" Alex asked.

"I don't know!" Sean exclaimed. "It just came out." He dragged a long french-fry through the ketchup pool he'd squirted onto the side of his plate. "You should try these. They are incredible!"

"My diet is already well out of balance with fat and carbohydrates. It will not help to add more carbohydrates," Alex complained.

"Just taste one! It won't kill you. Here. Here's a little one without ketchup," said Sean as he held a small piece of potato in front of Alex.

Alex reluctantly put the morsel into his mouth and chewed. "Considerably more sodium chloride than is needed," he said just before a shocked look came over his face. "Did you know these were fried in animal fat?" Alex grabbed a napkin and spit the offensive food into it.

"Really?" Sean asked, munching another fry drenched in ketchup. "I wonder if that's what makes them taste better."

"It is barbaric!" Alex blustered. "Slaughtering animals simply to...." He stopped himself.

"Having a little culture clash while hanging out with the cavemen?" asked a bemused Sean.

Alex looked embarrassed. "I am sorry. I am aware that the human body requires the consumption of protein, and you have yet to learn how to synthesize it efficiently in this era. I was momentarily repulsed by having something that was once a living, breathing creature in my mouth."

"Dude, it was a French-fry," Sean said unsympathetically. "Apparently fried in lard but still like 99% potato."

"You should not say 'Dude'. That term is rarely used in this time."

"Everything OK?" Louise asked as she returned with another tray bussed from one of the booths.

"Smashing!" Sean said enthusiastically.

"I thought Peter looked a little upset," observed Louise.

"Righto! Ummmm... Peter must have been drinking too fast and it just iced up his noggin," Sean improvised.

"Iced up his noggin," Louise repeated as she laughed. "I do so enjoy hearin' you say stuff. We call that a 'brain freeze' in American."

"Louise! Are you going to get those dishes washed before you leave?" came a stern voice from down the counter.

"Yes, sir," replied a contrite Louise in a sing-song tone. "I was just makin' sure everything was OK with their food." She lowered her voice as she spoke to Sean and Alex, "I'd love to chat some more, but I better not get Ritchie too riled up at me."

Louise picked up some plates she had stacked earlier and slid them carefully into a large under-counter sink near the middle of the bar. She then took the stacks of glasses to a smaller sink that was closer to Sean. Sean moved down two stools, dragging his plate along with him. He leaned forward for a better look at what Louise was doing. The smaller sink was full of suds, but also had two cylindrical bristle brushes peeking out. Louise had a glass in each hand and was plunging them both over the brushes. From there, she dipped them into an adjoining sink which was filled with clear water to rinse any residual soap. She'd laid out a clean, white tea-towel on the rear counter where the rinsed glasses were stacked, bottom side up.

Sean pointed to the sink with the built-in brushes. "That's a bit clever, id nit?"

"It sure speeds up washin' the glasses... which is a real good thing, since I probably wash every glass in this place twice during a shift."

"Business is good, then, is it?"

"I can't say if Ritchie makes a whole lot of money or not. Lots of people just come in for a Coke. A hundred Cokes is ten to fifteen dollars, dependin' on how many people go for the fifteen center. While that's not bad money for you or me, I got no idea how much it costs to run a business like this," Louise said all the while dunking more glasses.

"What's happenin', Lulu?" came a voice passing behind Sean.

"Hey, Toto," Louise answered then turned back to Sean. "That's Tony. He's Ritchie's oldest son. He's a senior this fall. He comes in most nights to help Ritchie close up. I only call him 'Toto' when he calls me 'Lulu'." She glanced up at the clock. "I'd better hurry up and get on those plates." She quickly dunked two more glasses.

Sean took another bite of his cheeseburger and chewed as he contemplated the wording for his next question. He was just about to speak when Louise turned to put two more glasses on the counter behind her. As she plunged the last two glasses onto the brushes, Sean made up his mind. "Louise, luv, what are you going to be doing with yourself when you get off work?" he asked, his stomach tied in knots.

She looked thoughtful. "Well, lots of times on a Saturday night a bunch of us will get together up around the park and then go do somethin' or sometimes just do nothin'. You 'n' Peter should come on up! I'll bet my friends would be as tickled to meet you as I was!" She paused. "If you didn't have any place else you were goin' already, that is."

Sean didn't know if he was disappointed or relieved that Louise didn't recognize his question as asking her out. They had already planned to go back to the park to try to meet his Dad, and maybe he was one of Louise's friends. In any event, he would get to spend some more time with her. "That would be smashing, luv. We'd be happy to meet your mates," he said cranking up his best smile.

She put the last two glasses on the shelf and moved down the counter to the larger sink and plunged her hands in, pulling up a plate. Sean moved back to his original stool, sliding what remained of his food with him.

"She's going to hook up with some friends in the park when she gets off work. This might make an easier way to get close to my Dad," Sean told Alex.

"It does seem to be a fortuitous opportunity," Alex replied.

"Fortuitous?" Sean scoffed. "I think it's a good thing you're using an English accent now. It fits your snobby weird language."

When Alex had no reply, Sean went back to devouring his burger. By the time he'd finished two-thirds of his mountain of fries, he felt pretty full. Alex had been taking tiny sips of his malt but hadn't nearly finished half of it. Louise glanced up at them and started drying her hands on a towel as she walked toward them. "Are you ready for your ticket?" she asked, already writing on it again.

"Yes, I don't think I can finish this huge pile of fries," Sean replied. "That was just amazing."

Louise glanced over at Ritchie, who was still talking to the beer-drinking man at the end of the counter. "Would you think it terrible of me if I snitched a couple of your fries? I haven't eaten since lunch... well, not counting the Cherry Coke on a break." Sean pushed the plate closer to Louise. With her back to Ritchie, she quickly snagged a couple shorter potatoes and popped them into her mouth. "I know that's just terribly unprofessional of me, but I'm gonna skip on dinner today, even though it's a payday."

"No, I really don't mind at all. Better than throwing them away," Sean said sincerely. "Take all you want."

"No, I'm good. Thanks. Just a little something to keep my tummy from growlin'," she said after swallowing. She placed the bill halfway between Sean and Alex. Sean picked it up and looked it over. Louise had returned to her sink of plates, adding the one she just removed from Sean. Sean's eyes widened when he looked at the total at the bottom of his slip of paper.

"Louise?" he called. "Are you sure you got this right?"

"Oh no!" she cried as she hurried back over. "Did I make a mistake?" She examined it carefully. "Fifty-five for the cheeseburger, twenty-five for the fries, and a fifteen cent Coke, plus forty cents for the malted. Tax is three cents on the dollar, so that's four cents. A dollar thirty-nine. That's right. Did you not know that the cheeseburger was five cents more?"

"No, that's quite all right. Sorry. My bad. Couldn't add right. Bit of a dunderhead, wot?" said Sean. "Sorry to have given you a fright."

"That's all right," she said, relieved, "Everyone makes mistakes. I'm surprised it wasn't me." She went back to washing dishes.

Sean elbowed Alex. "A dollar thirty-nine!" he said in a hoarse whisper. "Can you believe it? A dollar thirty-nine! It would have been under a buck if you hadn't gotten that malt!"

"I apologize for my extravagance," Alex said sincerely.

"Are you kidding? All this food for a dollar thirty-nine? It's amazing!"

"There are several years of inflation from now until 1995."

"But that's just crazy to get a whole meal for under a dollar... and I couldn't eat it all! Dude, my Dad's a lucky dog to have prices like these."

"You must realize," Alex said patiently, "that it is all relative."

"What do you mean?"

"They also have much lower incomes. A 1969 dollar is worth about four times what your 1995 dollar can purchase. The median household income in 1969 is approximately $17,000.00. That will grow to $63,000.00 by 1995," Alex explained.

"Yeah, yeah," Sean said, waving him off. "I'm sure I had that in some class, but somehow it's just numbers until you really sink your teeth into it." He tried to finish his Coke, but found that his straw had collapsed. He took the straw out and tipped up the glass. Louise grabbed it as he set it down. She dumped the ice into an empty sink followed with a brisk plunging of the glass on one of the brushes. Sean wondered how many sinks they had behind that counter. He also wondered about his straw and took a closer look. "This is made of paper," he said to Alex.

Alex connected to his computer. "Plastic straws became the popular replacement for paper straws in the 1960s. You might also be interested to know that there is a resurgence of paper straws in your near future, when environmentalists become more concerned about all of the plastic going into landfills. Those paper straws, however, are of a different design, and more durable than this one. Perhaps Ritchie's is simply reticent to change."

Louise had returned and was standing in front of Alex. "I'm sorry, Peter. I don't mean to be a pest, but would you like a to-go cup for the rest of your malted?"

"No," Alex answered, "that will not be necessary. I have..."

"That would be super, luv!" Sean interrupted. "Ta so much!"

Louise quickly poured the remainder of Alex's malt into a waxed paper cup. She just as quickly plunged the empty glass into the sink and bounced it up and down on the brush. Sean waited until she had rinsed it and placed it on the towel to air dry. "Could I also get a fresh straw?" he asked. Louise spun around, grabbed one of the larger straws, and handed it to Sean. She stood beaming at them, rocking on her heels a little.

"Oh!" Sean said when he'd figured out the body language. "Sorry." He moved over to the cash register.

"How was everything?" Louise asked automatically.

"Smashing, luv," Sean enthused, then glanced at Alex before adding with a grin, "really popped the kipper!"

"Well, I'm so glad you liked it... at least I *think* that means you liked it," she giggled.

Sean chuckled along with her as he gave her the five he had. Louise tucked it into the register and counted his change back to him. "Three dollars and sixty-one cents makes five." Sean handed a dollar back to her. She stared at it but didn't take it. Sean's face turned red and he added another dollar. "Nigel!" She said in a loud whisper. "What are you doing?"

"Ummm... tip?" Sean said, not sure what he had done wrong.

Louise looked around to make sure no one was listening. "Nigel," she whispered, "I don't think you understand American money. That is *way* too much to tip! I hope other people don't take advantage of you not knowin' what's right."

"Ummm, what would *you* say is 'right' in this case?" Sean asked cautiously.

"Well, I gave you back sixty-one cents in change, so you could keep the quarters, and tip me the eleven cents... the quarters are those bigger ones."

"That's not even ten percent! Here, take this quarter," he said as he forced it into her hand. "Oh, and catch this," he said as he flipped the second quarter in the air. She reacted quickly and caught it, but stared open-mouthed at him. "That one is karma," he proclaimed, "for refusing the tip from that young family."

"Nigel, that's sweet, but I can't...."

"Tut tut! You don't want to start and international incident," he interrupted, "do you?"

She grinned. "No, sir!"

"There you go! Carry on!"

She looked down at her quarters. "You are just the *sweetest* thing..." her voice choked a little. "I need to go change, if you could wait for me for a few minutes, we can all walk up to the park together," she said, then dashed to the back of the room.

Sean looked at Alex with puppy-dog eyes. "I think I'm in love."

"I have observed that you appear infatuated with Louise, but it is very impractical to say that you are in love. We will only be here for a few days at the most, and when you return to your own time, Louise will be old enough to be your mother," Alex replied logically.

"I know *that*!" Sean snarled, "I didn't mean 'I wanna marry you' love... just 'I wanna get closer to you and spend some time with you' kinda love."

Alex cringed slightly from Sean's snarl. "I am sorry," he said. "I do not have any data to allow me to assess the various levels of love for teenagers in the 20th century."

Sean felt regret that his explosive personality cowered his descendant yet again. "No, I'm sorry I snapped at you," Sean said contritely. "I shouldn't let it get to me when you spout logic. I can't expect you to react the way Raj or Kevin would. That's just not you." He paused and waited for Alex to look at him. "Can I ask you something, though?"

Alex nodded.

"You said that I may be ignorant, but not stupid, right?"

Alex nodded.

"After I thought about that for awhile, I guess I figured out what you meant. Just because there are lots of things that you've learned that I haven't, doesn't mean that I can't learn."

Alex nodded.

"So," Sean summed up, "if you think I say something stupid, remember that you don't actually think that I'm stupid, and maybe...just *maybe* what I said that sounded like something stupid only seemed that way because you don't know what I mean."

Alex thought for a moment, then started to speak.

"Whup-up-up-up," Sean interrupted, holding his hand in Alex's face. "Before you say something logical, I'd like to add that when you hear me say something that sounds stupid, the *last* thing you should do is try to explain to me why what I said was stupid."

Alex waited to see if Sean was going to continue. When he didn't he asked, "May I ask a hypothetical question regarding the situation with you and Louise?"

"Sure."

"You insinuated that your friends Raj and Kevin would have reacted differently than I did. From the inflection of your voice, I assume that you believe their reactions would have been preferable to mine."

Sean thought it over, then nodded.

"What then," Alex asked, "would Raj or Kevin have said in a similar situation, reacting to your statement of being in love?"

Sean looked away as he tried to visualize what Alex had proposed. "OK," he said, "Raj would probably say, 'Again?' and Kevin would say something like, 'I saw her first.'"

Alex pondered Sean's answers before continuing, "What would then be your reaction to such statements?"

"Then we'd probably all laugh about it."

Alex closed his eyes as he tried to make sense of what his ancestor had said. "Your friends would have recognized that your profession of love was hyperbole, and they would make light of your statement?"

"Hyperbole?" Sean gave Alex an 'are you serious' look before continuing, "Yeah, OK, yes! It would be a normal reaction to make a joke about it."

"Then in summation, you would prefer that I refrain from pointing out that something is illogical. Furthermore, I should say something that would induce a humorous reaction."

"Yeah, I don't know about the second part," said Sean. "Your humor leaves a lot to be desired. But you've got the first part figured out."

"I will attempt to alter my behavior."

Sean glanced to the back of the room to check for Louise. When he didn't see her, he looked around aimlessly for something to pass the time. The counter in front of the cash register was stocked with candy bars. Although the labels looked a little different, he recognized Snickers, 3 Musketeers, and several other familiar brands. Then he started picking up some that he didn't know.

"Look at these," he said to Alex. "Zagnut. Bun. Black Cow. Denver Sandwich. Hollywood. With psycho names like that, no wonder they're not around anymore. Check this one out—Zero—is it supposed to be no calories or what?" He saw Alex do his 'I don't know, but the computer does' twitch.

"It consists of caramel, peanut butter, and almond nougat, covered in white fudge," Alex recited.

"That sure doesn't sound like zero calories."

"Perhaps it is a reference to the white color?"

"I think I'll buy one just to check it out."

Louise emerged from the women's restroom, carrying a large paper bag. She'd barely taken a couple of steps when a loud wolf whistle came from one of the men at the pool table. She glanced his way, but quickly looked back forward and continued walking.

"Hey, Bama Girl! Looking good!" one of them shouted. "Hey, I got something for you," he added. He had put his pool cue between his legs and stroked it lewdly.

Louise stopped and turned toward him, speaking loud enough for everyone in the room to hear, "My mama told me that when boys do things like that it's to make up for feelin's of inadequacy." She started to walk away, but the man reached out and grabbed her by the arm.

"What'd you say?" he snarled.

Sean had heard the wolf whistle and from across the room had watched the drama unfold. He started briskly toward Louise, unsure of what he was going to do when he got there, but feeling he had to do something. Before he was even halfway across the room, a blur shot out from behind the counter and Tony was standing within striking distance of the man as he brandished a baseball bat with both hands.

"Say the word, Louise," Tony said without taking his eyes off the man.

Several tense seconds passed as the man and Tony eyed each other. Sean reached the small crowd, still unsure what to do. The second man who had been playing pool slowly moved over beside his friend, holding the middle of his cue, waving the large end in small circles in the air, his eyes focused on Tony. Tony's eyes showed no emotion, but the muscles in his jaw were rigid. The man released his grip on Louise's arm and stepped back half a step, eyes still locked with Tony's.

"Louise?" Tony prompted.

"Well," Louise started softly as she rubbed the red mark on her arm where it had been in the man's grip, "I guess maybe Mr. Parker has just had a few too many beers."

Parker let his pool cue clatter to the floor as he held his arms away from his sides, open palms facing forward. His friend also took a step back and leaned his cue against the pool table. The muscles in Tony's neck relaxed a little. Sean took a deep breath, unaware that his breathing had gone shallow as adrenaline coursed through his body.

Parker forced an insincere smile to his lips. "See," he said, "everything's cool."

Tony's grip on the bat relaxed a little. "It's cool after you apologize to Louise," he said evenly.

"What?" growled Parker, his eyes narrowing.

Tony re-tightened his grip on the bat. "Apologize," he said calmly.

"For what?" Parker sneered. "For whistling at her? She's asking for it parading her cute little ass around in those tight little shorts."

"Apologize," Tony repeated, but through clenched teeth the second time.

Parker glared fiercely at Tony for a few seconds, then switched his gaze to the floor turning slightly away from Louise and Tony. "Sorry, Bama," he muttered angrily.

"Her name is Louise," Tony stated calmly.

"I know that!" Parker spat, looking hard at Tony again.

"I think you should call her by her real name, and try that apology again."

Parker's face turned red with rage. Tony's face showed determination, but no real anger.

Parker took a deep breath. "I'm sorry... Louise," he said, truly regretting that he'd ever laid eyes on her.

"Thank you, Mr. Parker," Louise said softly to the floor, "Maybe you can go back to enjoyin' your game of pool."

Parker looked at Tony. Tony nodded and let the bat rest loosely on his shoulder. The men returned to the pool table as Louise walked away. Tony walked next to her but backwards, not taking his eyes from Parker. Sean fell into step on the other side of Louise and they moved toward the cash register.

"Thank you, Tony," Louise said quietly. "I don't think he would have really done nothin' but I appreciate you standin' up for me."

Tony shook his head, "Louise, you're too softhearted toward losers like that."

"Mama taught me to always look for the best in people."

"I don't think that counts for jackasses," Tony replied tersely.

"He has his troubles, too," Louise said charitably. "The whole town knows that his wife kicked him out two weeks ago."

"Yeah," answered Tony, "and the whole town but *you* knows he deserved it."

"I should have just kept walkin' instead of tauntin' him about his man parts," Louise said solemnly.

Tony's face split into a huge grin, "Come on, Louise. That was the best part!"

Ritchie leaned over the counter when they got close. "You all right, Louise?" he asked.

"Yes, sir," she replied, then added, "May I have my pay, please?"

"Sure thing," answered Ritchie as he started toward the cash register.

Louise, Tony, Sean and Alex all clustered near the other side of the cash register. Tony eyed Sean and Alex suspiciously. "What are you two hanging around for?" he challenged.

Louise put her hand on Tony's right arm which still held the bat. "It's OK, Tony," Louise assured him. "They're going to walk up to the park with me."

"Are you sure you want to go with strangers, Louise?" Tony asked, still eying Sean and Alex.

"Don't you trust my judgment of character, Tony?"

"Thirty hours, Louise?" interrupted Ritchie.

"Yes, sir," Louise replied, "That's what I counted up."

"Three fives OK?" Ritchie asked.

"If it wouldn't put you out too much," Louise said shyly, "could I get five ones and two fives?"

Ritchie counted out the bills and handed them across to Louise. She stuffed the fives into her left front pocket and the ones into her right front pocket.

"Normal time on Monday?" Ritchie asked.

"Yes, sir! I'll be here!" Louise answered cheerily.

Ritchie closed the cash register and started back to the end of the counter where the large man still sat with his collection of empty beer bottles. "Tony," he hollered as he walked, "you want to get the ketchup bottles topped off?"

Tony glanced between Louise and Sean. "You sure they're OK, Lulu?"

"Oh, Toto!" Louise said, giving him a little push, "Go fill your ketchup bottles!"

Tony walked away from them after giving Sean and Alex one last harsh look.

Sean opened the door and waited for Louise and Alex to walk outside. When he'd stepped onto the sidewalk and closed the door behind them, he softly said, "Wow."

"That was a near dust-up, I should say," Alex commented. "Rather awkward for a bit," he added in his perfect British accent.

"That's one way to put it," Sean mumbled.

"I'm sorry you had to witness that," Louise apologized, "People 'round here don't normally act like that. I don't want you to get the idea that Mercer's a bad town."

"Louise, luv," Sean said, "You just paint a rainbow over everything, don't you?" He took the cup from Alex and handed it to her. "Here, I nearly forgot."

She looked up at him. "Nigel! You can't just take Peter's malted and give it to me!"

"He was finished," Sean assured her, "The only reason I had you put it in a to-go cup was so you could have it. I mean, really, luv, if all you've had since lunch is two french-fries..."

"And a Cherry Coke," Louise added.

"And a Cherry Coke..." Sean repeated. "You've got to be hungry. Fresh straw, too, remember?"

She looked over at Alex. "Are you really done with it, Peter?"

"Quite," Alex replied. "It was frightfully good, though. Please, drink up."

Louise took the cup from Sean and sipped from the straw. "Mmmmm, that is soooo good," she purred, "I'm so glad I put three pumps of chocolate in. I just love chocolate."

They walked up the street without a word except for Louise's occasional *Mmmmms*. Sean gave her quick sideways glances to appreciate the transformation from waitress Louise. The only other sound besides *mmmmm* as they walked was the consistent slapping of Louise's pink flip-flops against her heels. Her shorts were indeed rather short, as Mr. Parker had pointed out. Sean thought of them as 'Daisy Dukes', though he was pretty sure that show hadn't yet aired in 1969. The edges of what was left of the blue denim legs were unraveled fringe. She wore a form fitting emerald-green tank-top snugly tucked into her shorts. By far, the biggest change in her appearance was her hair. When released from the clip she was wearing, it hung halfway down her back. She had tied a matching emerald scarf around her head forming a band about an inch wide at her forehead. Her hair spilled over most of the scarf, hiding most of it except at her forehead and where it was tied into a large bow with long tales in the back. Louise's scarf was the only element that Sean considered 'hippie clothes'. That fleeting thought again caused him to feel uncomfortable with his own strange garb.

As if cued from his thoughts, Louise spoke. "I like the colors in your tie-dye, Nigel. Did you do it yourself?"

Sean glanced at Alex before replying, "No, ummm, bought it on the beach when we first were in California. Just off the boat, knocking about."

"It looks good on you," she commented.

"Thanks... ummm... you have lovely hair," Sean said, thinking he should return the compliment.

Louise's cheeks were tinged with pink as she gave him a quick smile. She tried to hide her blush by returning her attention to the malt.

They crossed the street to the park and paused by a trash barrel as Louise finished and tossed the cup in. She pointed toward a large gazebo in the center of the park. "I think I see some people up there. Let's check." Before they could move, a car honked two short blasts as it sped up the street. Louise waved enthusiastically. "Y'all get to meet my very best friend!" she gushed to Sean and Alex. Sean's gaze bounced between Louise and the light blue Thunderbird convertible driving up the street.

"Please tell me her name isn't Thelma," Sean said through a grin.

Louise looked curiously at Sean. "No, it's Jane. Why would you think it was Thelma?"

"No reason," Sean said. "Something about the car, I think."

"That's her uncle's T-Bird," said Louise. "I wonder why she has it. Come on. She's probably heading for the bandstand, too."

Louise set a brisk pace which Sean matched effortlessly with his longer strides. As they neared the gazebo, Louise broke into a faster trot, angling toward the girl who was also moving rapidly toward Louise. They greeted each other with high pitched squeals and hugs. A boy about their age sauntered slowly behind the girl who had rushed to meet Louise. Louise trotted over to him and gave him a hug, too. A bit of ice hit the bottom of Sean's stomach when he saw them kiss. The boy wasn't much taller than Louise, and had sandy brown hair that covered his ears and hung to his collar.

The other girl waited for the couple to reach her. She was about 5'6', trim, an odd color of brown hair hanging down in two braids, blue eyes, and had a prominent nose which shifted attention away from her smile and eyes. A pair of gold wire-rimmed glasses with circular lenses barely larger than her eyes sat on that nose.

Louise linked arms between the newcomers and headed toward Sean and Alex, smiling infectiously as she brought the two groups together.

"Nigel, Peter, this is my very best friend, Jane Carmichael," Louise said with practiced Southern charm. "Jane this is Peter Lindsey and Nigel..." She paused and put her hand briefly over her mouth. "Oh my goodness... Nigel I didn't ever hear your last name."

Sean stared at her blankly as she looked expectantly back at him.

"Davies," Alex said. Sean breathed out a sigh. He'd suddenly gone blank on his assumed name.

"Nigel Davies," Louise continued smoothly.

"Nice to meet you both," Jane nodded toward each of them.

"Cheers," said Alex.

" 'ello, luv," Sean said sullenly.

"And this," continued Louise brightly, "is my boyfriend, Micky."

"My *little* brother," Jane added with a wry smile.

Louise giggled. "Jane likes to lord it over Micky. She's eighteen minutes older than him."

Twins, thought Sean as he glanced at Alex and thought of Nicole and Alexis. *Real ones, though.*

Micky and Alex shook hands. Sean then took Micky's offered hand, trying to hide any sign of jealousy. "What's happenin'?" Mickey grunted.

"G'Day, Mate," Sean replied.

"Nigel is from New Zealand and Peter is from England," Louise announced. "They're cousins!"

"Far out," mumbled Micky with far less enthusiasm than Louise.

"Groovy!" Jane said with genuine warmth.

"So... twins..." Sean said, trying to think of something to say. He wondered why the two newcomers spoke 'hippie' but Louise didn't.

"Yeah," Jane replied, "I'm the cute one." Micky stared daggers at her. "...*and* the smart one."

Louise gave Jane a playful shove. "Stop bein' mean to my boyfriend!" she complained.

"So how'd you two wander into the middle of nowheresville?" Micky asked flatly.

"Hitchhiking across the United States," Alex said. "Taking a listen to local bands when we can. Musicians, ourselves, you see."

"That's cool," Micky said blandly as his head bobbed.

"So what instruments do you play?" asked the ever enthusiastic Louise.

"I play guitar," Alex said, "Nigel plays various wind instruments, mostly flute. He sings like a bird, though." Sean's eyes flew wide open as he turned to Alex.

"Far out!" chimed Jane. "So, Peter, what part of England are you from?"

"Liverpool," Alex answered.

"I wondered... your voice sounds so much like Paul McCartney," Jane said. "Paul is so dreamy. Ever hear them live?"

"I have, actually," Alex said modestly. "December 1963, not long before they made their first trip to the States."

"Did you see them at the Cavern Club?" asked an engrossed Jane.

"No, unfortunately. Me mum said that was no place for decent lads. I was only 13... nearly 14," Alex said. "I saw them at the Empire. That was

61

where they played their last Liverpool concert two years later. Too big after that to come back, I reckon."

"I watched them on TV the first time they were on Ed Sullivan. I was almost 12. I was mesmerized," Jane said.

"You mean you sat there and screamed along with all the girls in the TV audience... and cried. Mom thought I kicked you or something," said Micky.

"You were just as goofy over the Monkees," Jane sniped. "So much that you changed your name to Micky."

"What was it before?" asked Sean.

"Mike... well, it still is Michael, but he managed to get everyone to start calling him Micky," Jane replied.

"Michael Carmichael?" asked Sean, trying to suppress a laugh.

"It gets better," Jane grinned. "His middle name is Carl."

"Michael Carl Carmichael?" Sean said, unable to hide his smile.

"Not cool!" Micky snapped. "Jane *Ophelia*!"

"Oh!" gasped Jane melodramatically. "You got me, Micky! Right in the heart!" She staggered with a hand over her heart as if dying, then punched him in the shoulder and laughed.

"Come on, Louise," Micky said as he tugged Louise away with him. "Let's sit on that bench over there and you can tell me about what a drag it was spending the day at Ritchie's."

"Oh my gosh, Micky," Louise said in her continually perky voice. "You wouldn't believe it, but there was almost a fight." Their voices trailed off as they walked away.

"Looks like Louise has left you in my capable hands," Jane said confidently. Sean frowned as he watched the retreating Louise, both disappointed and irritated that she had a boyfriend. "I suppose I shouldn't hassle Micky so much," she said as she also watched them walk away, "but it's just *so* easy!" She turned her attention back to Sean and Alex. "Hey, looks like you got here about the same time as me, so I guess you haven't met anyone else."

"No, we have not, as of yet," replied Alex.

Jane started walking toward the gazebo, quickly looking back at Sean and Alex, giving her head a 'come on' jerk. They followed her to the gazebo.

"What's happening?" Jane asked brightly of the three guys sitting on the north wall.

"Not much, Jane," one of them replied. "What's up with you?"

"Keeping mellow," she returned.

"Cool."

"How come you got your uncle's T-bird?" asked another.

"Check this out," Jane said with a grin. "Uncle Carl is having a bash at his place tonight, OK? So he asks me to come help him clean it up. Says he'll pay me. So I spend six hours cleaning his dump and when I get done, I ask him about the money. He says he doesn't have it right now, 'cause he spent it all for beer and booze for his party." The three guys laughed. "So I see his car keys by the door and grab 'em. As I head out the door, I says to him, 'you'll get your car back when I get my money' and I was outta there."

"Aren't you afraid he'll call the cops on you?" asked the first guy.

"Nah. He's cool with it. He's not going anywhere tonight since everyone's coming to his place. He'll take up a collection to pay for the kegs and I'll take his car back tomorrow and get paid. It's all cool."

"And she'll have fun fun fun til her uncle takes the T-bird away," sang the second guy, breaking into a falsetto.

"Scott," Jane said, "I don't think *Beach Boys* is really in your repertoire." His friends laughed. "Hey, I want you guys to meet some friends of Louise's. This is Peter Lindsey from England and Nigel Davies from New Zealand."

"Far out," said the third guy.

Jane gestured toward the three. "This is Jimbo, Scott, and Juan." All five launched into a series of greetings and handshakes, ending with Alex and Juan.

"*Hola, Juan,*" Alex said in perfect Spanish, "*¿Cómo estás?*"

"What?" said Juan, blankly, "Oh! Spanish... I don't speak it. Hey, I'm not Mexican or anything. Juan is just my nickname. My real name is John Kelly."

Sean's jaw dropped. "Dad?"

Chapter Four

"She seemed so sweet and kind / she crept into my mind"

"**D**ID YOU say, 'Dad'?" asked John.

Sean froze. He hadn't considered that any of the three in the gazebo could be his Dad. None of them even remotely looked like the Jack Kelly he knew.

After several tense seconds of silence, Alex spoke, "Sounded like it, I must agree. It is one of those New Zealand quirks I have learned to accept. What he actually said was *n'd'a'id*. Get it from the Maori people, right?" He directed the question to Sean.

Sean looked blankly at Alex, still stunned. "What?" he stumbled. "Oh, yeah Mallory..."

"The Maori are indigenous to New Zealand," Alex continued. "Nigel always had a fascination with their tribal cultures and picked up some language along the way. *N'd'a'id* means "I do not understand". I will assume Nigel is wondering about how you came to have a Hispanic nickname."

"Righto," said a recovered Sean. "Sorry about that, lads. Just slipped out." He turned his back to the three guys and leaned close to Alex's ear to whisper, "Is any of that true?"

Alex smiled and whispered back, "Some."

"Well," John started reluctantly, "I got it in Junior High, and it just kind of stuck."

"Oh, come on, Juan," Jimbo prodded. "Tell the whole story."

"They don't care about the whole story," John said dismissively.

"Sure they do," Scott joined in. "It was in gym class. The gym teacher was also the football coach, and I think he was scouting to see who might be candidates for a future team. We had to run a course he'd set up outside on streets around the school. It was about six blocks; I think. Juan was more of a chubby kid in Junior High, and when everyone else had finished, Juan was still a block and a half away. Coach yelled at him, 'Come on, Juan...*vamos...* before *mañana.*' It's been Juan ever since."

John stared daggers at Scott.

"Well, now that we've got *that* out of the way..." Jane quipped. "These three are trying to get a band together," she said to Sean and Alex, "and..." she continued as she turned back to her three friends, "*these* two are also

64

musicians. Maybe you guys can learn something from each other."

"That would be smashing!" piped Sean.

"I've got my guitar and amp in the car," offered John as he stood up. Alex nodded, and John started toward the street. It was the first good look Sean got of his Dad since the gazebo had them all in shadows. He was shorter than Sean expected; at least three inches shorter than Sean, which made him six inches shorter than the Jack Kelly he knew. Sean tried to examine what it was that made 'Juan' so unlike his Dad. Even though Scott insinuated that he wasn't as chubby as he had been in Junior High, he was still somewhat overweight. He looked much softer than his Dad, but maybe it was because he looked so young. Not any younger than the rest of them, it was just that... well, that was his Dad! The mop of curly brown hair spilling over his ears and onto his collar looked all *wrong*. His Dad always kept his hair short and well groomed. Sean didn't know what he had expected, but it certainly wasn't what he saw.

John returned, lugging a guitar case in one hand and an amp the size of a suitcase in the other. He set them down in the gazebo and pulled a cord from the back of the amp, then bent down to plug it into a socket in the lower part of the gazebo wall. He flipped a switch on the amp.

"That's what I thought," he said. "They keep the power turned off except for during 'official' performances or speeches."

"Where's the on switch?" asked Jimbo.

"I think there's a box outside, but I'm pretty sure it's padlocked," said John.

"Bummer," commented Jane.

"There may be a way to get around it," John said as he looked around the domed ceiling.

There were light bulbs forming four corners at the edge of the dome and one more in the very peak of the dome. John located a light switch on one of the columns that held the roof. He flipped it, and all five lights came on. He flipped it back off, knelt by his guitar case and palmed a small object.

"Jane, are you feeling adventurous tonight?" John asked.

"That's a loaded question. What are you planning?" she replied.

"Well," he continued, "you're probably the lightest of all of us. If you stand on my shoulders, you should be able to reach one of the four light bulbs."

"Probably, but so what?" asked Jane.

John opened his hand. Jane glanced at it, then up to the lights. "OK," she shrugged.

"What is it?" asked Sean.

Jane handed the object to Sean. "It goes in the light socket and adds two power receptacles," she answered.

Sean examined the small piece of plastic and metal. It had the screw shape of a light bulb on one end, a light bulb socket on the other end and two double-prong electrical ports in between. He handed it back to Jane. "Why do you have one of these in your guitar case?" Sean asked his Dad.

"For situations just like this," John said with a smile. "There's a six foot extension cord in there, too. Now, if someone can help get Jane up on my shoulders..."

John bent part way down next to the gazebo wall. Jane kicked off her flip-flops and Scott helped her up onto the wall. She gingerly stepped one foot onto John's left shoulder, then with both hands against the pillar, she carefully moved her other foot onto John's right shoulder. As he slowly stood up, Jane inched her hands up the pillar.

"OK," she said, "That's good. Don't move."

With her right arm tightly wrapped around the pillar, she reached her left out the short distance to the light bulb and started unscrewing it. Sean hadn't previously noticed that Jane was wearing fringed blue-jean shorts similar to Louise's. They weren't quite as short, which he decided was probably a good thing considering the angle she was presenting to five teenage boys. He had to admit it wasn't an unpleasant view. Jane had rather nice legs.

"Got it," she said as she pulled the light bulb out. She held the socket extender in her right hand, her right arm still crooked around the pillar. Once she had screwed the bulb into it, she reached back out to screw the whole unit into the gazebo socket. Scott held up the extension cord.

"Jane, here's the cord," Scott said.

"I'm *not* looking down," Jane replied.

"Just reach your left hand down," said Scott, "and I'll slap it into it."

Jane grabbed the cord and plugged it into the newly modified socket. "Now get me down!" she ordered. "Slowly!"

Back on the ground she slipped her flip-flops back on.

"Brava!" Alex said. Jane took a bow.

John plugged his amp into the extension cord and flipped on the lights. He paused dramatically at the amp's switch then flicked it. A red light glowed. A small cheer and a smattering of applause erupted from the little group.

"So, who should go first?" John asked. "Guests or home team?"

"We can go first if you like," offered Alex.

"What?" squeaked Sean.

"If you could pardon us," Alex said apologetically, "we need to step off a bit and plan what to play."

Alex calmly stepped from the gazebo with a wide-eyed Sean at his heels. When they were a few paces away, Sean could no longer contain himself. "Are you *crazy*? We can't do this!"

"Of course we can. I think we should perform Cream's *Sunshine of Your Love*. It has a dominant guitar part that will not seem unimpressive without a bass-line. It would sound better with drums, of course," said Alex thoughtfully.

"Let me make sure you heard the first part of what I just said," Sean continued in panic mode. *"Are you crazy*? I don't know *Sunshine of Your Love!"*

"Assuredly, you do," said Alex calmly. "It was a hit in 1968. You know all of the hit songs from 1967 through 1969. If you would calm yourself, you will realize that you know it quite well. You could perform that song in your sleep as it were."

"I thought loading the song thing in my head was for like a trivia contest," said a marginally calmer but still intense Sean. "I didn't know you planned for us to play something!"

"I had not specifically *planned* for us to perform, but prepared for such a contingency. Now, take a deep breath, calm yourself and think about this song. It begins: 'It's getting near dawn'. Think it through."

Sean took the recommended breath and tried to quell the fear that prodded at his stomach. He rethought the lyric Alex had given him and 'when lights close their tired eyes' popped into his head. Then he could hear the opening guitar riff and he went through the lyrics again, but this time he heard them sung in his head, just as if it had been a song that he had listened to over and over that he knew so well he could hear it *exactly* in his head. "Holy crap!" he said, "I *do* know that song!" He concentrated again, and facts about the song came to him. "Wait a minute. The guitarist for Cream was Eric Clapton? He's still considered a primo guitar player in my time. How are you going to fake Clapton? Do you even play guitar?"

"Once I had worked out the musician scenario, I spent several hours learning to play all the instruments of a 1960s era rock band."

"Several *hours?*" mocked Sean. "It would take *months* to get good at even one. Besides, guitar players have to play long enough to develop calluses on their fingertips to be able to hold the strings down correctly."

"It would be difficult for you to fully understand what I mean when I use the term 'learn'. It is an intense loading of the brain from the computer. In this instance, it required a degree of muscle memory training also for the physical aspects," explained Alex. "Nanites in my fingertips will simulate proper pressure for the strings."

"Are you serious?" said Sean, in awe. "You can hook up to the computer for a few hours and know how to play guitar, and physically be able to play it? That is so unfair! ...But really cool and I'd love to try it."

"Now then," Alex said as he turned toward the gazebo, "shall we go perform?" Sean hooked his arm and pulled him back.

"There's one more little detail," started Sean. "When you said I sang like a bird, were you imagining the bird to be a crow... because I can't carry a tune."

"Thank you," said Alex as he dug into his pocket. "I nearly forgot about these." He held out his hand to Sean. In his palm were two ivory colored gumballs.

"What's this?"

"Take one and place it on your very back molar and bite down. Then do the same with the other one on the other side of your mouth."

Sean took the first ball, placed it and bit down. He nearly screamed when he felt it move and tried to spit it out, but it had already locked onto his back tooth and stopped moving. "What the hell was that?" he shrieked.

"I will demonstrate once you get the second one in place," Alex said as he handed the second ball to Sean.

"It *moved!*" complained Sean.

"Yes, the tech has to position itself to optimally point to the back of your throat, avoiding tonsils and uvula. Please put the second one in."

"It *moved!*" Sean hissed. "I don't *like* things moving in my mouth!" He took the second ball. "It's creepy!" He shuddered as he put the second device into position and bit down.

"Now, to demonstrate, I need you to softly sing the scale."

"You mean, like, do re mi?"

"Yes," said Alex as he twitched a connection to his computer. "You will need to enunciate."

Sean opened his mouth to attempt to sing the scale, and couldn't believe his ears. The tones came out perfectly. "That is beyond awesome!"

"Please remember to substitute 'far out' when you find yourself wanting to say 'awesome'," Alex corrected. "We should return; they will be wondering what caused our extended absence. Remember, the computer is pacing the song. Think about how it should sound and follow the guitar. Softly sing it using your own vocal chords to become fully engaged in forming your mouth for the tones. The tech and the computer will provide the proper volume and pitch, you provide the words. You must enunciate."

Alex turned again to head back to the gazebo. This time Sean followed him but had to fight off his rising panic. He'd never performed a song in front of people before, and he knew he couldn't sing. But, apparently he *could*, with help from Alex's toys, if only he could shake his stage fright.

John handed his guitar to Alex. "I tuned it while we were waiting. You can check it if you like." He passed a microphone to Sean, "I keep a small mic in the back cavity of the amp. It's not the best quality, but I've got it plugged into a separate channel so we can adjust the volume with the guitar. No mic stand... sorry."

Alex slid his right arm through the guitar strap and cradled the guitar. "Nigel, can you give me an 'E', please?" Sean looked blankly at him. "Nigel has perfect pitch," he explained to John then turned to Sean and slightly opened his mouth and raised his eyebrows. Sean opened his own mouth, and Alex signaled his computer to echo the requested note off the back of Sean's throat. "Very close," Alex said, then made a slight adjustment to the lowest string and went through the same process with the five other strings. Once satisfied, he hit a chord sharply, and quickly released. "Can you maximize the bass in the amplifier, since we lack a bass guitar?"

John adjusted one of the knobs on the amp. "Try it now," he said.

Alex hit the same chord again and nodded approval. "Ready?" he asked Sean.

No thought Sean as he nodded meekly. Alex quickly strummed the opening four strokes, moved down to the lowest string for the following three bass notes, followed by three notes up higher, sliding and holding the second note. He repeated the same sequence. As he went into his third repetition, Sean could feel the back of his throat pulse, but he hadn't opened his mouth. Alex stopped.

"Sorry," Alex apologized to the onlookers. "We have not done this in awhile." He looked at Sean. "Do you remember when to come in now?" Sean nodded.

Alex started again, and when he reached the third repetition, Sean opened his mouth and softly sang, "*It's getting near dawn.... when lights close their tired eyes...*" Alex expertly put in the guitar riff at the end of each phrase as the tech provided the proper pitch and volume for Sean's 'singing'. "*I'll soon be with you my love.... to give you my dawn surprise...*"

Louise and Micky returned when the music started. Louise enthusiastically started dancing and Micky reluctantly joined her. Jane started swaying with the beat and slowly danced closer to Sean.

Sean was surprised the first time Alex leaned into the microphone on the chorus to add a perfect harmony, "*...waiting so long..... where I'm going... In the sunshine of your love.*" Sean began to relax by the second verse and started shaking his head a bit with the beat to get his long locks to whip around. When Alex went into an extended guitar solo at the end of the second chorus, Sean was considerably looser and started moving more with the beat and even miming 'air guitar'. Jane edged closer to him as she gyrated to the beat. Sean watched in fascination as she sometimes jerked her arms up as if throwing salt over her shoulder. Though unfamiliar with that move, he attempted to mimic her. She smiled warmly and moved a bit closer.

Distracted, he missed the first word of the third verse, which was actually just the second verse repeated. Jane was very close and he could smell her perfume. She enthusiastically moved with the beat, smiling as she locked her eyes to his. When he came to the part, "*...I'm with you my love.... it's the morning and just we two...*" she winked at him playfully. His cheeks flushed and were still slightly rosy a minute later when they finished the song.

There was a polite smattering of applause, but Louise rushed up and grabbed Sean and Alex each by an arm and bounced up and down on the balls of her feet. "Oh my goodness," she gushed, "you all are amazing! You sound just like the radio!"

Sean beamed at Louise. Her enthusiasm was intoxicating. Jane's eyes flitted between Sean and Louise. Her own smile faded and she slowly backed away to stand closer to Scott and Jimbo.

"Wow," said John meekly, "You guys are *good*. We're nowhere near that good." Alex slid out of the guitar strap and handed his instrument back to John. John held it by the neck. "I don't know after that if I want you to hear us. I guess we should have gone first so it wouldn't be such a letdown."

"No need to be modest now," encouraged Alex, "give us a listen."

"I'm not being modest," said John. "You guys are ten times better than us."

Sean stepped closer to his Dad. Even though they were equal in age right now, he still thought of him as his Dad. "I'd really like to hear you play," Sean said sincerely, a little emotion crept into his voice as he wondered why he never knew his dad even played guitar.

John eyed Sean carefully, sensing an honest desire that he found baffling. "OK," he said, slipping the guitar strap over his shoulder. "Just to explain more... Scott's the drummer, Jimbo is the lead singer and plays rhythm guitar, and I play lead guitar and sing backup... and we really need to find someone on bass."

Sean handed the microphone to Jimbo. John strummed a few chords as they put their heads together to discuss what song to do.

"We're going to do *'Bad Moon Rising'* by *Creedence Clearwater Revival*," Jimbo announced.

Sean instantly heard the song playing in his head, as if someone had turned on a radio. John started playing the opening chords and Sean could tell it was just a little off.

Jimbo started singing, "*I see the bad moon arising.... I see trouble on the way....*" Jimbo had a pretty good voice but sounded nothing like John Fogerty. Louise swayed a little and clapped along, not dancing this time since the tempo wasn't really a dance tempo.

As they listened, Sean edged a little closer to Jane to catch her scent again. "Excuse me, luv," he said, "I was wondering about your perfume. I don't think I've ever been around that particular scent before."

Jane lifted her eyebrows. "Really?" she said with the hint of a smile. "You must lead a very saintly life for a musician." She saw his confusion. "It's patchouli oil. Most people think it smells a little like pot."

"Oh," replied Sean with a nod, not really following most of what she said.

"Don't you call marijuana 'pot' in New Zealand?"

"Umm... no," Sean said, deciding she would believe however he answered, "I've usually heard it called 'weed' at home." That part was true... even if the location of 'back home' was a lie.

Jimbo was on the third verse, "*Hope you got your things together.... hope you are quite prepared to die.... looks like...*" Suddenly the sound went dead. Scott had flipped the light switch off.

"Cop car coming up the street," Scott announced urgently.

John quickly slid his guitar off and put it in the case. Jane tugged on the extension cord and brought it down. John said, "Everyone just be cool."

"What?" Sean asked, amazed by the sudden flurry of activity. "You can't play music?"

"I guess technically, no," John said. "That's why they keep the switch to the electrical boxes locked... but mostly the cop just likes to hassle us."

"Hassle?" asked Alex.

"He's looking this way pretty hard," Scott reported. "I think he's going to go around to park and pay us a visit."

"Scott, over the east wall as soon as the pig reaches the corner," Jane said decisively. "Now!"

Scott vaulted the wall. John had his guitar case over the edge almost before Scott hit the ground. Jimbo held onto the amp waiting for Scott to get a free hand. Sean was impressed by how smoothly they executed their tasks and wondered if they had done this before.

"OK, everyone stay cool," Jane repeated. "Don't say *anything* until the pig specifically asks you a question. Scott! Keep an ear open in case you need to move the stuff around."

"Got it!" Scott said from the other side of the wall.

"I am still unclear as to why the local law enforcement wishes to 'hassle' you," said Alex.

"You were right, Scott," Jane said over the wall, ignoring Alex. "He's parked. Stay down and be ready to move." She turned to Alex, "You've seriously never had any cops hassle you just because of the way you look?" Alex shook his head. She looked at Sean, who also shook his head. "Wow, I want to move to *your* country." She returned to taking charge. "OK, everyone just have a nice little conversation with someone you're standing next to. All smiles and happy now. Here he comes."

"I'm real sorry about this," Louise said softly to Sean and Alex. "You two are really gonna think we live in a terrible town, but it's really not that bad."

Jane suddenly raised her voice and spoke melodramatically, "So I said, '*thank you*, Mom! That was wonderful for you to teach me how to make a seven layer cake. Now, I can only hope that *someday* I'll have a husband to enjoy it'." She turned toward the approaching policeman. "Well, good evening, Officer Dietz! To what do we owe the pleasure?" Her lips stretched in a pleasant smile, but she couldn't mask the scorn in her eyes.

"Miss Carmichael," nodded Dietz as he stepped closer, eyes flitting from face to face, "and who else do we have here? Your brother... Miss Rimmer..."

"Good evening, Officer Dietz," Louise responded politely.

"Kelly," Dietz continued. Sean's stomach seized when he heard his name. "Groff... so where's the third stooge?"

"We're waiting for him," offered John. "He's supposed to meet us here."

"And who are these two?" demanded Dietz, eying Alex and Sean.

Alex stepped forward and put out his hand, "Good evening, officer," he

71

said warmly. "My name is Peter Lindsey and I am from... owww!" Jane had stomped on Alex's foot.

"Oh, sorry, Peter," Jane said to Alex then turned to Dietz. "Out of town. They're from out of town."

"Friends of ours," John added. "We met them at a concert. They've just come over for a visit."

Alex opened his mouth to speak again, and Sean put an elbow into his ribs, followed by a minimal shake of his head.

"Where, exactly, did you 'come over' from?" Dietz quizzed as he glared at Sean.

"Omaha," John interjected. "That was where we went to the concert... Omaha."

"They can't speak for themselves?" Dietz asked. "*Where* in Omaha?"

"Eighty-eight Thirteen Johnson," Sean said quickly, hoping Johnson was a common enough name for a street in a city that size. "Just off Eighty-Eighth Street," he added, hoping there was also an Eighty-eighth Street.

The policeman glared at him, looking slightly up from his shorter stature. "Don't they have any barber shops in Omaha?"

"Officer Dietz," Jane jumped in, "you're going to give our friends the impression that Mercer is a little redneck town."

Dietz immediately got into her face. "I don't care *what* your friends think, *Missy!*"

"Is there a particular reason you've decided to visit us tonight, officer," John jumped in, trying to draw him away from Jane. "Instead of driving around patrolling our fair city? Keeping us safe from all sorts of evil that surely lurks in the shadows?"

Dietz shifted to put his face inches from John. "You smart mouthing me, Kelly?" he growled.

John didn't flinch. "No, sir. Just wondering."

Dietz continued to glare as he considered his next move. "I had a report of loud music coming from the park. Rock music... the kind hippies like to listen to."

"There must be some mistake," offered John calmly.

"You saying you weren't playing loud music?" barked Dietz.

"How could we?" asked Jane, spreading her arms out wide.

"I'm pretty sure you know that the town keeps the electricity locked up," John added. "We couldn't play loud music here if we wanted to."

Dietz rubbed his chin. "How do I know you didn't break the lock?"

"You could go look," John suggested.

"Maybe I will," growled Dietz.

"I think it's on the north side," shouted Jane, turning slightly to the east wall as she spoke.

Dietz stepped out of the gazebo and started around to the north side. John went with him. Jane peeked over the south side and smiled down to

72

Scott. Scott flashed her a thumbs up.

"As you can see, sir," John said loudly, "the lock is still in place. No electricity in the gazebo."

Dietz stood up and started around to the east end.

"You know," John shouted, "Earlier a car with out-of-state plates drove around the park, playing their radio kinda loud. They went *all the way around!*"

Jane leaned over the south side. "Go!"

In a moment, they all saw Scott carrying the guitar and amp, sneaking past the opening of the gazebo in a crouched position.

"Maybe that was the loud music someone reported, sir," John again shouted, now on the south side."

"I'm not deaf, Kelly," grumbled Dietz. They finished the circuit of the building and stepped back into the gazebo. "I can tell by looking at you that you're up to something."

"No, sir," said John politely, "we all just decided to meet here. As soon as Scott gets here, we're going to go bowling."

"Bowling?" barked Dietz. "You expect me to believe you hippies are going to go bowling?"

"Why not, sir?" continued John. "Perhaps it runs in the family? I'm sure you've seen the picture of my Dad behind the counter in the bowling alley. The one when his team won the 1957 league championship? Third win in three straight years, I think. Was that the year your team got fourth place, Officer Dietz?"

"You think you're so smart," spat Dietz.

"No, sir, just observant," smiled John.

Dietz tried his best to look intimidating. John remained calm. The officer had held an evil eye momentarily on each person before he spotted something in the shadows. "What's this?" he said, crossing to Sean and Alex's backpacks.

"Backpacks," said Sean levelly.

"Open 'em up!" ordered the policeman.

"Do you have a warrant?" asked Jane crisply.

"Got something to hide?" snarled Dietz, his face inches from Jane. "Drugs, maybe?"

"No," said Jane calmly, "Just wanted to remind you that we live in America, not Nazi Germany."

"Don't talk to *me* about America, Missy!" roared Dietz. "I was killing Nazis before you were born!"

"And yet you seem to have forgotten what you were fighting for," she said icily.

"I sure as hell didn't put my life on the line so a bunch of long-haired hippies can burn the flag!" barked Dietz.

"And those Nazis you killed," Jane continued crisply, "were probably

73

just some German factory workers brainwashed by propaganda into thinking they were doing what was best for the Fatherland. Or worse, probably some scared little German farm-boy who didn't know *what* the hell he was doing there and just wanted to go back home."

"You sympathizing with the Nazis?" sneered Dietz.

"No," Jane answered calmly, "just trying to make sure any flag-wavers realize how stupid war is. Especially the current one in Vietnam."

"You little commie-loving pinko..."

"Constable," interrupted Alex, "I would be more than happy to divulge to you the contents of my bag."

"You talk like a limey," said Dietz suspiciously, turning to Alex.

"I do indeed, sir," answered Alex.

"Why might *that* be?" pressed Dietz.

"Well, that's the funniest part of *all*," interjected Louise as she stepped between them. "When we got to talkin' to these two at the concert, turns out Peter's Daddy and my Daddy were both in Korea at the *same time!*"

"How's that make him a Brit?" challenged Dietz.

"Well, I haven't *got* to that part yet," continued Louise. "His *Mama* is from England. She was over in Korea with the USO, entertainin' the troops... you know, with Bob Hope and all. She met Peter's Daddy and just fell smack dab head over heels in *love* with him. They got married and moved back to Nebraska when the war was over."

"That sounds like the biggest line of bull..." started Dietz.

"Actually, I do not believe I purchased one of those," Alex interrupted, "but if you wish to look, you might find one in all this camping gear somewhere." He opened the backpack and dumped everything out with a clatter. Sean followed suit and emptied his own pack.

"While I'd love to continue our fascinating discussion of political ideologies, we don't want to keep you from your duties," Jane said as she fluidly folded herself to the floor. "And we were just getting ready to do our meditation." She tucked her legs into the lotus position and held her hands out to her sides with middle fingertip and thumb touching, palms up. The others glanced at each other, smiled and sat down with her, trying with limited success to fold their legs like Jane's.

"Meditation?" howled Dietz.

"You should try it," offered Jane. "It would help lower your blood pressure." She closed her eyes and took a deep breath through her nose. "Ommmmmmmmmmm."

All the others joined in, "Ommmmmmmmm."

"You all need to be put in a loony bin!" yelled the exasperated Dietz.

Jane opened her eyes to briefly look up to Dietz. "You're harshing our mellow, sir." She closed her eyes again. "Ommmmmmm."

"God save us from this generation!" declared Dietz bitterly as he stormed out of the gazebo.

"Ommmmmmmm," chanted the group.

After a few more minutes of chanting, Jane opened her eyes. When she saw that the police car had moved on, she started laughing. The others joined in when they heard her. "What a pig!" Jane said as she unfolded from the lotus position and gracefully stood up in a single liquid motion. The others got to their feet far less gracefully.

"I do not understand the reason for the subterfuge regarding my residency," Alex said.

"Since you two are hitchhiking, I didn't know if you actually had visas," replied Jane. "Dietz would have loved tossing you in jail and trying to get you deported."

"Clever girl," said Sean with a nod. "I'm impressed, luv."

Jane gave him a crooked smile and a quick wink. "I told you I was the smart one."

Scott's head popped up over the east wall. "I take it the coast is clear?" He lifted the guitar case above his head. John took it and set it down, then immediately took the amp that Scott hoisted over. Scott then zipped around to the opening on the west side.

"I guess the concert's over for tonight," John said. "Good thing Dietz didn't ever look up." He pointed to the modified light. "Jane, can you help get the socket?"

"Sure," she replied, kicking off her flip-flops. Moments later she was back in the air on John's shoulders, level with the light and removing the socket. "What's everyone want to do now?" She asked once she was back on ground level.

"I understood you to say that you were going bowling," said a confused Alex.

"No, man," chuckled John. "That was just to hassle Dietz back. My Dad's bowling team *always* beat his. I knew talking about bowling would get a rise out of him."

"We could scoop the loop awhile... see if anything is going on and, you know..." offered Scott as he put finger and thumb to his lips with a quick inhale.

"I don't know, man," responded Jimbo doubtfully, "I think Dietz is pissed at us. He'd probably figure out some reason to pull us over for a tail light or something."

"We could go out to the lake," suggested Jane.

"The police won't bother you there?" asked Sean.

"Nah," said Micky. "It's outside city limits. And as long as no one is acting obnoxious, the County Mounties will leave us alone."

"County Mounties?" inquired Alex.

"Yeah," replied Micky. "You've already met the Town Clown. The County Mounties are sheriff's deputies."

"Not nearly as evil as your Sheriff of Nottingham," added Jane with a wry grin aimed at Alex.

"We could go hang out at my Dad's fishing spot," John offered. "He's got a pop-up camper on a small trailer that he just leaves out there for when he wants to go fishing. It's a little ways off the road, and there's also a boat dock not far from it."

Everyone looked around at each other and shrugged.

"Sounds good," said Scott.

"Works for me," added Jane.

"I'm in," said Jimbo.

"It'll be fun!" piped the ever-perky Louise.

"Cool," said John. "Two cars? Jimbo, Scott, with me. Peter, you could ride with us if you want. Jane, you've got Micky, Louise and Nigel?"

Sean felt conflicted. On one hand he wanted to ride with his Dad, but, on the other hand, he didn't know if he'd ever get the chance again to ride in a vintage T-bird convertible. Deciding that fate had already assigned his seat, he nodded approval.

As they were repacking their backpacks, Alex leaned close to Sean and whispered, "I checked the computer. 'Town Clown' and 'County Mounties' are slang terms for police officers."

Sean held back a laugh. "So are pigs," he whispered back. "In case you didn't look that one up."

By the time Alex and Sean reached the cars, everyone else was already loaded up and waiting for them. Jimbo was in the front seat of John's 1961 Chevy Impala, which was mostly light green, except for a black left front fender. The right front fender had several spots near the headlight that had rusted out. The back right door was slightly dented. Alex got in and sat directly behind John. "There does not seem to be any safety restraints," he remarked as he shut his door.

"Any what?" asked John. "Oh! Seat belts? Yeah, they're back there somewhere. You'd probably have to dig them out of the seat. Nobody uses them."

"Many traffic deaths could be prevented with the use of safety restraints," offered Alex.

"Be my guest!" John said. "Stick your hands between the seats and pull on anything that feels like a seat belt."

Alex glanced over at Scott and noticed he didn't buckle in. He quickly reviewed John's history and found that he didn't have any motor vehicular incidents as a teenager. He decided that he would blend in better by assuming their norms.

When Sean got to the T-bird, Micky and Louise were in the backseat. He opened the passenger door and slid in. Micky was directly behind him, and Louise was sitting in the middle, snuggled up to Micky.

"Is the lake far?" asked Sean.

"About 7 miles north of town," Jane replied as she started the engine.

She looked over to Jimbo hanging his arm out of the window of the Impala. She mashed the accelerator a couple of times and the T-bird gave a throaty roar. Jimbo gave her a thumbs up. Once John had backed out and was headed up the street, she backed out and followed him.

"How big is this lake?" Sean asked, trying also to remember if he'd already seen it on one of his family visits to Grandma.

"I don't know," Jane shrugged. "Not huge. Big enough to ski on. Lots of little coves to fish from. It's an OK size, I guess."

"Do you ski?"

"Some. Uncle Carl had a pretty sweet speedboat for a couple of years. Sold it to buy the T-bird. What about *you*, Nigel? What do you do for fun in New Zealand?"

Sean tried to choke down the panicky feeling that hit him. With Alex unavailable to bail him out, he had to quickly think of safe answers. "Ummm, I don't know..." he stalled. "There's the music of course." He tried to think of British things. "Cricket....soccer... well, you call it soccer, we call it football."

"Far out," Jane said, nodding. "So is cricket cool? I mean... it's kind of like baseball, right?"

Why did I say cricket? Sean internally screamed at himself. *I don't know enough about cricket to explain it.* "Ummmm, yes and no," he stumbled. "I mean, mind you, I don't know all that much about American baseball. They both use a bat and a ball, of course..."

They pulled to a stop at the intersection of the highway.

"You don't get carsick, do you?" Jane asked Sean.

"No."

"Not squeamish on a roller coaster?" she asked as a wicked grin played on her face.

"No. Why do you...."

Before he could finish the sentence, Jane jammed the accelerator to the floor. The back tires screamed as the motor roared and the car fishtailed onto the highway. Jane pulled her foot from the accelerator briefly then floored it again and the tires briefly squealed in second gear. The engine reached a higher whine and shifted into third as she rocketed around John like he was standing still. She continued to push the engine, quickly picking up speed before she backed off and let it cruise. Sean glanced over at the speedometer. He wasn't sure, since he was looking at an angle, but he thought it read 85.

"I *love* this car!" she yelled to the open sky. "It was worth six hours of drudgery to get this car!"

Sean briefly pictured Susan Sarandon at the wheel and hoped there weren't any cliffs close enough to drive off.

"Get it under the speed limit, Jane," Micky yelled from the backseat. "You never know if there are any cops out."

"Sorry, Micky," Jane said sarcastically. "I hope you didn't soil yourself. How about you, Louise? You doing OK?"

Louise stretched two fists in the air as high as she could reach. "Yee-haw!" she yelled.

Sean turned back to look at her. Her hair and the tail of her headband was flapping behind her. Her smile was stretched from ear to ear and her enthusiasm made Sean feel a little more daring. He grabbed the top of the windshield and stood up. The wind immediately stung his face and his own long hair rippled behind him as the car sped down the highway. It was exhilarating! He squinted his eyes against the wind, gasping a breath from the torrent that sped by him.

Jane slapped him in the ribs. "Down boy!" she ordered. He dropped back down into his seat. "I didn't want you to go rolling over the top when I brake. It would be bad to create an international incident by running over you." Sean put his hand on the dash to stop his forward lurch as Jane quickly decelerated. She manually downshifted into second as she left the highway to turn onto a graveled road. As soon as she had completed the turn she mashed the accelerator again. Gravel and a cloud of dust flew from behind their tires as the car fishtailed for several yards.

"Jane!" Micky shouted. "Uncle Carl will kill you if you wreck his car!"

"If I'm going fast enough, he won't have to," Jane shouted back as she shifted to third.

Sean's stomach churned as he wondered if Alex would take his body back to 1995 or if they would bury him here in 1969. His thoughts continued to stray to morbidity and he wondered how Alex would explain his death to his parents? Or since Alex was his descendant, would he cease to exist if Sean were killed? Mercifully the car slowed.

"You're looking a little green, Nigel," Jane said. "Too much?"

"Perhaps just a bit, luv," Sean tried to answer bravely. "Saw me life pass before me eyes and there wasn't really quite enough to watch."

Jane laughed. "We need to let Juan catch up anyway. We're almost to the lake and I need to follow him to find his Dad's fishing spot."

Jane turned at the marker that pointed toward the lake, pulled the car to the side, and stopped for the few minutes it took John to pass them. She followed as they both slowly made their way down the twisting road that meandered around the lake. After several twists and turns, John pulled off the main road onto a rutty side-road that led down into a small cove. Jane followed warily. The spur's gravel was sparse, little more than dirt. They had to carefully maneuver through some fairly deep ruts.

John pulled onto the grass and Jane pulled in beside him. A short distance closer to the lake stood a two-wheel trailer bed with a pop-up tent.

Sean breathed a sigh of relief as he decided no one would have to figure out where to bury him. He looked over to his Dad's car as it unloaded. Jimbo and Scott were on the closest side and he noticed they each had cigarettes. It surprised him to also see his dad smoking. The Jack Kelly he knew not only didn't smoke but became indignant any time he even had to be around second-hand smoke. Shocking as it was to see his Dad with a cigarette, his mouth dropped when Alex got out, also puffing away.

John strode toward the trailer with everyone else shuffling along behind him, unsure of where they were supposed to go. Sean angled to intercept Alex, finger aimed at the cigarette in Alex's hand.

"What is *this?*" he said sharply.

"I believe they said it was a Winston," answered Alex.

"I don't care what brand it is! What are you doing with it?"

"Smoking," Alex said levelly. "I do not understand why you are confused. People still smoke cigarettes in your time, even though a lower percentage than 1969."

"You flip out because you put a French-fry that was cooked in lard in your mouth, but you have no qualms about smoking?"

"There are no animal products in cigarettes."

"Smoking can kill you!" Sean said, loud enough that Scott and Jimbo turned around to frown at him.

"Oh!" said Alex. "You are concerned about the carcinogenic effects. It is not an issue. By the 23rd century, everyone has filters in the upper part of their tracheae. The air that reaches the bronchial tubes is completely purified, no matter what toxins are in the air."

"So you suck smoke into your mouth and then down your throat, but it doesn't get to your lungs?"

"Correct."

"So I suppose you also have a slot in your throat so you can change out dirty filters?"

Alex chuckled. "That is an amusing idea; however, the filter is continuously cleaned by..."

"Nanites!" Sean said at the same time as Alex. "Of course. What would you do without nanites?"

"Your question is the logical equivalent as if I were to ask you what you would do without white corpuscles."

The side conversation ended abruptly as they joined the others at the campsite. Sean tried to place a mental bookmark to bring the topic back up at a later time.

John plunged the upper half of his body into the camper and pulled back with a lawn chair in each hand. "There's only two chairs and a little folding camp stool." He ducked back in and plucked the stool along with a spray can. "If we stay here very long, you'll probably want to use some of this mosquito repellent." He handed the can to Jane, who immediately started spraying her legs and arms. She handed the can off and it went from person to person as everyone followed her lead. When Louise got it, besides spraying herself, she also sprayed her fingertips and went around dabbing everyone behind the ears.

"You'll want a little here, too," she said. "Mosquitoes just love ears!" When she reached Alex, he pulled away.

"I do not need chemical repellent," he said. "Mosquitoes will not attempt to feed from me. It would be a waste of the product."

"OK, Peter," Louise said with a helpless shrug. "If you've got welts and you itch all over tomorrow, don't say I didn't try to help you."

When she had moved on, Sean sidled close to Alex and whispered. "Don't tell me. Nanites!" he said. "I suppose they grab the mosquito's pointy little nose and break it off before they can suck any blood."

Alex chuckled again. "You have the most entertaining hypotheses tonight," he said mirthfully. "The mosquitoes and any other insects for that matter, are repelled by high-frequency vibrations from the pseudo-body suit. They will not come within three meters of me."

"Hey," said John as he came out of the camper again, "my Dad left a cooler out here."

"Any beer in it?" asked Scott hopefully.

"No," replied John, "but I was thinking we could go back to town and stock it with pop if we're going to hang around here all night."

"Or maybe we could find someone to buy us beer!" said Scott enthusiastically.

"How about getting some hot-dogs and we could start a fire for a little weenie roast?" suggested Jimbo.

"And marshmallows!" chimed Louise.

"Who's going to pay for all this?" sneered Micky.

"And get some Hershey bars and some graham crackers and we can make s'mores!" continued Louise with ramped up enthusiasm.

"Everyone can just chip in a few dollars," John suggested.

"I didn't bring any money," complained Jane. "I *thought* my Uncle Carl was going to pay me."

"I got paid today," said as she dug into her left pocket. "Here's five for Jane and me!"

"I've got three," said Scott.

"I'll go three," echoed Jimbo.

"I'm putting in five and taking back two," said John.

Sean glanced at Alex and finding him motionless, dug out his own wallet. "I've got a twenty. You can take six out of it for Al... Peter and me... since everyone seems to be tossing in three dollars each."

John took his twenty and handed him back the two fives and four ones already collected. Everyone turned to Micky.

"What?" Micky said. "You've got twenty bucks! That'll buy way more hot-dogs than we'll be able to eat!"

"Don't be a drag, Micky," said Jimbo, "everyone else put in three bucks."

"If we find someone to buy beer we'll need every penny we can get," added Scott. "You know they'll make a profit buying beer for minors. Probably charge us at least double."

"If we don't spend it all, we'll distribute what's left back to everyone," said John.

"Fine," grumped Micky as he dug out his wallet. "Here's three dollars."

"Are we just going to eat charred hot-dogs off a stick, or are you going to get buns?" asked Jane. "And are you going to get ketchup and mustard?"

"And pickle relish!" exclaimed Louise. "I like pickle relish!"

"Always the practical one, Jane," sighed John. "OK, we'll see what all we can get. Everyone cool with Coke?"

"Beer!" yelled Scott.

"If we don't find any beer... everyone cool with Coke?"

"I like Dr. Pepper," Louise offered shyly.

"How about if I get a six of Coke and a bunch of Shasta flavors. I think the Shasta Black Cherry is kind of like Dr. Pepper, Louise," John said, then pointed to Sean and Alex. "How about you two?"

"Coke's great, mate!" said Sean.

"Ginger beer?" asked Alex. Sean rolled his eyes.

"Ummm, I think Shasta has a Ginger Ale," said John. "Not sure if that's close."

"Beer!" yelled Scott again.

"*You* can look for someone to buy beer," said John. "OK, we should be back in half an hour or so."

John picked up the cooler and went to his car and stuck it in the trunk. Jimbo and Scott hopped into the Impala. Sean considered asking to go, since no one else had claimed the fourth seat, but John had already started the car.

"Do they *always* do everything together?" asked Sean as the Impala backed up onto the rutted road.

"Pretty much," answered Jane. "Didn't you catch the pig's Three Stooges reference? Or does someone from New Zealand even know who the Three Stooges are?"

Sean looked to Alex for guidance. Alex twitched. His eyes went wide and he twitched again. When his descendant's face turned panicky, Sean decided to wing it. "Yeah," he said, "lots of American movies and TV get imported back home." He glanced back to Alex and became concerned when he saw how pale his face had become. "Will you excuse us for a moment?" He hooked Alex's arm and walked him toward the lake.

"What's going on?" hissed Sean.

"I...I cannot reach it," said Alex, nearly sobbing.

Chapter Five

"it's just a shot away / it's just a shot away"

C AN'T REACH what?" asked Sean.

"The computer on the S.T.E.," Alex whined. "We have gotten too far away!"

"Is that all?" said Sean, relieved. "I thought something terrible had happened."

"It has!" insisted Alex. "I have *never* been unable to access a computer when I need to. Never in my entire life!"

"Calm down," said Sean. "You were fine five minutes ago."

"I did not *know* five minutes ago," snapped Alex.

"So, we spend a couple of hours roughing it," said Sean lightly. "Out in the boonies in Iowa. It'll be good for you!"

"*No!*" shouted Alex, his face hardened, and he stormed off toward the road. Sean took a step to follow him, but stopped. He'd never seen his descendant so emotional, but decided Alex could take care of himself. He rejoined Jane, Louise, and Micky.

"Everything OK?" asked Jane.

"Right. Spiffy. Just fine," said Sean. "Me cousin is just feelin' a bit oogly. Said 'e needed to take a walk."

"Was it something we did?" asked Jane. "He seemed kind of stoked when he left."

"Eh, no worries," said Sean with a shrug, hoping to lighten the mood.

"Is it because of the hot-dogs?" asked Louise apologetically.

"Hot-dogs?" Micky snorted.

"Yes," replied Louise, "Peter is a...." She paused, looking to Sean for permission, then continued when he didn't react. "...vegetarian."

"So?" sneered Micky.

"Well, he might not feel comfortable around everyone eating hot-dogs," reasoned Louise.

"No," Sean said, "It's not that. *He* won't eat a hot-dog, but he won't care that everyone else does."

"Then do you know what's bugging him?" asked Jane.

"Yes," said Sean with a wry smile. "He misses someone."

"Who?" asked Louise.

"Steffi," replied Sean, struggling to keep a straight face.

"A girlfriend?" asked Louise.

"You wouldn't believe how close they are," said Sean, amused with his private joke.

"How long have they been apart?" asked Jane.

"I'm afraid I haven't kept track," Sean ad-libbed. "It doesn't seem that long to me, but, blimey sometimes the separation just seems to get to him."

"Aww! That is so sweet!" cooed Louise.

"Yeah, he's a bit of a duffer, wot? He's knackered for sure," Sean said with his thickest accent.

The three others looked at him blankly and nodded as if they understood him.

"Well, I hope he'll be all right," said Louise.

Micky lost interest in the conversation and went into the camper to explore. "Hey, Louise!" he yelled. "C'mere. You gotta see this."

"What?" she replied.

"Well, you have to come in here to see it," coaxed Micky.

"What is it?" she said as she slid through the tent flap, then immediately squealed. "Micky!"

Jane hooked Sean's arm. "OK," she said. "Why don't we go look for the dock?" She pulled him briskly along toward the lake. "I think it's off to the right down here."

Louise squealed again and laughed. Sean looked over his shoulder. "Are they going to..." his voice trailed off.

"Do the nasty?" asked Jane brightly. "Nah! Not that Micky won't try.... *again*. Louise has an invisible chastity belt, and Micky does *not* have the key."

"What do you mean?"

"Louise's Mom has a really strong influence over her that I don't think Louise is fully aware of. Her Mom's a Southern Baptist. Like from the south, hardcore Southern Baptist. Louise isn't going to give it up until her wedding night."

"Then why are we leaving?"

"They still get loud. Who wants to listen to someone else make out? Especially when it's your best friend and idiot brother. Plus, eventually Micky will push a little too far, and Louise will tell him to stop it, and then Micky will beg, and she'll keep saying 'no' and then he'll get mad and yell at her, and they'll have a little fight."

They walked along the edge of the lake and the camper disappeared behind the rolling terrain.

"You sound like you've been through this a time or two," said Sean.

"Oh, yeah," sighed Jane. "Too many times. Hopefully, this won't be one of those times when she needs to cry on my shoulder."

"Louise deserves someone better," grumbled Sean, then wondered if it was a mistake to bad-mouth Micky to his sister.

"Someone like you?" asked Jane, her voice turning frosty.

"Wot? Me?" over-acted Sean. "Blimey! No."

"Oooooo," sniped Jane. "I want to play poker with you. Your cheeks get pink when you lie."

Sean's cheeks flushed fully red as they walked several paces in silence.

Jane broke the awkward silence. "I'm sorry," she said sincerely, "That was mean of me." Sean remained silent, and Jane continued. "I guess I sometimes let jealousy get the best of me." Sean looked over at her but still didn't speak. "It's OK if you fall for Louise," she sighed, "Every guy does. What's not to love? She's just easy to fall in love with."

"I'm not *in love* with her," Sean said crisply. "I only just met her a couple of hours ago."

"OK, so love's not the right word. But I saw the way you looked at her in the park when she was all excited about your song. I should be used to it by now. She just has that effect on guys."

They reached the dock and Jane continued without breaking stride. Sean took two steps and froze. Jane walked to the end and sat down.

"Is this safe?" asked Sean.

"Sure."

"Didn't it feel all wobbly to you?"

"Yeah."

"That doesn't bother you?"

"It's a floater. Haven't you been on a floater before?"

"I guess not," Sean said as he tightrope walked toward Jane. He gingerly shifted his weight with each rocking step."

"So it can adjust to the lake whether it's bank full or low. The deck flooring isn't attached to the posts. The posts are in slots, and the flooring can go up and down as the lake does. Barrels under the deck float it. That way the end of the dock's always the right height for the boats."

Sean caught himself before he could say awesome. He shifted to current terminology. "Far out," he said as he sat down beside Jane. He sat silently mesmerized by the little waves that rippled in the retreating sunlight. "Why's Louise your best friend?" asked Sean, still lost in the water's soothing motion.

Jane stared at Sean while she considered his question. "I suppose initially because she needed me," she finally said. "She was in the seventh grade when she moved here. I was in eighth. We call that junior high here... I don't know if you use that term. Anyway, kids immediately teased her because of her accent. It was thicker then than it is now if you can believe that." She shrugged. "I decided to be nice to her since no one else would. I guess since I knew what it was like to be teased; it was kind of a kindred spirit thing."

Sean looked up from the waves and locked eyes with Jane. "Why were you teased?"

"Come on, Nigel!" said Jane indignantly. "The Color-Me-Barbra nose?" Her gaze hardened as she added, "And don't bother saying you didn't notice. Your cheeks will give you away."

"I don't understand the 'Color-Me-Barbra' reference."

"Streisand? The singer? You don't know who that is?"

"Yes, vaguely," Sean said as *My Funny Valentine* began playing in his head.

"I sometimes study pictures of her to see if I can get any makeup tips to help minimize my schnoz."

Sean studied her face again and decided she was overly critical of herself. As he took a closer look, he noticed there was something about the shape of her face and brightness of her blue eyes that made her seem familiar to him, but he couldn't quite place who she reminded him of.

"Wow! You don't have to *stare* at it!"

"I'm not. Just now, while looking at you, it seemed you reminded me of someone."

"If you say Jimmy Durante, I'm pushing you in the lake."

Sean didn't know who Jimmy Durante was, but didn't bother to ask. "No, it's just an impression. I can't quite put my finger on it." He turned back toward the water. "Maybe it'll come to me later." They sat quietly and listened to the waves gently slap the dock.

"As soon as I get a job and save up ten thousand bucks, I'm getting a nose job," Jane said determinedly.

"I think you're overreacting."

Jane glared it him for a moment, then turned herself away from him at a right angle. She slipped her shoes off and dangled her feet in the water. Sean watched as she occasionally brought a foot up to flip some drops of water above their heads. He wondered if she expected an apology, though he didn't think he had any reason to apologize. After a few moments of silence he took off his own shoes and socks and for the first time actually appreciated the outlandish bell-bottomed jeans Alex crafted for him. The legs easily inverted up to his thighs, baring his legs to his knees. He slid over to Jane's left side and dipped his own feet into the water.

"I imagine Barbra Streisand has made more than ten thousand bucks by now," Sean ventured.

"So?" Jane said petulantly.

"So, she didn't rush out to get her nose done."

No reply, but Sean felt that he at least got her thinking.

"Maybe she realizes that she's more than just a nose," he continued.

A hint of a smile played on Jane's lips.

"Maybe she realizes that there's a lot of things about a woman that can be attractive," he added, then kicked some water up onto Jane's leg. "If that woman doesn't get all hung up on her nose."

Jane kicked water back at Sean's leg. Sean escalated with a bigger splash. Jane shrieked but retaliated with a return kick that splattered Sean's shirt and face. They stopped politely taking turns as an all-out water war began. They both laughed and tried unsuccessfully to dodge the churned water, and then the splashing stopped almost as quickly as it had begun. As their laughter died away, they found themselves looking into each other's eyes. Jane's gaze flitted briefly to Sean's lips then back to his eyes. She leaned her face slightly toward his.

Sean's heart skipped a beat as his own gaze shifted to Jane's lips and back. He saw her eyes again flick to his lips as she leaned a little closer. When he glanced down again, he saw that Jane's lips had slightly parted. His brain raced. *Does she want what I think she wants?* His right arm slid gently around her shoulder as he slowly leaned closer to her. She tilted her head and raised her chin; her lips were reaching for his. She closed her eyes.

"There you are!"

They both jumped at the sound of Alex's voice. The spell was broken, and Sean let his arm drop away from Jane's shoulders and they leaned away from each other. Jane suddenly became engrossed with an inspection of the end of her left braid; left hand raised to separate even more from Sean.

"I thought I heard splashing and some laughter, so I headed this way," Alex said as he came closer.

Sean kicked his right leg straight out and sent droplets of water flying. Alex strode onto the end of the dock.

"When I returned to the campsite, it appeared that Micky and Louise were having a bit of a row," Alex continued. "Hello! A bit wobbly here," he said as he took a few steps onto the dock. "So anyway, I thought it best to come find you lot... and here you are."

"Here we are," Sean echoed gruffly, hoping Alex would detect his anger.

"Well then, getting a bit of soaking on those tired feet. Clever idea," Alex observed.

"Are you all right now?" Jane asked.

"Fine, thank you," replied Alex, "Why do you ask?"

"Oh, sorry if I'm prying," apologized Jane. "Nigel told us about your separation."

"Did he?" Alex asked nervously. "What exactly did he tell you?"

"He said that you missed Steffi," Jane said.

"Steffi?" Alex's voice cracked.

"Sorry, mate," Sean jumped in. "I mentioned how you missed your *girlfriend*, Steffi. They were concerned about you storming off, so I explained how you sometimes can't take the separation."

"What? Oh... quite," stumbled Alex. "Quite right, I do miss that bird."

"You seem to be in a much better mood now," Jane noted.

"Indeed," Alex confirmed, "Nothing like an evening constitutional to clear the head."

"Well, I'm glad things are better," said Jane as she pulled her legs onto the dock and slid her flip-flops on. "We should probably get back I case I need to referee."

Sean sprung to his feet, and offered Jane a hand. She put her hand in his but didn't but didn't pull up with it as she gracefully stood. Sean grabbed his socks and tucked them into his pockets and slid his damp feet into his boots, leaving the laces free.

As they walked back to the campsite, Sean repeatedly gave Jane sidelong glances. She faced forward, her smile had evaporated and she seemed almost weary as they trudged along. Sean felt more than a little confused. He had earlier thought he felt an attachment to Louise, and then he had nearly kissed Jane. *Maybe there's something to this "free love" era,* he thought. *Maybe everyone's just a lot looser about kissing each other... and possibly other things, too.*

He felt disappointed that he hadn't kissed Jane. She was a fascinating, complex person, and barring a few hippie idiosyncrasies, kind of cute. He shook his head briskly to try to shake off his thoughts of her. It was crazy! A few hours in 1969, and he was thinking about hooking up with two different girls. He forced a reality check. Both girls would be about his Mom's age in 1995. He closed his eyes and tried to age them mentally. *Surely there's some kind of time-traveler rule about not dating people your parents' age.*

Even before the tent came fully into sight, the sound of an argument reached them.

"Why don't you two hang back at least until I can get the screaming stopped," Jane requested.

Sean gave a quick nod, and then he and Alex came to a halt, allowing Jane to continue solo toward the camp. Sean waited until she was several yards away. "So, are you OK now?" he asked quietly.

"Right as rain," Alex replied cheerily. "Which, by the way, will begin in approximately one hour."

"What will begin?"

"The rain."

"So now you're a meteorologist?"

"No, I walked through it."

"It's going to rain in about an hour, and you've walked through it?"

"Yes."

"I'm a little confused."

"Where did you think I went?"

"To walk off whatever weird mood hit you when you couldn't get to your computer."

"No!" Alex exclaimed, "I went to retrieve the S.T.E. I brought it back here."

"You walked all the way back to Steffi?"

"Yes, once I realized we had traveled past the range of the computer, I had to rectify the situation."

"You walked almost eight miles? You weren't even gone half an hour."

"I could have returned sooner, but I thought I should give the appearance of taking a walk."

"So does this body-disguising suit also give you super speed?"

"No, it took me nearly four hours to reach the S.T.E. Do I need to remind you what the 'T' stands for?"

"OK, I got it. You spent four hours walking back to Steffi, but you erased three and a half hours on the way back here."

"Erased is not proper terminology, but I will not correct you, since that irritates you."

"And you did anyhow, but I'll let it go this time," said Sean. "So you got rained on?"

"Yes," replied Alex. "A rather forceful rain, and well over an hour in duration. Excessive thunder and lightning. Very dramatic. I would estimate local accumulation of perhaps five centimeters. I suspect in an agrarian community such as this, it will be appreciated."

"You're dry as a bone," Sean commented. "How'd you manage to walk through an hour of rain and not get soaked?"

"This time credit *does* go to the pseudo-body suit. It can repel water."

"Like a raincoat?"

"Not if I correctly understand your terminology. The pseudo-body suit can emit –using terms that you might use– a weak force field. It repels most objects at about three centimeters from the suit."

"Please tell me that gets invented in my lifetime!" exclaimed Sean.

"No. Sorry."

"Of course not. The really cool stuff is all in the future," Sean grumbled. "You know the saddest thing, though? You've got all this really awesome technology, and you don't even appreciate it."

"That is simply a matter of familiarity... and you should not say 'awesome'."

"Bunk! If I had half the cool stuff you have; I'd be psyched about it my whole life."

"In the same manner that you appreciate immediate access to relatively pure water by turning a tap? The way you appreciate light whenever you want it at the flick of a switch? Or perhaps the way you marvel traveling two hours in an automobile the distance you would spend more than a day to reach by horseback?"

"You can't compare that kind of simple stuff to the cool technology that you have," argued Sean.

"How do you imagine your great-great-great-great-great grandfather would react if you could show him those 'simple' things?"

Sean thought it over. "I suppose he would think it was all pretty amazing," he reluctantly admitted.

"Or possibly have you hanged for practicing witchcraft," suggested Alex.

"So is there anything that you *do* think is amazing?"

Alex paused to look Sean in the eye. "Yes," he replied, an edge of emotion in his voice, "talking about this with you."

Sean stared blankly at Alex. He hadn't seen that coming. He coughed and cleared his throat. "OK, I think Jane's probably had enough time to get the lovebirds patched up. Let's go before you get all mushy on me again." He quick-stepped the remaining distance to the camp, forcing Alex to trail him.

When they reached the camping area, there was no one in sight. Sean moved closer to the tent and could hear sobbing and Jane's voice trying to soothe Louise. "Everything OK?" he asked.

"Give us a few more minutes," replied Jane.

"Is Micky in there, too?" Sean asked.

"No," answered Jane, "he lost it when I called him an insensitive jackass, and he bolted." Louise's crying grew louder.

"All right," Sean replied. "Hey, we'll go look for some firewood. Be back in a few minutes."

"Thank you <sniff> Nigel," Louise sobbed.

Sean walked away from the tent, shaking his head. "Poor kid," he mumbled to himself, then turned to Alex and said, "Let's go look for some firewood."

"I noticed several dead branches on the ground between here and the S.T.E.," Alex mentioned.

"Maybe we'll need that hatchet after all," Sean said. "How far away is Steffi?"

"Less than half a kilometer. There is considerably dense vegetation. The cloaking function is nearly unneeded."

Sean dragged one of the lawn chairs over to where they had put their backpacks. He opened his and pulled out one of the extra shirts. He dried his feet with it and wiped at the inside of his shoes before putting his socks and shoes back on. Alex retrieved the hatchet from his own backpack.

"OK, scout," challenged Sean, "see if you can find your way back to Steffi."

"The link to the computer automatically gives me the range and directional signals," said Alex as he started walking away from the camp.

"Just for fun, why don't you turn them off and see if you can find your way back without it."

"I already have the coordinates."

"Then I guess this will be easy," Sean scoffed. "Man, being a Boy Scout in the 23rd Century must be boring. Do you get merit badges for advanced nanite manipulation?"

"What is a 'boy scout'?"

"It's a youth paramilitary organization," Sean lied. "They must have gone into deep cover in your time, but when they're ready, they'll come out of hiding and take over the world."

Alex stopped. "This is the dead branch that is closest to camp. Shall we hatchet it?"

"Sure," grinned Sean, "Hatchet it."

Alex began swinging the hatchet at the midpoint of the limb, but struck the wood at a perpendicular angle. Each stroke landed several inches from the last, making rows of small notches.

"Here," grumbled Sean, "Let a caveman show you how." Sean took the hatchet and began striking the wood at forty-five degree angles, each blow alternating ninety degrees from the last. Chips flew with each blow. When he was about halfway through, he put his foot on the big end and pulled toward himself with the smaller end. The piece snapped off. "You can only do that when it's pretty dry. If it were greener, we'd have to chop the whole way through." He dropped the log and looked back toward the campsite. "You know, it would probably make more sense to drag bigger pieces back and chop them up nearer the tent."

"What quantity of wood will be required?"

"I don't know. Probably four or five branches this size. How much farther to Steffi?"

"As we stand, we are nearly equidistant to the campsite and the S.T.E."

"I want to see where you parked it."

Alex nodded and started walking again. In a few yards, they entered thicker brambles.

"You may wish to be cautious," said Alex. "Many flora have sharp protrusions."

"Thorns?"

"My suit protects me, but I would imagine that they could do damage to either your clothing or your epidermis."

"Skin?"

"Yes," replied Alex. "Why do you insist on less descriptive monosyllabic terms?"

"Why do *you* insist on always using more complex words than you need?"

"Perhaps there is not a satisfactory answer to either of our questions." Alex stopped and pointed to a clump of brambles. "There. You could see the S.T.E. right through there if it were not cloaked."

"Remember how you found something about my Dad and his band in the local newspaper?"

"Yes."

"Could you look up something about Louise?"

"If it exists. What are your search parameters?"

"Can you just look for anything that has both Louise and Micky's names in the same place?"

"Certainly. I believe the police officer referred to Louise as 'Miss Rimmer'. Do you think I should search for Micky or Michael Carmichael?"

"Can't you do some kind of either/or search?"

"Certainly," Alex said, "That would require an additional 86 nanoseconds more than a single search."

"Instead of spending ten to fifteen seconds talking about it?"

Alex pointed at his ancestor and smiled. "Though your intentions were merely to be sarcastic, there is a solid logic construct at the core of your statement."

"Just do the stupid search!"

Alex twitched a query. "Zero results are returned for that search."

"OK," said Sean. "Try Louise Rimmer and engagement."

Alex twitched. "Yes. The article begins, 'Mr. and Mrs. Arnold Rimmer announce the engagement of their daughter, Louise Elaine Rimmer to Mr. Charles Arthur Jones, son of...'"

"So *not* Micky!" interrupted Sean.

"It appears not."

"Good! She deserves better than Micky!"

Alex considered Sean's remark. "You do not know that Charles Jones is better than Micky."

"Are you..." Sean stopped as he thought. "True," he finally agreed begrudgingly, "but I know Micky would be bad for her... so not-Micky is better."

"Your logic is flawed. You have no data to compare."

"I don't care," snapped Sean, and then more calmly said, "Is there a picture?"

"Yes."

"If we go inside Steffi, can you project it?"

"Yes."

"Then open up, I want to see it."

Alex pushed through the brambles and opened the S.T.E. Sean followed.

"Ow!" yelped Sean.

"I told you that the flora has..."

"Thorns! Yes. I know." He sucked a drop of blood from his thumb. "First hand. Now scoot over and show me that picture."

Alex displayed the upper half of a newspaper on the forward screen.

"Wow!" exclaimed Sean, "The resolution is awesome! It even looks like newsprint!"

"Would you prefer to examine a three-dimensional artifact?"

"Of what?"

"This particular issue of the *Quincy County Gazette*."

"Are you serious?"

Rather than answer, Alex touched the screen and twitched instructions to the computer. A full sized newspaper suddenly floated in front of Sean's face.

"If you attempt to hold it, it will react to you," Alex explained. "You will not have tactile sensations, but it will behave as if you were holding the original artifact."

Sean reached his left hand for the floating object and closed his fingers on the spine side. He couldn't feel a newspaper, but in every other sense it seemed that he had one in his hands. He put his right hand on the opposite side and mimicked the motion used to turn the page. It made a slight rustling sound as it turned.

"Just when I think you've shown me the coolest thing you've got, you bring something else out! This is insane!" Sean enthused. "So what page was the engagement on?"

"It was page ten."

Sean flipped through the pages until he held the paper open to the page with Louise's engagement announcement, just as if he were looking at a real newspaper. He glanced at the corner. "The date on the paper is April 10, 1975." He skimmed through the text. "It says a June wedding is planned. Can you do a search for Louise again and limit it to June 1975?"

Alex twitched. "No results."

Sean was puzzled for a moment. "Try July 1975."

"Yes. The last issue of the month has her wedding announcement on page nine."

"Can you put *that* paper in my hands?"

Alex twitched, and the paper that was in Sean's hands shifted. He flipped the ghostly pages until he reached page nine.

"They got married on June 21st. I'll bet it didn't go into the paper until July because they had to wait to get the wedding photos back." Sean scanned through the text of the announcement. "Louise's younger sister was the maid of honor. Two other bridesmaids whose names I don't recognize. Huh. I wonder why Jane wasn't a bridesmaid? Says the groom is a May graduate from the University of Nebraska, majoring in agribusiness. Looks like a nice enough guy in the picture. I wonder where they are now? Well, I mean my now. Where are they in 1995?"

Alex twitched. "I have several thousand results with the name Charles Jones in 1995. It appears to be a relatively common name. Perhaps with more information we could narrow the results."

Sean shook his head. "Nah. I'm being stupid. It's not like I could look her up in 1995 and say, 'hey, remember me? I met you when we were both 16, and guess what? I still am.' I guess I just wanted to know that she's happy." He attempted to fold up the ethereal newspaper. "OK, you can make this go away." Alex twitched, and the paper was gone. "We should get some more wood and head back."

Just as Sean and Alex reached the campsite, each dragging a good sized dry branch in each hand, the Impala pulled in next to the T-bird.

"Outta sight!" John proclaimed as he got out. "Firewood!" All three of them had cigarettes again, and Sean was again annoyed to see his Dad smoking.

John and Jimbo helped Sean and Alex carry the branches down near the pop-up camper, and Scott hefted the ice chest over to the campsite.

"So did you get beer?" asked Jane.

"No!" grumbled Scott. "What a drag, man. I wanted to keep driving around until we found someone that could buy it for us, but Juan wanted to get back here."

"But we do have ketchup and mustard," John announced. "And pickle relish, Louise."

Sean glanced at Louise and saw that her eyes were still a little red, and her smile wasn't running at its usual bright wattage, still she grinned a little at the mention of the relish.

"And buns and chips," added Jimbo, who returned with a big paper sack. He tossed a bag of marshmallows at Louise. "And marshmallows and graham crackers... and *Snickers* candy bars."

"*Snickers*!" complained Louise, "You were supposed to get *Hershey's*!"

Jimbo reached into the bag and pulled out a handful of flat chocolate bars. "Just kidding!"

Louise threw the bag of marshmallows at Jimbo's head, her bright smile returning.

"Where's Micky?" asked Scott. Louise's smile melted away as quickly as it had returned.

"He went for a walk," Jane said tersely. "I think he was going to check to see if there were any Snipe around here," she added with a mischievous smile.

"What are Snipe?" asked Alex.

"You've never been on a Snipe hunt?" asked the suddenly grinning Jimbo.

"He's from England, Jimbo," said Jane with a wink. "They probably don't have Snipe in England."

"Then we should take him on a Snipe hunt for sure, once it gets dark," said Scott.

"I do not believe in hunting animals for sport... or any other reason, for that matter," protested Alex.

"We don't hurt them," explained John. "We just catch them and release them."

"Then what is the purpose?" asked Alex.

"Snipe are a rare and beautiful bird. You'll want to see one in the wild," said John.

"But they only come out at night," added Jimbo.

"And you lure them into a gunny sack with a flashlight," continued Scott.

"It's kind of a Midwestern rite of passage to catch one," said Jane.

"I think it's mean," said Louise.

"Well, hey ho, then," proclaimed Sean. "Bit of a jingo, wot? We'll have a go!" Then he whispered to Alex. "Look it up on your computer, and be glad it's going to rain."

"I am unable to translate much of what you said," Alex whispered back. "What does 'bit of a jingo' mean?"

"It's New Zealandish for snipe hunt," whispered Sean. "I don't know! I'm starting to get into this foreigner stuff. I can make up whatever I like, and they don't know what I'm saying, but are too polite to ask."

Alex twitched a connection to the computer. "Snipe hunts are merely a ruse!" he whispered to Sean. Sean rolled his eyes.

"So who wants to start the fire?" Sean asked loudly.

"Jimbo was actually a boy scout, so we'll let him run the show," said John.

"Technically," Jimbo announced, "we should dig a fire pit and surround it with rocks." He looked around. "But there's a pretty big bald spot right over there. We can just set it up there."

They all set to work breaking up branches, chopping the larger pieces that wouldn't break. Jimbo left briefly, returning with a basketball sized handful of dry grass. He put it in the middle of the patch of grass-less dirt and started stacking small twigs around it. He put a lighter to the grass and began methodically feeding the flame with the twigs. He carefully blew on the twigs until they caught fire, then he added in larger twigs and kept building until he had the large chunks of wood in flames. It took nearly half an hour, but his efforts produced a roaring blaze.

John borrowed Alex's hatchet and found some green branches that were straight and long enough to hold the hot-dogs over the flames. He stripped away the bark and sharpened the points.

While everyone busied themselves with either the fire or prepping the hot-dogs, they were oblivious to the darkening sky until there was a deep rumble from the distance.

"Was that thunder?" asked John.

"Yes," replied Alex, "there is a major storm headed this way."

"Maybe it will go around us," Jane said hopefully.

"No," said Alex assuredly, "it will drop a considerable amount of precipitation at this location."

Everyone looked at Alex, curious as to why he was so sure of himself.

"Oi!" said Sean, "Me cousin's from England. An Englishman can smell a storm as sure as a sheep is wooly."

The attention shifted to Sean, then slowly heads agreeably bobbed as they decided that maybe they had heard that it rained a lot in England. As if in confirmation, another rumble of thunder sounded.

"Let's get some dogs in the fire," said John.

He distributed the sticks he had prepared and quickly all five of them extended hot-dogs toward the flames.

"So, where are you two going from here?" asked John.

Sean glanced at Alex, then answered, "East."

"Just 'east'?" asked John.

"Our intent is to make it to the Catskills in New York, before August 15th," said Alex.

"Wow, man, really?" said Scott, "You're hitching to *Woodstock?* Far Out!"

"That is so groovy!" enthused Jane, "That's supposed to be one mind-blowing happening."

"Man!" said John, "So many cool bands at one concert. *Creedence*, the *Dead*, *Airplane!*"

"*Hendrix, Joplin, The Who!*" added Jimbo.

"I heard they were still trying to get the *Beatles* and the *Stones*," said Scott, "and *Zeppelin.*"

"Tickets are like twenty to twenty-five bucks," said John, "I wish I had that kind of bread."

"Come on, Juan," said Scott, "even if you did you wouldn't go all the way to New York."

"When are you leaving here?" Jane asked Sean.

"Not really sure, yet, luv," replied Sean. "We might rest up a bit for a day or so if we can find a soft place to stretch out."

"Where do you usually sleep?" Jane asked.

"Oh, here and there," Sean continued. "Sometimes just out on the ground. Sometimes we find some kind people who take us in and give us a bed for the night." He glanced at his Dad, hoping that he would get an offer since he knew for a fact that his Grandma had an extra bedroom.

"Well," John started slowly, "I guess it would be all right if you slept here in the tent. It might not be as good as a real bed, but better than sleeping on the ground."

Sean was less than pleased with his Dad's humble offer. He pulled his hot-dog from the fire and headed toward Louise.

"That is very kind of you, indeed," Alex said to John as Sean walked away.

"Got a bun ready, Louise?" asked Sean.

She pulled a bun from the plastic bag and held it open as Sean slid the hot-dog off the stick, then tried to hand the bun and dog back to him.

"No, that's for you, luv," said Sean.

"Well, aren't *you* the gentleman?" smiled Louise.

She went to the Impala where they had set ketchup, mustard and relish on the hood, using it as a makeshift table. She had just finished applying all three when Micky shuffled back into the camp area.

"Micky!" exclaimed Louise. Micky sauntered slowly over to Louise, hands in pockets, head down.

"I'm sorry, Louise," he said when he reached her. "I was out of line."

"I'm sorry, too, Micky," replied Louise, "I guess maybe I got a little hysterical. Want my hot-dog?" She held it out to him. Sean's blood boiled as he watched Micky take a bite.

"Louise, did you put pickle relish on this?" Micky complained, "You know I don't like pickle relish!"

Sean imagined himself stuffing the hot-dog up Micky's nose.

"Here, Micky," said Jane gruffly as she approached, "Fix your own." She slid the hot-dog from her stick onto a bun and slapped it into her brother's hand. "Come on, Nigel, let's cook two more."

Sean reluctantly followed her back to the fire and they both threaded cold dogs onto their sticks just as Scott, John, and Jimbo headed to the Impala for buns and condiments. Alex accompanied them asking them questions about Snipe.

"Trust me," said Jane, "you don't want to listen to their 'kiss and makeup' drivel." She held her stick out over the flame. Sean moved to the other side of the fire and put his second dog over it. He watched reflected flames dance in Jane's glasses and again felt that she reminded him of someone. "So, Peter left a girlfriend back home... how about you?"

An image of Nicole popped unbidden into Sean's head, and almost immediately morphed into Alex. His stomach lurched. "No," he replied, "no one in particular." They both silently watched the flames lick at their hot-dogs, and Sean tried to purge the image of Nicole/Alex from his thoughts.

"So... are you going to stay?" Jane finally asked.

"Hmmm... oh, yes, I suppose we are," Sean replied. "I'd hoped for something a little less rugged, but this will do."

"Sorry I can't offer anything better. My parents would like totally lose it if I brought hitchhikers home."

"Wot? Couldn't you say, 'look mums what followed me home, can we keep them'?"

Jane laughed. Sean found the sound of her laugh both soothing and at the same time exciting. He was mesmerized by the flames still dancing in her glasses. A rumble of thunder sounded ominously closer than the last one.

"Do you think Peter is right about the rain?" Jane asked.

"He's rarely wrong about anything," complained Sean.

"Then I guess the party might get cut short tonight."

"And I was *soooo* looking forward to the Snipe hunt," said Sean sarcastically.

Jane grinned. "You know?"

"Yes. I guess New Zealand has its share of pranksters, too."

"Are you going to tell him?"

"Is there a reason not to tell him?"

"There's always tomorrow night," Jane said, suggestively bouncing her eyebrows.

"Tomorrow night?"

"Well, if you're staying around, we could get together again tomorrow night," said Jane. "All of us, I mean," she added quickly.

Sean thought he detected a bit of color blooming in Jane's cheeks and flashed back to their near kiss. "That would be nice," he said, "I'd like to get together again." He paused, waiting until her eyes met his. "All of us, I mean," he added with a wink. He smiled when he saw that her cheeks definitely colored.

She suddenly jerked her stick from the fire. "Bummer! I wasn't watching what I was doing," she exclaimed. "It's burned black!"

Sean handed his stick to her. "I'll trade you. I happen to enjoy charred hot-dogs."

"That's OK, I'll just do another one."

"No, seriously, I love a blackened dog."

"Liar."

"How can you say that? You don't know my preferences."

"If you like them black, why have you been so careful to keep yours on the edge of the flames?"

"Well..." Sean stalled as he tried to think of a plausible lie. "I generally like to get them heated all the way through, then finish them off by blackening the outside."

"Liar!" She said again. "You are *such* a liar!" Her cheeks dimpled from her smile.

"All right," Sean confessed, "How about if I say I'm not too picky and I'll trade you just because I'm being nice."

"That might be a little more believable," Jane nodded, then added, "Are you sure?"

Sean grabbed her stick and handed his to her. "Positive."

Jane glanced at her traded dog, then at Sean. Her mischievous grin softened to a warm smile. "Thank you," she said softly, not taking her eyes from his.

"You are most welcome, m'lady," Sean replied with a hint of a bow. "Shall we bun them?"

They joined the others by the car where most of the group munched chips or drank Cokes as Scott embellished a tale of the elusive Snipe.

"And Snipe are curious birds," Scott said melodramatically, "if you bang on something to make a loud clang they'll come running toward you to see what it is."

"Extraordinary!" exclaimed Alex.

"When they get close," Scott added, "you shine a flashlight at them and they'll run right at it. That's when you scoop 'em up in your gunny sack."

"What an unusual behavior for a wild creature," said Alex.

"You want ketchup?" Sean asked Jane after already drenching his black dog in red.

"No, thanks," she replied. "I'm a mustard and relish girl."

A bolt of lightning flashed quickly followed by a peal of thunder.

"That's getting closer," John noted.

"We haven't done s'mores yet!" lamented Louise. "Peter hasn't had a thing to eat!"

She set the remainder of her hot-dog on the car hood, ripped open the bag of marshmallows and threaded three marshmallows on one of the sticks leaning against the front fender.

"He won't eat those," said Sean. "That stick still has animal fat on it from the hot-dogs."

Louise stared blankly at Sean, then turned to Alex. "Really?"

"Sorry to be such an annoyance," apologized Alex.

John broke the end off one of the other sticks and sharpened a new point. "There you go," he said as he handed the shortened stick to Louise, "virgin wood."

Louise threaded three more marshmallows on the new stick and passed it to Alex before rummaging in the grocery sack. She pulled out the graham crackers and opened them, then unwrapped a Hershey bar and set it on a graham cracker. "We need something we can set close to the fire that we can set this on so the chocolate melts." She looked around the group and got shrugs and shaking heads.

"Let's check your survival gear and see if anything will work," Sean said to Alex. He opened the backpack and rummaged around, pulling out the pan. "We could turn this upside down and set the crackers on it."

"That will work great!" bubbled Louise. She took the pan and set it as close to the fire as she could tolerate, balancing the graham cracker and chocolate. Satisfied that it would melt enough, she turned to Alex. "Have you ever toasted marshmallows before, Peter?"

"No, I have not."

"Well, the trick is to get close without gettin' too close, and then you've got to rotate the stick, so you get them all golden brown all way around." She stuck her stick expertly near the flame. "Like this."

Alex watched for a few seconds, then attempted to replicate Louise's actions. In less than five seconds, his marshmallows were flaming fireballs.

"Blow them out!" shouted Louise.

Alex was frozen as he stared at the flame at the end of his stick. Louise grabbed his stick and blew on the flaming marshmallows. Though the fire went out, the marshmallows were blackened ash. "They appear to be highly combustible," commented Alex.

Another bolt of lightning flashed overhead, followed immediately by a crack of thunder. Louise jumped, then looked to the sky.

"Maybe I should do yours for you," she offered as she slid the three charred marshmallows from the stick to the flames. "Someone else want to take this stick?" she asked, holding her stick out. Scott took it from her and went back to the fire with it. She quickly threaded three new marshmallows onto Alex's stick. "I would normally let you keep tryin' until you got the hang of it, but I'm not sure how long we got before the rain starts." She went back to the fire and began carefully browning the fresh treats.

"I'm going to get the top up on the T-Bird," Jane said.

Sean watched in fascination as the front of the trunk slowly rose on hinges at the back until it was perpendicular. A white soft top slowly unfolded itself out of the trunk and crept toward the windshield, forming a smooth surface when it reached its destination. The trunk then slowly lowered itself back into position. Jane rolled up the windows and got out of the car. "OK, at least the car will stay dry on the inside."

"Groovy," said Sean, trying out the term he considered a hippie word.

"I'm gonna do another hot-dog," said Jimbo. "Anyone else want one?" He skewered a dog with his stick. John joined him.

"I get to drive home," Micky abruptly stated to Jane.

"In your dreams," Jane replied flatly.

"Come on," coaxed Micky, "It's just the three of us. You'd look stupid chauffeuring me and Louise."

"Louise can sit up front with me."

"Just let me drive!" he demanded.

"No! I worked for this car, I'm going to drive it!" said Jane emphatically.

Micky stared coldly at his sister, then turned and went down to the fire, leaving Sean and Jane alone by the cars. Jane reached into the potato chip bag and pulled out a couple of chips, munching one as she looked down toward the flames. Sean reached into the ice chest and pulled out a Coke. "Want one?" he asked Jane.

"Hmmmm... not really in the mood for Coke," she replied. "What flavors of Shasta did they get?"

Sean dug back into the ice and pulled out various colored cans. "Grape, Lemon-Lime, Orange, Ginger Ale, Strawberry..."

"Strawberry sounds good," Jane interrupted.

He handed her the can and started to open his Coke. He paused when he noticed that the ring top seemed a little odd. He looked to Jane's can and watched as she pulled her tab all the way off. She slipped the loose ring into the opening.

"Something wrong?" she asked.

"No... well, seems the bloody can is a bit different from back home."

"Oh, do you still have the kind you have to use an opener?"

Sean didn't know what she meant, but decided to bluff. "Yeah. So you just give this ring a tug until the whole thing comes off? Brilliant." He pulled the top free and considered whether he wanted to dunk the little piece of metal like Jane had. "Isn't it a bit risky to put this into the can? I mean... what if you drink it?"

"I suppose that's possible," Jane chuckled, "but I've never heard of that happening to anyone."

Sean wished he had access to Alex's computer. He was willing to bet that it *did* happen to someone before 1995 and he assumed a lawsuit prompted the pop-top design change to what he was used to.

"How long have you been away from home?" Jane asked.

Just a few hours, Sean thought, *but it seems like more.* He took a long drink from his Coke as he tried to fabricate a reasonable answer. He looked at his can. It *did* taste different; it wasn't just the glass bottle. "I haven't really kept track of time," he finally replied, "I guess it was about a month ago when we came into port in Los Angles."

"That is so far out!" Jane said. "I mean, you just are off doing your own thing. Radical!"

"It's been a bit of all right, it has."

"I can dig it. I wish I could hitch to Woodstock."

"Why don't you?"

"My parents are like too uptight to handle that, complete squares. They'd have the State Troopers on me before I got halfway across Iowa."

"Bummer," said Sean, again trying out the local lingo.

"Yeah. Maybe someday. Just one more year of high school. I mean, once I'm in college I can do stuff without the old man looking over my shoulder."

"So you're going to University?"

"Yeah. Probably Iowa State. Make sure your band tours there some day and you can look me up."

"Hey, you two," shouted Louise. "You want a S'more? The first one's about ready."

Sean was anxious to observe Alex with such alien food. "Let's at least go socialize, wot?" he said to Jane. They walked over to join the group around the fire.

"OK, Peter," Louise instructed, "get a plain graham cracker and then get the one from near the fire that has the Hershey bar on it." She was holding her stick with the evenly toasted, beautifully golden brown marshmallows in front of Alex. "OK, now when I lay the marshmallows on the chocolate, you trap them with your other graham cracker." Alex did as instructed, and Louise withdrew a slightly gooey stick. "Now just kind of smoosh them together 'til the marshmallow oozes out a little," she encouraged, "That's good! Now you're ready to eat it!"

Alex gazed in wonder at the soft marshmallow and chocolate oozing from the edges of the crackers, then he noticed that every eye was on him. He gingerly nibbled at the corner.

"That's no way to eat a s'more!" admonished Louise. "You've got to get a bite of everything together."

Reluctantly, Alex took a bigger bite. He found the crackers to be crunchy, the marshmallows gooey, and the chocolate had a surprisingly warm creamy texture. As he rolled it all around in his mouth, he decided that the sensation was quite pleasant. The flavors and textures all seemed to be harmonious.

Louise couldn't contain herself. "Well? What do you think?"

Alex glanced at Sean and discovered he was watching him as closely as everyone else. "Yummy," he said.

"I *knew* you'd like it!" said Louise triumphantly as Sean laughed.

"However, this is a rather large portion," Alex commented. "Perhaps you should take some of it, Louise."

Louise took the s'more with both hands, expertly broke the crackers in half, and pulled the gooey marshmallows apart, trailing little white threads from both halves. She quickly licked the side of the larger piece and Alex watched then mimicked with the half she handed back to him.

"There's two more Hershey bars already gettin' soft, and Scott's got some marshmallows almost ready. Somebody else should get some goin'," said Louise.

Jane grabbed a stick and poked three marshmallows through the tip, then held them near the base of the fire, away from the flames.

Louise took a bite of her s'more, then held it out for Micky to take a bite. Sean turned away from them. He tried to focus on the fact that Louise was going to marry someone else, and at some point she was going to dump this jerk. He watched Jane as she meticulously rotated her marshmallows near the hot coals of the fire and wondered if many twins were as different as the Carmichaels.

A fork of lightning streaked across the sky followed immediately by a clap of thunder. A stiff breeze began blowing from the southwest and more lightning crackled high over head.

"Oh, damn," said Jane as she jerked her stick from the fire and blew out her flaming marshmallows. "The wind blew flames into my marshmallows and they caught fire."

Sean grabbed a plain graham cracker and plucked one with a melting Hershey bar from the pan. "Here," he said, "I like burnt marshmallows."

Jane's eyes narrowed as she stared into his. "Are you lying to me *again*?"

"No," Sean insisted, holding his right hand and cracker up in surrender, "I really *do* like them a little burnt. I don't have the patience to get them all golden and gooey, so I kind of learned to like the burnt sugar taste."

Her face remained skeptical. He crossed his heart with his cracker and then returned it to surrender position. She shook her head and laughed. "Are all New Zealanders as crazy as you?" she asked as she laid the marshmallows across the soft chocolate.

"I have to say, luv, that I have never met anyone from New Zealand as crazy as me," Sean said, "and that's the truth." He captured the marshmallows with the top cracker as Jane pulled her stick away.

A few large raindrops started falling. Those that hit the fire sizzled as they instantly turned to steam.

"I think we'd better go," said John, "in case it really pours. It won't take much to make this little side road muddy."

Scott quickly put his marshmallows on the last Hershey cracker and started toward the Impala. Jimbo plopped things back into the grocery sack as he finished his second hot-dog.

"Just leave everything out here in the camper, Jimbo. That way they'll have something to eat in the morning," John said. "Be sure to tie the flaps down tight and you should stay dry," he said to Sean and Alex.

Sean snapped his s'more in two and handed half to Jane.

"What if *I* don't like burnt marshmallows?" she teased.

"Then just keep it as a souvenir of that crazy New Zealand boy you met in the summer of 1969."

She frowned. "Aren't you going to be here tomorrow?"

"Yes, but I thought you might find something better to do."

Lightning again danced across the sky with accompanying thunder.

"I want a better goodbye than this. We'll just say tonight was called because of rain... that's a baseball term, if you don't recognize it."

John, Scott and Jimbo slammed the Impala's doors and the engine roared to life. Micky and Louise hurried toward the T-bird.

"Come on, Jane," shouted Micky, "let's go!"

"You'll be all right?" Jane softly asked Sean.

"Let's hope so," he replied flippantly.

She gazed into his eyes, smiled, then took a big bite of s'more. Sean smiled back and mirrored a bite with his half.

"Yummy," said Sean.

Jane crinkled her nose. "If you like burnt marshmallow."

"Drive carefully," insisted Sean.

"In your dreams," Jane said with a laugh as she started toward the T-bird. She looked back over her shoulder and waved. "See you sometime tomorrow."

More raindrops began to fall and Sean headed for the camper as he watched the T-bird back out and drive away. He looked toward the fire and saw Alex still standing next to it.

"What are you doing?" Sean shouted.

"Observing the reaction of fire with rain. It is quite fascinating."

"So, people from the future don't have enough sense to come in out of the rain?" said Sean as he ducked through the tent flap.

"I have already experienced this same rain," Alex replied.

"Oh yeah... force field," Sean said softly to himself. "He's got such cool stuff."

Sean peaked out from the tent flap for a few moments, wondering how long Alex would stand out by the fire in the rain. He finally shook his head and closed the flap. There was a lot he didn't understand about his distant descendant. Sometimes Alex seemed like an all-knowing brainiac, sometimes he didn't have a clue about things that seemed simple to Sean, and sometimes he stood out in the rain.

Sean plopped down on one of the cots, hoping it wasn't the one that Micky and Louise had been on. It wasn't exactly cushy, but it was comfortable enough. He lay back as he listened to the patter of the rain on the tent and the occasional rumble of thunder. It was rather soothing. He yawned, and was immediately annoyed with himself. It wasn't *that* late. If the storm hadn't rolled in it would probably still be light. Then he realized that if he'd spent the last few hours back home, it would be after midnight. He tried to reconcile the time differences, not only the years they had moved, but also the hours that needed adjustment to make his natural body rhythms in sync.

He thought about his Dad and how different he seemed, both in appearance and the way he acted. Smoking? That was unexpected, so was the guitar thing, but that was interesting. He wondered why he didn't have a guitar at home, and when he'd stopped playing. Obviously the band thing didn't work out. He decided his Dad hung out with OK friends, connected at the hip with Jimbo and Scott, but how was he linked to Louise and the Carmichaels? And *that* trio! *They* were something. Louise, so sweet and bubbly, Micky a self-centered jerk, and Jane.

Jane. A smile came to his lips as he thought of Jane. There was something about her. He still couldn't think of who she reminded him of, but he liked her brashness, especially when she introduced herself as the cute *and* smart twin. Actually, he had to agree with her self-assessment. What else did he like about her? She was confident. She handled the cop smoothly. The whole hippie meditation thing was hilarious. Then there was her driving. Apparently skillful, but scary as hell. Maybe it was the T-bird that brought that out?

He rolled to his side. Had she kind of been flirting with him? Dancing closer when he was singing; playfully calling him a liar about the hot-dog and marshmallow. He closed his eyes and thought of their moment at the dock. What had really happened there? He felt some kind of chemistry with her, and it seemed like she was signaling him to kiss her.

His eyes snapped back open. "Stupid 5G-grandson had to show up at just the wrong time," he muttered. "But what did she mean by, 'I want a better goodbye than this.'? What did she have in mind?"

The patter of the rain became a heavier, constant white noise. He closed his eyes and thought about sitting with Jane at the dock, imagined not being interrupted and getting to kiss her. He smiled as he drifted off to sleep.

Chapter Six

"...caught up in sorrow, lost in the song..."

THOUSANDS of diamonds sparkled on the lake's surface in the morning sun. Sean felt a warm peacefulness even in the crisp stillness of daybreak, losing himself in the gentle lapping of the water against the dock.

"Are you coming in, or not?" asked Jane. Surprised, he turned to his left and saw her head bobbing just above the water's surface. "It's warm. Come on."

He didn't remember coming to the dock, and neither did he remember Jane coming back. He looked down at himself and was baffled to see he was wearing his swim trunks, which seemed wrong, since he hadn't brought swim trunks to 1969. He checked the temperature with a foot, then slid into the water. It *was* warm and felt fantastic.

"Remember the last time we were at this dock?" she said as he glided toward her. "There was something I wanted from you," she added in a sultry voice. She clasped her hands behind his neck and pulled herself tightly against him. She felt slippery-soft and warm and...

"You're naked!"

"Hey, it's the sixties," Jane said nonchalantly. "What can I say? Summer of Love. Dawning of the Age of Aquarius. Make love, not war. One small step for man, one giant leap for mankind."

"What?"

"Never mind. Kiss me!" she demanded as she lifted her face closer to his. "Oh, wait a minute," she said as she took the few strokes needed to reach the dock. "This damn nose keeps getting in the way." He saw her put something on the dock before floating back to him, her head turned away. "Now how about that kiss?" She said and quickly whirled around.

There was a horrific bloody hole where her nose should have been. Sean screamed.

He gasped as he sprung awake on the cot, his heart pounding as he sucked in short gasps.

"Have you awakened in there?" called Alex from outside the tent.

Sean looked all around, disoriented. He realized he was in some kind of tent, then began to relax as he took stock of his surroundings. Swimming with Jane had only been a dream, or more of a nightmare by the end. As the cobwebs of sleep cleared, he thought more about where he was, then about *when* he was. A moment of vertigo hit him and for a second he felt like he was falling as he realized how impossibly far he was from home. *Which is more insane?* he wondered, *The dream with Jane ripping her nose off, or the fact that I really am in 1969?*

"Yeah, I'm awake," Sean answered groggily.

Alex unzipped the tent flap and came in. "I thought I heard you cry out."

"Yeah, weird dream."

"That is a relief. I was afraid you might have been attacked by indigenous vermin or carnivorous insects."

"Or a snipe," Sean laughed as he wondered what type of insect Alex imagined. "So what time is it?"

"Six twenty-seven."

"I'll assume A.M."

"Yes."

"I *never* wake up that early without an alarm clock," Sean said, "Why are *you* up?"

"Your circadian rhythms are still in your home time zone," Alex suggested. "I generally sleep only four hours per day, though I did sleep five last night. The exertion of walking twelve kilometers must have triggered a longer anabolic nocturnal dormancy."

"OK, it's too early in the morning to be saying stuff like 'antibiotic doctoral normalcy' or whatever. If you'd be so kind as to take me and my 'Canadian rhythms' to *your* home time zone, I would gladly strangle your English teacher."

"Circadian," corrected Alex, thinking it prudent to not correct the other phrase. "And I learned 20th Century English the same way you learned the music of this era. There is no person to strangle. Even if there were, I do not believe you are capable of homicide."

"Don't push your luck," Sean grunted. He glanced at the other cot, which looked untouched. "Where'd you sleep?"

"In the S.T.E."

"Wow, that must have been comfortable," Sean said sarcastically as he imagined trying to sleep in a golf cart.

"Very."

"You've got to be kidding."

"No," countered Alex, "I can set the cabin gravitational field to null allowing my relaxed unconscious body to float in a modified fetal position."

"I'm sleeping on this lousy cot," groused Sean, "and you're floating in the ultimate-in-softness zero G?" He sighed. "I'd tell you that I hate you, but you'd take it wrong."

"Why do you hate me?" squeaked Alex.

"See, I knew you'd take it wrong," said Sean. "Never mind, just chalk it up to 20th Century conversation that you don't understand."

"I do not understand 'chalk it up'."

"It means 'add to the list'... you can chalk that one up, too."

"That would be recursive."

"Fine. Good. Wonderful. We need more recursiveness in the world." Alex looked at him blankly. "Well, since we're both awake, maybe we should think about breakfast."

"I have already prepared and consumed my morning meal," Alex stated. "Would you like me to prepare one for you?"

"Are you talking about that tasteless glop that kind of looks like yogurt?"

"Yes, Formula Ten."

"With all the balanced proteins and fats and vitamins and stuff?"

"Yes," replied Alex. "I will go get you some."

"Don't bother. I'd rather just eat some cold hot-dogs."

"That is nutritionally unbalanced as well as an oxymoron."

"Oxy-what did you call me?"

"Oxymoron. When contradictory words are used together. In this case, a hot and cold dog."

Sean squinted at his descendant. "I'd accuse you of yanking my chain, but I'm pretty sure you don't know how." Alex started to respond, then closed his mouth, perplexed. "Yeah," said Sean, "I know, you don't understand 'yank my chain'. Boy, whoever loaded your slang dictionary was one taco short of a combo platter."

Sean met Alex's confused stare with an especially toothy grin. Alex twitched a connection to his computer. "Deceive a person, usually in a playful manner," stated Alex gruffly, "and lacking in intelligence." He frowned. "That seems unnecessarily critical and judgmental."

"Sue me. I'm not a morning person. Especially at this time of the morning. Where'd you get those answers? I mean, why does your computer even have all that stuff?"

"Other time-historians have collected data. Most information that refers to this particular time-period is readily available in a loadable format, unlike earlier eras. The format is something you will call eBooks in your near future, if not already. Also, our scholars have downloaded the internet—again using your terminology—every six months from 1990 through 2000. From there it became monthly through 2005, then weekly until 2015. From that point forward, we were able to conceal a connection to the internet with one of our own century's computers hidden in a government data center. We then were able to record any changes to the internet in real-time and store it until our technicians retrieved it. I have the internet from 1990-2000 on my computer, as well as other pertinent reference works."

"You have ten years of the internet on the computer in Steffi?"

"Eleven, but yes," replied Alex, "It is only a few exabytes."

106

"To use your own phrase... I have no idea what that means."

"How much data can your computer at home store?" Alex asked.

"How big is my hard drive? It's 80 megabytes."

"Oh," he said with surprise, "I did not realize it was so limited."

"I know what a gigabyte is, though... 1000 megabytes, which is a billion bytes, right?"

"Yes," verified Alex. "An exabyte is a billion gigabytes."

"A *billion* billion bytes? That's *insane!*" Sean exclaimed. "You referred to a decade of data as only being a few exabytes. So how much more data can the computer in Steffi hold?"

"It is a standard portable computer, capable of handling 500 exabytes stored at a molecular level."

Sean blinked twice. "Molecular level? I don't think I can get my head around that before breakfast," Sean marveled. "And since you've convinced me that I shouldn't eat a cold hot-dog, let's see if we can figure out how to get that little camping stove of yours to fire up."

"That is an excellent suggestion," Alex agreed. "It will be interesting to observe how you heat food on another fire-based device."

"Yeah, speaking of fire... what was going on with you and the fire last night?" asked Sean. Alex gazed blankly back. "OK, how about if I ask you 'why you were standing in the rain by the fire?'."

"Oh! To observe the dynamics of the two elements in opposition. The heat from the flame initially vaporized the raindrops before they could reach the base of the fire. However, once the precipitation fell more rapidly, some drops were able to pass through and strike the wood, lowering the surface temperature, thus allowing even more rain to penetrate the cooler flames. Eventually, the rain extinguished the blaze with the ultimate result permeating the wood, thus making it no longer combustible."

"Or as any *normal* person would say, you watched the rain put the fire out."

"That is merely the result!" protested Alex. "The process is more complex and interesting to observe in stages!"

"Slightly more interesting than watching paint dry," quipped Sean. He gave his descendant a questioning look. "Have you never seen a campfire?"

"No," replied Alex. "It is not an efficient use of energy for light, heat, or cooking, and it increases the carbon footprint."

"What's a carbon footprint?"

"Have you not started using that term, yet? My apologies for introducing it to you, but I am confident you will soon hear it with increasing frequency. In this particular case, the combustion of wood literally puts carbon into the air, mostly as carbon dioxide, but some carbon monoxide, as well."

"Fire good!" grunted Sean. "Og like meat from fire! Taste good!" Alex was again perplexed. "Just playing the caveman again for you," added Sean in his regular voice.

"Let me pose this question: If you were 200 years in your past and could observe an everyday task that is obsolete in your own time; would you not find it intriguing?" asked Alex.

"Like what?"

Alex twitched a query to his computer. "Plowing a field with oxen or horses. Weaving cloth on a loom by hand. Spinning wool or flax into thread."

Sean tried to visualize those tasks. "OK, I guess I *might* watch any of those things being done... for a little while." He noticed Alex was frowning. "And I'm sorry if I offended you by making fun of you watching the fire." He thought of the flames dancing in Jane's glasses. "I guess when I think about it, it does have a mesmerizing effect."

"I also reacted badly," confessed Alex. "I should not have become emotional in defending my actions."

"OK, good, we both messed up and are sorry. Before you go further and get mushy again, I'm going to set up that camping stove."

Sean retrieved the small stove from Alex's backpack, sat down on the ground, and started tinkering with it. "I think all I have to do is unfold these sides, make sure the propane tank is tightly connected and valve open, then light a match and turn on the burner." He ran through the steps and was rewarded with a hissing blue flame. "That was actually pretty easy."

He grabbed a small frying pan from the backpack, sat it on the flame, and retrieved dripping hot-dogs from the mostly melted ice chest. "You sure you don't want to try one?" Sean chided as he dropped two dogs into the pan. "It's pretty central to our way of life. Baseball, hot-dogs, and Mom's apple pie! Hey, that reminds me... when it comes to trying things, what's up with you and cigarettes?"

"That is a 'why' question, correct?" asked Alex. Sean nodded. "It seemed to be a social norm, so I joined in to ingratiate myself with the others in the automobile. I again invite you to imagine yourself in the past. If you were in the 19th century at a Native American ritual, would you refuse to partake when they passed a pipe around the circle?"

"I guess not," shrugged Sean. "But cigarettes are bad news. I can't believe my Dad was smoking one. He is like Mr. Anti-smoking now... again, by 'now' I mean back in 1995."

"Perhaps it is peer pressure," suggested Alex. "If he later changes his peer group, smoking may become a taboo in the new group."

"You mean like when he goes to college and hangs around with a different crowd that doesn't smoke, he stops smoking to be like them?"

"That is one hypothesis. Studies suggest addictions have a stronger hold on some people than others. We can assume your father is not predisposed to a nicotine addiction."

Sean rolled the sizzling hot-dogs over to heat another side. "So does *anyone* from your time eat meat?"

"There are pockets of people who reject technology and attempt to subsist in primitive ways. Like what you might refer to as tribes. Those people keep animals to eat," said Alex disdainfully.

"Wow!" remarked Sean. "That is the snarkiest I have ever heard you talk. Do you look down on me for eating meat?"

"No. I accept that it is part of your culture in this century, and food synthesizers have not been fully developed yet. You do not yet have as many options for obtaining protein."

"So you object because the 'tribal' people in your time *do* have the option to have a perfectly balanced diet of tasteless glop, but still choose to eat a juicy steak." Alex scowled at Sean but didn't reply. "What do you mean fully developed? Are you saying someone in my time is working on a food synthesizer?"

"The experimentation with genetically enhanced foods is a cornerstone of food synthesis. That has already begun in your time-period."

"Genetically enhanced food? Yeah, that's not so popular."

"New ideas are frequently unacceptable when they vary too far from the status quo."

Sean grabbed one of the hot-dogs and popped it into a bun. "Well, I'm not going to eat any genetically enhanced food," he said as he covered his hot-dog in ketchup then took a big bite.

Alex silently turned away from Sean and went into the camper tent. Sean shook his head and rolled his eyes then finished eating his hot-dog. He plunged his hand into the icy waters of the chest searching for a Coke. Unable to find one, he settled for a Lemon-Lime Shasta, hoping it might taste like Sprite. *Close enough*, he thought as he wolfed down the second hot-dog without a bun or ketchup.

"OK," Sean shouted toward the tent, "The savage animal-eating ancestor has finished. You can come out now."

"I have nearly completed my task," replied Alex.

"What task?"

"Gathering samples that may have your grandfather's DNA."

Sean popped his head through the tent flap. "Doing what?"

"Gathering samples that may have your grandfather's DNA."

"I heard you the first time."

"Then why did you ask again?"

"OK, language breakdown. Sorry. *Why* are you gathering samples?"

"It will extend the S.T.E.'s navigational capabilities further into the past. You knew that was one of the objectives of this trip."

"But I thought we were going to get it at the farm."

"That will not be necessary if I can obtain it here. I have collected several different hair samples, and since your grandfather placed this camper here to fish, there is a greater than 99 percent chance that the majority of those hairs are his."

"Yeah, but what if you've got the wrong hair. You might get Micky or Louise, or even one of Grandpa's fishing buddies."

"I will test all of them, but only one will have a familial match to your father's DNA."

"Might be Grandma.... or my dad had an older brother and sister. It could be one of them."

"That is not how DNA works. One can identify the difference of gender and familial relationship when comparing two samples of DNA."

Sean was crestfallen. "Oh," he said meekly.

Alex noticed Sean's mood change. "I have said something wrong. Did I relate excessive details in the explanation of DNA comparisons?"

"It's not that," said Sean softly. "It's just that I thought I was going to get to see my Grandfather that I'd never met. He died before I was born, you know."

"Your father did not invite us to his house."

"I know."

"I do not believe he has reason to alter that decision."

"I know," Sean sighed.

"I cannot think of another reason for us to go to his house."

"Great. Me either."

"Also, it did not appear that you were very successful in befriending him."

"He's just different than I thought he'd be," Sean complained. "He's so *not* like my Dad. He's shorter, fatter, and with that long hair he looks scruffy and stupid. He smokes... he's just... different."

"From my observations, it appeared that you put more effort into getting to know both Louise and Jane."

"OK! OK! Got it! My fault! Shut up!" Sean bellowed.

Total silence fell. Within a few seconds, birds in the trees started singing again, but inside the tent, Alex was frozen. Sean whipped away from the tent, kicked Alex's backpack, then picked up the camp stool and flung it aimlessly. He scooped up a fist-sized rock and heaved it against the closest tree. The birds went silent again. He stomped through the remains of their campfire, scattering the pieces that hadn't burned.

"OK, Sean," he quietly said to himself. "Dial it back a little." He took some deep breaths but kept walking around in circles around the campsite, hands on hips. "It doesn't do any good to yell at Future-Boy. It just freaks him out, and he cringes." He took more deep breaths. "Why does he push my buttons?" He thought about it as he paced. *It's because he's always so damned logical. Worse than that... he's logical, and he's almost always right.* He took more deep breaths and circled some more, starting to feel a little calmer. "I'd better go back in there and make sure he didn't pass out from fright." He forced his face into the semblance of a smile and headed for the tent.

"I'm sorry I screamed at you," Sean said as he popped back into the tent.

"No!" said Alex firmly, "Not this time!"

Sean was shocked. He'd never seen his descendant take charge so forcefully. "Excuse me?"

"You are not going to apologize again!" Alex said sternly.

Wow, thought Sean, *he is majorly ticked off!*

"I have analyzed..." Alex began brusquely, then stopped. "I have contemplated..." he stopped again. "I have been thinking about what has transpired." His eyes met Sean's. "I *feel* like..." He looked down, unable to hold the gaze. "...I have irritated you by observing and reporting facts. I have allowed logic to always take precedence over emotion even though I am fully aware that you operate at a much higher emotional level than I do. I was particularly egregious in my cavalier attitude regarding your father and grandfather."

"Egregious?" laughed Sean. "Cavalier? Dude, your English program needs some serious adjustment."

"I am issuing an apology and your reaction is to find fault with my choice of words?"

"Wait... that was an apology?"

"Yes."

"You're apologizing because I yelled at you?"

"No, I am apologizing because I am the catalyst that precipitated your angry reaction."

"OK, first let me school you about apologizing... at least to me. Cut way back on the 'egregious', 'cavalier', 'catalyst', and 'precipitated', OK? Just say, 'dude, I'm sorry I'm an emotionless dork from the future' and be done with it." He faced Alex's vacant stare. "No? How about 'I'm sorry I'm an emotionless dork with no sense of humor'?" He blew out a breath. "It was a *joke*... to ease the tension?"

Alex's face remained blank. "Referring to me in a slanderous way is humorous?"

"Yeah, it's called teasing. But let's get to second before I explain humor to you *again*. Second, you don't have to apologize for getting yelled at. I've been with you enough to know that you are 90 percent Vulcan, so I have some responsibility to not go ballistic just because you're acting like your logical self."

Alex started to speak.

"Hold it!" Sean ordered, putting a hand in Alex's face. "Third, we've got a pattern going. I'm emotional and volatile. You're logical and annoying. We're going to clash. I need to get a better grip on my temper and you need to look around to see if you can find anything that resembles feelings."

Alex again tried to speak, but Sean repeated his hand gesture. "Just one more thing. I want credit for using the word, 'volatile' in a sentence instead of hot-headed."

111

After a brief moment of silently staring at each other, Alex asked, "Where do I place this credit for your use of the word 'volatile'?"

"In my 'Sean is a caveman' account. You know, you add points on for when I go ballistic or do primitive stuff like eat meat. Then you take points back off when I do something intelligent like use a better vocabulary. At the end of the week, I get my caveman score."

Alex looked questioningly at Sean, then smiled. "You are once again using humor to defuse strained interpersonal tension. I am beginning to detect a behavioral pattern."

"See? Now I can take points off the 'Alex is an emotionless dork' account, because you actually figured out on your own that something was funny."

"What is the purpose of these scores?"

"At the end of the week, whoever has the highest score has to buy the other guy a pizza."

"I do not want a pizza."

"Ha! Like you could win anyway," Sean scoffed. "OK, if you happen to win, I'll buy you a pack of cigarettes."

"I also do not want a pack... wait... you are employing humor again."

"Wow! More points! I might be in trouble with this week's score."

Alex looked at the big grin on Sean's face and returned a warm smile. "You are a fascinating person, Sean Kelly."

"Yeah, well, I forgot to mention that you also get more dork points when you get mushy, so watch it," Sean said. "OK... so back to the science project. What do you have to do to test the DNA in those hairs?"

"Take the samples to the S.T.E. to process."

"Then let's do it," urged Sean.

"You do not need to accompany me."

"Come on. You're going to trot out some new futuristic thing that I haven't seen. I'm not going to miss that."

"There actually is nothing to see."

"Are you trying to keep this secret?"

"No. The processing is accomplished internally. There truly is nothing to observe."

"Well, I'm bored anyway, so you can pop up that 3D newspaper reader again, and I'll play with that. Hey, could I fold it up into a 3D hat?"

"Very well, you may accompany me," said Alex. He exited the tent and started toward his time-ship. Sean trailed behind him.

"How about comic books? Can you do 3D comic books on that thing?"

They picked their way through the underbrush until they reached the cloaked ship. Alex opened it and slid in. Sean plopped down beside him and watched as Alex opened up the display and manipulated some symbols. A small tray slid out from beneath the screen.

"How many secret drawers do you have in this thing?" Sean marveled.

"They are not secret."

"Hidden then. You can't see them until they pop out."

"Several. About a dozen, I believe. I have never actually activated them all at the same time to count them."

Alex placed his collected hairs into the tray and touched the screen. The tray slid back into the panel and virtually vanished. Sean inspected the seamless area that had just swallowed the tray.

"That is so cool how it just kind of seals itself. No cracks, nothing. No one could tell there was a drawer behind there." Alex ignored him as he busily manipulated other icons on the screen. "How long will this take?"

"That will depend on the number of samples," Alex replied, "and since we are not certain of the quantity of unique samples there are, I cannot tell you."

"Seconds? Minutes? Hours?"

"Minutes, I believe. I will estimate between ten and thirty-five minutes."

"OK, so let me play with the 3D reader. Since you don't have any comic books, I guess I can read up on Woodstock. Dude, I was surprised that they all knew so much about it. All I know is a bunch of hippies went to this massive outdoor rock concert. Sex, drugs, and rock and roll!"

"If we were back in 1995, I could increase your level of nanites, enabling you to accept a download of all the data required to become an expert on the subject of Woodstock."

"Yeah, I think I've already got more nanites than I want. How 'bout if I just do this the old-fashioned way and read about it?"

"What do you propose to read?"

"I don't know. Something with current events, like a news magazine. Yeah, like *Time!*"

"I do not understand how time will assist your quest for information."

"*Time! Time Magazine*. It's a weekly news magazine that has been around for like forever. If you can pull up the *Quincy County Gazette*, surely you've got *Time Magazine* in there somewhere."

Alex manipulated some controls and a red-bordered magazine cover with *Time* in the masthead popped onto the forward screen. "Is that what you require?" he asked.

"Yeah. How do you select the date?"

"What date would you suggest?"

"I don't know. August 1969."

"There are five issues with that date."

"The first one, then. I said it was a weekly."

"August 1, 1969," Alex said as he displayed the cover on the screen.

"How about the 3D thing."

Alex touched the screen and simultaneously connected with a direct command to the computer. A holographic copy of *Time* instantly floated in front of Sean. He grabbed it and started flipping through the pages.

"Here's an article about Apollo 11. Oh, wow! I forgot. That's like just a few days from now." He flipped some more. "Here's something called Chappaquiddick. Sounds like some Indian tribe or something." He scanned the article. "It's about Kennedy. Ted Kennedy. Some scandal about driving a car into a river and some girl drowned. I don't think I've heard about this. It happens the day before the Apollo landing." He read through the whole article. "So, it looks like everyone thought he'd be in line to run for President, and this scandal kind of sunk him. Well, not completely, since he's still a powerful guy in the Senate in 1995." He flipped some more pages. "Vietnam stuff. I guess that was in the news all the time. More Apollo stories. I don't see anything about Woodstock. Maybe they didn't cover it beforehand. Can you jump to the first issue after Woodstock?"

"That would be August 22, 1969," Alex said as he mentally prompted the computer to change the issue Sean was holding.

"That is so cool. Man, something like this would sure make school reports go easier."

Sean started flipping through the pages of the newer edition.

"Huh, more stuff about the moon. So that was still a big deal. More stuff about the Ted Kennedy thing. More stuff about Vietnam. Night of Horror... what's that about, some horror movie just come out?" He scanned through the article. "Holy crap! When you said this era was full of violence you weren't kidding! Somebody killed and mutilated some Hollywood actress and her friends. This is weird! The investigation is on-going. Do you know if they ever caught who did this?"

"What are the names of the people who were murdered?"

"Sharon Tate, Jay Sebring, Abigail Folger, and I don't know how to pronounce this other name."

"I will search those three names," Alex said as he twitched a query. "Several people were convicted in the murders, but the principal name of reference is Charles Manson."

"Seriously? This is the Manson murders? I've heard of that nutcase. He's still in prison in 1995. Read this! This was sick and brutal and twisted. When did it happen?"

"August 9, 1969."

"Just a few weeks," Sean said softly, then enthusiastically added, "We could stop this!"

"No. It happened," Alex replied. "It was an evil deed, but it happened."

"Why? Why do you think something like this isn't worth stopping?"

"History is not to be changed," Alex stated dispassionately.

"Come on! How can stopping a murdering psycho be a bad thing? What worse thing could happen if we saved those people's lives?"

"Charles Manson may kill someone else, and the consequences of that death or deaths may have a catastrophic impact somewhere in the future. We cannot know. Perhaps he would not be captured, and a multitude of other people will be killed. He appears to be psychotic."

"So we take him down, before it happens," Sean suggested.

"Take him down? What does that mean?"

"Kill him before he kills!"

Alex audibly gasped. "You would be capable of murdering someone?"

Sean paused as he thought about what he said. "I don't know." He shrugged. "There must be some way of stopping him. Tell the cops."

"They would have no reason to capture or hold Manson if no crime has been committed."

"But it's *going* to be!"

"Sean, your argument is irrational."

"And your argument is heartless," Sean fired back. "How can you not want to stop this?"

"Why this one?" Alex countered. "There have been countless murders throughout mankind's history. Where is the justice in selecting only this one incident, and not any of the others?"

Sean mulled over Alex's point. It was true that no one could stop every murder.

"It's just not fair!" He complained less passionately. "We know about this before it happens."

Alex twitched a connection to his computer. "Tonight in Detroit, Michigan, a 23-year-old woman named Jennifer White will be murdered. Her husband eventually charged. Also tonight in New York City, a 17-year-old is knifed to death. It is assumed to be gang related, but no one is ever convicted. In Chicago, Illinois, a 44-year-old man is killed in his own home when he attempts to stop a burglary. He is killed with his own handgun. In Los Angeles, California, a..."

"Stop it!" Sean shouted. "Why are you telling me about all these murders?"

"They are historical events," Alex said coolly, "Things that happened before either of us will be born."

"So?"

"But they have not yet happened in the point of time we currently occupy."

"Obviously, if you said it'll happen tonight."

Alex took a deep breath and turned slightly away from Sean. "It is not fair. We know about this before it happens."

"*What?*" exploded Sean. "Don't parrot me! What are you trying to get me to say? That I'm wrong? No! I'm *not* wrong! It *isn't* fair!"

Alex sat stone still, afraid to even look Sean's way. He could feel Sean's icy gaze boring into him. He held his breath, waiting to see if Sean was going to continue to lash out. When he didn't, without looking up, Alex spoke in a flat tone just above a whisper. "I want you to say that you acknowledge that these incidents, no matter how heinous, are historical. I need you to understand that time-travel is used only to observe and learn about the past, not attempt to reshape the future by changing what happened."

Sean continued to stare at Alex, but weighed his words and considered the logic behind them. For the moment, he hated that logic, felt fury toward Alex for being so emotionless. Then he exhaled the breath he had planned to use for his next verbal assault and tried to let go of the anger. When he did speak, it was with a calm voice that nearly matched Alex's tone. "At least tell me that you feel bad for those people. All those people that you listed. The ones that are alive right now, but will be dead tomorrow. Tell me that you at least feel bad that your Time-Traveler non-interference rule keeps you from helping any of them."

Alex looked up at Sean. "I do not think about them," he stated frankly. "I have no positive or negative feelings for any of them. It is all a matter of history."

"Do you really *want* to understand me?" Sean asked with renewed passion. "Do you *want* to know what it is like to be living in the 20th century? You say you do. You say that's the reason you made contact with me instead of just watching me."

"That is true."

"Then *feel* something for those people!" Sean urged. "I'll help you. Imagine that tomorrow you are standing in front of that teenage knife victim's mother. Now tell her you could have saved her son, but you didn't. That middle-aged guy in Chicago. Tell his wife you knew what was going to happen, but you did nothing. Let's assume that the woman in Detroit has two small kids. Tell them why you decided it was better for them to not have a Mom anymore."

The two stared at each other as a single tear rolled down Alex's cheek.

"To me," Sean said softly, "that has *got* to be the worst thing about time-travel. Knowing something bad is going to happen, and just letting it happen."

A second tear rolled down Alex's other cheek. "I cannot!" he sobbed. "I cannot change things! It is the first law!"

Sean reached out and put a hand on Alex's shoulder and gently rubbed it. For a split second, he even considered giving him a hug. "I can see they drilled that into you pretty good. I get it. I understand the logic. I just think it sucks." Alex continued to sob softly, and Sean began to feel guilty for pushing him too far. "You know," he mused, "on all of the *Star Trek* episodes I've ever seen, the only time they mention the Prime Directive is when they're going to break it."

Alex looked over to Sean with questioning but still glistening eyes.

"Hey, speaking of *Star Trek*," Sean continued in a lighter tone, "Does it look to you like the main color in this tie-dyed shirt is red?" He followed with an overly toothy grin and raised eyebrows.

Still confused, Alex blinked back tears. "Humor?" he asked softly.

"See, there you go scoring more points on me," Sean joked.

"Why?"

"Hey, I only wanted you to feel a *little* bad," Sean asserted, "I didn't mean to *crush* you. Just trying to lighten things up again."

"I do not like this feeling."

"Yeah, I know, it's..." Sean started, then stopped with a jaw drop. "Please tell me this isn't the first time that you've ever cried."

"It seems unlikely," Alex replied as he thought about it. "I am sure that as an infant I would have cried. I believe that is normal for infants since they have no verbal skills."

"You don't remember ever crying?"

"No. Do you remember things from your infancy?" Alex asked.

"So you never fell off your bike and skinned your knee?"

"I did not have a bike, and children in my era wear protective clothing that makes epidermal abrasion nearly impossible."

"Sure they do," said Sean as he rolled his eyes. "Never watched a movie where the boy's dog or Bambi's mom gets killed?"

"I am unfamiliar with your references. Who is Bambi?"

"Never mind," sighed Sean. "Hey...look...I didn't mean to... you know...mess you up like that... and... Sorry."

Alex looked at Sean wistfully. "It is, however... interesting. You have felt this way before?"

"Oh yeah!" Sean affirmed. "More times than I could begin to count."

"How do you..." Alex searched for the right words, "stop the feeling?"

"I don't. It just kind of goes away... eventually. I guess I just make myself do stuff, or think about other stuff... but, then later when I remember... well... it can still feel bad. I doesn't just go away. That's why I started joking around. To get you to think of something else. Kind of move the pain off to the side."

"You are a very complex person," Alex said, then forced a wry smile, "...for a caveman."

"Wow! Major point score! You actually made a joke... kind of." Sean saw the screen flash out of the corner of his eye and turned to it. "What's that?"

"I believe the DNA analysis is complete," Alex answered as he used two fingers to pull a box off of the screen and enlarge it. "Yes. As I hypothesized, most of the samples are from your grandfather." Alex squeezed that box smaller and pulled out a second box. He dragged data from the DNA report into the new box, then closed it.

"What's that one?" Sean asked, pointing to a blue cube on the screen.

"That would be you. Since I set the match point to your father's DNA, you match half, thus blue."

"What's that one?" Sean asked, pointing to another spot on the screen.

"That is your grandmother; also a half match. The arrangement of the alleles let me know that it is female DNA."

"And that one?"

"You said your dad has a brother?"

"Yes."

"Without a closer examination, I would say with a 97 percent confidence level that it is your uncle."

"How about that little orange one at the bottom?"

"No relationship to your father, but a partial match to someone else in the database."

"Like who?"

"I do not know without searching it further. It appears that someone else who has been in your grandfather's camper is somehow related to one of my other ancestors."

"Wow! That's kind of a surprise. Don't you want to know who?"

"It is irrelevant to the task of recording your grandfather's DNA. Besides, we have no idea who all of the contributors are. Perhaps one of your grandfather's fishing buddies is also a relative of mine. At that level, I have 512 Great-great-great-great-great-great-great-grandparents."

"Wow! That's a lot of ancestors! What if it's Micky?" teased Sean.

"I will save the data. If you wish to obtain a specific sample of Micky's DNA, perhaps we can check it later. Although I am not entirely certain that I care to know if Micky is a distant relative."

Alex moved the data into a new file and closed all the windows and shut down the display.

"OK... I guess you're done with that. So what do you want to do now?" asked Sean.

"I believe I wish to sit on the dock and meditate on our conversation."

"You sure that's a good idea?"

"No, but I intend do it anyway," Alex said decisively. "What will you do?"

"I don't know," replied Sean. "You got any 20th Century science fiction in your database? I could read."

"It is possible. It would be easier to determine if I had an author or title to query."

"I've been reading Robert Heinlein. So far I've read everything of his that our library has, but there's a bunch more."

Alex twitched a connection. "Yes, I have full text of several Robert Heinlein novels."

"How about *The Cat Who Walks Through Walls*? I thought that sounded good. The title's a little quirky. Might be interesting."

Alex nodded, twitched, and touched the screen in front of him at the same time. A book floated in front of Sean.

"I gotta say," said Sean as he reached out for the book, "that's got to be one of your cooler toys. Too bad it doesn't extend beyond Steffi... or does it?"

Alex thought for a moment. He touched the screen in front of them and manipulated a few icons. A drawer slid out from the area below revealing a pair of glasses. "You remember," he said as he scooped them up, "the little 3D ball that Katherine showed you?" Sean nodded. "I believe I can transfer this book into the glasses and you could then take it with you. As long as you wear the glasses, it will appear that you have this book."

"Why do you have these with us?" Sean asked as he took the glasses.

"When we return to 1995, I will use them to download the movie we were supposed to watch into your visual cortex. Your memory will tell you that we watched the movie."

"I guess that's why you only sleep four hours a night. You have to sit around thinking of all these wacky details to manage my split brain." Sean put the glasses on. "Now what?"

Alex moved some icons on the screen, then closed it down again. "Get out," he said, "You should still be able to see the book in your hand."

Sean stared at his hand as he climbed out, the book remained in it.

"Awesome!" Sean said, then corrected himself, "I mean, Far Out!"

The two picked their way back to the campsite, Sean occasionally checking his hand to make sure the book was still there. "I guess you don't have libraries in the future," he said.

"We have buildings, their prime function more like your museums, to store the few printed artifacts that are still in existence. For those who still wish to read, all of the content is stored on the computer network to make it easily accessible."

"I don't know if I would like that or not."

"The change is gradual," Alex explained, "When new technologies arise, generally the older technologies they replace remain until after the death of all of the people who preferred the former version."

"That's a cheery way to look at progress."

"Is that not better than forcing everyone to embrace new technologies against their will?"

When they reached the campsite, Alex continued to toward the water. "I believe you will enjoy your book," he said. "Especially if you have read several other titles. It appears Heinlein attempted to draw as many characters as possible from all his previous stories into this one."

"You've read it?"

"I just downloaded his major works as we were walking. Plus some commentary by Heinlein scholars."

"You should try actually *reading* sometime," Sean yelled to Alex's back. "It's better to let the story unfold than to absorb the whole thing, then remember it."

"He is very reckless with his time-travelers. They need some restraint," Alex shouted back.

Sean settled into one of the lawn chairs and started reading. He was soon enthralled in the fantastic story of a talented author's imagined future. When he reached the part where Mike reappeared—he was the self-aware computer from *The Moon is a Harsh Mistress*—he wondered if the computer housed in Steffi was similarly self-aware. It was kind of a scary thought, as he imagined when Alex connected to his computer that it might be actually like talking to another being. Sean loved stories with artificial intelligence and sentient robots or androids and wondered if Alex knew any androids personally in his own time.

He was a little more than halfway through the book when he heard a sharp *beep-beep* from the main road. He looked that way and caught a glimpse of yellow through the trees. He pulled off the glasses for a better look and his book disappeared. He hoped it would hold his place so he wouldn't have to start over, then wondered if he should have activated some kind of a virtual bookmark.

He stood and began to walk toward the main lake road. Part way up, he could see that the patch of yellow was actually a bright yellow Volkswagen beetle with a huge blue flower painted on the door facing him. He immediately recognized the feminine form walking toward him. Jane.

"Hi!" she called to him. "I wasn't sure if you'd hear the horn or not. I didn't want to drive down in here and get stuck, the bug's not a good mudder. That was some storm last night. I'm glad we got out when we did."

The gap between them closed quickly as they both walked toward each other.

"Jane. Good to see you," Sean said, smiling brightly.

"What did you think of our Iowa thunderstorm? Do you have storms like that in New Zealand?"

New Zealand? Sean had forgotten to put on his fake accent. He hoped Jane hadn't noticed from the short greeting he gave her.

"Yeah, sometimes we get a bit of a wonker what comes off the sea," Sean improvised, laying his multinational accent on thick. "That was a bit of a wooly dingo last night, though."

"I hope you stayed dry," Jane replied without asking how a thunderstorm was like a dingo.

"No worries, luv. Buttoned up like a roo in his mum's pocket," Sean rambled, pleased that these wacky phrases readily popped into his head. He briefly wondered if there really *were* Kangaroos in New Zealand, but since he didn't know, he hoped Jane didn't either.

"Where's Peter?"

"Oh, he's knocking about somewhere. I fink he was down at the dock."

Being close to Jane again and mentioning the dock caused Sean's thoughts to drift back to their near kiss. He wondered if she was thinking the same thing when he noticed her cheeks suddenly had a pink tinge. She smiled shyly as she looked down. Quickly recovering, she produced a paper bag she had hidden behind her back.

"I thought you might be tired of hot-dogs," she said, handing the bag to Sean. "It's a ham and cheese sandwich. I made peanut butter and jelly for Peter. I hope that's something he eats."

"Just as long as no animals were harmed in the making of the sandwich," Sean joked.

"No. Just some peanuts and grapes, I guess," Jane laughed.

She put her now empty hands behind her back and rocked on her heels. She was wearing flip-flops again, blue denim shorts and a simple olive green T-shirt. Sean liked the way it looked on her. Her hair was pulled back in a single ponytail hanging halfway down her back, and with the sun shining brightly overhead, Sean noticed that her oddly colored brown hair had blonde roots.

"Well, anyway, I thought you might like some sandwiches," she said as she continued to rock, also swinging her hands a little. "I guess I should go."

"Do you have to?" Sean quickly asked. "I mean, would you like to come down to the campsite and sit for awhile? There might still be another strawberry Shasta."

"Well, I don't know," she said nervously, then met his eyes and smiled. "I guess so. For a little while."

"Brilliant!" Sean declared as he hooked her arm to usher her back down the hill.

"I guess a lot of the flower children who live in communes are vegetarians," Jane suggested.

Flower children? Who are they? Sean wondered.

"Have you or Peter ever lived in a commune?" she continued.

Maybe she's talking about hippies? "No. Stayed in one overnight, though. The first week when we were still in California," Sean lied.

"What was that like?"

I am getting in way over my head. Where's Alex when I need him? "It was all right, I guess," he bluffed.

Sean could feel Jane steeling herself for more questions. "So... is it all... like...um...drugs...and free love and stuff?" she asked, unable to hide a blush.

I don't know! Isn't that kind of what hippies were all about? How can I change this conversation? "Um... yeah... I guess so," he mumbled, trying to sound disinterested.

Jane battled with her curiosity and embarrassment, but pressed on. "Like... you know...right out in the open? Or..."

Sean glanced at Jane, her cheeks were flaming and she stared straight ahead. "I can't rightly say, luv. I was really nackered from the day's walk about. I had a bite to eat and just wandered off to a quiet place and zonked out."

They reached the campsite and Sean dragged the two lawn chairs close together.

"So... then you didn't... um..." Jane stammered as she sat in one of the

121

offered chairs.

"No, luv," Sean quickly affirmed. "Completely zonked. Slept like a stone."

"Have you ever....?"

Sean busied himself digging into the ice chest which held only cool water around the remaining cans now. "I'm sorry, luv, I was wrong about the Strawberry. All out it seems. Want to give the black cherry a go? They're still a bit chilled."

"Um... sure."

He handed her the can and returned to his inspection of each can. "I can't decide between the orange and the grape. What do you reckon?"

"Um... I don't... I guess..." Jane murmured.

"Orange it is, then!" Sean proclaimed as he popped the top and sat in the chair beside her. He decided it was time to steer the conversation away from Jane's questions. "I hope it's not too forward of me, luv, but I noticed in the sun that your hair is..." he touched the part in his own hair.

"Oh... yeah," Jane said, "Umm, I'm naturally a blonde. Kind of sandy blonde."

"Decided to give it a go as a brunette, wot?"

"Not exactly," Jane responded with some reluctance. "It wasn't *planned* that way."

"How'd you mean?"

"I actually started out bleaching my hair. I wanted it really white-blonde for the summer."

"Didn't like it?"

"No, I did! I thought it looked really groovy," Jane insisted, then paused. Sean looked at her expectantly. "And... well... I made the mistake of going swimming at the swimming pool." She paused again. "The chlorine turned it green." She blushed.

Sean bit his lip to keep from laughing. He couldn't believe she wanted to talk about hippie sex, but was embarrassed by green hair. He thought of all the different colored hair he saw daily at his high school. "Well, that's not so bad, then, is it?"

"Green! I couldn't go out in public with *green* hair!" Jane complained. "So anyway, Louise helped me out with a henna rinse. We had to do it several times to get it to cover, and it's still kind of a weird color. Henna normally gives a red-brown look. I guess the green makes it this grotey brown."

That explains the odd color. "No, it looks fine!" Sean assured her.

"Well... better than green," she pouted.

Maybe not. Sean looked at her and tried to imagine green hair and decided he kind of liked it. Then he tried to imagine her as a blonde, and the feeling returned that she reminded him of someone.

"Nigel. You're staring."

"Hmmm," Sean thought aloud, then refocused. "Oh, sorry, luv.

Remember I told you that you reminded me of someone? I was trying to imagine you with blonde hair." He skipped telling her about the green hair vision.

"Oh," said Jane. "Sorry, I just always feel like when someone stares at me, it's because of my nose."

"Why do you make such a big deal out of your nose?"

"Because it's there, and it *is* kind of a big deal!"

"But there's more to you than just a nose."

"I'm seventeen, Nigel. This Fall starts my last year of high school, and I've never been asked on a date."

"Never?" exclaimed Sean, honestly surprised.

"Well... Juan kind of pretended to be my date for Prom," she recanted. "See, we've been friends since grade school." She smiled at the memory. "A little bit competitive since we were both 'smart kids'. I remember in third-grade we had a Spelling Bee for grades 1-3. Juan was the second-grade champ and I was the top for the third-grade. The first-grader went out right away... didn't really have a chance, but Juan and I went several rounds, both of us desperate to be the best of the best." She gazed off into the sky.

Sean was amazed that his dad had gone out with Jane, even if she didn't seem to count it as a date. "Who won?"

She laughed. "That's the funny thing. I don't remember. I think I did. We seemed to always be competing in school over the years, but now I don't remember keeping track of who won what." She still stared off into space.

"You know," Sean ventured, "It's OK to have a date with a friend."

"Yeah, maybe," Jane said wistfully, "if it hadn't turned out to be such a disaster." She sighed deeply before continuing, "Some of the 'popular' senior girls decided it would be fun to harass us. Juan's always been nervous around pretty girls—well, except for Louise, but Louise can make anyone comfortable—anyway, some of them surrounded him at the punch bowl and started drilling him with questions. Stuff like, 'is tonight the night, stud' and 'did you remember to reserve a room at the motel' and other junk like that. Made him so nervous that he spilled punch on his shirt. I told him that I had a headache and the noise from the dance was making it worse, just so we could get out of there. Then as we were leaving, one of the clique loudly said, 'Can you believe that she came with that roly-poly sophomore?' She knew we could hear her. Man, I am so glad those bitches graduated." She winced slightly as she glanced at Sean. "Pardon my French." She finished brusquely, "Not that there's not a pack of them in every class, you know."

Sean's thoughts went straight to Megan and her entourage and he wondered if that was just something that spanned any generation. "I'm sorry you had such a rough go," he offered sincerely. He paused before nervously adding, "I think you're rather attractive."

Jane gave him a look that said, 'please, don't patronize me'.

Sean continued, "You have very nice eyes, and I think your glasses are spiff. You have nice lips, you..." He stopped when she formed a straight line with her index fingers, framing her nose as the midpoint. "Oh, come on, Jane, give that a rest! It may not be your best feature, but it's not like you're the Wicked Witch of the West!" A moment of panic seized Sean as he wondered if the *Wizard of Oz* was made before 1969. Deciding it must have been, he continued, "And I don't mean to embarrass you, but I think you have..." He paused to think. *What's a nice way of saying hot body?* "...a lovely figure." *Wow, that sounded kind of lame.*

Jane's cheek's flared and her eyes dropped to her feet. The corners of her mouth crept into a smile. "Thank you," she murmured. She glanced up at Sean and then immediately back down. "Unfortunately, I was kind of a 'late bloomer' in that department. I remember all the attention the girls who were 'early developers' got in Junior High. When you're nearly fifteen before you start to fill out, it's already too late... at least in a small-town High School. You've already been put in a box and there's no way out."

"What box?"

"Outsiders... misfits... I don't know if it has a name... but I'm in it."

They sat quietly, each thinking about their own complicated dynamics dealing with people in their schools.

"Tell me the truth, Nigel," Jane said seriously. Sean looked up and found that her eyes were locked on his. Her intensity made him uncomfortable and he nearly looked away. "Do you think after I get my nose done that boys will find me attractive?"

He stared into her searching eyes, hoping he'd say the right words. "I've already said that I find you attractive now. I believe I qualify as a boy." Their eyes remained locked. Jane searched Sean's face for any hint of guile.

When she was satisfied that he meant what he said, she looked back to the ground. "When you go back to New Zealand, can I go with you?" Fear gripped Sean's stomach and he began to babble incoherently. "Kidding," Jane said with a wry smile. She stood. "I probably should go." She started walking away, then stopped as an idea struck her. She turned. "Nigel, do you have drive-in movies in New Zealand?"

"I have actually never been to a drive-in movie," Sean answered, attempting to skirt the New Zealand part of the question.

"The drive-in over in Colgate has 'buck night' on Sunday nights. It might be fun to round up a car full of people and go. It's only twenty-five miles from Mercer."

"What's 'buck night'?" Sean asked.

"Oh! Sorry. As many people as you can cram into a car gets in for a buck... a dollar. They show older movies that everyone has probably already seen, I guess that's why it's so cheap. I don't know, maybe they make money on popcorn."

"Sounds...interesting."

"So, you want to go? You and Peter, of course."

"I can ask him," Sean offered. "Want to wait while I find him?"

"No, that's OK," Jane replied. "Why don't I come back in a couple of hours? That'll give me time to round up some people, and you and Peter can decide if you want to join us."

"What time is it now?"

"Eleven-thirty. I'll try to be back no later than two," she said as she started walking back to her car.

"Hey, I meant to ask you what happened to the T-Bird?"

She turned and walked backwards as she replied, "It turned into a pumpkin."

"I thought pumpkins were orange," Sean teased.

"It's not quite ripe yet," Jane fired back.

Sean smiled. He loved her quick, witty reply. "Drive safely in that pumpkin, luv," he said as he waved to her.

"I'll do the best I can," Jane replied then took three more backward steps, and with a quick grin added, "... luv." She immediately whirled around and set off briskly for the road.

"And thanks for the sandwiches," Sean shouted to her back.

She kept walking, but waved her arm above her head in a backward goodbye. She soon disappeared around a small copse of trees. Sean listened until he heard the engine start. He could see a little flash of yellow through the trees as the VW pulled away and vanished from sight.

Sean was somewhat surprised that Jane said it was eleven-thirty already, but he also knew he easily lost track of time when engrossed in a good book. He considered returning to his book, but decided since Alex had been away for several *hours* he should check on him, so he started walking toward the dock.

A pang of irrational fear suddenly gripped him as he imagined Alex doing the dead-man float in the lake. He had no idea if his descendant could swim. If Alex drowned, how could he get back to 1995 without him? The panic eased when he realized that the crazy super-suit from the future would probably keep him from drowning. For all he knew, Alex could calmly sit at the bottom of the lake and not even get wet. Then guilt set in for thinking of himself being trapped in 1969 before considering Alex's well-being.

He breathed a sigh of relief when he got close enough for the dock to come into view. Sitting at the very end, facing the water sat the long-haired and outlandishly dressed shape of the person everyone in 1969 thought of as Peter Lindsey. He called out, "Oy! Cousin Peter!" but Alex didn't move or acknowledge him in any way.

Sean closed the distance and stepped gingerly onto the dock as it swayed under his weight. "Hey, man... you are looking *far out*... into the lake. As long as you've been sitting there on those boards, I'll bet your butt is looking *groovy*. Hey, before I came over here, you were really *out of sight*." He emphasized his three hippie phrases, quite pleased with himself and his little puns.

Alex still did not acknowledge him. Sean carefully walked to the end of the dock. "Dude, what are you doing?"

"I told you of my intent when we parted, I have been thinking," Alex said without moving.

"And what have you been thinking about, all this time, oh brainiac from the future?"

"The assumptions I made regarding the knowledge most needed to function well in this time were lacking," Alex said in a monotone as he continued to gaze at the ripples on the lake.

Sean waited a few moments to see if Alex would continue. "Wow," he mocked, "several hours out here and that's all you've come up with?"

"I have also absorbed and assessed the entirety of the *Star Trek* mythology."

"*All* of it?" Sean asked, utterly amazed.

"Yes," Alex affirmed. "The television episodes, the movies, the books, scholarly commentary..."

"OK, I can see that would take several hours."

"The total transfer time was slightly more than half an hour. I have been contemplating several topics that were recurring, as well as examining the depths of the philosophies."

"I can't believe you can pack that much stuff in your brain at all, let alone in less than an hour."

"You might be surprised by the capacity of the human brain, even unaugmented."

"I don't know," Sean replied. "After you partitioned my brain to be able to lock away the memories I have of being with you, I guess I can believe anything."

They were both silent several moments before Alex spoke again, "I believe I have a better understanding of your attitudes toward me, particularly regarding logical decisions."

Sean sat down near Alex, leaving enough space for a large third person to sit between them, and joined him staring out at the water.

"Even though it is obvious," Alex expounded, "that Vulcans—as well as the android in the later series—function at a higher level of intelligence, they are generally not in command. Any time a human ignores the recommended logical course of action in favor of his own intuitive feelings, the human is generally correct. Some of the characters in the original series are openly critical of the Vulcan for being emotionless, particularly the physician. The android in the second series seeks to obtain emotions as he feels incomplete without them. I believe all these fictional themes contribute to your own attitudes regarding logical decisions."

Sean nodded slowly as he digested Alex's comments. "I can see how you could *logically* reach that conclusion," he said with a wry smile.

"You consider my emotionless reaction to information to be a character flaw."

"I don't know if I think of it as a flaw... more like just annoying," Sean said, still grinning.

"Perhaps it is a flaw," Alex uttered softly.

"Wow! Did not see *that* one coming," Sean exclaimed.

"I have also been thinking about the tens of thousands of people who die violent deaths in this year alone. Wars, murder, suicides... hundreds because of alcohol impaired automobile drivers." They both sat quietly and Sean allowed the words to sink in. "I always only regarded them statistically. Never allowing myself to consider individual pain and loss. Perhaps more than one hundred thousand people negatively impacted by the untimely death of friends or family members... just in a single year. How much does that pain shape the future? Perhaps someone who could have contributed something wonderful to society becomes emotionally crippled and unable to reach their potential." Alex fell quiet again.

Sean's smile faded completely away. "Dude, maybe you're tipping the other way a little too far," he said in a hushed tone.

Alex finally pulled away from his lake vigil and turned toward Sean. "I also have a better understanding of why they instilled us so strongly with the First Law. Why the thought of my attempting to change something actually terrifies me. Regarding each of the thousands of lives lost as individuals, rather than statistics, triggers thoughts of how easy it would be to use time-travel to interfere. How tempting it would be to attempt to make improvements."

"So... do you want to go save that woman in Detroit? Or the gang banger in New York? Or the old guy in Chicago?"

Alex turned back to the lake. "Yes."

"Wow!" exclaimed Sean. "I don't know what to say..."

"But I am not going to do so."

"You know, whether you're being all logical or emotional, it's really hard to follow your thinking."

"When I think of the fragility of human lives... individual lives, I also think of the fragility of the space/time continuum. How easily it could be shattered," Alex said wistfully.

"So you still aren't going to change anything."

"Correct."

"But now you are going to feel bad about it?"

Alex turned back to Sean. "I will have a different perspective."

Sean stared at him for a few moments, shook his head briskly, and then stood up. "OK, I think I'm going to go back to my book and eat my ham and cheese sandwich."

"Where did you obtain this sandwich?" Alex asked.

"Oh, I almost forgot why I came over here. Jane stopped by. She brought us each a sandwich and asked if we wanted to go to a drive-in movie tonight."

Alex twitched a connection to his computer. "A large outdoor screen for viewing motion pictures from vehicles arranged in rows. Each vehicle is provided a small audio speaker that hangs inside their window. The format was most popular during the decades of 1950 and 1960. There was a resurgence of the concept in 2045 using a large outdoor holographic projector."

"Why do you tell me some stuff from the future, and act like other stuff is a deep dark secret?"

"The holographic drive-in is inconsequential, both to your life and in general. It was too expensive and the image was not as vivid as the enclosed theater alternative. It was a short-lived phenomenon."

"I'll bet it was," Sean agreed. "So do you want to go tonight? I think it would be a riot."

"I was going to propose that we return to 1995. I have your grandfather's DNA, and we do not appear to gain anything from further observation of this time-period."

"That's why we should go," Sean insisted. "It will be an excellent opportunity to observe the behavior of teenagers in 1969 doing something in a typical sixties social setting."

Alex weighed the options. "Perhaps," he finally said reluctantly.

"Great!" Sean slapped him on the back. "Let's go eat those sandwiches."

"You know I will not eat ham and cheese."

"Jane made you a PB&J. So unless you are morally opposed to grapes being crushed and peanuts being ground up, you can eat it. Great change of pace from your tasteless goo."

Alex stood and they walked back toward the campsite.

"I believe you have more interest in being with Jane than experiencing a sixties' social setting," Alex proposed after walking most of the way in silence.

Sean blushed. "Maybe."

"It validates my decision to approach you in feminine form. You seem very receptive to befriending females," Alex commented. "Are you disappointed that Louise is romantically attached to Micky?"

"You know... whether logical or emotional, you still aren't very tactful."

"I am merely making observations."

When they arrived back at the campsite, Sean retrieved the bag of sandwiches and pulled his out. "Here," he said, handing the bag to Alex, "you can observe me eating a sandwich." Alex removed the second sandwich from the bag as Sean plunged into the no-longer-icy ice chest. "You want something to drink? The choices are getting slimmer. I guess I'm going to have to go with grape. There's that ginger ale that my Dad got for you."

"I will try it," Alex replied. "Does it feel unusual to refer to someone your own age as your Dad?"

Sean rolled the question around in his mind. "Haven't really thought about it that way. I mean, I guess I don't really *feel* like he's my Dad, since he's so different, but, on the other hand, I *know* that he is... or at least will be. Interesting question."

They both sat in the lawn chairs.

"I have not heard you address him by his name," Alex commented.

"Yeah, now that *is* weird... the whole Juan thing. He goes by Jack in 1995, and Grandma always calls him Jonathan. I guess he probably shook off the Juan label in college. College must be the big transformation years; changes his name, stops smoking, meets Mom. Maybe that's when he loses weight? Since I didn't ever know he was overweight, I don't know when that happened."

Sean popped the top on his grape Shasta and took a bite of his sandwich.

"How does actually meeting him compare to what you imagined?" asked Alex.

Sean chewed as he thought. "I guess the physical appearance is the biggest surprise... well, not counting the smoking. He's so much shorter... and... softer, I guess. The long hair just looks bizarre on him."

"It appears that you have an amicable relationship with your father in 1995, yet you do not seem to particularly like this younger version of him."

"I don't know," Sean shrugged, taking a sip of his drink as he thought. "Maybe I assumed he'd be cooler. Jane pretty much labeled him as a misfit."

Alex tasted his ginger ale and wrinkled his nose. "Why do you prefer to drink highly sweetened carbonated water?"

"I don't know... it tastes good. I like the taste of Coke a lot more than this grape. Even weird 1969 Coke."

"But why not simply drink unadulterated water? Humans need to rehydrate to maintain the body, but the excessive sugar content of these drinks will stimulate overproduction of insulin and caffeine functions as a mild diuretic when ingested in large quantities. It is not an efficient way to rehydrate or keep blood sugars level."

"Coke tastes better than water," Sean proclaimed.

"Many studies suggest that sugary drinks were linked to a rise in the occurrence of obesity in the general population from the mid-twentieth century through the mid twenty-first century."

Sean glared at Alex. "Has anyone in your time done a study on how eating and drinking tasteless foods increase the boring speech level in the general population?"

"Your father is not cool, and I am boring," Alex said frostily as he shot to his feet. "Perhaps *you* are overly judgmental."

Sean was about to take another bite of his sandwich, but was stopped by the outburst. Alex generally had a neutral face, occasionally a smile, but his clinched jaw was accented with a frown. Sean hadn't ever seen that before.

"Something bugging you, 5G grandson?" He set down his drink and sandwich then stood.

Alex stared back. He rapidly blinked several times, started to speak, and then pulled his lips into a thin line. "This visit does not seem to be going well," he finally huffed. "I have spent a negligible percentage of the time here making any worthwhile observations of this era as we have been isolated in this primitive wilderness setting. You suggested last week that it would be interesting to study the relationship of a father and son existing at the same age; however, you have had very little interaction with him. Your attention seems to be focused on meeting females. I, myself, have spent hours staring at a lake and attempting to understand the philosophy of a fictionalized supposition of the future... which was ludicrously incorrect in several assumptions." He paused for a breath, then added, "I think we should return to your time."

Sean gauged Alex, trying to discern the best response to his unusual outburst. "Things not going your way, Grandson, so you want to take your ball and go home?"

"I do not *have* a ball, and I said return to *your* time, not *mine*," Alex snapped.

"Sorry, I forgot you take everything literally. That's just something my Dad said to me as a little kid when I was throwing a tantrum."

"I am *not* throwing a tantrum!" Alex ranted, stamping his foot with the word 'not'.

"Oh, you *so* are. I wish I could take a video of this," Sean chuckled.

Alex's eyes narrowed and his lower lip protruded ever so slightly. Sean couldn't keep from grinning which served to irritate Alex even more. "You....you..." Alex stammered, "you... you can be... *very* frustrating!"

"This is priceless," Sean laughed. "There isn't a way to get the magic 3D glasses to record video is there?"

"Frustrating and... insensitive...and... smug... and..." Alex's face burned red and his breathing became heavy and irregular.

Sean's smile vanished. "OK, settle down," he advised, "Don't blow a gasket."

"I do not *have* a gasket," Alex growled, still huffing and puffing.

"OK, hang on, let me think of a way to say this literally," Sean said, holding his hands up, palms forward. "Maybe you should sit back down and try to breathe a little more slowly and deeply. Count to ten... or calculate the square root of Pi or something."

Alex sat. "How many decimal places?"

"Oh, I don't know... let's say about a hundred."

"1.7724538509..."

"Just to yourself is fine," Sean interrupted.

Alex stared blankly for a couple of seconds. "Now what do I do with the calculation?"

"That was a hundred decimal places? OK, umm... try a couple thousand."

Alex's face went blank again as he stared straight ahead for a little more than 30 seconds. He turned back to Sean. "Completed. What do you wish to do with this calculation?"

"Nothing," Sean replied as he sat. "It's just a diversion to calm you down. And seriously, you can do two thousand decimal places that fast?"

"Why would calculating the square root of Pi to two thousand decimal places calm me?"

"I don't know... but it worked, didn't it?"

Alex blinked a few times as he mulled it over. "It appears it did. Perhaps the shift to something as purely logical as mathematics?"

"Works for me," agreed Sean. "Hey, I know that I've been trying to coax you to find a little more emotion, but I hadn't planned on this reaction."

"Nor I," Alex admitted. "I do not fully comprehend what has happened."

"Well, my Mom has the psychology degree, but offhand, I'd say something pushed you into the deep end of the emotions pool without a floaty ring."

Alex blinked several times. "Do you purposefully use terminology that I do not understand when you speak to me?"

"I could ask you the same thing," Sean replied. "Let's just call it a little language barrier."

"I have queried 'floaty ring' and it appears to be a child's water toy. I fail to see how it would add or detract emotional status."

"You don't need a *literal* floaty ring," sighed Sean. "OK, let's break this down. You're in over your head dealing with some emotional issue. That would be the deep water. You don't know how to cope, so you are flailing around. The floaty ring would be something you could hang onto to help you deal with it... keep you above water."

"Do you have access to such a device?"

Sean clamped his eyes shut and rubbed his temples before responding, "It's not a device. It's not like your magic nanites that fix everything." He stopped and struggled to find a better explanation. "OK... like I go out and shoot hoops when something's bugging me." Sean paused again, made a face like someone had stuck a lemon in his mouth, and then reluctantly continued. "But my Mom, the psychologist, is always trying to get me to *talk* about what's bothering me. Supposedly that helps."

"You are suggesting that if I verbalize what bothers me, that will somehow decrease the bad feelings that I have?"

Sean looked heavenward, trying to think of a way around what he knew he should say. "Yes," he groaned.

"I do not want to be here," Alex reported flatly.

"Where is here? This lake? Iowa?"

"1969."

131

"Really? I thought other than the gas station guy and the cop hassling us—apparently just because we look like hippies—that it's been a pretty good trip. Although I'm not excusing their behavior, I gotta agree with them that we *do* look stupid. C'mon, give it another day. Tonight might be interesting. Sixties era teenagers at a drive-in movie. How could we miss that? Another chance to observe how strangely different they are, and in a period-exclusive environment." Sean waggled his eyebrows when he finished.

"I do not want to spend another night here!" exclaimed Alex.

Sean noticed that Alex's breathing had become erratic again. "OK," he said in a measured tone, "I think we're back in the deep end. I'll probably regret playing psychologist, but... do you know *why* you don't want to spend another night here?"

Alex began to tremble. His jaw clenched and his muscles tightened. Sean thought he was about to explode, but he suddenly looked away and down at the ground. "Because of them," he said softly.

"Because of my Dad and his friends?"

"No... not them," Alex snapped, then quietly added. "Jennifer White, Jorge Sanchez, Walter Bogdanowicz."

Sean's brow furrowed. "Who?"

"Jennifer White, in Detroit. Jorge Sanchez, in New York. Walter Bogdanowicz, in Chicago."

Sean puzzlement broke with a sudden sinking feeling in his stomach because he didn't know what to say. "Oh," was all he could manage.

"I do not want to be here when..." Alex paused when his voice cracked. "...when they die."

They both sat silently for what seemed like forever to Sean. His mind churned, looking for some helpful words, but nothing seemed quite right. Sean picked up his drink, sipped, then took a deep breath. "I'm sorry I made you think of them as individuals." Alex stared at the ground. "Sorry that I made you feel like you should do something to stop it." Alex glanced at him briefly, then back to the ground. "Look, it's not your fault. You don't kill them."

"But I *could* do something to stop it," Alex shouted, his voice cracking again.

"Do you know how to stop a gang fight?" challenged Sean, "You'd probably just get yourself knifed. Think you can stop the guy that beats up his wife? Can you overpower a burglar that is apparently strong enough to take the guy's gun and shoot him with it? You could easily get killed in any of those situations and not help any of them."

Alex continued to stare at the ground.

Sean changed tactics. "OK, you know that stuff I said earlier? Totally a lie," he asserted, "The gang-banger's mom isn't going to miss him. He ran away from home five years ago, and the only time she's seen him since was when she came home and caught him burglarizing her apartment. Not only did he steal her stuff, he slashed her face with his knife. That woman in Detroit? She doesn't have two little kids. She and her husband are both drug addicts, and he comes home and catches her in bed with someone else. Kills her in a fit of rage. The guy in Chicago? He's actually a mid-level boss in the mob. Turns out he was skimming and they put a contract on him, planning to make it look like a robbery. His wife even gave her hubby's gun to the hit man to help with the burglary story."

Alex stared open-mouthed at Sean, totally fascinated by this new information, then suddenly frowned. "You are simply fabricating that information," he said angrily.

Sean shrugged. "You're right. I am." He locked eyes with his descendant. "Just like I did the first time I told you about them. We don't know who these people are... whether they're good or bad or something in-between, and if you're committed to your non-interference rules, then we should just leave it at that. We don't know. Their deaths may be a tragedy to those around them, or maybe the world is better off without them."

Alex stared at Sean with childlike wonder. "How do you do that?"

"Do what?"

"Fabricate a plausible scenario that is in direct conflict with the original situation that you described."

Sean shrugged again. "I dunno. I just make it up. I guess it's something that Raj and I do a lot when we're just goofing around. Like make up stuff about people we see in the cafeteria. Put together wild stories just for the fun of it. We both try to come up with a more outlandish story."

"You fabricate stories for the sake of entertainment?"

"I guess you could call it that."

"Can you do it again?"

"What? With the same three people but like a third scenario?"

"Yes."

Sean gazed into space, scrunching his mouth up as he thought. "I guess so." He thought a while longer, then launched into his stories. "Turns out the gang-banger is an undercover cop, but his cover's blown, so they fake his death so he can go back out on the streets with a new identity. That guy in Chicago was actually in the witness protection program. The mob finds out, and they are going to snuff him, but the feds get wind of it first and fake his death then relocate him in another city." Sean paused to take a drink. "Ummm... OK, the woman in Detroit was actually abducted by aliens, they cloned her, killed the clone and left the body behind to be found." Sean paused for another sip, then he looked directly at Alex. "How was that?"

"The first two seem plausible."

"Give me a break!" Sean groused, "It's hard to come up with three new things with such short notice."

"Alien abduction?"

"Yeah! You know what? *That's* probably the only one I got right. You

133

should check into that one. Those aliens'll probably need a couple hundred years to study their abductees to find all mankind's weaknesses. I'll bet like the year after you get back to your own time, they'll invade."

Alex smiled. "You continue to amaze me, Sean Kelly. I believe I now have a better understanding as to why you initially imagined I was either an alien or a robot from the future."

Sean picked up his sandwich and took a bite. "Maybe I was right about that, too. You've never proved you're *not* a robot." Sean finished eating as Alex quietly watched him. "Not too bad," he said, licking his fingers, then wiping them on his jeans. "Could have used a little more mustard." Sean pointed at the unopened baggy sitting beside Alex's chair. "Not going to eat your sandwich?"

Alex looked down at it then back to Sean. "I believe I prefer Formula Ten."

"You're going to hurt Jane's feelings."

"Why would my dietary preferences cause her distress?"

"She made that especially for you, carefully trying to accommodate your bizarre vegetarian needs. At least take a bite so you can tell her that it tasted good."

Alex picked up the baggy and gingerly removed the sandwich. He lifted one piece of bread to examine what was inside. Sean rolled his eyes. Alex reluctantly bit down on a tiny corner section and chewed pensively. "Besides the natural fructose from the grape, there appears to be massive amounts of added dextrose. It is a testimony to the resiliency of the human body that more people in this century didn't develop diabetes from the foods they consumed."

"You are like the ultimate picky eater. Give me that sandwich." Alex slid it back into the baggy and handed it to Sean. "You'd better not say stupid stuff like that when Jane asks how you liked it." Alex recoiled slightly. "What *are* you going to say when she asks you about it?"

Alex looked away briefly, then looked timidly back at Sean. "That it was yummy?" he squeaked.

"And thank her for being so considerate," Sean advised firmly. Alex nodded. "OK, she said she'd be back in a couple of hours, so I guess I'll go back to my book until then. Here's my proposal. If my Dad is one of the group going tonight, we go with them to the drive-in. If not, we can hop into Steffi and head back to 1995. Deal?"

Alex thought it over briefly before answering, "That seems acceptable."

Sean slid the 3-D glasses on and looked around the campsite. "Where's my book? It's gone!"

"Look in the upper left corner. You should see a tiny blue triangle."

"OK, yeah, I see that."

"Close your left eye and while looking at the triangle blink once with your right eye."

Sean followed the instructions. "Now there is a ball floating in mid-air."

"I did not realize that sub-routine was still active. Sorry. The corrective procedure is to close your right eye and blink once with your left eye, which should remove the ball."

"Yeah, OK, that worked. The ball's gone."

"Now close your left eye again and blink twice with your right eye while looking at the triangle."

"OK, got it! Great! Hey is this kind of like right and left mouse clicks in Windows?"

"Mouse clicks?"

"Yeah, never mind," Sean said as he flipped pages until he found where he had left off. As he settled back into his book, Alex began to walk away. "What are you going to do now?" Sean asked.

"I am returning to the S.T.E. to ingest mid-day nourishment."

"Eat lunch. Why can't you just say 'eat lunch'?" Sean complained. "No, never mind, that goop you eat doesn't really count as lunch. Hey, why don't you actually *watch* a couple of episodes of *Star Trek* while you're in there, instead of just absorbing them." Alex didn't reply but kept walking. "Or you could go back to the dock and contemplate life, the universe and everything. Hey, there's an idea. The BBC did a six or seven part series of *The Hitchhiker's Guide to the Galaxy*. You could watch that." Alex was just barely visible in the underbrush he pushed through. "OK," Sean shouted, "Good talk!"

Chapter Seven

"So close, so close / And yet so far"

T HE *BEEP-BEEP* of a Volkswagen interrupted Sean's reading. He craned his neck left and right to catch just a glimpse of yellow through the trees. "Fifteen minutes more and I'd have finished," he muttered as he stood. He pulled off the 3-D glasses, tossed them on his chair and started walking toward the main road. Partway up, Jane came into view and waved a big hello, hand over her head tracing large swooping arcs. Sean cupped his hands around his mouth and shouted, "So, is it a go, then?"

Jane put a cupped hand to her ear. "What?"

"I said," Sean started, then waved it off until they were closer and didn't need to shout. "I said, 'Is it a go, then?'"

They both slowed their pace until they stopped with a comfortable but close distance between them. "The drive-in? Yeah, I think I got it finally worked out," Jane chirped. "Louise can't go... and that's a drag... her mother doesn't like her going to movies any time, but especially not on a Sunday... plus she has to work the breakfast shift tomorrow at Ritchie's. Micky's not going since Louise can't go. Juan, Jimbo, and Scott were going to go, but if you and Peter go, that pretty much fills a car. Oh, did Peter decide to go?"

"Yeah, he said he'd give it a look."

"So anyway, that'd make five guys and me, and I said I wasn't going to be the only girl, so Scott said he'd bring his on-again-off-again girlfriend, Karen, so I guess that means she's on-again, but then that would make seven. Which I guess *could* work, but it would be a little crowded." Jane drew in a deep breath and flashed Sean a smile.

"You're not going to try to stuff seven people in that little yellow tin can of yours, are you?"

"No!" Jane laughed as she playfully punched Sean's arm. "We're not taking the VW! We'll either go in Juan's Impala or Scott has a 58 Plymouth. That thing is a boat! Either can easily handle six people, and I guess we *could* get four in the backseat, but it would be a little snug. Of course, that's kind of the idea with Buck Night, you pack the car and party. Anyway, Jimbo said he might drop out."

"You've been busy, luv. Good job!"

Jane tucked a stray strand of hair behind her left ear and turned her gaze to a small evergreen. "Does that word ever mean anything to you?" She asked coyly.

"What word is that, luv?"

"Love."

"Um... yeah," Sean stumbled. "Sure, I reckon... sometimes."

She turned back to look him in the eyes. "But if you call any girl 'love', what do you call a girl that you *do* love?"

"Not sure what you mean, lu... Jane," Sean stalled.

Jane smiled. "It's OK. You can call me 'love' if that's what you're comfortable with. But I mean like Peter called Steffi 'bird'. I assumed that was an English term of endearment. I was just wondering what *you* said when it was someone special."

"Oh... right, um... well, some of me mates back home..." Sean's mind raced to try to think of something plausible. "... they sometimes call their girl 'ladybug'."

"Ladybug?" Jane chewed her lower lip and nodded. "That's kind of cute. So what do these 'ladybugs' call your 'mates'?"

"I suppose you'd be meaning in polite company," Sean laughed nervously. Jane smiled back with another nod. Sean's mind raced. *Crap, what goes with ladybug? Nothing! Maybe something cutesy, like a teddy bear.* "I've heard a few call their guys 'koala'." He immediately regretted opening his mouth.

"Koala?" she mouthed as she mulled it over. "Um... OK, that's.... different... but cute, I guess."

"Yeah, cute and cuddly... that's a koala, all right," Sean babbled. "Of course, a goodly bunch of me mates are also kind of furry... so that fits 'em, too." That bit of nonsense produced the desired result—Jane laughed. Sean loved the sound of her laugh. It made him feel warm and comfortable. His nervousness dissolved away. "You think I'm joking?" Sean ad-libbed boldly. "Me mate, Georgy is right furry!" He cupped a hand behind each ear. "Whopper ears, too. He really does look a lot like a koala."

"Oh, stop it," Jane laughed.

"Got a really bad habit of gnawing on eucalyptus leaves, though." Sean mimed chewing a big wad of tobacco and pretended to spit to the side.

"Liar," Jane laughed as she punched Sean's arm again.

"Ow!" Sean complained, "You're going to give me a bruise."

"Sorry," Jane purred, "Here, I'll kiss it and make it better." She took his arm with both hands and made a loud smack with her lips as she touched them to his upper arm. She continued to hold onto his arm as she lifted her eyes to his. "Better?"

Sunlight glinted from Jane's glasses, but Sean was dazzled by her smile. "Much better," he whispered. As he fell into the depths of her blue eyes, Sean's thoughts drifted back to their almost-kiss at the dock. "Good thing for you that you didn't hit me in the face," he teased.

She glanced from his eyes to his lips, then back to his eyes. "Yeah," she murmured, "good thing." She stopped breathing as her gaze flashed quickly between his lips and eyes, and then with a sudden gasp, she dropped his arm and looked away. "I should probably go," she said rapidly to the ground.

"Umm, yeah... OK," Sean mumbled as he mentally cursed another missed kiss and wondered why his timing seemed to be off. It was a short mental dress-down, as his practical side quickly took over and told him it was a good thing. He reminded himself that Jane was actually a year older than his Dad, and chastised himself for having feelings for someone who probably had kids his age back in 1995. "Hey, I wanted to thank you for the sandwiches. We really appreciated them."

"Oh, um, sure," Jane replied as she took a step back and shyly looked back up at Sean. "I'm glad you liked them."

"Yeah, they were great," Sean rambled, beginning to feel tension between them.

"Great," Jane said, looking away again. They each silently examined different spots on the ground for several anxious seconds. "Well... I should go," Jane repeated, taking a couple of steps backward.

"Um, what, um, time tonight?" Sean inquired awkwardly.

"Oh!" Jane stammered. "Umm...I'm sorry. I, uh, think we are going to leave for Colgate around eight. Do you, um, want to go into town before that? I mean, you know, to get something to eat before we go, or, um, like go in now? Or do you uh, like, need to talk to Peter? Or..." her voice trailed off to nothing, then she looked up at Sean. "Where is Peter?"

"Oh, he's out and about somewhere. Hard to keep track of him, really. He's probably off someplace pining for Steffi. As for supper, no worries there, luv. There's still the odd hot-dog lying about. Peter can nosh on some crackers and marshmallows and such."

Jane crinkled her nose. "Are you sure? That doesn't sound appetizing."

"Yeah. No worries."

"OK, then," Jane said, taking a couple more steps backwards. "Then I guess we'll come get you a little before eight."

"Looking forward to it... the drive-in. Bit of Americana, wot?" Sean turned to start back to the camp.

"Nigel, I..." Jane said as she took a couple quick steps toward Sean. Sean spun around, and she froze in her tracks.

"Yes?"

"I..." She looked into his eyes then back to the ground. "I might come by earlier to pick you up and take you into town. That might work better for Juan and Scott."

"OK," Sean said as he wondered if she meant to say something else.

"Maybe 7:30?"

"Sure. We'll be ready."

"OK, then. Great," Jane said as she started walking backwards again.

"See you about 7:30, then."

"Right. See you then."

"You're sure you're all right out here?"

"Yeah. Nice an' peaceful like, id nit?"

"OK, then. Later." She turned and started up the hill. Sean watched her for a moment before turning back to camp.

When he reached the camp, he threw himself into one of the chairs and brooded about Jane. He tried to assess logically why he found her so attractive. At first, she looked like a take-charge kind of girl, but he'd also seen her seem almost shy, especially at their most recent encounter. He loved her quick wit, and despite her hang-ups about her nose, she was cute. She had nice legs... really nice legs and it seemed like, in 1969, it was fashionable to show a lot of leg.

He mentally slapped himself as he realized his rational assessment was shifting to warm gooey feelings. There was no logical reason to pursue any feelings for her. She was his Dad's friend and apparently had been since grade school. His *Dad's* friend. His Dad's *age*. This was his Dad's *time,* and he wouldn't be around much longer. He didn't belong in 1969; so nothing could really ever develop with Jane, and he certainly couldn't look her up back in 1995. Then the serendipitous thought hit him. She might have a cute daughter his age. Who knows?

The next time he saw her would most likely be the last time he'd see her. It wasn't likely there would be any quiet, intimate moments, in a packed car, when he might be tempted to kiss her again. He shook his head briskly, whipping his long hair around, trying to shake out all thoughts of Jane. Then he picked up Alex's 3-D glasses and reloaded his book, flipping the empty air as he found the page he was on.

Less than twenty minutes later, he clapped his hands together, closing the hologram book, then took off the glasses. "Well, that was kind of a weird ending," he muttered to himself. He wondered if the cat in the title was a reference to the kitten, Pixel, or simply a metaphor for something else. If it *was* a metaphor, he wasn't quite sure what it meant. He could see why Alex made the remark about the Time Corp needing restraint, as they were rather cavalier not only about their trips to the past but also the even more bizarre multiple alternate timelines. He decided to ask Alex if there really were alternate realities in parallel timelines, but first he'd have to find him.

As he tromped through the underbrush toward Steffi, he again wondered if the computer part of the time-machine was sentient like the one in the book he'd just finished. It took only minutes to arrive at the clump of brambles that was the final barrier to the S.T.E. He tried to take the last few steps quietly, but could scarcely avoid snapping twigs. He was just inches away before he could even make out the outlines of the cloaked vehicle. Grinning mischievously, he banged Steffi's invisible roof.

"This is Officer Grzbzfz of the Intergalactic Time Cops," Sean bellowed in a gruff, bass voice. "This vehicle is parked illegally! I'm going to need to see your license and registration!"

The door slid open, and Alex's neutral face peered out. "I have decided to cease further inquiries for an explanation of such unusual outbursts. I am classifying them as humor and filing them for later study," he uttered expressionlessly.

"I missed you, too," returned Sean sweetly. "Hey, Jane came by. Looks like we *are* going to the drive-in tonight. You, me, Jane, my Dad, Scott, Scott's girlfriend, Karen, and maybe Jimbo."

"Karen, not Louise?"

"Yeah, Louise can't go, but Jane insisted that she was *not* going to be the only girl in a car full of guys, so that's where Karen comes in, I guess. Can't really blame her about wanting at least one other girl along. So anyway... looks like we're going."

"I assumed you were rather confident of that outcome," Alex said, "I did not think you would make a wager on an event that you thought truly random."

"Whatever." Sean rolled his eyes. "Move over. I need to check something." Alex moved more to his right and Sean slid in.

Sean tapped the forward screen. "Can you make this into a video mirror again?"

Alex complied with the request and they each stared at mirrored images of themselves. Sean ran his fingers through his hair, watching himself on-screen. He pulled a handful to perpendicular, then let strands fall from his hand as he watched his reflection.

"This is disgusting," he said as he crinkled his nose. "I can't go out like this. Why didn't you tell me my hair was a wreck?" He lifted his arm and sniffed. "Ugh! I need a shower! No wonder Jane backed away from me so fast. Why didn't you tell me?"

"Tell you what?" Alex asked in a meek voice.

"That I stink!"

"I did not know. I have olfactory filters that remove unpleasant odors. I would not be able to function in this era if I were unable to remove the objectionable smells."

Sean stared open-mouthed at Alex. "You're kidding me. No, of course you aren't." He moved his face close to Alex and took an overt sniff. "And you don't smell like anything. So which is it this time? The super-suit or your freakin' nanites?"

"You are unhappy that I do not have an unpleasant odor?"

"No, but right now I'm jealous," Sean said. "So how's it work?"

"It is not only the pseudo-body suit. All clothing from my era are permeated with nanites that remove sloughed off skin cells and bacterium," Alex explained. "However, I believe that historically there is evidence that the hippie culture eschewed regular hygienic practices as part of their back-to-nature philosophy. You are much more authentically representative than I."

"I don't care what hippies do. Just because I look like one, I don't have to smell like one. I'm not going to be packed wall-to-wall in a car full of people smelling like this."

"What do you propose?" asked Alex.

"In the first place, it was bad planning to not pack some deodorant and cologne for this little trip. That would have helped. But at this point, besides picking some up, I need to think of where I can catch a shower around here."

"Some ancient cultures, like the Romans, had public baths as part of their society," Alex offered.

"That's not much help when we're in 1969 Mercer, Iowa," Sean groused. "OK, here's what we do first. Let's hop over to town and find some place to buy some deodorant, soap, shampoo, and cologne. Maybe while we're doing that, I'll think of some place that I could grab a shower. If not, we might have to find a secluded cove at the lake."

"If you wish to be near the commerce area of Mercer, perhaps we should return to the space under that bridge I initially selected," Alex proposed.

"Do we have to walk all that way again? How about we just park in some back alley? It won't take that long to pick up a few items."

"I would not feel secure in leaving this vehicle abandoned in a populace area, even with the cloak engaged."

"Fine. Drop me off and hover or something."

"That is an acceptable solution," Alex agreed, then opened the control panel to set the necessary commands. After only a few seconds he asked, "Where do you propose I drop you off?"

"Was that it? We're already here?"

In response, Alex set the craft to pseudo-transparent. The main street of Mercer was about fifty feet below them, and the afternoon sun was above.

"OK, kill the lower half of the projection screens so I don't feel like I'm falling out of the sky," squeaked Sean. Alex limited the external viewing to the top half of the S.T.E. "Much better. Now then, if you drift up the road a little..." Alex gently tapped a blue icon. "Yeah, right there. I thought I remembered a drug store just up from Ritchie's and across the street." Sean scanned the area. "How about there?" He pointed to the alleyway behind the stores. "See that dumpster? If you drop down there, I can get out, and no one would see."

Alex maneuvered Steffi into the position Sean had pointed out. When they were a foot off the ground, he opened the door. Sean hopped out but stuck his head back in. "Just circle the block a few times until I come back out." Alex looked at him blankly. "Fine. Don't be conventional. Just hover somewhere, and I'll come back to this spot when I've got everything." Alex nodded, then closed the door, effectively vanishing.

Sean went down the alley a few yards before finding an opening between buildings that led to the main street. Once he was on the sidewalk, he turned back up toward his target.

When he reached the drugstore, he grabbed the door handle and tugged, surprised that it didn't open. He rattled it a couple of times, then stepped closer to peer into the store. The lights were dim, and he couldn't see anyone inside. As he stepped back, he noticed the 'Sorry we are Closed' sign on the door. Below that were the posted hours which ended with 'Sunday – Closed'.

As he walked up the street, he noticed that all of the stores and shops appeared to be closed. He scanned across the street to find that each building displayed a similar 'Sorry, we are Closed' sign. Ritchie's was open, but he didn't see how smelling like fried food and cigarette smoke would be much of an improvement. Still further up the street, there were a few cars parked near a corner store and Sean decided to investigate.

Just before he reached the corner, a woman and young child came out from the store's corner opening. A man carrying a brown paper bag and wearing a white bib-apron followed them. They all walked to one of the cars, and the woman opened a back door. The man set the bag on the back seat and closed the door. "Thank you, Mrs. Brant," he said politely.

"Thank you, Terry," she replied as she helped her toddler into the car and slid in herself.

Sean fell into step behind 'Terry' and followed him back to the corner opening. As the automated door swung shut after the man entered, Sean read the sign painted on the top half of the glass door before it swung back open with his approach.

Lyle's IGA

Hours:

6am – 8pm Mon – Fri

8am – 10pm Sat

1pm – 5pm Sun

"Grocery store," Sean murmured to himself, "not here during my lifetime, but it should have the stuff I need. Who knows? Maybe my purchases will be enough to keep them from going out of business."

He went in and found carts lined up near the door. Since he only wanted a few small things, he scanned the area until he spied a stack of blue hand-carried baskets and picked one up. The store was small—at least compared to any grocery store he'd been in—and it didn't seem to be as bright and the aisles felt narrower. The first was wider than the rest and was lined with fresh produce. Sean turned to walk the cross-aisle just behind the checkout stands and did a quick scan of each perpendicular aisle as he passed. The end-cap of the next-to-last aisle had bright colored boxes that caught his eye, particularly the orange box with the large *Tide* that covered two-thirds of the front. Laundry soap. He turned, stopping briefly in front of the section where the *Tide* was featured. Everything was in boxes, and most of them were small. He wondered if liquid laundry soap was a new product. The only plastic jugs he saw in the area were labeled *Wisk* and *Clorox*.

He moved on down the aisle, filing away his curiosity about the changes in laundry soap. Just a few steps away he found bar soap. There were several brands he'd never heard of, so he grabbed a bar marked *Dial*, since that was still around in 1995. He wondered if the one called *Lifebuoy* floated better than the others.

Next to the soaps he found a few shelves of shampoo. Again, he saw nothing that he had ever used and thought it weird how the products that he knew weren't there, and the displayed items had unfamiliar names. He finally spied a *Johnson's Baby Shampoo* and put it in his basket. Though he hadn't used it personally, he'd at least seen TV ads that promised 'no more tears'.

He skipped over the next section that seemed geared toward women, but stopped when the items on the shelf changed to shaving cream. Next to the shaving cream, there were a few bottles he guessed to be cologne. Again, nothing he'd heard of, except one, but he didn't consider *Old Spice* to be age appropriate. It was definitely for an older crowd. The first one he took from the shelf was simply for the novelty of the name, *Hai Karate*. But when he opened it and took a sniff, he decided that he knew why it wasn't around anymore. He didn't particularly like *English Leather*, either. It vaguely reminded him of horse saddles. There was one named *Canoe* that wasn't too bad, but he decided to select *Jade East*. It was bright green and, overall, he liked the scent. It was kind of sweet, but a little spicy and not too overpowering. It would do.

It seemed logical that deodorants would also be in this section, but he didn't see any. There were more canisters about the same size as the shaving cream on the other side of the cologne and after-shave sections. Then he spotted a familiar name on one of the canisters—*Right Guard*. It was a golden-tan cylinder with a black lid. The name was in white surrounded by a black rectangle. Below that, a smaller red box featured tiny white lettering for the word 'deodorant'.

Sean pulled the cap off. It was an aerosol spray just like a can of spray paint. He vaguely remembered that before the ban of fluorocarbons that spray cans were used for a lot of products. His curiosity was again aroused, and he wondered when people started getting nervous about the ozone layer.

"Need some help with that?"

Sean looked up and toward the end of the aisle. A man in his late twenties or early thirties had been mopping the floor but had stopped and was leaning on the top of the mop handle.

"No, I'm good," Sean said, then returned to looking at the different brands on the shelf.

"I just thought maybe someone like you didn't know how to use one of those," the man said in a tone that wasn't as helpful as his words.

Sean looked his way again, noticing this time that the man was dressed in the same type of apron as the one he'd seen outside, but obviously was not

'Terry'. The man slowly strolled toward Sean, using the mop almost like a walking stick.

"Someone like me?" Sean asked with a slight edge of defiance in his voice.

The man stepped closer, and Sean took in more visual clues. He wore his hair in a crew cut and had a tattoo of an anchor on his forearm. Sean wondered if he was a Popeye fan. The man's head was slightly tilted back, leading with his chin as he walked, his chest was puffed out and he had a swagger to his step. He had the semblance of a smile on his face, but no one would mistake it as friendly.

"Yeah, I heard hippies are allergic to soap and water, so I figured deodorant would be beyond your comprehension." He stopped inches from Sean's face, and since he was a couple of inches shorter, he had to look up slightly to stare menacingly into Sean's eyes.

Sean felt his anger rise, and thoughts of a quick right hook to the guy's jaw flashed through his mind, but they merely glared at each other. Sean's eyes flitted to the man's tattoo and visions of stereotypical Navy brawls he'd seen in movies replayed in his head. He decided it would be a good time for reason to trump emotions. He glanced down again, this time to the man's name tag.

"Well, 'Dean'," Sean said coolly, "I'll be sure to tell your manager how helpful you've been." With eyes still locked, he dropped the *Right Guard* into his basket.

Dean's face was rigid; his jaw clenched as he spoke, "I don't think I've seen you around before. You just passing through?"

"I've got some family in the area. Just a short visit," Sean said evenly, not letting his eyes drop.

"Maybe your family can treat you to one of our fine barber shops," Dean mocked.

"I'll have to see if we can fit that in," Sean replied, struggling to keep his voice neutral. "I think I've got everything I need today. Thank you so much for your assistance, Dean, but especially your warm hospitality." Sean faked a smile just before stepping away from Dean.

"Enjoy your *short* stay," Dean called after him.

As Sean walked toward the checkout, he wondered what was going on in the town of Mercer. When he had visited when he was younger, everyone seemed not only friendly, but also helpful. *Of course, that was several years from now,* he mused. *Will be several years from now?* Time-travel grammar was still confusing to him. *Why were people so hostile because of the way I look?* He admitted to himself that if he met someone decked out like a hippie in his own time that he'd think they looked stupid... but to be belligerent? That would never cross his mind.

Sean was still lost in his thoughts when the checker had told him his total. He absentmindedly handed her a twenty and was again amazed to get most of it back in change. *Everything* was so cheap! Someone roughly his age had put each item into a large paper bag as quickly as the checker had rung it up. Sean suddenly realized there was no scanner. He glanced to the next checkout lane and saw that each item had its own price sticker attached, and the clerk entered the series of numbers individually for every item. *When did bar-codes start?* he wondered. *When did 'paper or plastic' start? This really is a different world than the one I know.*

The teen handed him his bag. "Cool tie-dye, man," he commented.

"Yeah, um, thanks, um... man," Sean stumbled.

The kid held up his hand in a two fingered 'V'. "Peace," he concluded before turning back to sack the next person's items.

Sean mimicked his hand gesture and mumbled, "Yeah, peace, um... man." *At least that guy was friendly. I'll bet he knows my Dad... probably goes to school with him.* Sean headed out the door carrying his large paper bag and decided he didn't want to go anywhere alone in Mercer anymore.

Walking down the street, he rolled up the top of the bag into a makeshift handle and carried it at his side. He briefly stopped at Ritchie's and peeked in hoping to get a glimpse of Louise, and then remembered she wouldn't be back until Monday morning. He crossed the street and walked between the two buildings back to the alley where he'd come out. There still was no one on the sidewalks and very few cars on the street. Mercer was not a hopping town on Sunday afternoons in 1969. He decided he could probably get in and out of Steffi right in the middle of Main Street and no one would even see him.

As he came around the dumpster, a door slid open from thin air. Steffi was about where he left her, nearly invisible except for the opening to the cabin. Sean slid in. "That was interesting," he said sarcastically.

"Did you locate all of the items you wanted to purchase?" asked Alex.

"Yup," Sean replied, "Plus a couple pounds of bigotry, no extra charge."

Alex was puzzled. "Either bigotry has a definition that I do not know or I am confused by the weight reference."

"Don't worry about it," Sean sighed, "Let's just rephrase it that this guy in the grocery store had some anger issues toward hippies, and oh, look... everyone thinks I look like one."

"Mistrust of others is difficult to remove from civilization," Alex said wistfully, "I am sorry to say that there are still elements of mistrust in my own time."

"No Utopia in the future, huh?"

"Perhaps in *my* future..."

"Yeah, maybe someday..."

"There was an episode of *Star Trek* that dealt with that issue in an interesting way. They portrayed racial intolerance using beings who were half-black and half-white. The animosity sprang from which half was a certain color..."

"Yeah," Sean interrupted, "I've seen that one at least a couple of times.

145

Good stuff." He shifted the conversation. "Well, setting hatred aside for a moment, I think I have an idea about where to catch a shower."

"I also have devised a solution. We can locate a secluded spot and travel back in time to that thunderstorm from last night."

"Yeah... I like my idea better," Sean countered. "So where is the one place that teenagers take showers when they are *not* in their own homes?"

"Should I research that question?"

"No, you're supposed to guess. Never mind. *School!*" Alex looked at him blankly. "Basketball courts? Locker rooms?"

"Your voice has the inflection of a question, but I am not sure what you are asking me."

"No. No," Sean groaned. "Never mind. There are showers in the locker rooms near a basketball court where high school teams play. We just need to find the high school."

"I can do that," Alex said as he twitched a query. "I have the street address gleaned from a recent issue of the local newspaper. I will show you on a map." He flipped a few icons on the screen in front of them and a map displayed across the front of the cabin.

"Awesome!" Sean exclaimed. "What's the red triangle?"

"That is the location of the school."

"And what's the blue dot?"

"That is our current location."

"Awesome! So you can just call up a map and track where you want to go? Dude, I so wish I had even a tenth of your cool future stuff."

"This technology becomes common in the earliest part of the twenty-first century."

"Seriously?" Sean exclaimed. "Awesome!"

"I suspect you will find it mundane before your thirtieth birthday."

"No way! Cool future stuff like that? That will *always* be awesome to me."

"While I believe that your enthusiasm is genuine—based upon your repetitive use of the word 'awesome'—I must point out that familiarity and constant use of any technology will dissipate the initial mystique."

"Whatever. Just fly us over to the high school," Sean commanded dismissively.

"We are already there," Alex reported. "While we were talking, we traveled to the selected endpoint."

"Never felt a thing," Sean remarked. "This is one smooth ride." He looked out at the large building several feet below them. "OK, follow my thinking here. It's Sunday, and it's summer, so there shouldn't be anyone in there. That's good. But it's probably locked up tight, so that's bad. First, we need to figure out where the locker rooms are." Alex pulled up an image that resembled an outline sketch of the building. "Why do you have plans for some random building in 1969?"

"I did not. I implemented an echo-sonogram of this building. The computer is displaying it as geometric line shapes."

"My plan was to peek through windows, but we can go with this," Sean nodded. "So we're looking for a large room with high ceilings."

"There are two."

"OK, zoom in on one of them." The area on the right side zoomed to fill the screen. "OK, what are those shapes? Seats? Yeah, I think that's an auditorium. Go for the other one." Alex moved the drawing to the other room. "That's gotta be it." Sean paused. "OK, this is that part that might get tricky. Can you move a little in another dimension and then reappear back here and be in a different spot, without doing a time-jump?"

"Yes," Alex affirmed.

"So I need you to do that, and reappear inside this gymnasium."

"If that is all you wish to accomplish, there is no need to shift dimensions."

Alex moved his ship to the side of the building that they had determined contained the gym and snugged up against the wall. He blanked out the view-screens and pushed some icons around on the display screen. "Part of this procedure can be visually unsettling," he explained. He again turned the view-screens back on. To Sean's amazement, he saw bleachers, hoops with nets, and a wooden floor painted with the lines and circles of a basketball court.

"So..." he started slowly, "we're inside... but you said we didn't have to shift dimensions..." he turned to look behind them. "...and you didn't knock a hole in the wall..."

"We passed through it," Alex explained.

"Passed through it? Like ghost-walking-through-walls pass through?"

Alex's face turned studious. "I do not know if I can explain this in a way that you can fully grasp," he began apologetically.

"You're not playing the 'magic' card on this one. Explain it in a way you think I can *partially* grasp."

"The density of an object is subjective to our perceptions." He paused. "Imagine a large glass container that is packed with oranges. It is filled to the point that one cannot put another orange into the container." Sean nodded. "Now imagine pouring peas into that same container, allowing them to shift into the spaces between the oranges. It may require jostling the container." Sean closed his eyes, then nodded. "Next we will add sand, which can also settle into spaces between the peas."

"Why are we putting oranges, peas, and sand in this big jar?"

Ignoring Sean, Alex continued, "Could anything else be added?"

"You're trying to trick me into saying 'no', but I'll bet there is something smaller than sand," Sean replied.

"Indeed. Next we will pour water into this container," Alex said, then paused.

Sean glared at him with restrained frustration. "Great, we have a container of wet, sandy, peas and oranges. What does that have to do with passing through a solid wall?"

"It demonstrates that the solidity of the wall is an illusion."

"OK... sounding more like you're about to play the 'magic' card now... *illusion*..." Sean stretched out the word 'illusion' sarcastically as he marked the air with imaginary quotes.

"The peas were able to move around the oranges, even though the container was completely full... with regard to the oranges." Alex paused to reassess his example. "On a molecular level, there is more space between the molecules and atoms than physical matter. If one were to shift the molecules of one object through those spaces of the other object, there is room to pass without collision."

"So, are you saying that like a bunch of people in a hallway are going one way, and another bunch is coming the other way, and the people just kind of weave their way through each other. You're able to do that with a solid wall?"

"That also is an acceptable analogy, and on a molecular level, the answer is 'yes'."

"How?"

Alex exhaled loudly. "That is not easy to explain." When he didn't continue, Sean raised his eyebrows as a prompt. "It is a peculiar type of harmonic vibration." He paused again. "I do not fully understand it myself, beyond theory that is."

Sean grinned. "OK, so 'magically' all of our molecules shake around all of the molecules in the wall."

"It is science, not magic," huffed Alex.

"It's crazy is what it is. What if we got stuck halfway through?"

"That is not possible."

"Just a few weeks ago, I'd have said 'not possible' to about nearly *everything* you pull out of your little futuristic bag of tricks... but I'll take your word for it." Sean tapped the screen on his left. "You wanna pop the door?"

Alex opened the door and Sean got out. "This should only take about ten minutes. Maybe you should read the owner's manual about your pass-through-walls gizmo while you wait."

Sean scanned the room and spotted a door marked 'boys' locker room', as well as a 'girls' locker room' on the opposite end of the gym. He took his newly purchased bag of toiletries and his clean shirt and underwear and went into the boys' locker room. There were some small frosted windows high on the wall that allowed enough light in to see the room dimly. He found a light switch by the door and flipped it on.

The walls were lined with tall gray lockers, most closed, some partially ajar, a couple with combination locks securing the lift-up handles. Long wooden benches stretched in front of the lockers, their corners and edges worn smooth. Several layers of paint showed through the latest coat, which was badly peeled. Sean wondered how many decades the benches had been sitting there, and how many guys had unknowingly sat on the spot previously occupied by their fathers or even grandfathers. He dropped his clothes and bag irreverently on one of the ancient planks.

Sean followed the wall of lockers to a wide opening in the far wall. It was as wide as three regular doors and had a concrete lip about six inches high rising from the floor. The room was windowless and dark except for the light that spilled in from the dressing room. He found another light switch on the left side of the doorway and clicked it on. The small room lit up. It was as wide as the dressing room, but only about eight feet deep. The walls were concrete, painted pale green, but also peeling to reveal several past color choices. There were six sets of small round metal wheels that he usually associated with garden-hose faucets. Shower heads curved out of the wall above each pair of handles. The concrete floor sloped gently toward three circular depressions covered with eight inch metal drain plates.

"Primitive," Sean mused, "and obviously personal modesty was not part of the design... but it'll work." He stood arm's length to the left of one of the fixtures and turned the left control counter-clockwise. "Not even labeled hot or cold... fifty/fifty chance I guess." He backed away from the spray and waited. He stuck his hand into the stream several times over a two minute period, but there was no warmth to the water. "Must be the other one." He cranked the left control off and opened the one to its right. Assuming he now had the correct line open for hot water, he went back out to the dressing room and started removing his clothes. Stripped to his underwear, he went back toward the shower and noticed a row of hooks along the wall right outside. "I guess the fastest guy hangs his towel closest." He immediately slapped his forehead with the palm of his hand. "Towel!"

He looked around the dressing room. It was barren; easy to see there were no towels left lying around. He started checking the lockers. They were all empty. "Great," he grumbled as he slid his jeans back on. He left the locker room and started toward the end that was designated for girls.

Alex popped his head out. "You appear disgruntled."

"No towel," Sean groused. "You don't have a little magic drawer that slides out with fresh towels do you? Or some kind of massive blow-dryer?"

Alex looked perplexed. "No," he replied, then added, "I am sorry."

"Yeah, didn't think so." Sean entered the girls' locker room and turned on the light. It was as spartan as the boys. "No frills?" He mumbled to himself as he started checking lockers. They were all empty as he worked his way down one side toward the shower room. Before he could start back with the opposite row of lockers, he saw a pink towel hanging from the hook farthest from the entrance to the showers. He pulled it off the hook and examined it closer. Not only was it pink, it also had a pattern of little white kittens. "I'm so glad Raj and Kevin aren't here," he sighed.

He returned to the boys' locker room and hung the towel on a hook closest to the shower, then went back to his pile of clothes and finished stripping down. Armed with his bar of soap and bottle of shampoo, he strode back to the shower room. He popped his soap and shampoo into a wire basket that hung from the shower head. His arm splashed through the spray... still cold. "Must have been right the first time," he muttered as he closed that valve and reopened the first one. As he waited, he wondered how far away the hot water heater was, then swore softly. He realized that as old as the building was, it probably had a central boiler room... and it probably was shut down for the summer.

Resigned to the fact that his two water choices were cold and cold, he took a deep breath and stepped under the frigid spray. "Auauaughgh," he screamed involuntarily as he pivoted around until he was thoroughly wet. He grabbed the soap and stepped away from the spray to lather. He meticulously soaped up every inch of his body, procrastinating the return trip under the icy spray. Taking another deep breath, he plunged back under. "Auauauaughghgh! Cold! Cold! Cold! Cold!" He gasped as he pirouetted under the spray until he determined he had removed all the suds. He doused his long tresses and again stepped away from the chilling torture.

He poured shampoo into his hand, remembered how much hair he currently had and doubled the amount before he began lathering his hair. It felt strange. There was simply too much hair. *How did people with long hair deal with this mess?* As he set the bottle back into the wire caddy, he noticed the instructions, 'lather, rinse, repeat'. He plunged his soapy head under the bone-chilling torrent. "Not bloody likely," he shouted.

Arctic ordeal completed, he dried off and hung the towel on a hook. "Goodbye, kitty! I hope you find your way home." He slid into clean underwear and his floppy bottomed jeans. He opened his bag again and took out his remaining items, deodorant and cologne. He popped the top from the aerosol can and contemplated how to use it. He test sprayed it away from himself and decided it behaved like bug spray or spray paint. He lifted an arm and pointed towards himself and sprayed, wondering how much to use. He let the spray hit him for several seconds. When he lowered his arm, his armpit felt sticky. "Too much?" he muttered. He fetched the towel and blotted under his arm. "Sorry, kitty, I thought our paths wouldn't cross again."

For his second try, he pumped tiny bursts of spray as he flapped his arm up and down checking for tackiness. Satisfied, he capped the canister and popped it into an open locker. "Happy birthday, somebody." Unscrewing the cap from the cologne, he sniffed it again. He kind of liked it. He put a couple of drops in his left hand and rubbed it around his chest, a couple more drops and he rubbed his face. He smiled at the cheery green bottle and glanced at the open locker, but decided to keep this one. He put it in his bag and slid into his clean t-shirt and sighed. It felt good to be fresh again.

Alex was sitting quietly when Sean returned. Sean tapped under his seat, and after a moment of blank-stare, Alex opened the slide-out drawer. Sean stowed his things with his backpack.

"That was twenty-two minutes," Alex droned.

"Ran into a few problems. Hey, can you make the screen into a mirror thingy again?"

Alex complied. Sean pulled a comb from his pocket and started to work on his hair. He quickly found that the comb got tangled in his wet, disheveled locks. He abandoned the comb and worked through the major snarls with his fingers. "This is insane," he complained. "I have a totally new respect for girls that wear their hair really long. What a pain." Eventually, he removed the tangles and got the comb through his hair. Satisfied with the look, he turned to Alex. "OK, I guess back to the camp at the lake and we wait. I think I'll sit in the sun and try to warm up and get this mess of hair dry."

Chapter Eight

"His name was always Buddy / and he'd shrug and ask to stay"

JANE WAS true to her word and picked up Sean and Alex at seven-thirty, but no one else seemed able to get organized enough to leave for Colgate by the planned eight o'clock. The park, near the gazebo, was again the designated meeting spot. Scott came by a few minutes after eight to make sure everything was still on, then left to pick up Karen. When no one else had arrived by eight-fifteen, Jane stormed off to find a pay phone. John Kelly showed up only minutes after she'd departed and when Jane later returned, she immediately started yelling at him for being late and ranted about not reaching anyone by phone.

It was eight-thirty when Scott returned with Karen. He parked next to John's car and everyone leaned against either the Plymouth or the Chevy as they negotiated the next phase of their plans.

"We can take Black Beauty," Scott offered.

Jane assessed his appearance and grimaced. "Are you sure you want to drive all the way to Colgate?"

Scott wore a silly grin, and though he faced Jane, he appeared to look past her. "I'm cool," Scott assured her. "I drove all the way from Karen's house to here with no problems."

Karen giggled.

"That's *only* six blocks," said Jane harshly.

"Really?" Scott snickered, "Seemed farther than that." He suddenly doubled over in a fit laughter that Karen joined in.

Jane rolled her eyes and turned to John. "Juan," she asked, "do you mind driving?"

"No, that's cool," John responded evenly.

"Nah, c'mon... let's take Black Beauty," Scott snorted as he choked back a laugh. Karen looked at him, and when his eyes met hers they convulsed into another fit of giggles.

Sean noticed that Karen and Scott's eyes seemed slightly unfocused, and wondered about their inability to manage ordinary conversation.

Regardless of focus, Karen had rather dark, pretty eyes. She also had a somewhat ruddy complexion and jet black hair that hung perfectly straight almost to her waist. Her petite frame stood about five feet tall in leather sandals. Sean suspected that she might be of Native American heritage.

Jane stood with arms crossed, openly demonstrating her displeasure. "Since Scott hasn't bothered," she snapped, "let me introduce you. Nigel, Peter, this is Karen Silver. Karen, this is Nigel Davies and Peter..." she paused, pursing her lips trying to recall Peter's last name.

"Lindsey," Alex filled in. He nodded toward Karen. "I am very pleased to meet you, Miss Silver."

Karen's eyes were locked on Alex's as she crossed to him. He swallowed hard as she stood inches from him, staring up with wide eyes. "Are you British?" she asked, her voice steeped in wonderment.

"Yes, I am," Alex answered, uncomfortable with her closeness, "Liverpool, actually."

"Actually!" Karen shrieked, trying to mimic his accent. She jumped up and down squealing with excitement.

"Um... yes," Alex stammered nervously, glancing around at everyone else.

"Oooo, say something else," Karen coaxed. "Like, say, 'the rain in Spain falls mainly on the plain'." Alex again scanned the other faces, looking for someone to rescue him. When no one did, he repeated the phrase for her with his perfect British accent.

"Oooo, I think he's *got* it!" Karen gushed, then hooked an arm behind Alex's neck and pulled him down into an enthusiastic kiss. "Mmmm," she purred when he finally pulled away, "British accents are soooo sexy!"

Jane grabbed Karen by the shoulders and steered her back to Scott. "Karen can be overly... *affectionate* at times," she said icily over her shoulder in Alex's general direction.

"Quite," Alex squeaked, his eyes wide as saucers on his bright red face.

Sean leaned into Alex's ear and whispered, "So, what's it like being kissed by a cavewoman?"

"Quite," Alex repeated, still staring emptily. Sean laughed.

"OK, here's the deal," Jane announced loudly. "Juan is driving and we leave when Jimbo shows up or in ten minutes, whichever comes first."

"I kissed a Britlishman," Karen giggled to Scott just before grabbing him for a kiss. "Now you've kissed someone who kissed a Bristleman."

"You said, 'britselman'," Scott whooped, then they both fell into hysteria.

Sean sidled closer to Jane and asked softly from the corner of his mouth, "Are they.....?"

"Kinda baked? I'd say so," Jane returned, not so quietly.

"Thanks for getting my d... er, Juan to drive."

"Hey, it's my life, too," she shrugged. A curious smile crossed her face and she leaned closer to Sean and sniffed. "Jade East?"

"Umm... yeah... too much?"

"No, I like it," she mused. "It's nice."

"And how many different colognes can you name just from a sniff?"

"Not many," she replied, pleased with herself for guessing correctly. "Louise gave Micky some for his birthday. I just happen to like the way it smells. I guess Louise did, too, although Micky won't wear it. He's an *Aqua Velva* man." She rolled her eyes. "Come on, Micky, it's 1969, not 1950."

"I'm glad you like it," Sean said. "Umm... you're wearing a different perfume tonight."

She smiled, "Mmm hmm. Can you tell what it is?"

"I'm not very good at that, I'm afraid."

"That's OK, it's something I whipped up myself. I stirred a little cinnamon into some musk oil. What do you think?"

Sean sniffed deeply. "Yeah, I guess I do get that hint of cinnamon. Rather nice."

Alex sidled closer to them. He appeared to be recovering his wits.

"I'm sorry about Karen," Jane told him. "She can be like, out there, sometimes."

"It was a bit surprising, I must admit," Alex commented. "Does that behaviour not upset Scott?"

"Who knows," Jane shrugged, "They're both a little..." she put a pinched thumb and index finger next to her lips and inhaled sharply. Alex looked at her blankly.

"Smoking weed," Sean said quickly, then clarified, "marijuana."

Alex nodded slowly, trying to take it all in.

"Jane," called John, "can I talk to you for a minute."

"Sure," she replied as she started walking toward him.

"So, perhaps a drug induced euphoria explains Miss Silver's actions," Alex suggested.

"Don't sell yourself short, Cousin Peter," Sean grinned, "that English accent just gets to some girls."

"I am very pleased to get to observe their behaviour," Alex declared. "It was an important part of the sub-culture of this time-period. It will be fascinating to monitor how well they function while under the influence."

"Yeah," Sean said dryly, "maybe *Scott* will kiss you next."

Jane returned. "Juan was worried about having enough gas. I told him we could all chip in. I hope that's OK with you."

"Sure," Sean replied.

"Might I say that you look quite fetching tonight, Miss Carmichael?" Alex offered graciously.

Fetching? thought Sean.

"Why thank you, Mr. Lindsey, you are too kind," she replied with just a hint of a curtsy. She looked to Sean and raised an eyebrow.

"Yeah," he stumbled, "You look great, luv. The Marcia Brady look is working for you." Jane's face went blank. "More of a Jan Brady, you think?" he countered. She lifted her eyebrows and shook her head slightly.

"Ah," Alex quickly interjected, "You are confounding her with your

Maori slang again, Nigel." He turned directly to Jane. "*Marja Braddy* means 'without braids'. Last night you wore your hair in braids. *Morvajhan Braddy* means, 'do you prefer braids'?"

"Oh," Jane nodded, "Thanks, Peter. At first I thought it kind of sounded like he said 'Marsha Brady', and I didn't know who that was."

Sean's eyes questioned Alex.

"A moment, Jane," Alex requested politely, "I need to clarify something with Nigel."

They took a few steps away. "What's the deal?" Sean hissed. "It's the same hairstyle as those girls in the *Brady Bunch*."

"She has not seen that television program."

"How do you know that?"

"Because it first airs in September of this year."

"Are you kidding?" Sean yelped. "I thought it was a 60s TV show."

"Technically it is."

"I mean, when I saw reruns of it, it just seemed so 60s, I thought they would all know about it."

"They probably will, in just a few months," Alex confirmed.

"OK, so I guess I owe you one for that save."

They returned to Jane.

"I'm sorry, luv," Sean offered, "I sometimes just wonk off into some odd slang phrases."

"That's OK," she replied, "I guess I should expect some language barriers, even if we do both speak English." She paused before coyly asking, "So *do* you like my hair this way?"

"Yes!" Sean gushed, "Of course! It's gorgeous!" He wondered if she had to use an iron to get it that straight. He glanced at Karen. *Maybe they* all *iron their hair?* "That's also an interesting umm, purse, is it?" He nodded toward Jane's shoulder bag that was made up of various colored twine artfully tied together to form a large pouch. The straps hung from her right shoulder with the pouch sitting on her hip.

"Isn't it groovy?" Jane said happily as she lifted it toward Sean for a closer look. "Louise made it. Macramé! I told her she should sell them, they're so cool."

"Louise must be very talented," Alex said, then launched into the history of the art of macramé. Jane nodded and tried to listen enthusiastically. Sean almost immediately tuned him out and used his lecture time to admire Jane. She wore leather sandals secured with leather thongs that wove around her ankles. What he first thought was a burnt-umber short skirt, was actually some type of shorts with widely flared bottoms that made it fan out like a skirt. They nicely complemented her forest-green top that billowed loosely over her skirt-shorts and tied in a bow behind her neck, leaving her shoulders and most of her back exposed. Her shoulders and neck were creamy-white against the dark straps. When he looked up to her face, she was chewing the

155

corner of her lower lip. He glanced quickly at her eyes then away. She had been watching him as he checked her out.

When Alex's history lesson wound to a close, Jane leaned closer to Sean's ear and whispered, "Do I pass?"

Sean's cheeks flamed, and Jane's eyes sparkled as her smile went wider. She happily held her gaze on him a few seconds more before stepping away to the center of the small group.

"OK," she boomed, "I don't think Jimbo is going to make it, so let's get in the car and get going. It's already 8:45."

"Shotgun!" yelled Scott.

"Fine," agreed Jane. "Scott and Karen up front with Juan. Peter and Nigel and I will take the back."

They had all been standing on the passenger side of the Impala. As John circled around to get behind the wheel, Karen slipped into the passenger front with Scott following her. Jane was first through the passenger rear door, with Alex following her in. Sean paused. He *could* also get in through the same door since Jane and Alex were already shifting over. With only a moment's hesitation, he closed that door and walked around the back of the car and opened the other door. Alex and Jane slid back the other way and Sean got in behind his dad, next to Jane.

"We should keep it boy, girl, boy in front *and* back," he suggested.

Jane almost said something, but then closed her mouth and simply smiled to herself.

"Who wants tunes?" Scott asked, pulling several plastic cartridges from the glove box.

"Let me see one of those," Sean requested. Scott passed one over his head and Jane passed it on to Sean. Sean rolled it over and over in his hands. It was roughly the size of a paperback book, with various notches, and one end was mostly open with a strip of magnetic tape sitting on pads and wheels. Pasted on the front was a picture like he would expect to see on a CD cover, as well as a list of songs.

"Don't you have 8-tracks in New Zealand?" asked Jane?

"I can't think of a soul back home who has any of these," Sean said with a private grin.

"Oooo," squealed Karen from the front seat, "Airplane!"

"Which one you want?" asked Scott, "*Crown of Creation*? Or *Surrealistic Pillow*?"

"Which one has *Somebody to Love*?" she trilled.

"*Surrealistic Pillow*."

"Then that one!" she insisted.

"We should probably like, take a vote," Scott said diplomatically, "Backseat: who wants which one?" He held one on each shoulder.

Sean and Alex looked blankly at each other. Jane's head turned from side to side, checking their expressions. "I don't think anyone back here cares," she said.

"Either is fine with me," John added.

"Far out!" whooped Karen as she jammed the cartridge into the player.

When the music started blasting, Sean turned and spotted a wedge-shaped after-market speaker behind Alex's head. From the concussive blasts he felt, he assumed there was one just like it behind his own.

"Do you like Jefferson Airplane, Nigel?" Jane shouted above the din.

"Yeah, Grace Slick's vocals are out of sight," he yelled in reply, then wondered how he knew to say that. He assumed it was Alex's programming in his head, which eerily enough also made the songs that played seem familiar. They didn't get to hear the entire album, though since Karen kept switching back to the same track with 'Somebody to Love'. She sang along with it and pumped her fists as high as the ceiling of the car would allow, rocking her head back and forth with the beat.

It was only a thirty-five minute ride to Colgate, but it seemed a lot longer than that to Sean. He'd given up trying to talk to Jane above the blaring music and roar of the air rushing through all four windows. He made a note to try to be thankful the next time he turned on the air-conditioner in his own car. He glanced over to Alex occasionally. His serenely neutral face irritated Sean. He supposed that his descendant had some kind of nanite filters in his ears to temper the volume.

"So where, exactly, *is* the drive in?" John asked as they came into town. He turned down the music. "I don't think I've ever been to the one in Colgate."

"On the north side of town," Scott replied.

"No, it's on the southeast side," Jane corrected.

"No, man! North!" Scott insisted.

"You're thinking of the one in Oakdale," said Jane.

"No I'm not!"

"Juan, you've been to the drive-in in Oakdale, right?" Jane asked.

"Yeah, but like, when I was a kid. The family went to see like *Flubber* or *The Nutty Professor* or something."

"And it was on the north side of town," asserted Jane.

"Maybe," John said noncommittally.

"So the one in Colgate is on the southeast side," Jane concluded.

"No, man," Scott protested, "it's on the *north* side of town!"

"Yeah," chimed Karen, "Scott's right!"

Jane slammed her head against the back of the seat and crossed her arms over her chest. Her lips bunched together in near pout. John glanced at her in the rear-view mirror, his eyes apologetic as he made a left turn onto one of the main north-south streets.

After ten minutes of driving around the north end of Colgate, John stopped at an intersection and put the car in 'Park'.

"So where is it, Scott?" John asked.

"I don't know, man," Scott lamented. "It should be around here somewhere. Everything looks kinda different."

"OK, Scott," Jane said, trying to sound helpful. "Think about other landmarks. Where is it from the big orange water tower?"

"Yeah, excellent idea, man," Scott nodded then closed his eyes to concentrate. "It's like four blocks north and six blocks west of the orange water tower. That's it!"

"In *Oakdale!*" Jane snapped. "Colgate has a *blue* water tower!"

Scott turned questioningly to Jane. He bit his lower lip and squinted his eyes in concentration. "You might be right, man," he finally said softly.

John pulled through the intersection and turned around in a driveway, pointing the Impala back south. "OK, Jane," he sighed, "all the way back to the highway?"

"Yes," she replied, "then turn left and follow it most of the way through town. I'll tell you when to turn."

"I probably should go ahead and get gas now. I don't know if any of the stations will be open when the movie's over. That'll be after midnight."

"Good idea," Jane agreed, then added louder, "Since we're already late and missed the start of the first movie."

Scott was oblivious that she had directed the latter remark at him.

As they pulled into a gas station, Sean started to pull his wallet out.

"Put that away," Jane said, "I've got this. You and Peter are our guests tonight." She quickly pulled three ones from her purse and passed it to the front seat. "Here's for the back seat."

"Jane, I've got money," Sean said indignantly.

"Yeah, but you'll probably need every dime of it before you get to New York. It's cool," said Jane.

"I still think Peter and I should contribute," Sean complained.

"Fine. You can buy me popcorn," Jane said sweetly as she smiled at him.

They had barely gotten back on the road when Scott started shouting, "Pizza! On the left! Pizza!"

"We're going to the drive-in!" Jane snarled.

"I'm starved," Scott complained. "And Cougar Corral Pizza is the best!" John drove past it. "Awwww!" Scott whined.

"The entrance to the drive-in is just up here on the right," Jane advised.

"I see it," John replied.

They pulled to the edge of the road where they could read the marquee before pulling in.

Buck Night!
Jane Fonda – Double Feature!
Cat Ballou – 9:00   Barbarella – 11:00

Scott struggled to read his watch. "Turn on the dome light," he urged. John flicked it on. "OK, it's already 9:45 and Cat Ballou's really stupid. I saw it a couple of years ago. Lee Marvin's a drunk gunslinger and Dobie Gillis is in it and every time there's a chase scene or something this white guy and black guy sing a song about Cat Ballou. It's a complete drag. If we go get pizza now, we can be back before eleven. You *know* that there's cars that'll leave after the first show's over and we can get a better parking spot if we go in then. Cougar Corral Pizza is like the best ever!"

"Pizza does sound good," Karen agreed when Scott took a breath.

John turned to look at Jane.

"Are you going to complain about not getting pizza all through the show if we go in now?" Jane asked Scott.

"Probably," he grinned.

Jane turned to Sean and lifted her eyebrows.

"Actually, luv," Sean commented, "The more he talks about pizza, the better it sounds."

Jane turned to Alex. "What do you think, Peter?" she asked.

"What exactly *is* a Cougar Corral?" he inquired.

"Colgate's school mascot is a Cougar, so that's where the name comes from. Other than that, it's just a pizza joint," Jane explained.

"It's the *best* pizza ever, man!" Scott asserted.

Jane rolled her eyes.

"I have no objection, particularly if others wish to eat," said Alex.

"You will *love* it, man!" Scott enthused.

"Fine," Jane sighed. "Let's go or we won't be back in time to even see the *second* show."

John pulled a U-turn and they drove back toward Cougar Corral Pizza.

Sean was surprised how busy the place was. They had to wait several minutes before a booth opened up. They had barely sat down when a waitress plopped some menus on their table and promptly darted away. The room was a steady hum of conversations as everyone tried to talk over the blaring jukebox. The six arranged themselves as they had in the car except Sean switched with Jane, putting her on the outside end. Scott was all the way inside on the opposite side of the table and Sean wondered if Jane's shift was designed to get as much distance from him as possible.

"What would you like to drink?" asked the waitress as she magically appeared.

"A pitcher of beer," Scott requested.

"That'll take awhile, I'm afraid," the waitress droned, her face reflecting her boredom.

"That's OK," said Scott.

"No, I mean a really long while," the waitress deadpanned. "From the looks of you, I'd say four to five years."

"Hey," Scott protested, "I'm twenty-one!"

"Show me six driver's licenses that prove that and I'll bring you a pitcher of beer and congratulate you all for looking so young."

159

Scott scanned the faces around the table. "Fine. Pitcher of Coke," he grumbled.

"I'll have a Tab," Karen said.

"I'll have a Tab, too," said Jane.

"I would prefer water," Alex said meekly.

"I'll get your drinks right out," said the waitress, adding, "My name's Suzie." Then she was gone.

Everyone began studying the menus. Sean found the low prices more interesting than the descriptions of the pizzas. He leaned toward Jane. "What's Tab?" he asked.

"Like Diet-Rite or Diet-Pepsi," she replied absently, not looking up from her menu.

"Not Diet-Coke?" Sean asked.

"I think Coke owns it, but it's Tab. There isn't any Diet-Coke."

Not yet, thought Sean.

"We should get an extra-large Kitchen Sink," Scott announced. "Minus the anchovies."

"Have you looked at the size of an extra-large?" Jane asked. "Turn around and look above the counter, they've got samples of the pans up there."

Scott briefly looked at the pans on display. He turned back nodding. "Looks about right."

"It's seven dollars!" Jane protested, "And it's huge! And Peter's a vegetarian! Not to mention, I don't like onions, green peppers, or olives."

"So you could like, pick those off your slice and give them to Peter."

Jane shook her head and rolled her eyes before turning to Alex. "Peter, do you want to split a small cheese pizza with me?"

"I am not particularly hungry," Alex replied.

"Nigel?"

"Truthfully, Jane?" admitted Sean, sheepishly, "The Kitchen Sink sounds pretty good to me."

"Karen?" Jane said across the table.

"I'm with Scott."

Jane nearly made a snide remark but bit her tongue. She looked at John.

"I like anything," John said with a shrug.

"OK," Sean said, taking control, "Why not a small cheese and a medium Kitchen Sink? I can go for a slice of each." He looked across the table to his Dad. John Kelly nodded approval. He looked at Karen. She shrugged. He turned to Scott.

"We need at least a large, man," Scott insisted.

"No, mate," Sean said firmly as he glared at Scott, "we *don't*."

"Whoa, peace, man," Scott said, hands up in surrender, "I'm down with that. Whatever's cool."

The waitress suddenly appeared with a tray of drinks, quickly set them down on the table and turned to leave.

"You forgot the beer," Scott chirped with a big grin.

"You forgot I'm not as stupid as you," she fired back.

"Well, I guess *you* don't want a tip," Scott sneered.

"Sweetie," she sighed, "I can tell by looking, you are *not* a tipper." And then she was gone.

"She didn't even ask if we were ready to order!" said an exasperated Jane.

"Let me out for a minute, luv," Sean said softly to Jane.

She stood to let Sean slide out, then sat back down, dejected.

Sean found the waitress across the room, busing a table. He slid into the booth and grabbed an empty glass at the far end of the table and set it on her tray. She glanced his way.

"Busy night?" he asked when she looked up.

"No thanks," she replied wearily, not hiding the frustration in her voice, "already got one."

He smiled. "Good one," he said warmly. "Listen... sorry about my friend being a jerk."

"I just don't have time for comedians tonight."

"I can see that," Sean replied sincerely. "But if you get our order in now, it will get us out the door that much faster."

"I'll get to your table in a few minutes."

Sean pulled out his wallet and handed her a five.

"Wow!" she said as she took it. "Who're you? Howard Hughes' long lost son?"

"No, just someone who appreciates when someone else is having a hard night," Sean said, thinking of Louise getting only fifteen dollars for a week of waitressing.

She pulled out her pad. "What'll you have?" she asked with more enthusiasm than she'd previously shown.

"Small cheese and a medium Kitchen Sink, no anchovies, please."

"And he says, 'please'," she mused. "What's a class act like you doing hanging out with the pot-head?"

"Friend of the family," Sean shrugged.

"Yeah, you can get some lulus that way," she nodded knowingly. "I'll get your order right in." She gave him a bright smile as she held the five up. "And thanks for this." She stuffed it in a pocket and whisked her tray away.

Sean strolled back to his booth with a spring in his step and a smile on his face. He decided he enjoyed the appearance of being rich. Especially when it only took five dollars... not to mention that it was technically Alex's five dollars. He'd have to remember to ask Alex to find out who this Howard Hughes was, obviously some billionaire. "She's putting our order right in," he said as he sat back down. Jane slid back in next to him.

It was 10:20 when the pizzas arrived. Scott had wolfed down half of the Kitchen Sink plus a slice of the cheese almost before anyone else had finished

161

one slice. Sean, Karen, and John ate most of the other half, with John and Sean also eating a slice from the cheese pizza. Jane ate one slice from the cheese, and Sean convinced Alex to also try a slice. When he'd determined no one else was going to go for the last two slices, Scott wolfed them down. By the time they had finished eating, and arguing about who should pay how much, it was 10:45 as they went out the door.

"See!" Scott proclaimed happily, pointing to all the cars coming out of the drive-in as they arrived. "I told you that a bunch of people would leave. Lots of them have kids in the car, so they're like, out of there."

John handed a dollar bill to the bored attendant as they crept past the entrance. They slowly approached the rows of already parked cars using only their parking lights, tires crunching the thick gravel. Dozens of cars were still coming toward them as they inched their way carefully onto the lot.

"Aw man!" Scott complained. "Look at all those losers pulling up taking the better spaces!"

"And you wouldn't have suggested that if we were already parked in one of the back rows?" asked Jane.

"Well, yeah, for sure... but I didn't think anyone else would think of that."

"I know," Jane said sarcastically, "it's *amazing* anyone else would think of it."

"Ooo, quick, find a spot, find a spot," Karen squealed, "the cartoon is starting!"

"That's an ad for the concession stand," Jane retorted disdainfully.

"How can you tell?" asked Karen. "Looks like cartoon characters to me."

"That's true," replied Jane, speaking as if to a child, "but when the characters are a hot-dog, a box of popcorn and a Coke, I don't think Bugs Bunny is going to show up anytime soon."

"Oh, I love Bugs Bunny!" Karen gushed.

Sean nearly laughed out loud when Jane crossed her eyes, let her tongue hang from the corner of her mouth and waggled her head behind Karen's back. He glanced over to check on Alex, who was smiling happily. He hoped Alex was getting some good notes from all this.

John pulled into one of the empty spaces, snuggled close to one of the poles that held the movie speakers, and turned off his engine.

"Come on, man," complained Scott. "We should drive around some more and see if we can find a better spot."

"We can see the screen fine from here, and it's only about twenty-five yards to the concession stand from here. That will be real handy, Scott, when those three glasses of Coke you drank work their way down," John advised wearily.

"Oh! That's a good idea!" said Karen abruptly. She turned to face the back seat. "Jane?"

162

Jane nudged Sean, who initially looked at her blankly before figuring out what she wanted. He opened his door and stood as Jane slid out. Scott also got out to let Karen exit the front. As the girls headed toward the restrooms, Scott lit a cigarette and leaned his elbows on the roof of the car. Sean got back in. When John noticed Scott was smoking, he also got out and lit up.

Sean leaned toward Alex. "Getting some good notes on all this?"

"The conflict and resolution of several issues have been quite fascinating," reported Alex. "It is difficult for me to discern to what degree the marijuana influenced any positions. One thing certainly confounds me. I was convinced that I had detected an animosity between Jane and Karen, yet they have left the vehicle together, as if they are friends."

"Yeah, that's a girl / bathroom thing," Sean suggested. "I don't think anyone who is a guy can ever explain that. What else?"

"The amount of food Scott consumed seemed excessive. I assume that was artificially induced."

"Don't really know the guy, but yeah, he seemed to be shoveling it in like he was starving."

"Karen, though smaller in stature than Jane, ate twice as much pizza."

"Oh, hey, pizza reminds me. The waitress thought I was a rich kid, and she asked if I was Howard Hughes' long lost son. When we get back, can you look him up for me?"

To Sean's surprise, Alex did his query twitch. "Net worth of $1.5 billion at the time of his death in 1976. Chiefly known for aviation and the movie industry. Right now he is in his reclusive period before his death, probably in Las Vegas, where he owns several hotels. There is some suggestion of mental illness that was largely untreated."

"Wait, I thought you had to be within 5 miles of Steffi to connect. How did you do that?"

"I decided I would be uncomfortable to be out of contact that long, so I determined how I will compensate."

"*Will* compensate?" Sean questioned.

"Yes, when we return to the lake, I will take Steffi back to this moment in time and follow to this town."

"So... Steffi is somewhere near here?"

"Yes."

"So another copy of you is here somewhere, too?"

"Not another copy," corrected Alex. "It will be me. I will have simply returned to this same time-period."

"Isn't that kind of weird?"

"In what way?"

"To be two places at the same time, just so you can have your computer link," Sean said incredulously. "And what does Steffi think of two of you trying to contact her at the same time? Any chance one of you will get a busy signal?"

163

"It is astute of you to recognize that as a potential difficulty. However, I will simply put myself into a neutral mental state once I arrive here. You might refer to it as a 'self-induced trance'."

Sean tried to picture Alex somewhere above them, flying around in a cloaked time-machine, staring into nothingness like a zombie. He shook the thought off. "OK," he finally said, "that hurts my brain to think about it, so I'm going to ignore it for now."

"As you wish," Alex said, ignoring Sean's exasperation. "I would like to pose another scenario to see what conclusion you would draw. Since it appears that the initial euphoria seems to be subsiding, do you believe Scott and Karen will inhale any more tetrahydrocannabinol to renew the effects?"

It took Sean a few seconds to translate to something he understood. "Are they going to smoke more weed? I don't know. If they try to light up in the car, I'm going to bail."

"Why?"

"Mainly because it's illegal. What if the guy in the next car is an off-duty cop?"

Alex fired off a query. "There is no record of your father ever being arrested for drug possession."

"I'm *still* out of here," Sean proclaimed. Alex eyed him curiously. "So what's *your* plan? You going to just sit there and watch them smoke weed?"

"I believe I would appear less conspicuous if I were to also participate. You are already aware that I am equipped to filter out any toxins in the air I breathe. It would have no effect on me."

"Wow, not often the scientist actually sits in the maze with the lab rats," Sean sneered.

"You seem irritated."

Sean took a moment to consider the accusation. "Maybe," he admitted. "I think listening to Karen screech off-key to *Somebody to Love* three times got me started. And... I don't know... this sixties' scene isn't really what I thought it would be like. My Dad seems... weird. I mean, he's out there smoking again. And at first I kinda thought Scott was OK, but now I'm thinking I don't like my Dad hanging out with him. All he seems to care about is beer and getting high." He shook his head and curled his lip. "None of this has gone like I thought it would. I thought we'd pop back in time and I'd hang out with my Dad at the farm or something. When we first got here, I even thought maybe I'd get to meet Grandpa Kelly." He paused as he searched his thoughts. "My Dad is just kind of... I don't know what. Bland? Not cool? Jane said that she and Dad are kind of misfits, at least at their high school. It's just all different than I thought it would be." He sat quietly for a few seconds then turned to face Alex.

"I do not wish to appear unsympathetic," Alex responded, "but I find that it is quite interesting how much different this era is from the one you live in. I hypothesize that it will also be quite different in the period where your

164

grandfather is sixteen. I had no preconceived expectations of this visit, which may be why it is more exhilarating to me."

"Yeah, great stuff, I'll bet," Sean said bitterly, "Caveman Sean invent wheel, very interesting. Go back another generation, Caveman John create fire."

"I do *not* view you that way!" Alex snapped; his clipped British accent highlighting the indignation in his voice.

"Sure you do," Sean argued. "You're ten times smarter than any of us... maybe a hundred times when you count tapping into your computer."

"I had assumed we were beyond this stage," Alex huffed, blowing out a frustrated breath. "It is my opinion that you currently are projecting your disappointment in your father onto me, assuming I feel the same way about you. Your interactions with Jane and Louise seemed to have been quite positive... but then you had no expectations of how *they* should behave. Conversely, in 1995 you have experienced years of observing Jack Kelly that colour how you expect *Juan Kelly* to act in 1969." Sean stared at Alex coldly. Alex continued, "Perhaps you should consider that *living* those years between now and when you begin to observe him as your father is what *makes* Jack Kelly to be who he is. *You* are not likely to be the same person in 2021 that you are now."

Sean's eyes softened as Alex's words began to sink in. "2021?" Sean said thoughtfully. "That seems so far away."

"It is the same span of time as 1969 to 1995."

"Yeah, but 2021? That just sounds like... I don't know. Moon bases. Colonies on Mars. Futuristic stuff like that. Flying cars. Talking computers."

"The twentieth-century science fiction writers tended to assume a quicker change than what actually comes about. There are no manned missions to Jupiter with a neurotic computer in 2001. And, I am sorry to tell you, there are no moon bases or Mars colonies by 2021. Perhaps the authors did not take into account government bureaucracy."

"What about flying cars?"

Alex furrowed his brow and was about to respond when the door behind Sean opened.

"OK if I sit on the outside?" Jane asked as she ducked her head in.

"Umm, sure... I guess," Sean said as he reluctantly scooted closer to Alex. Jane slid in beside him and closed the door. Sean pointed to the large Styrofoam cup she held. "More Tab?"

"No, just a cup of ice," she replied, then shook it so he could hear the ice rattle.

"What's that for?"

"You'll see," she said coyly, "after the movie gets started."

The front doors both opened and Juan, Karen and Scott all piled in.

"Previews are starting," John announced as he retrieved the speaker hanging from the short pole. He rolled his window part way up and hung the

165

speaker on the glass. "Everyone hear it OK?" he asked as he played with the sound and tone knobs.

"Max it out!" Scott yelled.

"I'm the one sitting right next to the thing," John complained. "I'm not going to blow an eardrum, Scott. Can you hear it OK or not?"

"Chill out, man," Scott returned. "Yeah, I can hear."

"Back seat?" John queried.

"I think we're good," replied Jane, looking over to Alex, who gave a little nod.

Trailers played for *The Wild Bunch* and *Midnight Cowboy* as 'coming soon'; followed by *Butch Cassidy and the Sundance Kid* and *Battle of Britain* 'coming this fall'; and finally *Easy Rider* in the 'coming next week' slot.

"I'll bet that's why they dug out these Jane Fonda films," John said, "The feature next week stars Peter Fonda."

"Are they like married?" asked Karen.

"No," John corrected patiently, "Brother and sister."

"Children of Henry Fonda," Jane added.

"Who's that?" Karen inquired.

"Didn't you see *Spencer's Mountain* when you were a kid?" asked Jane. "Or any of a dozen old westerns that have been on TV."

"He was just in one last year with Lucille Ball," John continued. "They'd both been married before and had a bunch of kids, like 20 or something." He shrugged. "It was a comedy."

"Yeah, but this one with Peter Fonda looks far freakin' out, man!" Scott proclaimed. "We should go see it next week. 'The story of a man who went looking for America, and couldn't find it'," he quoted.

"That's what you and Peter need," Jane said to Sean as she pointed toward the screen, "a couple of motorcycles."

"Yeah, man," Scott enthused, "Born to be wild, man! That'd be so cool! *Vroom! Vrooom!*" His hands gripped invisible handlebars.

"Shhhhh," shushed Karen, "the movie's starting!"

All six of them grew quiet and stared at the screen as the feature began, but the lull was short-lived.

"What is that?" asked Scott, "A robot?"

The screen showed a human shaped object tumbling inside a fur lined spacecraft. Sean thought it was pretty cheesy special effects. It reminded him of an MST3K set.

"Far out!" Scott marveled, "it's a woman, and she's doing a striptease in space! Is this rated X?"

"No," said John, "it's M."

"M?" Sean asked, "What's M?"

"For mature audiences only," Jane explained. "So you're not going to *see* anything, Scott."

"She's floating around naked and I'm not going to see anything?" Scott scoffed. "Oh, man, move those letters!" The opening credits covered much of the actress as the theme music played.

"Told you," Jane sneered.

"Yes!" Scott crowed, pointing at the screen. "That was a boob. That was a definite boob!" Karen punched him in his left shoulder. "Ow!"

"Don't be looking at other women's boobs!" she demanded.

Sean chuckled to himself as he thought about the 'peace and free-love' mantras touted as icons of the sixties.

Jane held out her Styrofoam cup above his lap. "Hold this, please," she said, then went digging into the bottom of her voluminous shoulder-bag. She pulled out a large clear glass bottle filled with something pink and twisted the lid off.

"What's that?" Sean asked.

"Boone's Farm Strawberry Hill," she smiled as she began pouring it over the ice.

"You got Boone's Farm!" blurted Scott as he cranked his head around.

Sean wanted to ask *what's that* again, but was afraid it might be something that was common knowledge. He looked to Alex who ticked into search mode.

"Ever had it before, Nigel?" Jane asked Sean.

"Umm, I don't think so."

"It's the best!" proclaimed Scott.

"Do you *like* wine?" Jane asked.

Wine? Over ice? He wasn't an expert, but he didn't think you poured wine over ice. He'd only had a little glass of wine once at his cousin's wedding... or maybe that was champagne? "Um, sure!" he bluffed. She finished filling the cup.

"You get first sip, then," Jane said.

"Great!" Sean said, trying to truly sound pleased. He took a sip. It was a lot like strawberry soda, with just a bit of bitter aftertaste... and a little warmth that buzzed its way down his throat to his stomach. "Really good," he added offering the cup back to Jane. She pointed to Alex. Sean turned and handed the cup to Alex. "Here you go, old man! Down the hatch, wot?"

Alex looked into the cup as he re-examined the data he had retrieved. It was 7.5% alcohol from fermented apples and the flavoring was both natural and artificial strawberry. He sipped it. It had a light carbonation and an excessive amount of what he assumed was dextrose, although possibly fructose. He attempted to hand the cup to Jane.

"Hey!" complained Scott, "I thought we were going counter-clockwise!"

Jane rolled her eyes, then nodded. Alex handed the cup over the seat to Scott, who took a huge gulp. "Oh, man! That is *good* stuff!" He took another big gulp before handing it to Karen. Karen tipped the cup but didn't take in quite as much as Scott had.

"Groovy!" she said as she passed the cup to John, who also took a moderate sip before passing back to Jane.

"Where'd you come up with this, Jane?" John asked.

"Uncle Carl had it left over from his party. He said he'd let me have it if I washed his T-Bird."

"Decent," John responded as he bobbed his head in an appreciative nod.

Jane took a good sized sip before handing the cup again to Sean. Sean assumed they were going to continue passing the cup until it was gone, so he took a bigger sip this time. He decided it wasn't quite as bad as the first taste. Jane put her hand on his wrist before he could pass the cup to Alex. She lifted the bottle and tipped in more wine until the cup was full again. She smiled, then recapped the bottle.

"Here you go again, mate," Sean said as he gave the cup to Alex. "Cheers!" To Sean's surprise, Alex chugged down a big gulp.

"Right on!" Scott said with admiration. "Party hardy!" He took the cup from Alex and again took two big gulps. Karen giggled as she took the cup from him. "Hey," Scott said conspiratorially in a mock whisper, "everyone cool if we spark another doobie?"

"Yeah!" Karen shouted as she pumped her hand to the ceiling, splashing wine and ice over Scott and herself. She giggled again and handed the cup to John.

"I'm cool with it," John said mildly.

Scott turned to the backseat. Jane nodded. He looked at Sean.

"What exactly is a 'doobie'?" Sean asked.

"A joint. Grass. Pot." said Scott, finishing with an overly enunciated "Mary Gee Wanna!"

Sean felt slightly panicked when he realized everyone else in the car was OK with smoking weed. He didn't even have Alex as an ally since his descendant was going to go deep into research mode. He glanced from person to person. His Dad! *His Dad* smoked weed! And Jane! She didn't strike him as a pothead... but then neither did his Dad. Maybe Juan Kelly really *wasn't* anything like his Dad... at least not yet. He couldn't think about it, he just needed to get out of there. "Umm... No..." Sean finally said after what seemed like an eternity but was actually only a few seconds. "No. Count me out." Four pairs of eyes were suddenly locked on him. "Umm... I'll just go walk around or something."

"For real, man?" Scott asked, almost in shock.

"Yeah," Sean mumbled, looking down as he spoke.

"You're headed to Woodstock, but you don't smoke dope?" gasped Scott, still dumbstruck.

"Yeah," Sean mumbled again, then pointed across Jane toward the door. "Umm, can I..."

"Oh!" Jane said as she sprung back to life and popped her door open. "Yeah... umm... sorry."

"But you're not gonna narc on us or anything, right, man?" Scott questioned.

Jane stood by the door while Sean slid out. "No. You can do whatever..." Sean stepped around Jane to let her get back in, but she closed the door. "Aren't you going to..." Sean said toward his feet as he turned back to Jane.

"Nah," she said nonchalantly. "I can take it or leave it."

"Really?" he asked as his eyes moved from the gravel to meet hers.

She smiled at him. "No big deal," she shrugged. "Anyway," she continued brightly as she patted her bag, "I didn't mention that I've got a second bottle of Strawberry Hill."

"You sure this isn't going to wreck your evening?" Sean asked solemnly.

"*Pthththt!* Like Scott and Karen haven't already mostly trashed it," she laughed. "C'mon, let's go somewhere less conspicuous."

"Where?"

"You'll see," she said with a flirtatious grin and started walking toward the screen.

Sean followed a few steps behind her, glancing into cars as they walked by them. He was a little surprised by how many couples were making out instead of watching the movie. He even thought he saw one couple in the backseat of a car that might have been doing more, but the windows were pretty steamed up. *Kind of a warm summer night to have the windows all up,* he mused.

The volume of the movie's soundtrack shifted as they walked along, passing speaker after speaker. Jane stepped from the graveled lot into a grassy area nearly directly beneath the screen. The huge picture was strangely distorted by the angle where they stood. When he looked back down, Sean saw swings, teeter-totters, a merry-go-round, and other playground equipment scattered around the small area. Jane had already crossed to the swings and was tugging at one of the chains hooked just above her head.

"What are you trying to do?" Sean asked.

"Moving the seat up," she replied. "I don't want to sit at little kid level."

Sean helped her with the other chain, and they raised the seat to a comfortable level, then together they raised the neighboring seat. They sat quietly for a few moments. The sound from all the tiny speakers behind them had an eerie cavernous echo.

"The sound is rather odd, sitting here," he commented.

"Picture's kinda weird, too," Jane added, pointing up. "Are those dolls with razor teeth attacking her?"

Sean shrugged, he couldn't get too interested in the movie. His thoughts were elsewhere. "Why didn't you get back in with your friends?"

She turned to him and stared deeply into his eyes before speaking. "I... I didn't think it would be very hospitable for all of us to just ignore you."

"Maybe it wasn't very gracious of me to leave."

169

"No. That's cool," Jane shrugged. "If it's not your bag... you know. I mean... you do your thing, and they do theirs and it's all cool."

"What about you? I saw you nod when Scott was asking about..." his voice trailed off.

She shrugged again. "I just assumed everyone was cool with it."

"So it surprises you that I'm not?"

"No," she said sharply, then looked away in thought for a few moments. "Maybe..." she said as she turned back to him. "I mean... you're hitching across a foreign country, going to this huge rock concert. You're obviously a musician yourself. I mean... the hair, the tie-dye, the cool patches on your jeans. So, yeah... I guess I did assume you'd smoke a little pot."

Sean stared at the ground and watched the shadows shift around from the changing light levels on the screen just above. Jane started swinging in a short arc. "Would it surprise you if I said I assumed you didn't?" Sean asked, still staring at the shifting shadows.

Jane dragged her feet to a halt. "Not as much as it surprises me that it seems to be such a *big deal* to you. Louise never smokes pot or even drinks, but she doesn't judge me. She's my best friend. What's your hang-up?"

"I'm sorry," Sean mumbled, unsure of how the conversation had turned and where to go with it next. "I just... I've never... my friends and I just never hang out with any of the kids that smoke weed. I guess I don't know what to do around a pothead."

"*Pothead!*" Jane glowered. "I'm not a *pothead!* You think anyone who just occasionally parties is a *pothead?*" Sean was overwhelmed by her outrage. "So, back in New Zealand, someone who smokes marijuana is a pothead and everyone else steers clear of them?" She started swinging again, but in much larger arcs.

Sean felt confused... conflicted. He questioned his position. Was *he* acting judgmental now? Like gas station guy? Like grocery store guy? He really liked Jane. She was witty, funny, smart... and apparently did *not* consider herself a pothead. Was it the word 'pothead' that set her off? Were these guys in 1969 somehow different from the ones he knew in 1995 who lived and breathed 4:20 as their goal for the day? His Dad had stopped smoking everything, as far as he could tell, so maybe whatever he did in the sixties wasn't that big of a deal. And truthfully, when he imagined the sixties, he *did* think of hippies and drugs and free-love. *Maybe it's just...what?* he wondered, *a different time... different place... different ideas?* It seemed like everything eventually turned out OK... or at least as OK as it ever gets. He simply didn't know what to think. What he *did* know was that he didn't want to alienate Jane.

"Jane?" he said softly. She continued to swing, staring forward as if he wasn't even there. "Jane, luv, could you maybe consider I used the wrong word?" She kept swinging, but he thought he saw her face soften. He decided to try tossing out some more nonsense words in 'New Zealand' English.

"C'mon, luv, give a wonk a dobbler, yeah?"

She grinned.

"Give a *what* a *what?*" she asked, trying to not laugh.

"A wonk a dobbler," Sean repeated soberly. "You don't say that in America?" He beamed his best smile at her, exposing all his teeth.

"I'm pretty sure you *know* we don't," she said, her swinging motion slowing. "Let me try to translate from context though. Give a guy... hmmm... a second chance... the benefit of the doubt? Dobbler kind of sounds like double, so I'm going to go with 'second chance'."

"Aces, luv! Spot on!" he proclaimed. *Of course, if she'd said 'benefit of the doubt', **that** would also have been correct.*

"But I'm *not* a pothead," she asserted with a frown.

"I don't even normally *use* that word," Sean insisted. "I just heard it from the waitress when I was trying to smooth things over with her. She called Scott a pothead, so I must have misunderstood the usage, I reckon."

"Yeah..." she considered, "Scott kind of *is* a borderline pothead... especially when he's with Karen... she *definitely* is one." She paused thoughtfully before continuing, "So what about Peter? He stayed with them. So are you cool with him smoking?"

No! "Well, you know, it's his thing I guess. I mean, if he wants to occasionally, then I'm cool," Sean lied, trying to smooth things over, regardless of his true feelings. "He doesn't do it that often, and he doesn't use any other drugs at all. You know what I mean?"

"For sure," Jane nodded. "So you're really not all freaked out by someone occasionally getting high? I mean, as long as it's not like... regularly."

"Oh, right on," Sean said, trying to mimic hippie-speak. "Like, I do my thing and you do your thing."

"You are you, and I am I, and if by chance we find each other, it's beautiful."

Sean looked at her curiously as he rolled the phrase around his head. "That's kind of... that was nice..."

"Oh! I thought *you* were starting to quote it."

Sean was lost. "Quote it?"

"Yeah, haven't you seen that, like, on a poster somewhere? It's around a lot."

"I guess not."

"Or what about this one," Jane said, then with eyes turned to the stars began quoting again: "*Go placidly amidst the noise and haste, and remember what peace there may be in silence. As far as possible without surrender be on good terms with all persons. Speak your truth quietly and clearly; and listen to others, even the dull and the ignorant; they too have their story.*

Avoid loud and aggressive persons, they are vexatious to the spirit. If you compare yourself with others, you may become vain or bitter; for always there

171

will be greater and lesser persons than yourself.

Be gentle with yourself. You are a child of the universe, no less than the trees and the stars; you have a right to be here.

And whether or not it is clear to you, no doubt the universe is unfolding as it should. Therefore be at peace with God, whatever you conceive Him to be, and whatever your labors and aspirations, in the noisy confusion of life keep peace with your soul. With all its shams, drudgery, and broken dreams, it is still a beautiful world. Be cheerful." She glanced at Sean, then self-consciously stared at the ground.

"Wow," Sean said softly, "that was amazing."

She blushed and smiled bashfully.

Chapter Nine

"She'd sigh like Twig, the Wonder Kid / and turn her face away"

"I T'S FROM *Desiderata*," Jane explained. "It's just the first part and then the ending. I had to memorize the whole thing for speech contest last spring. I got a 'one' at regionals, but just a 'two' at state. I think the state judges thought it was too hippie-dippy-out-there."

"It's beautiful," said Sean.

"You haven't heard that one either? They're both like on posters all over."

"No... I guess things are different back home," Sean said wistfully, thinking he was discovering more and more just how different.

"It must be kind of hard to be half a world away from home," Jane sympathized.

"Yeah, I guess. Sometimes this just seems like a faraway time and place."

Jane stood abruptly. "Hey, I'm tired of the swings, let's try the teeter-totter."

He trailed after her, discovering that she had already straddled one end of the closest board. He pushed down on the upper side, easily leveraging her weight as he slung a leg over. He scooted as close to the handle as he could. "You're going to have to slide back some more to get it to balance." She did as requested and finding equilibrium, they gently bobbed up in down. "I haven't done this since I was a kid."

"Good to know that they have teeter-totters in New Zealand," Jane acknowledged, "or do you call them something else?"

"Jibbelty-Jabbers," Sean deadpanned.

"Really?"

"No," he laughed. They continued to bounce up and down. "Think anyone over in their cars is watching us instead of the movie?"

"I don't know," she mused. "It seemed from the cars we passed that lots of people weren't even watching the movie."

"You noticed that too?"

"Hard not to."

After quietly bouncing up and down for a couple more minutes, Jane pointed behind Sean. "Nigel, let's go take a look at that one."

"OK. Careful with the dismount. Slide forward." She moved up and Sean put his hands behind himself and moved one leg off. He gently lowered her down and she stepped a leg over and was off.

"I hope that wasn't *too* unladylike."

"Nope. Very smooth," he assured. "Might have been a little trickier if you were wearing a skirt like I thought you were at first. What do you call that, by the way?"

"This?" she asked, pulling the lower seams outward. "Gauchos. They're kind of like culottes... but 'gaucho' sounds cooler."

"Well, they're very sexy," he said, and almost immediately regretted his candor. *Was that too forward?* She hooked her right arm through his left. *Maybe not.*

"Thank you," she murmured with a blush.

She led him over to another playground apparatus. It was low to the ground and shaped kind of like a flying saucer.

"What's this?" Sean asked.

"I don't know. Something kids climb on. Kind of looks like a flying saucer."

"Even more than the one in this movie," Sean scoffed.

She sat on the lip of the playground UFO, facing the screen. When Sean sat beside her, Jane reclined onto the upper curved shape of the saucer. "I guess we could watch the movie from here." Sean slid down onto an elbow, keeping his head above hers.

"I guess," he agreed.

"You don't look too comfortable."

"I don't want to appear too forward."

She slid up onto an elbow, leveling her face to his.

"Nigel," she said thoughtfully. "Yesterday... on the dock... before Peter came over..." She paused, moved her face slightly closer to his. Her eyes flicked between his eyes and his lips, then she suddenly sat upright. "Want some more wine?" she said abruptly as she went digging into her bag.

"Umm, sure," Sean replied, raising up next to her. He wondered if he had missed again.

"It's a little warm, of course," she said as she twisted the cap off and took a swig. "I should have snagged the cup of ice."

He took the proffered bottle from her and tilted it up, taking in a mouthful of warm, sweet strawberry wine. "It's fine," he lied, handing the bottle back to her.

"Liar," she said just before tilting it back for a big gulp.

"You call me that a lot!" he laughed, taking the bottle again and drinking.

"I do not," she countered. "Only when you lie."

Sean tipped the bottle back again before handing it to her. "Fine. It's better cold."

They continued to pass the wine back and forth as they halfheartedly

174

made an attempt to watch the movie.

"It wasn't really lying," Sean eventually proposed, "I was just trying to make the best of it for you."

"Very shiverless of you shir," she attempted formally, then shook her head briskly and tried again. "Very civilous... silverless..." she giggled, then with a determined look, slowly enunciated each syllable, "chiv-al-rous of you, sir!" She took another big drink, held the bottle up to the screen to see it was nearly empty. "Here," she urged, handing it to Sean. "Kill it."

He took the bottle and looked into her unfocused eyes as she grinned a goofy grin. "Miss Carmichael," he announced, "I believe you are intoxicated." He drank the last swallow.

"Re-dick-you-muss," she giggled, "I'm just a teensy bit happy."

Sean had little experience with alcohol and decided that he felt a little more relaxed himself.

Jane tilted her head back to look up at the screen. "Look," she pointed, "that guy has feathers and wings." She squinted to give the scene further scrutiny. "Do you think he's a bird-man, or an angel?" She flopped back against the curve of the saucer. "I think he looks like an angel... but this is some kind of silence friction movie, isn't it?" She closed her eyes to concentrate. "Probly a bird-man-alien."

Sean laid back against the curve alongside Jane. "Looks like a guy with fake wings tied to his back," he quipped.

"Aw come on!" She punched his shoulder. "He's cute!" Jane took her glasses off and nearly stabbed Sean in the eye with them as she put them on him. "You need glasses, buddy! He's cute!"

Looking through her glasses, the screen was a mass of blurred colors. "You're right, he looks much better now."

"Told ya," she crowed.

He pulled the glasses off and started to hand them to her when it suddenly hit him. For all the times that he snarked about Clark Kent not being recognized as Superman; he couldn't believe that he'd been tripped up by the glasses! Her nose and hair were still different, but he finally figured out who she reminded him of. It was Alexis. She took her glasses from him and put them back on.

"Holy Hannah, she's naked again!" she shouted, pointing to the screen. "In a giant bird's nest. I think she just did the bird-man-alien-guy."

Sean didn't bother to look up at the screen, he was intently studying Jane's face. He could now mentally remove the glasses and change the straight brown hair to sandy curls. The nose was a little more difficult to adjust, but there was no doubt... she looked a *lot* like Alexis.

A frightening thought popped into his head. "Umm, Jane," he said and waited until she looked at him. "You might think this a very odd question, but... you're not *Alex*, are you?"

She furrowed her brow as she tried to concentrate. "I don't think I'm going to get this one without some clues. So is that like New Zealandish for smart-aleck or something?"

"No... just Alex."

She puzzled some more, then whispered, "Is it like some kind of New Zealand code word for virgin?"

"No!" he groaned, "I just want to make sure of something. You never go by the name Alex, or Alexis, or Nicole, or Katherine, do you?"

She scrunched her face up as she gave serious consideration to his confounding question. "Nope," she finally declared. "Should I?"

"Definitely not!" Sean laughed.

"OK... good," she proclaimed with one sharp nod. "So is it my turn now?"

"Your turn?"

"Nigel," she said, trying her best to be serious, "Do you ever go by the name Andrew, Phillip, Richard, or..." she paused as she tried to come up with another name. "...or Raphael?" She giggled.

"No," he replied, then laughed with her.

"OK... your turn again!" She poked his chest with her index finger.

Sean enjoyed seeing her silly side but decided to shift the line of questioning. "Jane... were you about to kiss me on the dock before Peter interrupted us?"

Her silly grin vanished with a gasp and she stared deeply into his eyes. "Yes," she breathed. She looked down at her hands before continuing cautiously. "Nigel... were you about to kiss me on the dock before Peter interrupted us?"

"Yes," he replied, his voice just above a whisper.

She edged her face closer to his, her eyes locked on his eyes. Sean leaned into her. Jane turned her head for just an instant to pull her glasses off and a fleeting flash of the 'nose nightmare' slipped through Sean's mind. He instantly dismissed it when her lips softly brushed against his. He tilted his head and pulled at her lips with his own. His heart skipped a beat when he heard her sigh as their kiss deepened.

Fireworks. Flashes. His brain actually tingled. Electricity coursed through his entire body. It was beautifully baffling; totally unexpected and completely different than any other kiss he'd ever shared. He pulled away. His eyes were open wide in amazement, hers were closed as if savoring a perfect dream. They both softly gasped.

Her eyes fluttered open. Her cheeks flushed scarlet but then dimpled from her broad smile. "I think I hate your cousin Peter," she said softly.

"Me, too," he agreed, then slid his hand behind her neck and pulled her into another kiss. She slipped her arm under his and around him, pulling herself closer. Sean considered pulling back to check if there were sparks arcing between them. She moaned softly as she hungrily pulled at his lips. Sean's brain was ablaze. His heartbeat thudded in his ears like a tribal drum.

She pulled away.

"Wow," she gasped.

He sucked in a deep breath and happily nodded. "That *almost* says it, but is there a word that is like 'wow' to the tenth power?"

She studied his face, her own turning serious. "Did you like... see... flashes... I don't know... sparks?"

She felt it, too? "Yes. It was... amazing."

"Is it... always like that?"

"Not for me. How about you?"

"Oh..." she glanced away from him. "I thought.... I thought you knew I'd... I'd never kissed anyone before." Her cheeks burned again.

"Could have fooled me."

"Really?" she asked shyly. "It was OK?"

"We've already been to 'wow' and 'amazing' and now you want to back it up to 'OK'?"

"I didn't know what to expect." She again turned her head slightly away. "I didn't want to mess it up... by not being very good."

He slid his fingers slowly through her hair. "Everyone has a first kiss. It's not something you study for like a test."

She nodded thoughtfully, then looked him in the eye. "What was *your* first kiss like?"

Tiffany flashed through Sean's mind... both the pleasure and the anguish. "It was... different," he said slowly. "Very different from this."

"How?"

"Well..." Sean stalled, unsure if he wanted to dredge up old memories. "The first girl I kissed kind of... controlled it all. Looking back, I was probably a little sloppy... and after *just now* saying it's not something you study for, I kinda think I was... her little student." He looked away from Jane. She put her hand on his arm.

"Will you show me how to be better?" she asked timidly.

"No," Sean snapped, turning back to her. She was visibly shocked by his sharp response, so he continued with a gentler tone, "Come on. You don't need an instructor. Let your instincts and feelings guide you." He took one of her hands in both of his. "Were you thinking about technique when kissing me just now?"

"At first..." she confessed, "then it just kind of... happened." Her lips curled into another dimpled smile. "And it was out of sight!"

"I thought so, too," Sean agreed. "Who needs technique?"

"So it wouldn't help if..." she paused, looked down slightly and bit her lower lip. "...I practiced?" Her eyes sparkled as she lifted them back up to his.

"I didn't say *that!*" Sean chuckled as he slid an arm around her waist.

She pulled closer to him again, her eyes darting all around his face as she moved her lips slowly toward his. He didn't move, just smiled as he let her find her own way. As her lips softly brushed against his, he let his lips part slightly. She angled her face to better mesh with his and plunged into a deep kiss. He met her equally and gently rubbed his hand across her bare shoulders. She whimpered and his brain was ablaze again, sparks flying. Together they reclined against the curve of the saucer. He pulled her even closer, tighter. Her arms were around him, also pulling. At last her mouth slid from his, her lips brushed against his earlobe. "Don't let me fall," she breathed into his ear.

Her hair had tumbled over his face. "Fall?"

"Off this flying saucer. Aren't we at least a hundred feet in the air?"

He slid his hand under her hair and gently stroked her neck. "At least."

"Can we land it far, far away on a deserted tropical island?"

He ran his fingers through her hair and traced the edge of her ear. "What if it runs out of gas before we get there?"

"Then we'll plunge back to Earth in a magnificent fiery crash!" She hugged him tighter.

"Maybe we should just land it back at the drive-in..."

She pulled back a little and tapped him on his nose with a finger. "That's not very romantic."

"But if we died in a fiery crash you wouldn't get to practice kissing anymore."

She lifted herself up so that she was above him. "You have an excellent point," she said just before hungrily attacking his lips again.

She's perfect, Sean thought. *She's fun, she's sexy, she's witty, she's imaginative...* His heart sank when reality slapped him in the face. *...and she was born about the same time as my parents.*

His head and heart were suddenly at war. He felt a pang of guilt about leading her on. But he couldn't deny how amazing it was to be with her, even though he knew that when the night ended he'd never see her again. The joy of the moment shattered like delicate crystal hitting concrete. He gently pulled back from the kiss, determined to set things right. "And think of all the other guys that would miss out kissing a wonderful girl like you."

She pulled back further so she could see his entire face. "Why would I care about what other guys might miss?"

"C'mon, Jane, you've got to get out there and kiss a lot of guys," Sean urged, attempting to sound both cheerful and encouraging. "Then one day you'll find someone who's just the perfect match."

Her smile melted away. "What if I already have?" she countered.

An icy prickling crept into Sean's stomach. "That's sweet, luv... but we're from two different worlds."

"We don't have to be," she insisted.

"Jane..."

"I've only got one year of high school left," she continued. "I could find a college to go to in New Zealand."

"Jane..."

178

"They have colleges, don't they? It would be a super place to start over."

"Jane, you..."

She talked over him. "Nigel, I've never felt like this about anyone. What if you're my soul-mate?" Sean's heart raced, the fear that had crept into his stomach gripped his throat. "You said you saw the sparks," she asserted. "You said that it's not always like that. What if that's because we're *meant* to be together?"

Full blown panic overran Sean's brain. He struggled to formulate words. "Jane... no... I... we..."

"*Be yourself,* she quoted, *"Especially, do not feign affection. Neither be cynical about love; for in the face of all aridity and disenchantment it is as perennial as the grass.* That's a part of *Desiderata* that I left out earlier," she explained. "I'm not feigning affection... were you?"

"I... I... no... but, Jane, there can't be anything long term about us."

"*Neither be cynical about love...* don't be cynical, Nigel. It doesn't *matter* that we've come from two different worlds. Our worlds have collided! Don't let the past or circumstances make you cynical! I believe in love, Nigel! I believe that love can overcome obstacles!"

But can it overcome lies? Sean thought, miserably. *You think you're in love with Nigel Davies from New Zealand... someone who doesn't even exist.*

"Think about it," Jane continued. "Just hours after we met... at the dock. I wanted to kiss you so bad. I don't even know you, but I feel like I do... like I've *always* known you. I felt it again when I brought you the sandwiches, and I think you felt it, too."

It was pointless to try to reason with her. She was on an emotional high with maybe a little boost of wine high. He was overwhelmed by her enthusiasm, enthralled by her spirit, and at the same time, crushed by the despair of their impossible situation. He'd leave soon, and when he did, in the few minutes spent to travel back to 1995, Jane would age twenty-six years. He would prefer to make her understand that they couldn't be together, but considered that it might be best to just vanish. Vanish and let time heal whatever heartache she might face.

"Jane, Peter and I..."

"I know!" she interrupted, "I know you're going to hitch to New York and go to an amazing three-day concert, and I'm completely jealous. I'm not asking you to not go." Sean relaxed a bit, hoping she could see reason. "But why couldn't you come back this way after it's over?" She started digging into her bag.

"Jane..."

"Here!" she handed him a folded piece of paper. "My address and phone number." He took the paper and stared at it, dumbstruck. "I know you probably won't have a lot of time... but maybe if you get stuck in some town for awhile you could send me a postcard." She beamed at him with sparkling eyes. She threw her arms around his neck and pulled herself into him. "Oh,

Nigel! This is the best day of my life!" She leaned back to look at him again, her hands resting on his shoulders. He smiled sheepishly, still not sure what to say to her. She glided smoothly into him for another long soulful kiss.

He had to admit that even with all of the anxiety he felt, when she kissed him... there were sparks! She pulled back again. "You can call me the minute you get back to Mercer. I'll figure out a better place for you to stay. I'll figure out a way we can sneak off to a secluded place, just the two of us." She paused, looked away from his eyes. Her cheeks flushed. "We can make love before you have to go back home. We'll knit our hearts together for the months we're apart." She looked back into his eyes. "As soon as I graduate I'll come to New Zealand and we can be together the rest of our lives."

Sean felt overwhelmed. Jane was serious... at least she thought she was. Truthfully, parts of it sounded pretty good and might even work out... *if* he really were Nigel Davies. She snuggled into him again, contentedly resting her head on his chest. Reflexively, he stroked her hair as he tried to think. He found it strange that holding her close actually had a calming effect and his panic level started to subside. He'd decided it was pointless to reason with her. If he just didn't think about how she might feel when Nigel Davies never returns, if he would live only in the moment... it felt good. He slid the paper she'd given him into a pocket of his jeans.

His thoughts drifted as the shifting colors and shadows washed over them and he wondered if it could be just a coincidence that Jane looked so much like Alexis. If Alexis was modeled by his future wife, as Alex had told him, was Jane somehow related? *What if Jane has a daughter that grows up to be my wife?* He cringed at the thought of having shared a romantic kiss with his mother-in-law. *That's one good thing about Alex wiping my memory,* he decided, *I won't have to face the memory of kissing my mother-in-law during every Thanksgiving dinner. But would she recognize me? Nah, that's at least thirty years from now. She won't remember one night with a stupid New Zealand guy that ended up breaking her heart. Besides, it probably really is just a coincidence.* He could hardly wait to ask Alex if Jane would become his future mother-in-law.

"Nigel? You still there?" Jane asked. "Penny for your thoughts."

"Hmmm? Oh, right. Ummm... just thinking about the odd turn of events that brought our lives across each other's paths."

"You don't believe in fate?"

"I don't rightly know, luv. I guess I haven't thought about it much."

She propped herself up on an elbow and began drawing on Sean's chest with her finger. "I do. I mean, there are billions of people on Earth. We started out on opposite sides of the world. It's almost like magnets that we were drawn together."

"It's pretty mind-boggling," Sean admitted.

"I can't wait to tell Louise. It will blow her mind!" She pulled herself into another hug. "I wish tonight never had to end."

They lay there quietly on the saucer-shaped kids' climbing toy. The sound from dozens of tiny speakers behind them echoed eerily and seemed as abstract as the distorted picture that danced above them. It was nice, Sean decided, it was nice to just be together... even if it was for only one night.

"I suppose we should go back to the car," Jane eventually said. She slowly sat up and smiled back down on Sean.

"Right," he said as he sat up, "don't want them to forget we were along and leave without us."

Her eyes sparkled as she looked deeply into his, and the moment was too charged for Sean to ignore. *OK, why not... one more kiss.* He pulled closer to Jane and soulfully kissed her. His heart fluttered when she sighed... and as his brain tingled, he imagined sparks dancing between his synapses. He reluctantly released her lips and slowly stood, pulling her up beside him. She locked her wrists behind his neck as she again stared into his eyes, her smile soft and warm.

"You are amazing, Jane Carmichael!" He proclaimed as he lost himself in her eyes. *Tonight I won't think about how hurt you'll feel when I never returned. Tonight I'll live in the moment.*

"You're my koala, Nigel Davies," she affirmed as she slid her glasses back on.

It took him a moment to recognize what she was talking about and he immediately regretted his hastily made-up stories about pet names in New Zealand. He knew what she wanted him to say in return, but he didn't think he could. He couldn't give her that much hope only to break her heart. He could see it in her eyes, the expectation, and the longer he said nothing, the more doubt was creeping in. It would hurt her tonight if he didn't say it.

"You're my sweet little ladybug," he responded. Her misty eyes sparkled and she hugged him tightly as she covertly batted the joyful tears away, banishing the remains with a quick finger across her cheeks. When she released him, she slid her hand into his and they started back toward the cars.

Tonight, he thought, *just tonight.*

She nudged against him, changing their course toward the concession stand.

"What are you doing?" Sean asked.

"You said you'd buy me popcorn," she replied playfully.

"That's right... I did."

He opened the door for her and followed her into the smell of fresh popcorn. They glanced around at the hot-dogs rolling, the racks of candy, and the bored guy behind the counter, who happened to be the only other person in the stand. Jane started digging into her bag for her wallet.

"Hey," Sean said sharply, "I said I'd get the popcorn."

"I know," she replied. "You can get the popcorn. I'll get the rest of the stuff."

"What 'rest of the stuff'?"

181

"Nigel? Have you *never* been around anyone with the munchies? This will cost a bundle... but I'm going to make them pay me back."

"No, that's OK. I've got this. I've got a ten burning a hole in my wallet."

"You're going to need that!" she protested.

"Not really," he countered, then leaned into her ear to whisper. "Peter is actually loaded. He's got way more money than we need."

"Really?"

"Cross my heart," he said as he drew an X on his chest.

"Well, you should still make them pay you back," she insisted.

"Let me worry about that, luv."

"OK," she said, palms up in surrender, but shaking her head as if he was crazy.

"So what are we going to get?" Sean asked.

"We'll start with two of the giant tubs of popcorn." She checked the prices on the overhead board, then compared drink cup sizes. "Two extra-large Cokes and one large Tab. Two large and one medium empty cup..."

"Those are a nickel each," the counter guy interjected.

"That's a rip-off!" Jane protested.

Counter-guy crossed his arms and shrugged. "I don't make the rules, man, I just work here. I can fill the medium with ice... no charge."

"Fine!" Jane snarled, then added, "Capitalist," under her breath.

"Want some candy, man?" counter-guy suggested.

Jane studied all the different choices. Counter-guy watched her, waited until she looked back his way then pointed both his fingers to the display behind him.

"Yes!" Jane exclaimed, "Three packs of Twinkies!"

"Huh!" crowed counter-guy, "Thought so!"

Counter-guy took Sean's ten, packed the drinks into a cardboard carrying tray, bagged the Twinkies, filled the giant tubs with popcorn, and handed Sean his change. Sean stared at the returned money, amazed that he got change back from his ten dollar bill.

"OK," Jane advised, "If you can get the popcorn, I've got everything else." She bit down on the rolled up end of the bag of Twinkies and picked up the drink tray. Sean grabbed a tub of popcorn in each hand.

This is a lot of popcorn! he marveled, *That alone would take most of the ten dollars back home.*

Jane pushed the door open with her hips and backed her way out the door with Sean following after her.

When they got to the car, they set everything on the roof. Jane opened the back door and a sweet, acrid smoke rolled out to greet them.

"What the hell?" Jane exclaimed.

"Get in the front, man," Scott called back.

Jane slammed the back door. "You're not going to believe this, Nigel,"

Jane groaned, rolling her eyes as she opened the front passenger door and slid in. "Pass me the food and I'll hand it out." Sean shifted everything from the roof to Jane, one item at a time. When the last popcorn was in, she slid over to the middle. "OK, come on in."

Sean glanced into the back seat as he got in. Alex, Scott and his Dad were seated shoulder to shoulder in the back with Karen reclined across them.

"Where's your shirt?" Jane demanded.

"It got hot in here, man," Scott replied.

"I'm not talking to you!"

"Chill out, Jane," Karen replied testily, "I've got my bikini on. I thought we might go swimming later."

"Oh, man!" Scott crooned enthusiastically as he stuffed in a second fistful of popcorn. "This is like the *best* popcorn, like, ever!" Most of the popcorn made it into his mouth.

Jane faced the windshield with arms crossed. "Little tramp," she mumbled.

"What's in the cups, Jane?" John asked.

"The two biggest ones are Coke, the other one is Tab. If you pour half into each of the empty cups, we all get one," Jane explained to the windshield. "And there's extra ice in the medium cup."

"I can't breathe," Sean coughed. "I've got to roll down the window."

"What's in the bag, man?" Scott asked, then gushed, "Oh Sweet Hari Krishna! I've reached Nirvana!" Cellophane rattled as Scott tore into a pack of Twinkies.

Sean hung his head out of the window searching for fresh air. Alex rolled his window down and stuck his head out, leaning forward. "I am quite pleased that we stayed for this," he said to Sean, "It has been fascinating,"

"I'll bet," Sean replied. He pointed back inside with a head nod. "Don't eat the Twinkies, by the way. They have industrial strength preservatives. You could bury one now and go back to your own time, dig it up and it won't have changed."

Jane nudged Sean. "Here's your Coke... luv." He turned back toward Jane and took it from her just as she was turning away from him toward the backseat. "Did you guys figure out the ice and splitting the drinks?"

"We're on it, man!" Scott replied, then added to no one in particular, "popcorn and Twinkie-fluff together is like, beyond, man!"

"I'm doing the drink splitting, Jane," John quickly added.

"Then maybe it will actually turn out right," Jane muttered as she returned to face the front.

The car on their right's engine started and moved to a different spot.

"OK, try this one, man," Scott said. "Get your mouth like totally packed with popcorn and then take a huge drink of Coke, then like hold it for a couple of seconds and then mash it with your tongue. It is like *so* far out. The popcorn just kinda like *disintegrates!*"

"Here's your Tab, Jane," John said as he handed the cup over the seat.

"Thanks," Jane replied as she turned to take it. "Oh for— Karen! Just eat the damn Twinkie like a normal human being."

"I'm just showing Scott how much I can put in my mouth," Karen replied with a sultry tone. "Wanna have a contest?"

"Gross me out!" Jane exclaimed as she whirled back to face forward.

"Come on, Jane," Scott taunted. "It's fun!"

"See," Karen sneered, "Scott likes it!"

"I'll bet he does," Jane grumbled softly to the dash.

As the feeding frenzy continued in the backseat, Jane tried to ignore them as much as possible. She had her Tab in hand, and one of the tubs of popcorn sat on Sean's lap. She leaned her head against his shoulder as she reached for some popcorn. "So how do you like the drive-in?" she asked with a grin.

"Bits of it have been quite lovely," Sean replied. "And then some bits have been rather loony."

"What bits were lovely?" she cooed with a mischievous grin.

"I think you know."

She snuggled closer. "Sorry about the loony parts."

"Not your fault," Sean replied, "Besides, Peter gets a kick out of the looney bits."

"Really?" Jane asked. "He seems pretty quiet to me."

"Oh yeah, right studious our lad back there. Tries to figure out what goes on in people's noggins."

"So, like a psychiatrist or something?"

"I dunno... maybe. Always pictured him as more of a stuffy History teacher."

"You know," Scott announced loudly. "All of the aliens in this movie just look like regular people... well, except for the guy with the wings... but, you know, weird futuristic clothes, but just... people."

"So?" commented John.

"So, like in most of the stuff on Friday night Creature Feature, the aliens were always creepy monsters. You know, slimy or tentacles or some other weird stuff."

"Your point?" John asked.

"So, like, what's everyone think? Are the real aliens like people or more like the old we're-gonna-eat-you type monsters?"

"*Real* aliens?" Jane sneered, turning toward the backseat.

"Yeah," Scott continued gravely. "Monsters, or just people?"

"Maybe some of both," John suggested.

"Whoa!" Scott exclaimed. "Never thought of that. That makes sense." He stared hazily toward the ceiling as he tried to picture both. "I guess we'll just have to wait until they get here to find out for sure."

"Maybe they're *already* here," John reasoned.

"Whaddaya mean, man?" Scott asked, struggling to comprehend this new idea.

"If they look exactly like us, then they could already *be* here," John warned.

"You mean, like they snuck in and are just kind of hanging out, like, watching us?"

John struggled to hide his grin. "Sure. Why not."

"Whoa... that's creepy," Scott said with a shudder.

"For all we know, Peter and Nigel might really be aliens."

"No way, man!" Scott argued, eying Alex carefully.

"They *say* they just came into town hitchhiking," John embellished, "but maybe they had just landed their spaceship on the edge of town and walked in."

Karen, who had returned to her reclining position with her head in Alex's lap, looked up at him suspiciously.

"Why would they do that, man?" Scott asked, leaning slightly away from Alex.

"I don't know," John said, trying to make his voice sound mysterious. "Maybe just to study us, or maybe they intend to grab us and take us back to their planet."

Karen quickly sat up and put her arms around Scott's neck, tentatively looking back toward Alex. "But," she protested, "he's got a British accent."

"Maybe he learned English by watching British TV," John proposed in a low menacing voice.

Sean looked back at his Dad and smiled. *So he was a bit of a joker at my age*, he mused.

"Then why's he got a cousin from New Zealand?" Karen asked, her eyes flitting nervously between Sean and Alex.

"Just a better cover story," John declared.

"Come on, man," Scott said, trying to nervously laugh it all off, "they're not from outer space."

"You'll notice neither of them has denied it," John said coolly.

Scott and Karen both leaned away from Alex.

"Come on, man," Scott pleaded, panic rising in his voice, "this is crazy!"

"Ask him," urged John calmly.

"What?" Scott said, truly confused.

"Ask him," John repeated.

"Ask him *what*, man?" Scott whined.

"Ask him if he's an alien," John coaxed.

Scott's eyes were like saucers as his head swiveled between Alex and John repeatedly. After several seconds, Scott swallowed hard and focused on Alex. "S-s-s-sooo," he stuttered, then swallowed again, "like, Juan says you haven't denied it... so like, are you an alien or what?" He clamped his eyes shut and hugged Karen tightly.

Alex watched him patiently, a bemused smile on his face. He waited several moments before responding. "I hope you will not find it too disappointing that I was actually born on this planet... just like you." Scott opened his eyes and exhaled a sigh of relief. "But nearly 250 years into your future."

Sean spun around to face his descendant. "Alex!" he hissed, "What the hell?"

"The future?" Scott gulped.

"Why are you telling them?" Sean shouted, near panic.

"Yes," Alex replied calmly to Scott, "2217 if you need a precise date." He turned to Sean, "and *Nigel*...it is part of the experiment." He stressed Sean's pseudonym.

Jane looked quizzically at Sean, then Alex.

"Why are you here?" Scott asked, his voice nearly childlike.

"Maybe something went terribly wrong in the future," John reasoned. "And the only way to fix it was to come back to the past and change something."

Sean's jaw dropped as he stared at his Dad. *How did he come up with that idea?*

"Fix it how?" Scott whimpered to John.

"I'd say he needs to remove someone who is at the source of the problem," John speculated. "And since he's already admitted who he is, I'd say it must be someone in *this* car... or maybe he's just going to kill *all* of us!"

Pandemonium erupted. Scott pushed against John, crying, "Let me out, man! Let me out!" Karen crawled over the back of the seat and whacked Jane's head with her knee as she tumbled through. John erupted into hysterical laughter. Alex calmly watched the chaos with a bemused smile. Sean's eyes darted between Alex and his Dad. He wondered why Alex had unmasked them, and how his Dad could possibly know the plot to *Terminator*? Jane jerked forward with a hand to her head where Karen kicked her. "I don't want to die!" screamed Scott as Karen continued to tumble forward toward the floor. She caught herself on the steering wheel, blaring the horn. John convulsed in laughter.

"That was great!" John gasped. "Oh man, Peter, that was amazing!"

Karen disentangled her arm from the horn, but her feet were against the ceiling, her skirt inverted around her midriff. "I guess it's a good thing you *did* wear your bikini," Jane commented dryly as she continued to rub the back of her head.

"And Nigel," John hooted, "that bit where you were pretending to be shocked that Peter said you guys were from the future... that was a great touch. Almost like you guys had rehearsed it!"

The driver of the car to their left started his engine and moved to another spot.

Scott gazed at Alex's calm face, then turned to see his long-time friend still red-faced from laughter. Jane eyed Sean suspiciously. He smiled innocently and shrugged his shoulders.

"So you're not going to kill us?" Scott asked Alex.

"No."

"And you're not really an alien?"

"No."

"And you're not really from the future?"

When Alex didn't immediately respond, Sean jumped in, "That'd be a good one, wouldn't it? If we had a time-machine, Peter, we wouldn't have to worry about how long it takes to hitchhike to New York, we could just pop into whatever and be there, yeah?"

"Oh man, Scott, you should have seen your face," John teased, getting some control over his laughter. "'Let me out man' and 'I don't want to die'... oh man, that was too much!"

Jane pushed Karen's legs down and away from her as she struggled to get back upright.

"Not cool, man!" Scott groused.

"Aw come on! You were the one that brought up aliens," John reminded him, "I just improvised from where you started. I didn't know that Peter and Nigel would play along so convincingly." He paused and his eyes twinkled. "Or maybe they *didn't*... maybe they still really *are* aliens!" He cackled hysterically again.

"Well, technically, anyone from foreign soil would be an alien to this country," Sean pointed out, hoping to keep things from getting crazy again.

Jane held up a nearly empty cup. "I'm sorry, Juan," she said, "but I think I spilled my Tab all over up here when Karen kicked me in the head."

"I didn't *mean* to," Karen snapped sourly.

"Yeah, I think there's Coke and popcorn all over back here, too," John reported, grinning and wiping the tears from his eyes. "I'll clean it up tomorrow. No big deal."

"You're a jerk!" Scott complained, punching John in the shoulder.

"Yeah," John smiled, "but you're a sucker."

Scott stared coldly at John for several seconds before breaking into a big grin. "Yeah, I guess that was pretty funny... now that it's over and we're not dead."

Several car engines started and headlights came on all around them. Credits started scrolling up the screen.

"Speaking of over..." Jane pointed to the screen.

"I guess we'd better get everyone back where they belong and head out," acknowledged John.

"Yeah... how about front seat just swaps Karen for Peter, and I'll drive home?" Jane suggested.

"I'm cool," John declared as he opened the back door and got out. Karen also got out, and Jane slid under the wheel and pulled the front door closed. "Seriously, Jane, I'm cool," John asserted, leaning through the window.

Jane patted his arm. "I know you are, Juan... but why don't you just sit back and enjoy your mellow?"

He considered her offer. "No hot-rodding?"

"Scout's honor," Jane promised, holding her hand in a piece sign.

"Were you a scout?" John asked.

"No."

"Good enough for me," John chuckled, handing his keys through the window.

Sean slid over to Jane. "Are you sure *you're* all right? Maybe I should drive."

She smiled at him. "I've already burned off my little buzz... I'm fine. And anyway, have you got an American driver's license?"

Sean thought of his license that Alex had hidden away and imagined showing it to a cop if he happened to get pulled over. "Good point."

Alex joined them in the front seat and they were soon on their way out of the drive-in.

"Can you pop in 'Somebody to Love'?" Karen called from the back seat.

"No!" Sean and Jane said simultaneously.

"Harsh," grumbled Karen, sitting back with crossed arms.

"So...umm... Juan, where did you come up with the idea of someone coming from the future to terminate someone who was the root of a future problem?" Sean asked.

"Hmmm? ...oh, from a movie I saw a couple years ago. Anyone else see it? *Cyborg 2087.*" He looked around. "No? Michael Rennie? Same guy that was in *The Day the Earth Stood Still*? Anyway, he's some cyborg that comes from the future and tries to stop the scientist that invents the stuff that makes cyborgs possible because everything is all messed up in the future. I think he even wore the same shiny suit that he wore in *The Day the Earth Stood Still.*"

"Yeah, what is it with people from the future and their shiny suits?" Sean quipped with a wink toward Alex. *So Terminator is a retread of a 60s movie? Weird... the things you find out when you visit the past.*

"Anyone wanna stop and get something to eat?" Scott asked.

"No!" Sean and Jane said simultaneously.

"Harsh," Karen confirmed with a nod to Scott.

"For sure!" Scott agreed. They rode silently for a few seconds. "How 'bout we light up one more joint for the road?"

"No!" Sean and Jane said together even louder.

"Man... front seat is a complete downer. You guys are a drag," Scott complained, then settled into making out with Karen the rest of the way back to Mercer.

"Juan," Jane called, "You got any tapes that are mostly mellow?"

"Let me think," John replied. He paused to mentally review the tapes he had in the car. "There's *The Associations Greatest Hits*... that's pretty mellow. I think it's in the glove compartment."

Alex stared blankly at the compartment in front of him, unsure how to open it. Sean reached over and popped it open. Alex pulled out a half dozen 8-track tapes and handed them to Sean. Sean shuffled through the titles, found the one by the Association, and returned the rest to Alex. He was relieved to find that the Jefferson Airplane tape was still halfway in the player, so he didn't have to fumble around figuring out which direction to stick the tape into the unfamiliar device. He removed the old tape and pushed on the new one until he felt it click. Music started immediately.

After just a few bars, Jane reached over and punched a button that changed the track. She rotated through all four tracks, then stopped on one.

"I think this is the one I want... coming up after this song," she said.

They cruised through the quiet countryside on the two-lane highway that led back to Mercer. The scenery that sped by was mostly telephone poles, bushes, and trees as well as the occasional darkened farm house whose inhabitants were long since in bed. There were no other cars on the road in either direction.

Jane broke through the solitude as a new song began to play. "This is it," she said as patted Sean's leg. He was still amazed to recognize songs from this era and actually knew the lyrics as well as if they were popular in 1995. He knew the one that had just started was called *Cherish*. He glanced at Jane and saw that she was either softly singing along or at least mouthing the words. She looked his way and smiled as she mouthed the words at the end of each verse to him. *...cherish me as much as I cherish you... ...make you see that you are driving me out of my mind.... ...touch your face, your hands, and gaze into your eyes.*

Sean also noticed, with some remorse, that she skipped singing along with the fourth verse. He sighed as he realized it was the verse most appropriate for him to sing to her. *Perish is the word that more than applies / To the hope in my heart each time I realize / That I am not gonna be the one to share your dreams / That I am not gonna be the one to share your schemes / That I am not gonna be the one to share what / Seems to be the life that you could / Cherish as much as I do yours.* His emotions overrode his reason as he let himself briefly wonder what it would be like if they *could* be together.

He was determined to ask Alex to find out more about Jane, as soon as they were back at the camp. Whether she would one day become his mother-in-law or not, he wanted to at least know that she was happy. *Would that make me feel less guilty about vanishing from her life,* he wondered. *Was she really as head-over-heels in love with me as she seems?* His thoughts tortured him. *Honestly, if we only lived in the same time, I'd be thrilled to have her as a girlfriend.*

"Girlfriend," he mouthed silently as he realized his current best hope for a girlfriend in 1995 was sitting to his right. *Insane,* he decided, *Totally insane. Jane's in love with Nigel Davies... who doesn't exist... and I'm in love with Nicole Townsend... who also doesn't really exist.* His head dropped back and he squeezed his eyes shut. It felt like they were all trapped in one of Shakespeare's mistaken identity plays.

Alex leaned into Sean's ear and whispered, "Do you believe Scott and Karen will actively engage in coitus with no regard for the proximity of the rest of us?"

Sean mentally rewound Alex's question several times as he attempted a translation. He glanced over his shoulder to the backseat long enough to witness Scott and Karen's intense lip-lock, then whispered back, "No, I don't think so... but I'm pretty sure that once they get back in his car, he won't be taking her right home." Alex nodded thoughtfully.

Jane had sung along with *Windy* and *Never My Love* before they reached Mercer. *Along Comes Mary* had just started as she pulled into a parking spot between Scott's Plymouth and her VW. The back door flew open before they came to a complete stop.

"Great party, man," Scott said enthusiastically as he and Karen scrambled out. "We'll have to do it again sometime. Catch you later." They were backing the Plymouth out before Jane had even shut off the Impala's engine.

"Juan?" Jane said, turning her head. "Are you awake?"

"Yes."

"How are you doing?"

"Very mellow."

"Cool," Jane nodded. She paused. "You think you can drive home?"

"Most definitely."

"I could take you home in Lemon Drop," Jane volunteered.

"I'm cool," John said. "It would not be cool tomorrow for my parents to ask where my car is. I'm good to go."

"Be careful," she admonished. "Pay attention. Think about driving. Don't think about other stuff, just driving."

John popped open the back door. "You're a good friend, Jane." He slammed the back door and opened the front. "But you worry too much." Jane got out and John slid in behind the wheel. Alex had already opened his door and was out, Sean was sliding his direction. "Hey, man," John said. Sean turned back to see his Dad's smiling face. "Nice meeting you, man."

"Yeah. Good to meet you, too... Juan," Sean replied, feeling his throat tighten just a bit.

"Be nice to Jane, OK?" John said. "I think she likes you."

It was tough getting fatherly advice from someone his own age... particularly when the person giving it really was Sean's Dad. "Yeah," Sean replied. "I like her, too. She's pretty special."

John flashed him a peace sign. "Peace, brother. Hey, if I don't see you before you take off for Woodstock..." He trailed off, nodding and grinning.

"Yeah, peace," Sean jumped in to fill the lapse, blinking to keep his eyes from tearing up. They sat nodding at each other for a few moments before Sean slid out.

So, just now, Sean mused, *just before we head back to 1995 I have a moment with my Dad.* He sadly shook his head. The trip to the past hadn't been anything like what he had anticipated.

"Act cool," Jane hissed over the car. "Act like you're still talking. Lean in."

Sean played along. "What's going on?" he called through the car.

"Dietz," warned Jane. "We need to act like we're hanging out, then before he can circle back around we need to get out of here." She stood and faced the street, smiling and waving as the Mercer patrol car rolled slowly by, Officer Dietz giving them a cold stare. "OK, Juan, we both go up the street, you turn left on seventh, I'll turn right. Keep zigzagging each block until you get to the west side of town, then you can backtrack to the highway and head home. Hopefully, he won't run into either of us, if he bothers to come back... which from the look on his ugly face, I think is likely."

Sean marveled at how quickly she could transform into the amazing "in-charge" Jane. She seemed to especially rise to the occasion when a policeman was around. Sean really liked this facet of Jane, but most of all, he enjoyed how multifaceted she was.

Alex climbed into the backseat of Jane's beetle and they soon were all headed the opposite direction from the police car's path. Jane took a zigzag course to the north and east. She soon hit the highway that swung towards the lake. "I hope Dietz doesn't stop Juan," she fretted as she shifted up to highway speed. They rode a few moments in silence.

"So..." Sean said when the quiet began to make him nervous, "Lemon Drop?"

"What?" asked Jane.

"Lemon Drop," Sean repeated. "You call your car Lemon Drop?"

"Yeah," she said, shrugging, "sometimes."

"That's cute. I like it."

"Do you have a car back home?"

"Ummm, yes," Sean mumbled, wondering if that was the smart reply.

"What kind?"

Uh oh, am I going to get trapped by not knowing what kind of car I should have in New Zealand? "Ford," he blurted.

"What year?"

I don't think I'm going to tell you 1987. "It's seen a few years from the old assembly line."

"You mean like an old junker?"

Sure, that sounds good. "Yeah, kinda."

"And do you have a name for *your* car?"

"No," Sean responded, "Not unless you consider 'piece of junk' a proper name."

Jane pulled onto the road that led to the lake.

"How can you expect a car to be dependable if you don't give it a nice name?"

"It's a machine, it doesn't need a name," Sean said defensively.

"Like Steffi?" Alex whispered.

Jane lovingly rubbed the dashboard. "Don't listen to him, Lemon Drop, he just hasn't met a decent car yet."

Sean glanced back at Alex long enough to give him an evil eye. "All right, luv, I promise to give my car a name when I get back home," he said to Jane. She smiled back at him and nodded approval.

They pulled onto the twisty road that curved around the lake. Jane leaned right to attempt to be in Alex's line of sight as she briefly twisted toward the back seat. "Peter, did you have a good time?"

"I must say," Alex replied in his crisp English accent, "it was a most delightful evening all round."

Sean rolled his eyes.

"It was very enlightening," Alex added.

"Enlightening," Jane said slowly, rolling the word around in her head. "Nigel said you like to figure out what goes on in people's heads. So do you, like, get more introspective when you're stoned?"

"Stoned?" questioned Alex.

"Under the influence, mate," Sean interjected, then held pinched fingers in front of his lips and loudly sucked in.

"Oh," Alex uttered, then stopped to consider the implication. "Yes, I would say that the presence of marijuana induced a higher level of introspection tonight."

"You know," Jane observed as she glanced at Alex's reflection in her rear-view mirror, "just looking at you, I don't think I would suspect that you're stoned. You must be able to, like, really contain yourself within yourself."

Sean and Alex both nodded thoughtful agreement, even though neither had any idea what Jane meant.

The little yellow beetle pulled onto the rugged path down into the cove and stopped.

"Think it's dry enough that I can get down to the camp and back up?" Jane asked.

"I wouldn't try it," Sean advised. "Peter and I can just walk down, no big deal."

She shut the engine off. Sean got out and pulled his seat forward so Alex could get out. Jane also got out and leaned on the roof, waiting until Alex was standing. "I'm glad you went with us, tonight, Peter. It was fun... and I'm glad you found it 'enlightening'," she said to him over the car top.

"It was very kind of you to arrange the outing," Alex responded courteously. They all stood quietly, glancing at each other. Alex continued, "I suppose we should get down to the camp, Nigel."

Sean locked eyes with Jane. Hers were pleading as her head barely nodded toward Alex. "Ummm, Peter, old man," Sean proposed, "If you wouldn't mind going ahead, I'll catch up to you."

Alex looked quizzically to Sean, then Jane. Jane flashed him a quick smile, then looked away. Even in the dim starlight, Alex could see her cheeks darken. "Oh," he said, "right, then. I should just be off, then, and give you two a moment." He started toward the camp.

"Peter," Jane called after him, "can you see OK in the dim light? I've got a flashlight."

"Not needed," Alex replied confidently. "I have excellent night vision."

Probably some kind of nanite sonar or super-suit night goggles, thought Sean.

As Alex disappeared into the shadows, Sean walked around the car and slid an arm around Jane. She smiled up at him, then burrowed her face into his neck.

"I wish I could spend the rest of the night with you," she confessed. "My parents know the movie got out late, but if I don't get home pretty soon, they'll freak out. They go to bed, but I think my dad just lays there awake until I get home... maybe my mom does, too."

"I suppose it *is* pretty late."

She crushed herself against him, then released and tilted her head to look up into his eyes. "Oh, Nigel," she sang, "it was just the best night." She hugged him again, then slid her glasses off and set them on the roof of her VW. Sean bent his face closer to her and she lifted her chin as she reached for his lips, unwilling to wait for them to come to her. They locked tightly, passionately. Sean's hand glided over Jane's bare shoulders. Jane slipped her fingers through Sean's long hair. They pulled at each other hungrily, released briefly, and then plunged their lips back together. As they released again, Jane let her lips slowly slide over Sean's chin and down his neck. He felt the sparks again, pulsing through his body. She snuggled in. "I've got to go," she finally sighed.

"I know," he replied softly.

"I don't want to."

"I know."

They had held each other quietly for several minutes before she took a step back. "How's *your* night vision," she gently inquired.

"Actually," he admitted, "if you wouldn't mind... I could use that flashlight."

She pulled her glasses on and got back into the beetle. In an instant, she handed the flashlight out the window.

"Thanks," he said as he took it and flipped it on.

She started the engine, then leaned out the window. "Goodnight, ko...." she stopped, a little embarrassed. "Nigel... I love you intensely, but it just feels silly to call you *koala,*" she giggled.

"That's OK, luv," he replied. "It just doesn't sound quite right with an American accent."

"But I do like it when you call me *ladybug*," she grinned, then blushed.

"All right... ladybug," Sean winked. "Goodnight."

"Goodnight," she murmured as she let out the clutch allowing the Volkswagen to inch forward. "I'll see you tomorrow... or I guess later today."

"Sweet dreams," he called as she pulled away.

The guilt he felt was crushing and he berated himself with every step back to the camp. Why did it feel so right to be with her, to hold her, to kiss her? It was selfish of him. Selfish to enjoy being with her when he knew that he was leaving and would never see her again. He trudged on toward the campsite, swinging the beam of the flashlight in front of his path, desperate to free himself from his miserable thoughts. He'd have Alex look Jane up... find out about her life. He'd feel better once he knew she was happily married with two or three kids... one of which might even become his wife someday. The thought of Jane becoming his future mother-in-law was intriguing... and a little bit creepy. The resemblance to Alexis was striking. Change the hair and the nose, lose the glasses, and she looked a *lot* like Alexis.

He had cheered himself up a bit. Even though Jane would feel hurt when she figured out that he was never coming back, her life would go on. She'd probably go to college, meet some nice guy who won't care about her nose and they'd fall in love. *She'll be happy,* he told himself, *it'll be great.*

Alex was sitting in one of the chairs when Sean reached the campsite. He stood, and was about to speak when Sean jumped in ahead of him. "What the hell were you doing telling them we were from the future?"

Though surprised by Sean's sudden tirade, Alex answered calmly, "It seemed a logical segue to what your father had started. Did you not find it fascinating how susceptible Scott was to suggestion... just normal suggestion, not what I can do."

"What if they believed you?" Sean demanded as he picked up the Coleman lantern and lit it.

"Given that the initial assumed context was that we were possibly alien lifeforms, I fail to see why they would have been any more susceptible to believe we were from the future. It was obvious that your father intended to evoke a humourous reaction to Scott's logically impaired reasoning; therefore, he would assume that I was taking part in the scenario he invented. Scott and Karen were emotionally set to believe whatever Juan told them, and of course you already knew the truth."

"That still leaves Jane."

"I will grant you that she had the most potential to correctly ascertain that we were from the future. However, it was my observation that she has become enamored with you, and therefore would not want anything to jeopardize her vision of who you are. Perhaps the greatest risk was when you called me 'Alex' rather than 'Peter'. However, I believe it went largely unnoticed in the pandemonium that ensued."

"It would have been nice to have had a heads-up before you launched into your little experiment."

"I would agree... however, the decision to participate in your father's ploy was serendipitous."

Sean wished he could connect to Steffi's computer for access to a dictionary for some snappy phrase to come back with, but he decided to change directions in the conversation. "So did Karen kiss you again while I was gone?"

"I was of the impression that she was going to, but it turned out her intent was to exhale smoke that I was to then inhale. It still seemed to be a rather intimate connection."

"Let me ask you something... when Karen kissed you earlier, did you see stars or feel sparks or anything?"

"I was certainly taken by surprise, but I do not believe I understand your reference to sparks or stars. After the initial surprise, I was concerned about any transference of bacteria. The human mouth in your century has over 600 different species of bacteria. Granted, most are either harmless or beneficial, but my mouth is my least guarded orifice while wearing the pseudo-body suit."

"Orifice? Wow! *That's* romantic! I think I can safely say that you probably didn't see any stars."

"Can you elaborate? I still am not sure what you are asking."

"Fine," Sean said, breathing out a heavy sigh. "I don't like to kiss and tell, but when I kissed Jane tonight, it was... different."

"Different from what?"

"From any other girl I've ever kissed. That's what I mean. I felt sparks in my brain. I saw little flashes that were like stars," Sean reminisced, grinning happily from the memory. "She said she felt it, too."

"Were you near any objects that could have given an electrical discharge?"

"No, we were sitting in the playground."

"Perhaps a static electricity buildup?"

"No, not that kind of sparks. Never mind... I can't explain it, and even if I could, I don't think you'd get it."

"Perhaps it was a phenomenon caused by a spike of adrenaline brought on by emotional intimacy at the moment of osculation, randomly firing synapses."

"OK, just forget it. I don't need a scientific examination," Sean growled. He calmed himself before he continued, "There is one thing I'd like to know... did I just make out with my future mother-in-law?" Reading the baffled look on Alex's face, Sean continued. "I figured it out. Jane looks a *lot* like Alexis. You said Alexis was modeled after my someday wife, so I thought maybe Jane is going to be her mother." Alex blinked several times before speaking.

"No," he reported flatly. "Jane will not become your mother-in-law."

"Are you sure?"

"I know your mother-in-law's name. It is not Jane."

"Maybe she changes her name."

"Unlikely."

"Maybe Jane has a kid and gives it up for adoption, and that kid grows up to become my wife. So then Jane is my biological mother-in-law, even if she isn't 'officially' my mother-in-law."

"You are formulating a very complex and highly improbable scenario based solely on a resemblance between Jane and Alexis. If you would scrutinize your hypothesis, you would realize how far-fetched it sounds."

"Look it up," Sean demanded.

"Look what up?"

"Whatever you can find on Jane's life. You know, like how we found out who Louise is going to marry. See what you can find out about Jane. I want to at least know that she's happy somewhere in 1995."

"You wish to know who she marries?"

"Yeah, and anything else you can get. Like does she have kids, have a career, where she lives in the future. Start with the local paper, like we did with Louise."

Alex twitched into query mode. Almost immediately the color drained from his face. "Gursk," he whispered.

"What?" Sean demanded.

"I am cross-checking," Alex snapped back.

"What is it?"

"*Quiet!*" Alex commanded. He became a statue, his eyes staring far into the distance. Then he suddenly turned away from Sean and dropped his head.

"*What?*" Sean screamed.

Slowly Alex turned back to Sean. His face was somber. His lips quivered slightly. "Jane Carmichael," he reported evenly, "is killed in an automobile accident in October of this year."

Chapter Ten

"As the present now / Will later be past / The order is Rapidly fadin'"

"**WHAT?**" Sean gasped.

"Jane Carmichael is killed in an automobile accident in October of this year," Alex repeated soberly. "October 10th."

"That's got to be a mistake," insisted Sean.

"I have cross-checked several sources."

"But... she's only seventeen..." Sean mouthed, bewildered.

"Age is irrelevant in an automobile accident," Alex stated flatly. "In 1969 there were more people killed on American highways than in the Vietnam War."

"We have to tell her."

"Tell her what?"

"About the *accident!*" Sean screamed.

Alex cringed slightly from Sean's angry outburst. "You want her to be aware of when she is going to die?"

"No, you idiot!" Sean shrieked. "To stop it from happening!"

Alex looked timidly at Sean, watched his chest heave as he breathed rapidly, saw his flared nostrils and fierce eyes.

"I thought you understood the first law of time-travel," Alex reasoned cautiously.

"We're talking about *Jane*, here," Sean threatened.

"History is not to be changed," Alex argued, almost chanted.

"We're not talking about Jorge Gang-banger or Old Guy in Chicago," Sean growled. "This is *Jane!*"

"Her death is a historical fact."

Sean glared at Alex. "You heartless bastard!" His voice was level with icy menace. "How *dare* you treat her like a statistic?"

Alex cowered, visibly shook as he thought carefully about his next words. "I am sorry that she will die so young. It is very tragic. It is certainly a waste for someone so vibrant to end so abruptly."

"Stop talking about it like she's already dead!" Sean exploded.

"She is dead for more than a decade before you are even born. You should never have even known anything about her... and you will *not* know once we return to your time."

Sean glared at him coldly. "You're not even a human being anymore," he snarled. "Years of 'civilization' and science has snuffed any spark of humanity out of you."

"You know that is not true," Alex refuted.

"Do I? I'm looking at someone who won't lift a finger to save a friend. That seems like pretty damning proof to me."

"We have already discussed this," Alex proclaimed, as if factually delivering a presentation in a corporate office. "There are millions of people spanning the spectrum of time that have died tragically before they have the opportunity to reach old age. It is an unpleasant side of life that we must accept. Even the science that allows time-travel cannot change untimely deaths for all those people."

"I'm not talking about 'all those people'," Sean raved, "I'm just talking about Jane!"

"I truly am sorry that she will die young. She is a very likable person."

"Then *change* it!" Sean demanded.

Alex fearfully studied Sean's stern face and braced himself. "No," he said softly.

"Then *I* will!" roared Sean.

"I cannot allow that."

Rage blurred Sean's vision. Without conscious thought, he swung a fist at Alex's face.

The next thing he knew, he was lying on the ground.

"How?" he asked once his senses had returned.

"I anticipated you might truly become violent over this incident. You will recall that I told you I put two fail-safe protocols into play before you could come with me to 1969."

"You used the blackout thing?"

"Yes."

"You bastard!" Sean spat.

"If necessary, I will return you to an unconscious status until we reach 1995."

Sean looked up at him, carefully weighing his options. "No... I guess that won't be necessary."

"That is good. I do not enjoy harming you."

"Good to know," Sean replied softly, his voice thick with defeat.

"I think we should depart as soon as I get back."

"Get back?"

"Yes," Alex explained, "Do you not recall that I am going to drop back a few hours in time and follow the car to the drive-in?"

"Oh, yeah," Sean recalled, "so you can stay in contact with the computer."

"Correct."

"So where is the 'other' you now?"

"I would assume that I am a little more than five miles away, waiting until this iteration of me departs from this section of time."

"So it will take you awhile to get back?" asked Sean, a plan bubbling in his brain.

"Not really. Once I walk over to Steffi and launch, I will return to this spot. It will seem like minutes for you, but, of course, it will be hours for me before returning from the drive-in."

"Could you just give me a little time alone?" Sean requested, "I just want to be alone."

"To grieve?" Alex asked gently. "... I understand." Although he wasn't really sure if he did.

"I'll just be in the camper. I'll come out when I'm ready... OK?"

"Yes. I will land here and wait until you come out."

"Thanks."

"I am truly sorry for your loss, Sean Kelly. It has been a shock to both of us, and it is very sad."

"Just... just leave me alone for awhile," Sean said as he grabbed the Coleman lantern and went into the tent.

Sean listened intently to gauge Alex's progress through the underbrush, then when satisfied he was gone, began searching the camper. "Come on, Grandpa Kelly... a pen, a pencil... something." He rummaged through the few items inside the tent, finding nothing. His last hope was the fishing tackle-box. He found fishing line, weights, bobbers, lures, hooks, and a pen-knife, but no pen or pencil. "Damn it, Grandpa Kelly... just a lousy stubby pencil... you couldn't have a lousy pencil?" He looked around frantically, anxious about how much more time he had.

He gave up his futile search of the spartan tent and went outside lifting the lantern high to shine around the campsite. He considered trying to use pieces of the charred logs, but decided it would be too smeary. He could see nothing that could readily be used as a writing instrument, but continued to look, hoping to avoid his other option.

Time was running out and he had to make a decision... it wasn't one he relished, but he could think of nothing else. He snapped off part of one of the sticks they had used for hot-dogs and sharpened a clean, sharp point on an eight inch piece. He took it back into the tent, pulled out the piece of paper with Jane's address on it, and reached into the tackle-box. He selected what he thought was, hopefully, the cleanest hook, poised it over his left thumb, breathed in and out several times to steel his nerves, then stabbed it into his thumb. He squeezed his thumb to express a large drop of blood and dipped the tip of the sharpened stick into it.

Ignoring the pain, he began the tedious process of squeezing, dipping, and writing a single letter. Squeeze, dip, write, squeeze, dip, write, he labored over the small piece of paper under the lantern light.

"Today is July 13th, 1969...."

Alex waited patiently for Sean to emerge from the camper. Although it had been only minutes for Sean, Alex had taken a short hop back to 8pm and then spent hours away, most of it hovering over the drive-in nearly comatose in a self-induced trance-like state. But during travel between Mercer and Colgate, he had time to reflect on the evening. It had been enlightening and even enjoyable to observe how mood and perception were altered with the usage of marijuana. Scott was easily convinced that Alex and Sean were from outer space.

It would have been an enjoyable end to their visit to 1969, if only Sean had not requested information about Jane Carmichael's life. Alex truly regretted that Jane would not reach that happy future that Sean had asked him to search for. He did have his own feelings for her, obviously not as strong as Sean's, but he found it pleasant to be with her. She seemed more mature and intelligent than her friends in general, particularly if he ignored her flagrant disregard for safety while driving.

Initially, he had supposed that it was Jane's own reckless abandon toward driving that would have been the cause of her early demise. But further scrutiny of the available data sources showed she was a passenger in a car driven by a Willie Brighton. One other passenger in addition to Jane was terminated, Willie and a fourth passenger were hospitalized with multiple fractures and contusions. The other survivor was Tony Caparelli, Louise's friend. The second fatality was a Randel Hunter.

Alex thought it odd that Jane was even in that particular vehicle, considering she had insisted there be at least one other female in the car when they went to the drive-in. He wondered what circumstances had led her to be in the ill-fated vehicle. According to the historical documents he had consulted, the crash occurred on a graveled country road as the vehicle lost control and rolled when it left the road while being pursued by a county deputy.

Alex also contemplated the other chain of events that affected this incident. Had Sean not earlier taken him into an emotional state with regard to the homicides of the three people he had randomly selected as statistics, his position about Jane may have been different. His emotional state had been pushed to the point of nearly convincing him to interfere, potentially stopping the historically recorded deaths. He wondered if he had initially entered into that emotional state upon the discovery of Jane's demise, might he have been more easily swayed to take action, especially with Sean's insistence.

It still caused Alex considerable distress that Jane would face a violent early death, and he certainly felt sorrow that Sean was so deeply hurt by his decision to allow history to unfold as it had been recorded. He would need to further examine his own balance between emotions and logic once Sean was returned to his normal life. It pained him to realize that the things he was learning were far from what he had anticipated.

The tent flap unzipped and Sean stepped out, carrying the lantern. Alex could see the anguish was still fresh in Sean's eyes. It had only been minutes since he experienced the confrontation that had been hours earlier for Alex. He didn't move as Sean approached him, stopping several feet away.

"Are you prepared to return to 1995?" Alex asked quietly.

"I'm not talking to you," Sean snarled.

Alex fought the reflex to cringe from the force of Sean's voice. He waited several moments before speaking again. "I have had time, since you last saw me, to ponder some things... and I wish to tell you something."

"Have you changed your mind about warning Jane?" Sean asked hopefully.

"No," Alex uttered cautiously.

"Then I don't care what you have to say," Sean growled.

"I shall tell you all the same," Alex retorted. "I wish to apologize for bringing you on this journey to 1969. It was ill advised, and I should have projected the potential negative repercussions. It was my own vanity that tempted me to observe you in a different era as well as allow you to meet your own father as a teenager. I had no right to make you a subject in an experiment."

"Like you hadn't already back in 1995!" Sean countered.

"It was ill-advised," Alex continued without acknowledging Sean's outburst, "for me to allow my own feelings toward you to cause me to consider extending your interaction with me on a peer level."

"You never considered me a peer!" Sean sneered.

"Therefore, I wanted you to know that upon returning you to 1995 and disconnecting your access to memories of what has transpired; that I will never again revive those memories for you. Furthermore, I shall take steps to extract the Townsend family from your life shortly after our return. I will vacate 1995 and allow you to live the rest of your life normally."

"Too bad you can't just completely wipe my memory of Alexis and Nicole."

"I had considered that, but it would be nearly impossible to reach everyone in the school to also remove their memories. It would then be odd for you to not know about Alexis and Nicole when someone else brought them up in conversation."

"Whatever."

"You recall that when we return, you will still be at the movies with Nicole."

"Looking forward to it," Sean said sarcastically.

"I will need your cooperation to place you back into position to seamlessly return you to that reality."

"As long as I don't have to do it cheerfully," Sean sneered.

"No, I do not expect you to be able to alter your emotional state as long as you are aware of who I really am and where we have been."

"Good to know."

"Are you prepared to enter the S.T.E. and return to 1995?"

Sean paused several moments before speaking. "Do they still have manners where you come from?"

"That question seems to be a non-sequitur."

"You know... a set of social graces," Sean continued.

"I do not believe I understand the reason for your inquiry."

"Things that your parents taught you about how to treat other people."

"Certainly there are still guidelines for social interaction in my own century."

"I was just wondering if you felt bad for popping out of here without even saying goodbye."

"That does seem regrettable..."

"I'd call it rude."

"However, due to the circumstances, it seems there is no alternative."

"I can suggest one." Alex gave Sean a quizzical look. "We can just pop forward a few hours and catch Louise at the diner and tell her we're leaving town. I can say that you've decided we need to hit the road early to be able to make it to New York in time for the big concert."

Alex weighed the suggestion. "Is it your intent to tell Louise something that will warn Jane about her situation?"

"*Situation?*" Sean spat, "Her death is a *situation?*" He calmed himself before he continued. "You'll be standing right there beside me... you've even got your voice-silencer deal. Besides, what could I say in a few seconds that could convince Louise that Jane needed a warning?"

"Then the purpose of this stop?"

"I just want to tell *someone* that we are leaving, so Jane won't immediately feel like I abandoned her without even a word. I can have Louise tell Jane I'm sorry that we're leaving like this. Is that too much to ask? To grant a dying woman a little less grief. She thinks I'm going to come back and somehow swoop her away to a new life in New Zealand. Let her hope that for a few weeks."

Sean looked pleadingly into Alex's eyes as Alex pondered his request. "Perhaps you are right," he finally agreed. "It would be... rude... to leave without any word."

"Thanks," Sean breathed. *That's the first hurdle*

"What do you propose as an optimal time to approach Louise?"

"I don't know," Sean shrugged, "I'd guess they open for breakfast around 6:00. Assuming most of their early morning customers have to be at work by 8:00; I'd guess if we got there a little after 8:00 that she might be able to spare us a few minutes."

Alex nodded.

They gathered all of their camping equipment and other belongings into their backpacks. Sean took one last look around, flooded with memories of Jane at the campfire, walking down the hill with the sandwiches, and their interrupted moment at the dock. He sighed and slid wearily into the time-machine. Alex closed the door, and moments later opened it again. Sean had barely noticed the dimensional shift, but his eyes told him they were in the alley behind the buildings across the street from Ritchie's and it was daylight. It was nearly the same spot Alex had selected when Sean went on his quest for soap.

As they entered the diner, Sean noticed that the smell of bacon almost masked the stale smell of cigarette smoke. The blue haze that hung over the pool table area had dissipated, though there were still a few smaller fresh clouds hanging over booths. Sean spotted Louise busing one of the booths and headed in her direction, Alex matching his stride.

Louise's face lit up with a bright smile when she looked up and saw them coming toward her. "Nigel! Peter!" she squealed. "I'm glad to see you all! Did you want some breakfast?"

"No," Sean replied, "we just wanted to let someone know that we were leaving, and thank you for your hospitality."

"Awww!" Louise pouted, "You're leaving?"

"Yes," Sean explained. "Peter thinks we need to get an early start to try to get across Iowa today."

"Well, did you get to go to the drive-in last night?" she inquired.

"We did indeed," confirmed Alex.

"Then you probably didn't get a whole lot of sleep. You didn't walk into town, did you? My goodness, you would have had to been up before the sun to make it into town."

"No, we were lucky," Sean lied, "We caught a ride in."

"Louise!" came a gruff voice from across the room. "I don't pay you to socialize."

"Aw come on, Ritchie! Five minutes? I've nearly got all the tables cleared. I'll skip my break later." Louise pleaded.

"All right," grumbled Ritchie, "Five minutes."

Louise turned back to Sean and Alex. "So did you have a good time last night? I wish I could have gone, it sounds like it would have been a lot of fun... but my Mama doesn't much like me even goin' to movies, let alone on the Lord's Day. I'm so sorry that you have to leave already. Are you sure you don't want to get something to eat? I could buy... if you don't want to spend your money... as long as you didn't order steak and eggs or something expensive."

Sean had to smile at her enthusiastic use of her five minutes. "No, we're fine, Louise. Just wanted to say goodbye. Tell everyone we had a super time here." He reached into his backpack. "Oh, and could you give this flashlight back to Jane? She loaned it to us." He gave a quick glance toward Alex as he held it out for her.

Alex snatched it away before she could take it. He looked the flashlight over, flicked it on and off, then unscrewed the top and dumped out the batteries. He peered inside.

"Something wrong?" asked Sean, relieved that he'd rejected his plan to put the note in the flashlight.

"No," replied Alex as he reassembled the flashlight. "Just wanted to make sure it was all in good working order. Unacceptable to return a borrowed item that we had damaged." He handed the flashlight to Louise. Sean took a small step backwards, hoping that Louise would behave as he expected. She didn't disappoint.

"Well, give me a hug goodbye," she squeaked as she reached for Alex, who was closest. She pulled him reluctantly into a bear hug. "I'll think of you Peter, every time a meet a vegetarian. I don't know how often that'll be, but I know I'll think of you every time."

Sean plunged his hand into his pocket and palmed the folded note while Alex was distracted by Louise's hug. When she released Alex and lifted her hands toward Sean, he stepped into the hug warmly. He wrapped his arms around her, squeezing and lifting her while he carefully tucked the paper under the apron's bow behind her waist.

"And Nigel," Louise chirped, "I don't know if I'll ever meet another Nigel—or anyone else from New Zealand—but you can bet I'll sure think of you if I do."

"And I'll never be able to look at another cute waitress without thinking of you, Louise," Sean vowed sincerely as they released each other.

"Now, Nigel, I don't believe for a minute that's true," Louise giggled, blushing a little, "but it was nice of you to say."

"Goodbye, Louise," Sean sighed "Tell Jane I'm sorry I didn't get to say goodbye to her."

"You two be careful out there on the highways," Louise ordered. "If someone looks like a psycho, don't you dare get in the car with them."

Sean and Alex turned and started toward the door. Sean turned back as they went out and gave Louise one last wave. His plan had gone OK so far, but there were still so many things that could go wrong. Worst of all, he would never know if he saved Jane's life or not. She would be one of the memories that Alex would remove. Still, he could hope.

Louise reached around behind her back and pulled out the hidden paper. She wondered why Nigel had been so secretive about it. It was folded several times, ending at about two inches square. "Jane" was printed on the outside in a very odd colored ink. When she had called about the drive-in, Louise was pretty sure that Jane was interested in Nigel. Now it appeared Nigel was also interested in Jane. She fought with her conscience about peeking at the note, but then rationalized that Jane would tell her about it anyway. She hoped it was real mushy.

She carefully unfolded the note all the way flat and smoothed the creases. It was written in that same odd colored ink. The first line read, "Today is July 13th, 1969." She skimmed the other lines and noticed there were several with dates in them.

"Louise," barked Ritchie, "Are you going to get back to work?"

"Yes, Ritchie," she replied as she tucked the note into her pocket. She hoped Jane would understand it, but it didn't make any sense to her, and it sure wasn't a very good love note.

Sean wearily slid into the S.T.E. and sighed deeply. It would be over soon. The good, the bad, all of it whisked away from his memories. He was mostly relieved but also had some regrets. It had been the amazingly impossible bittersweet adventure that he could never tell anyone about.

"Do you wish to do anything to prepare? The last time we took a voyage this long you were in rather bad shape upon arrival."

"Can you turn off the British accent?" groused Sean, "We're done with that."

Alex twitched briefly. "Thank you, I had forgotten I was using it," he said, returning to a Midwestern United States accent.

"When you threatened to knock me out for the whole trip, were you serious?"

"It was not an action I wished to take, but I would have, if necessary."

"Then do it."

"Pardon me?"

"Do it. Knock me out."

Alex blinked rapidly. "I do not understand."

Sean refused to make eye contact with him. "I don't feel like fighting whatever weird thing hits my brain this trip, just put me out."

"Are you certain?"

"Yeah."

The next thing Sean knew, the door was sliding open and it was dark outside.

"We have arrived," Alex said softly.

"Great," Sean mumbled with unenthusiastic sarcasm. Alex handed him a box. "What's this?"

"It is best to catch your hair when it detaches. I do not want loose hairs all over the ship."

"So how do we do this?"

"Generally the same way we attached them. If you would lean forward and scoop your hair into the box, I will issue the release command."

Sean leaned over the box and felt the hair come sliding off. The first thing he noticed was how much lighter his head felt—cooler, too. Alex took the box from him. "If you could step out, I will eject the tray from under the seat so you can get your regular clothes back."

Sean pulled the tie-dyed T-shirt over his head, tossed it at Alex and grabbed his blue shirt from the drawer. He slipped it on, buttoned it, then took off his jeans and put his khakis back on. "What about the mud caked on my shoes?"

"If you will remove them, I believe I have a solution."

Sean took them off and handed them to Alex, who put them into yet another drawer that had appeared from a seamless panel. "This will sonically vibrate all of the particles from your shoes."

"Normally I'd say something about 'cool toy', but I just don't care anymore." In a few moments, the clean shoes came out and Sean slipped them back on. "I guess that's everything."

"Not quite," Alex corrected as he handed Sean the 3D glasses. "Please sit back down and put these on. I need to upload the movie into your brain."

"I'd forgotten about the movie," admitted Sean. "At least it's bound to be better than the one at the drive-in." He put the glasses on.

"This is somewhat involved because I need to load it into a portion of your brain that will retain it after you have been disconnected from your memories of me and where we have been."

"Hey, my brain is a playground," Sean said sarcastically, "mess with it all you want."

"This will require a toggle password. Are you ready?"

"Sure."

"Relax," Alex advised. "Brad Pitt Popcorn."

Sean's head recoiled slightly as the download streamed from the glasses. "Brad Pitt Popcorn."

Sean looked over at Alex. "What are you waiting for?"

"It has already completed."

"I don't think so. I don't know anything about *Hackers* except for a trailer I've seen."

"It will toggle back into your memory when we are in the theater and after I have placed you back in your normal memory."

"OK," Sean said skeptically, "you're the mad scientist."

"We need to go, I have planned to return just before the end of the movie, but I have only allotted ten minutes beyond travel time back to the theater to get into position."

Alex took the glasses from Sean and put them away. Sean stood and when he had turned back, found that it was Nicole who slid out of the S.T.E.

"You're looking lovely as ever, Nicole," Sean mocked.

"Sean, I promise you," Alex replied in Nicole's melodic voice, "it will all be over soon."

"Yeah, and I get to fall all head-over-heels for you again once I think you're this beautiful girl... after you make me forget what you really are."

She flipped on her illuminator and closed up the S.T.E. The beam-less light lit up the ground as if it were daylight in a small moving circle. "Please, might we simply walk back to the theater?"

Sean started walking, following the moving circle of illuminated ground. "Promise me again that you won't let me kiss you," he pleaded.

"I will not let you kiss me."

"Thank you."

After a brisk ten-minute walk, they entered the theater.

"We will need to purchase more popcorn and soft drinks," Nicole advised as she moved toward the concession stand.

"I trust you to cover all the bases," Sean yawned, not walking over with her.

When she returned she handed him a Coke and they walked toward the auditorium. Sean remembered that he had put the ticket stubs in his shirt pocket, days ago. He pulled them out and flashed them to the bored ticket taker, who had last seen them less than two hours before. He nodded at them wordlessly.

They quickly found their auditorium and went to the back row and sat down.

"That is not the correct seat," Nicole whispered. "You need to move one more to your left."

"Are you sure," Sean whispered back.

"Yes." Nicole handed him a nearly empty popcorn bag. "I need your drink, please."

Sean took a big sip before handing it over. He watched Nicole dump most of it into the trashcan near the door. She returned the all-but-empty cup, sat down, and then took the popcorn bag from him. "Guess you've got money to burn if you're dumping stuff," Sean commented.

"It is necessary to have what would be plausible remains of what was purchased before the motion picture began. Remember, it is now Friday evening and we have been gone from these seats for approximately one hour and forty minutes; not several days."

"So now what?"

"In just a few moments," Nicole instructed, "you will believe you have spent the last 100 minutes watching this film."

"And *then* what?"

"I do not know *what* you have planned for the remainder of our date."

Sean heaved a deep sigh. He remembered that he was determined to kiss Nicole tonight. "Please... don't let me kiss you."

"I have already told you that I would not."

"OK, then I guess let's do this." He glanced up at the screen and watched a guy and girl in a swimming pool. It was on a rooftop, and they looked out onto some tall buildings that spelled "Crash and Burn" in the windows. "I'm going to remember seeing this movie?"

"Yes," Nicole assured him as the credits started rolling. "Mobo Gerga store LX seventeen eight." Sean's head dropped slightly to the left. She rapidly added, "Brad Pitt Popcorn."

Sean blinked a few times. "What?"

"I said, 'did you want some more popcorn?'" Nicole lied.

Sean felt a little odd. He thought he had just sat down, but it was obviously the ending credits on the screen... and he did see the movie. It was actually pretty good. "Umm, no, thanks," he said, still watching the credits popping over the swimmers as the music swelled.

"Did you enjoy this film?" Nicole asked.

"Yeah," nodded Sean, "It was pretty good. A little espionage, some excitement, a little bit of a romance. How 'bout you, what did you think."

"I thought it was rather enjoyable... although I question whether they would have been able to gain access to those company computers with their personal computers."

"I guess. Makes a good story though." Sean stood. "Ready to go?" Several people were already in the aisle, exiting.

"Yes, if you are ready."

They walked out of the auditorium and into the lobby area.

"I guess it was pretty obvious that the guy and girl hackers would end up together, even though she was playing hard to get."

"Hard to get?"

"Yeah, you know, she acted like she didn't like him at first."

They walked out into the night air, it felt a little cooler than when they had entered.

"Are you warm enough?" Sean asked.

"Yes, I am comfortable. Thank you."

They strolled slowly toward the parking lot. "So, do you like movies that end all happily ever after, you know, with the guy and girl together."

Nicole didn't respond for several steps. "Yes. That is nice. It is designed to make the viewer feel that their own lives can turn out happily."

Did she have to analyze everything? "Anyway," Sean said, "I thought it was more of a movie that a girl could like. Not just all action and excitement. Although there was plenty of that." He abruptly stopped. Nicole looked at him, noticed the puzzled look on his face. "I could swear we were parked right there." Sean pointed at an older, burgundy Monte Carlo.

Nicole looked over to the row of cars where Sean pointed. He was correct. The car was *not* where it had been left earlier.

Sean began to look around, quickly moving from row to row, dodging cars that were leaving. He came back to Nicole. "I'm *sure* it was this row. What happened to the car?"

"I concur that this is where it was parked," Nicole agreed.

"So either Kevin got back early and came and snagged the car or someone stole it!"

"Why would Kevin take the car from you?"

208

"I don't know... as a joke? Even though it's a crummy joke, I hope that's the answer and not that someone stole it."

Sean stood with hands on hips, scanning all around the parking lot. The midnight blue Avenger was nowhere to be seen.

"We could acquire a taxicab to transport us home, and then you could call Kevin to ascertain that he does indeed have his vehicle. If not, I believe you will need to contact the police."

"I don't have any money for a cab," Sean complained. "I spent it all on tickets and popcorn."

"I can pay for the taxi," Nicole volunteered.

Sean looked pained. His ego rejected the thought of having to accept money from a girl, especially when they were on a date, but he didn't have a better solution. "OK," he groaned.

They went back to the box office to request that they call a cab. The girl glared at them as if they'd asked her to sign over the rights to her first-born, but in the end she grudgingly called the cab company. "They said they've got a car in the area... five minutes or so," the girl relayed to them.

"Thanks," said Sean. "I appreciate it."

The girl shrugged and returned to reading her *Cosmopolitan*.

"Want another Diet Pepsi?" Sean asked, calculating that he had just enough money to pay for it.

"No, thank you," Nicole replied.

"Want to play a video game?"

"Not really." She gave him an appreciative smile.

Sean looked off into the night. It seemed darker and gloomier than it did the first time they left the theater. Nothing was going as planned and the growing gap in the conversation spurred his insecurities. "I wonder how the football game turned out. Kevin was pretty psyched about it. Of course, he gets pretty psyched about every game." Nicole didn't respond. "Next week is a home game," he added nervously, "Maybe we could go to it."

Nicole had left a long pause hanging before she spoke. "That might be possible... dependent upon the amount of homework assigned next week."

Sean instinctively wanted to berate her for even thinking about homework on a Friday night, but remembered how serious Nicole and Alexis seemed to be about their classes. "Sure," he finally said.

He searched the street, willing the cab to appear. It had already seemed like an eternity standing there in silence. Mercifully, the car finally pulled up and they got in.

"Where to?" asked the driver.

"It would be most logical to drop you off first at your house," Nicole suggested to Sean.

"No," Sean disagreed, "we can just go to your place and I'll walk home from there." He gave the driver Nicole's address.

"I'll pay you back for the cab... maybe sometime next week," Sean declared while staring at the back of the driver's head."

"It is not necessary," Nicole replied. "You purchased the movie tickets and refreshments, I do not mind contributing to pay for the ride home."

"But we shouldn't have *needed* a ride home," Sean insisted. "I'm going to kill Kevin... unless, of course, if it turns out someone really did steal his car."

As the cab pulled into Nicole's driveway, Sean desperately rummaged his brain for a way to turn the current situation into a happier ending. He stood back and looked away while Nicole leaned into the cabbie's window, then handed him some money. The cab backed out and disappeared around the corner.

Sean walked Nicole slowly toward her door. The house was completely dark.

At least Aunt Katherine or Alexis wouldn't be spying on us, thought Sean. *Unless they're purposefully hiding in the dark so they could peek out a window.*

He didn't care, it was time to regain the evening. "I had a great time, Nicole," he said enthusiastically, then added, "Well, except for the car disappearing part."

"Yes," she replied, "it was an enjoyable evening. Thank you, Sean Kelly for taking me to the movies."

"You are most welcome, Nicole Townsend," Sean smiled. It cheered him up to play their little formal-full-name game."

They had reached the steps leading to the front door. *It's now or never.* Sean put his hands on Nicole's shoulders. Hidden beneath the guise of Nicole Townsend, Alex was torn with emotions. He had grown very attached to the ancient ancestor, and wished they could be together more, but he had promised Sean that he was going to ease Nicole away and not trouble him any longer. His feelings drove him to a snap decision.

"Bush Taft Ford Grant!" said Nicole suddenly.

"What?" asked Sean.

"It does not matter... you will not remember." She stepped up onto the bottom step, giving her a tiny height advantage, wrapped her arms around his neck, and pulled into a fiery kiss. Sean staggered back a half of a step when she released him.

"Wow," he finally gasped. "What was *that* for?"

"I must confess," replied a now embarrassed Nicole, "that was for me."

"Hmmm," reasoned a now confident Sean, "then maybe I should get one for me?" He leaned back into her, but she put a hand to his lips.

"No," she objected, "sorry... I made a promise."

"A promise?" asked Sean. "What promise... and to who?"

"To you, though you cannot understand... but first, I have to ask... any stars or sparks?"

"What?" Sean looked confused.

"No, I expected not," Nicole murmured as she stepped back down from the steps. She grabbed each of his hands and put them back on her shoulders where he had placed them moments ago. "Bush Taft Ford Grant, *erase!*"

Sean felt an instant of lightheadedness but ignored it as he leaned slowly into Nicole. At the last second, she turned her head, and his kiss ended up on her cheek. *Perfect! A terrible ending to an already not-so-great evening.* He wondered if she was just being shy, or did she really not have the feelings for him that he had hoped she would?   It was both discouraging and embarrassing... and it was time to go.

"Well, good night," he said quietly. "See you at school Monday." He turned and started walking away.

Darkness hid the tear that slid down Nicole's face and Alex struggled to steady her voice. "Good night..."

She stood there and watched as he walked away down the sidewalk. When Sean had gotten a few houses away, she hurriedly crept down the walk and turned the other way, silently rounding the corner to where the cab was waiting. She got in. "Thank you for waiting," she said.

"Hey, fifty bucks buys you a few minutes," the cabby replied. "No problem. So where do you want to go now?"

"Back to the theater, please."

"Back to the theater?" the cabby said, his voice didn't hide his confusion. "OK. It's your fifty. Back to the theater we go."

As they neared the Cineplex, Nicole leaned forward, "Actually, if you could drive past the theater and turn left at the next intersection." When he had made the turn, she waited until they were almost to the vacant lot. "Stop here, please."

The cabbie pulled to a stop and turned his head toward Nicole. "Here?"

"Yes, thank you."

"There's nothing here."

"That is true, but this is where I wish to get out."

"I don't know," the cabbie warned, "I don't know if I feel right about putting you out here. It might not be safe."

"I assure you, I will be fine," Nicole insisted, "Do you need more money?"

"No, you're good there... but are you *sure* you want out here?"

"Yes," she replied and opened the door.

"You be careful, little lady," he advised just before driving off.

When his cab turned the next corner, Nicole pulled out her illuminator and started across the vacant lot to where the cloaked S.T.E. waited. She opened it, slid in, and was quickly on her way back to the house she had left only minutes earlier. She thought about Sean as she drifted above the streets. They were confused thoughts.

Alex shifted back to himself from the Nicole disguise. He struggled with all of the thoughts that flashed through his brain, only to decide that there were no logical solutions to emotional problems. Logically, he was correct that taking Sean into the past was not a good decision... and yet, despite the problems, he felt a warmth of happiness as he thought about their adventure. Sean was certainly a catalyst to spark reactions that he would never have even considered. He wondered if he could adapt his own methods to include some of the situations that Sean inspired.

He sighed. It would not be the same.

The next step was to turn from thinking of the past to thoughts of how best to return Sean's life to normal. Alexis had been only mildly disruptive, but with Nicole, he had created something in Sean's life that he now truly regretted. It had worked as designed, Sean became very interested in being with Nicole. He heaved another sigh. That was the intent, but now with hindsight, he saw how wrong it had been to manipulate Sean's emotions.

Nicole had to go... immediately. He formulated a plan to use Alexis to report to Sean that Nicole decided she needed to return to New York to assist with their mother's care. It might hurt him that Nicole didn't even say goodbye, but Alex had learned an ancient idiom about ripping a Band-Aid off quickly. Twentieth Century medicine was so primitive.

As he approached his house, he noticed a shadowy figure at the front door. He adjusted to night vision and magnified to discover the shape was Sean, and he seemed to be rather aggressively banging his fist on the door. Alex quickly slid Steffi against the garage door and passed through it. He hopped out once inside. "Lights," he commanded, but nothing happened. "House! Lights!" he said more firmly... still no reaction. He pulled the illuminator from Nicole's purse and turned it on.

Something was wrong. Things were missing.

Sean continued to hammer on the door. "Nicole," he cried, "Alexis, Katherine... anyone!"

Alex opened the garage's door into to the house and trotted toward the front door, sweeping the illuminator around as he went. The rooms were empty. He quickly reverted to the Nicole disguise and switched off the illuminator before opening the door.

Tears raced down Sean's face.

"What is it, Sean?" Nicole asked. "What is wrong?"

"You know me?" he sobbed. "You know who I am?" He face was twisted with pain and fear.

"Of course I do."

"Were we just on a date?" he howled hysterically. "Did we just get back from a date? Did we see *Hackers* at the movie?"

"Yes," she cautiously assured, her voice betraying a creeping fear.

He grabbed her shirt with both hands, popping the top button open. "Where do I live?" he demanded maniacally, "*Where do I live? WHERE. DO. I. LIVE?*"

"Sean, you are hurting me," she squeaked.

He shook her, a second button popped open. *"Just answer the damned question! Where do I live?"*

"Just down the street," Nicole cried.

He released her. He stared with vacuous eyes, then slumped to sit on the step, leaning against the door frame. "That's what *I* thought..." he muttered hoarsely.

Nicole sat down beside him, gingerly taking his hands in hers. "What do you mean?"

Sean stared out toward the street. "That's what *I* thought," he repeated, then turned to look at her. "That's what *I* thought." Tears streamed from his eyes.

Utter panic began to grip Nicole, but she pressed on, "Tell me what happened," she said gently.

He looked at her, blinking the tears, trying to focus. He shook his head side to side, his mouth hanging open.

"Please," she coaxed, "Please tell me what happened."

His eyes returned to their empty vigil of the street as he started to speak. His voice quivered, had the tone and cadence of a madman. "I walked down the street. I was upset that you didn't kiss me. I walked down the street. I got to my house. I *thought* it was my house. I really did! I *thought* it was my house. I walked up to the door. It felt like it always did. It felt the same, looked the same. I put my key in the lock and it wouldn't turn. I pulled it out, put it in, tried again. It wouldn't turn. There were lights on, so I rang the bell. Maggie didn't bark." He looked wide-eyed at Nicole. *"Maggie didn't bark!"* He turned back to the street. "The door opened a crack and I could see this girl's face. She was looking under the chain lock. It was... it was... she's a freshman... I've seen her before. Ashley, I think. So I said, 'what are you doing here?' and she says, 'can I help you?' and I said, 'sure, tell me what you're doing here.' She says, 'babysitting, if it's any of your business.' I said, 'Babysitting? Babysitting who?' Then she says, 'who *are* you?' So now I'm getting a little pissed. 'Sean Kelly! I *live* here! What is this some kind of *joke?*' Then she says, 'I don't know who you are, but you sure don't live *here!*' and she slams the door. I immediately start banging on the door. 'Come on! What is this, some kind of joke?' She pops the door back open a crack, 'look, I don't know where you live, I don't know if you're drunk or high or what... but you don't live here. Go away or I'll call a cop.' Then she slams the door again."

He shook his head again, slowly, side to side, still staring at the street. Nicole squeezed his hand. He glanced at her face. With her eyes, she asked him to go on.

"So, I don't know what to think. Is someone playing a joke? Or is something really wrong? Has someone tied my parents up and are robbing the place? I ran across the street to the Wilsons. They're older, and the lights were already off, but they've lived on the street forever, so I know they'll help.

I rang the bell and waited. No answer. I rang the bell again, several times and finally a light comes on. Mr. Wilson opens the door. He's wearing a robe over pajamas. He just looks at me. So I said, 'Mr. Wilson, something is going on over at my house, and I don't know what it is.' Then he says..." Sean's voice cracked and he sobbed as he continued, "he says.... 'Who are you?' So now I'm really freaking out, because, he'd never play along with a joke. 'Mr. Wilson... I'm Sean Kelly. I've lived across the street since I was seven years old. You know who I am.' Then he looks at me really strange. 'I don't know where you think you are, or if you're hopped up on dope, but there's no one by the name of Kelly in this whole neighborhood.' Then he slams the door in my face. I don't know what to think. So I ran back down the street and banged on your door."

He stared at the street silently, his cheeks drenched with tears. He turned back to Nicole. "You know me, Nicole... right?" he wailed. She nodded. "Am I crazy?"

"No," she whispered as she threw her arms around him. "Sean, hold on to me, I really do not know what is going to happen to you when I do this."

"Do what?"

"Mobo Gerga retrieve LX seventeen eight."

Sean sucked in a loud gasp. He started convulsing and gasping like a drowning man. Nicole held tightly to him so he couldn't break free. "Gursk," she swore softly. "Sean, you are hyperventilating," she diagnosed with authority, "breathe with me," she commanded, "Deep slow breaths. In. Out. In. Out."

He followed her breathing pattern and gradually the shaking subsided. Nicole eased away from him to look him in the eye. His mouth hung open as he slowly turned his head from side to side. His eyes glistened with tears and stared unseeingly.

"We need to go inside," she announced, standing and pulling him up. She pushed the door open and tugged on Sean. He blundered through the door on wobbly legs. When the door was closed, Alex dropped the Nicole disguise.

"Do you know who I am?" Alex asked firmly, turning on the illuminator and shining it toward himself.

"Yes," Sean mumbled. "Alex... from future." He looked around stupidly. "Your furniture... gone."

"I know," Alex reported authoritatively. "I need to get you to the S.T.E. I believe you might be in shock. I can do diagnostics and hopefully treat you."

"Wha happent," Sean slurred as he stumbled toward the garage.

"From the evidence I have observed, it appears we have changed something in the past. Something drastic enough to create this reality where neither you nor I live. It is possible that neither you nor I even exist."

Chapter Eleven

"I'm not a man who likes to swear / but I never cared for the sound of being alone"

"DON'T EXIST?" mumbled Sean, "Are we in purgatory?... or limbo?"

"No, we are still in Grover's Corners," Alex said calmly, steering Sean into the garage.

"Don't understand... if we don't exist, how are we here?"

"We are here, because we returned to a beacon I set, plus one hour," Alex explained as he maneuvered Sean into the S.T.E.

"Where are my parents? Where's Maggie?"

"That I do *not* know."

Sean held out a hand, flipped it over, and then repeated the action with his other hand. "It feels like I still exist."

"Of course you still exist," Alex stated as if talking to a third grader.

"You said we might not exist."

"In this timeline. I have not yet verified that theory."

"Because something changed in the past?"

"That is my initial hypothesis. I will need to confirm it."

"Are we going to fade away?"

Alex looked at him and began to wonder if the shock of returning Sean's full memory had caused brain damage. "No. Unless I do not understand what you mean by 'fade away'."

"Like Marty McFly. He started to fade away when the past got changed."

Alex twitched a query. "That is a fictional character in a movie!"

"A movie about time-travel," Sean argued, attempting to justify his position. "Ida thought you'd watched movies 'bout time-travel 'fore you actually went anywhere."

"Sean, you are not making any sense."

"*I'm* not making sense?" Sean sneered, "*You're* the one said we might not exist."

Alex placed a hand gently on Sean's shoulder. "I need you to relax while the computer evaluates your physical and mental states."

"Relax?" Sean screamed. "My parents are gone, there are strangers living in my house, your place looks burglarized, and you expect me to *relax?*"

Alex involuntarily cringed from Sean's outburst. "Perhaps it would be best if you were unconscious."

"Now wait a minute, don't..." Sean threatened, just before darkness swallowed him.

Sean felt much calmer when he next opened his eyes. He was still sitting inside Steffi and Alex was beside him. "I have re-purposed some of the nanites," Alex stated, "that had linked to your extended memory to adjust the dopamine and serotonin levels in your brain. You should feel calmer. I am unsure if that also means that some of your memory is lost."

Sean tried to check his memory. He knew who Alex was. He knew he'd been in the past. He knew something had happened that must have changed the present. It all seemed to be there. "No, I think I remember everything," he said.

"You would not be able to remember that you forgot something," Alex pointed out.

Sean thought it over, then nodded. "I guess I see your point."

"While you were unconscious, I also did several diagnostic procedures," Alex expounded, "Shifting out of this dimension and running tests over the three months prior to this date as well as three months following. The only DNA trace to you is this present iteration of you. There is *not* another Sean Kelly anywhere else in this time zone. It is not a matter of geographic displacement, it is a matter of existence. It appears you were never born." Sean's eyes grew wide as he sucked in a breath. Alex continued. "Since I have your father's DNA, I also checked for him at the same time. During the entire six months I examined, he was in various locations close to Ames, Iowa. It appears that is where he lives in this altered reality."

Sean crinkled his face. "Altered reality?"

"Yes. That is the best terminology to explain this phenomenon, unless you prefer Alternate timeline?"

"I don't care what you call it," Sean yelled. "How do we get back to *my* timeline reality thing?"

"We cannot. It does not currently exist."

"I don't get it," Sean blurted, "we come back and pop into the movie we were watching before we left. Everything looks the same. My house is there, it's just that I don't live in it... wait..." Sean's voice became more thoughtful. "...so that's why Kevin's car wasn't there."

"It could not be there," Alex affirmed, "since you did not exist for him to loan it to you."

"But Kevin and Raj still exist in this timeline?"

"Yes, I see no reason that they would not."

"So maybe *they* know where I live."

Alex studied Sean for several moments, then spoke to him again as if addressing a child. "Kevin and Raj would not recognize you because they never knew you."

"No. No. No," Sean insisted. "I'm here!" He slapped himself on the chest. "How can I not exist?"

"You do exist," Alex said patiently. "You just do not exist in this altered reality."

Sean squeezed his eyes shut. "I exist... but I do *not* exist." He threw his hands in the air and shouted, "How does that make any sense?"

"You were traveling outside of the timeline as it changed," Alex explained, "You existed in 1969 when we left. As we came forward in time, events that were different from the original events took place. One of the outcomes of those different events is that your father lives in Iowa, another is that you were never born. Had I traveled alone to 1969, and triggered whatever has caused this change, you would not exist anywhere. You exist by virtue of being with me when the events were altered."

"What about *you?*"

"I also would not exist if I were to return to my time. As your descendant, I could not exist if you did not exist."

Sean squeezed his eyes shut again and pushed on his temples with the heels of his hands. "I'm *really* having trouble with this 'exist, but don't exist' thing."

"It is a complex concept," Alex agreed, "and I am sorry that you are struggling with it. However, I suggest that we now focus on discovering what created this rift, and returning to 1969 to repair it."

Jane, thought Sean. *Could saving Jane's life have done all this?*

Alex continued, "I believe our best course of action is to interview your father to ascertain any information that might determine what has caused him to be where he is."

What if Dad married Jane? I mean, they were just friends... but what if that changed if she lived?

"I have formulated a plan that I believe will allow us to question your father about his past."

Should I tell Alex what I did? But I don't really know for sure that's what caused this.

"We will need to acquire a video camera and gain stealth access to an unoccupied hospital room. We have limited funds. I do not know if we have enough currency to purchase the camera."

"Why not use your credit card?" asked Sean.

"I did not take it with me to 1969. Therefore, it does not exist. However, even if I had, I would not be able to use it as it would not be viable in this timeline."

Sean was confused. "Why not?"

"Katherine Tuttle also does not exist. Thus, a credit card in her name would trigger fraudulent use."

Sean smacked his forehead with his hand. "This is getting complicated!"

"I wish I had been more frugal with the currency that I do possess," Alex said absently.

"Maybe we can get a video camera at a pawn shop," Sean suggested. "But what's with the hospital room?"

"I will explain in detail when we are on the cusp of that step," Alex assured. "Is there a pawn shop in this town, or will we need to travel to Kansas City?"

"There's actually two of them in town. One's just a few blocks from Wal*Mart." Alex brought up a map, located the pawn shop, touched the blinking dot, and then changed to an image of Sean in his hippie guise on the front view-screen. "What's that for?" Alex altered his own appearance to mirror that of the long-haired Sean. "OK, that gets high marks in the creepiness department." Alex made further adjustments to his appearance, making his hair a little shorter with streaks of gray, adding a few wrinkles around his eyes and to his brow. Skin from his cheeks flowed slightly downward and he added the trace of a double chin. "And now even *higher* marks for creepy... *what* are you doing?" Alex made his skin a little paler with a gray cast and darkened circles around his eyes.

"I am attempting to fabricate what Nigel Davies would look like, aged another twenty-six years."

"Because?"

Alex didn't answer, he opened one of the drawers in the front panel and took out a small stack of twenties. "If you can conserve as many of these as possible when you make the purchase," Alex said as the door slid open. It was daylight.

"Where are we?" asked a dazed Sean.

"I believe you refer to them as 'strip malls'. We are on the back side of the pawn shop. It is Saturday morning, approximately 11:00 am."

Sean peeked out and saw they were next to a dumpster. "I didn't even feel the jump."

"Oh, we were already at this time. I moved forward while you were still unconscious, once I determined we would have better options for purchasing a camera during the day. Steffi moved to this location while I was altering my appearance." He stroked his left cheek as he examined his new likeness. "I believe I need to accent the gauntness." He handed Sean the stack of money. Sean took the cash and slid out.

Several minutes later he stumbled back around the dumpster, hands outstretched, feeling for the cloaked vessel. A door opened in thin air and Sean quickly slid in. He appeared to vanish when the door closed.

"I got three videotapes," he said as he pulled them from a plastic bag. "I didn't know how many you needed for your little secret project. Holy Cow! What happened to you?"

"Does my appearance suggest that I am ill?"

"You look like you're *dead!* What did you do?"

"I have been altering my appearance to be representative of someone dying of a terminal disease. I believe cancer was the most prevalent malady in your time that had a tendency to emaciate people as it progressed. Would you be convinced by looking at me that I was in the final stages of a cancer induced termination?"

"No, I think I would say you looked like you're ready to be in a zombie movie."

"Perhaps the lesions are too vulgar?"

"Yeah," said Sean, crinkling his nose in disgust. "And maybe not so much gray in the skin, and not so skeleton-like, and where did the hair go?"

"I thought minimal remaining strands of hair would suggest that I had undergone radiation therapy."

"I think it makes you look more like the Crypt-keeper. Seriously, put back some hair."

Alex made Sean's recommended adjustments and looked at himself in a real-time projection on the front view-screen. Satisfied, he brought up a wire frame view of a large building.

"What's that?"

"The hospital. I need to find a room large enough to materialize Steffi inside." He pointed at the screen. "What do you suppose this room is?"

Sean looked at it. "It looks like it has gym equipment in there. Maybe physical therapy?"

"That would not be in use at approximately 2:00 am, would it?"

"I don't think so."

"Then hold on to your stomach," Alex said only seconds before making the short jump in time and space.

Chapter Twelve

"Hide my head I want to drown my sorrow / No tomorrow, no tomorrow"

"**E**XPLAIN TO me again why I'm supposed to be a cameraman for a British TV show," Sean asked.

"Not British, for New Zealand Television," corrected Alex.

"But you're still British, right?"

"Yes! I thought you understood that part. I am still Peter Lindsey, merely advanced in age by twenty-six years, the same as your father."

"But I'm supposed to be Nigel Davies, *Junior* and I just happen to be a New Zealand TV cameraman?"

"Yes, you will not need to speak, unless spoken to."

"And my Dad will look right at me and not know that I'm his son, Sean Kelly?"

"In this altered timeline, he apparently does not have a son named Sean Kelly."

"This is crazy!" protested Sean.

"Simply follow my actions and narrative, and attempt to say as little as possible."

"You're sure he lives here, on this farm?"

"Yes," Alex sighed, "The DNA beacon has led us here, it is infallible."

"And you think my Dad is going to believe that the rest of our TV crew just dropped us off here and went back into Ames?"

"Though unlikely, it is still what we will claim is true. The absence of any other probable scenario will make it more believable."

"OK," Sean reluctantly agreed. "I still think this is going to blow up in our faces, but I'm going to let you run the show... I will speak when spoken to."

They got out of the cloaked S.T.E., walked around the detached garage, and started toward the front door of the farmhouse. When they reached the door, Sean stood back a few steps to run the video recorder. Alex knocked on the door.

"What if he's not here?" whispered Sean.

"I thought you were only going to speak when spoken to," reprimanded Alex.

"That's *after* some..."

The door swung inward and a tall, pretty teen-aged girl was framed in the glass of the storm door. She wore blue jeans and a green *Back Street Boys* T-shirt that accented her fiery red hair. She pushed the storm door open a few inches. "Can I help you?" she asked confidently.

"Yes," Alex said in his clipped British accent. "Is this the home of Jack Kelly?"

She looked them both over carefully before responding. "My dad's name is Jonathan Kelly," she said warily.

"May we speak with him, please?" asked Alex, showing the girl a polite, benign smile.

"Are you selling something?"

"No," assured Alex.

She pointed to Sean. "What's the deal with the camera?"

"It is for a documentary," smiled Alex cheerfully.

"Of what?" the girl demanded. She crossed her arms and stared coldly at the camera.

"I hitchhiked across the United States in 1969 and I am retracing my route, attempting to also speak with people that I met along the way."

The girl frowned at him. "You're doing a documentary, with a home video camera, held by a teenager?" she said with disdain as she looked toward the road. "Where's your car?"

"Actually," Alex replied, remaining cheerful, "there is more to my crew. They dropped us off and have gone into Ames to locate lodging for tonight."

"They just dropped you here and drove off before they even saw if you got into the house?" she scoffed. Her eyes narrowed.

Sean couldn't stand to remain silent. "Oi! Girly! Get back in the bleedin' 'ouse and tell your old man there's a limey out front lookin' to chat wiff Juan Kelly!" Her mouth dropped open, but fire ignited in her eyes as she glared at Sean. "Go on with ya! And be sure to say '*Juan* Kelly'," Sean added roughly.

The girl clamped her mouth shut into a frown, huffed, and slammed the inside door.

"That got some action," Sean grinned, pleased with himself.

"Are you certain she will not return with firearms?" asked Alex.

Sean smiled mischievously. "If she does, you run to your right, I'll go to the left. Keep your head low and run a zigzag pattern."

"I cannot tell for certain, since you are smiling in a rather devious manner, but are you seriously suggesting that it *is* possible we will be fired upon?"

"I guess anything's possible," Sean shrugged.

The inner door swung open again and Alex jumped back a step. Sean looked up at the man pushing the storm door open. It was his Dad! It had only been a few days since Sean had seen him, not counting his younger self in 1969, but seeing him at the door made him want to rush up and hug him.

He choked down his hurt feelings when Jack Kelly looked right at him without a glimmer of recognition. When Jack looked at Alex, his face showed a hint of recognition.

"Hello, Juan," Alex said warmly. "Been a few years, mate."

Jack squinted his eyes, still not quite putting it together. "No one has called me 'Juan' since high school... but we didn't have a British foreign-exchange student, so I'm not quite sure why *you* would use that name."

"Fair enough," Alex acknowledged, "It *has* been twenty-six years and a bit. Think back to July of 1969. One weekend a couple of foreigners on their way to Woodstock wandered into your town, played a little music, stayed in your dad's camper, went to the drive-in the next night..."

A smile crossed Jack's face. He nodded. "Yeah," he said through a grin, "I remember that now. You played my guitar. Pretty amazingly, as I recall..." He continued to nod.

"Peter," Alex prompted.

"Yeah, Peter! Right!" He shifted his gaze to Sean. "And... and..." He snapped his fingers to try to jog his memory.

"Nigel," Alex said softly.

"Nigel!" Jack repeated loudly, "Nigel! Right. Peter and Nigel!" His eyes narrowed as he examined Sean. "But this can't be Nigel... unless he discovered the Fountain of Youth."

"Actually, it is," Alex claimed, "Nigel Davies... junior."

"Wow!" Jack exclaimed. "You're the spitting image of your dad... I think. He had longer hair, of course. You know, it was a lot of years ago, but I *think* you look just like how I remember him."

Sean struggled to keep a smile on his face. His Dad barely remembered Nigel Davies... but obviously didn't recognize his own son at all. He felt hollow as if suddenly orphaned, but kept it all hidden behind a manufactured smile. He vowed to himself that somehow, they would put things back the way they should be.

"So actually, Juan," Alex said, attempting to move the conversation along. "I'm doing a documentary based on my earlier travels across the U.S."

"It's Jonathan, now," Jack said. "No one calls me Juan."

Jonathan, thought Sean. *Not Jack? Why the difference?*

"Right, then... Jonathan..." Alex replied. "I also have a short video to show you, if we may."

Jonathan was initially perplexed, then reacted graciously. "Oh, well, certainly... come in! Come in! Can I get you something to drink?" He stepped back to let them in. The girl stood just behind him, her arms crossed, jaw set, chin slightly elevated. Her eyes burned a hole in Sean.

"I would not say 'no' to a cup of tea," Alex quipped as he went up the two cement steps and through the front door. Sean followed him, still running his video camera. He nearly jumped when the girl's sour face filled the screen.

"This is my daughter, Caitlin, whom you've already met," Jonathan said to Alex.

"You have a lovely daughter," Alex said pleasantly, "Nice to meet you, Caitlin." He nodded toward her.

"Two, actually," Jonathan corrected, "Fiona is away at college. And a son! Sean."

Sean's heart skipped a beat. He looked to his Dad for acknowledgment, but Jonathan simply led them into his living room and asked them to sit. Sean continued to stand and operate the camera.

Alex said there's not another Sean, thought Sean, *I guess he doesn't know everything.*

"Michelle?" Jonathan shouted. "Have you got a minute to come in here, dear? There's someone I'd like you to meet."

I don't get this, Sean puzzled, *Mom's here, Dad's here and Sean's here. So all that's different is that I have two sisters and live in Iowa. Why does Alex think I don't exist?*

A tall redhead came into the room.

That's not Mom!

"Honey, you're not going to believe this," said Jonathan to the woman who had just entered. "This is someone I met briefly when I was in high school. Peter...." He started snapping his fingers.

"Lindsey," Alex supplied as he stood and offered a hand to the woman crossing to him.

"Lindsey!" declared Jonathan. "He was hitchhiking to Woodstock and came through Mercer and stopped for a couple of days."

Alex squeezed her offered hand gently. "Lovely to meet you, Mrs. Kelly."

"Nice to meet *you*, Mr. Lindsey," she replied politely. "I *love* your accent."

"Peter, please," said Alex. "My old dad's name is Mr. Lindsey."

"And did your 'old dad' raise you somewhere near the banks of the Mersey?" she asked, attempting a British accent with the phrase 'old dad'.

"Spot on, Mrs. Kelly!" Alex said with a nod. "Liverpool."

"Michelle," she replied with a mischievous grin, "Mrs. Kelly is my mother-in-law."

"Fair enough... Michelle," winked Alex. "What led you recognize my particular accent?"

"I've become fascinated with all of the regional accents in the UK," confessed Michelle. "I suppose I watch too much *Masterpiece Theater*. Of course, as a lifelong fan of the Beatles, it wasn't hard to pick yours out."

Sean didn't like her. Nor did he like that Alex was so easily warming up to her, and he *certainly* didn't like it that his Dad married another woman with his Mom's name.

"Sean," called Jonathan. "Come on in here."

Sean's head snapped toward his Dad when he heard his name, but his Dad wasn't looking his direction. He followed his father's gaze to the young boy peeking around the doorway.

"He's a little shy around strangers," Michelle advised.

"Come on in and meet some people," Jonathan coaxed.

The youngster edged around the door and fled to Caitlin's lap, the option furthest from the strangers.

"Sean is seven," explained Jonathan. "We thought we were finished with just the two girls, but then..."

"Then," interrupted Michelle sharply, "we decided we needed a little boy to round out the family." She gave Jonathan a warning glare, then turned to young Sean and smiled at him. "He just loves his big sister, Caitlin." The boy buried his freckled face in Caitlin's chest.

The elder Sean's heart ached. He wanted to be back with *his* family, but he also had a twinge of jealousy for this *other* Sean. Many times as he grew up, he wondered what it would be like to have a brother or sister.

"That is a fine young lad," commented Alex.

The boy turned back around. "You talk funny," he declared.

"That I do, lad," laughed Alex. "Not from around here, you see."

"Where's Nigel senior these days," Jonathan asked Alex.

"Still in New Zealand," Alex replied, a somber tone crept into his voice. "Christchurch, for the moment... in hospital."

The mood in the room shifted.

"Is something wrong?" inquired Jonathan, also somberly.

Alex stroked his chin thoughtfully before replying. "I believe if we show you this video, it would best answer that."

Jonathan was curiously concerned, but stood and pointed to the television across the room. "We can turn on the TV and put it in the VCR if you like."

Alex held his hand out to Sean, who reached into the camera bag that hung from his shoulder. He pulled out a tape and handed it to Alex, who in turn passed it to Jonathan.

Jonathan crossed the room, turned on the TV and VCR and slid the tape in. He switched the TV to channel 3 and waited. When an image came up, he pushed the pause button on the remote he'd picked up. "Did you want to say something about this before it starts?" he asked Alex.

"No, I think it explains itself," Alex replied. "But perhaps the youngsters might wish to go elsewhere."

Jonathan addressed his daughter, "Caitlin, could you and Sean go into the kitchen and boil some water and find some teabags for our guests?"

Caitlin stood, glared at her father until she was sure he registered her displeasure, then took Sean by the hand and left the room. Jonathan sat on the couch across from the television and Michelle sat beside him. She patted his leg, her face openly showing concern. Alex selected an adjacent chair and sat, Sean remained standing, continuing to record the events in the room. Jonathan looked toward Alex, received a nod, and then pushed the play button on the remote.

The haggard face of the elder Nigel Davies looked out at them from a hospital bed. He smiled wanly, then coughed before speaking. "Juan," he started, his voice raspy. "How have things been? I hope you are doing better than me." He coughed again. "If you are watching this, then Peter managed to track you down. Still in Mercer, Iowa, or have you moved on?"

Jonathan flashed a quick grin, his face reverting to somber features as he watched the obviously ill man on the screen. Michelle patted his leg again and attempted to force her own smile.

"No point in dragging this on. As you can see by looking at me, I been going through a rough patch... cancer." He coughed again before continuing. "Six months, say the doctors... a year if I am lucky. Not feeling all that lucky right now. Sometimes I think the blasted treatment is harder on me than the damned disease." He paused, forced a smile for the camera. The tape was obviously stopped as the image jumped before he continued. "Right, so that bit is out of the way. Now you know why I look like hell. I imagine you might also be feeling sorry for me right about now, and I would thank you kindly to stow that away." His smile took on a more authentic appearance. "I have had a good life, you can be sure. I went back to the family farm in Chertsey and before long met a lovely girl and started a family. The kids seemed to just keep popping out of my sweet Mary, bless her. Nigel, here, is the youngest of five." He pointed at the camera as he said Nigel's name.

Before he could speak again, he launched into a harsher fit of coughing. The recording was apparently stopped again as there was a sudden flip to Nigel once again smiling for the camera. "Sorry about that. Now then, to get to the point. One of my fondest memories is of the summer of 1969, hitchhiking across the United States. Quite the adventure, and to take it with my cousin Peter put a bond on us for life, to be sure. Woodstock itself was a crazy five days that will never be forgotten. We got there on Thursday afternoon, and there were already tens of thousands of people there. I suppose you have seen the Woodstock movie. It almost captures how wild things were... but not quite. I thought I might have seen myself in one of the crowd shots, but who could really tell? Nearly half a million people, they later claimed, stomping around in the mud." He went into another coughing fit and the tape jumped again. "Well, that is enough about Woodstock, anyways. The other amazing thing about that summer was all of the wonderful people we met along the way. Tell you the truth, there were some pretty terrible people, too, but I think they just are not worth remembering. As my days are winding down, I think back on that summer and those people. I can remember nearly everyone's name, and it sure seems to me I can picture each of them in my mind."

There was another jump in the videotape. "My cousin Peter came to see me when he heard I was terminal. We kept in touch over the years and had a few visits in person. I guess he thought he could come see me one last time."

The smile on the screen was genuine. "I got him to talking with me about that summer and all those people. We started putting together a list of names and places. I think it was about then I said something daft like, 'it would be great to see some of that lot again' when Peter gets this look in his eyes. 'I think that would be a marvelous idea,' he says." Another cut in the videotape. "Anyway, long story short, Peter volunteers to go back to America and track down as many people as he can find and put them on tape for me to see. Did I tell you that Peter is a wealthy old sod what has his own production company? He films commercials and the like for the telly. Can you imagine making a living, playing at that? I been milking cows morning and night for twenty some years and *he* turns up a fortune, making people buy stuff that they did not even know they were needing."

He paused a moment, blinked his eyes several times to fight back tears. "I joke with him, but I sure am pleased as can be that he did so well. Salt of the earth, my cousin, Peter." The tape flickered again. "Right. They tell me that there is a bit in the middle what goes to everyone, and now this is me again talking to Juan. Juan, I hope this message finds you well and happy, and I would sure be grateful if you would be willing to tell me a bit about your life on the tape. It will be great to see so many people from my memories one last time and hear about where life has taken them. And Juan, just in case you have family listening, I will skip over the crazy night at the drive-in movie. I would guess you do not want to tell them about that." He smiled warmly again, looking out from the screen as if directly to Jonathan. "God love you, Juan."

The tape went to static. Jonathan shut it off.

Everyone in the room sat quietly for several moments, then Jonathan stood, crossed to the TV and shut it off. "Would you like me to rewind the tape?" he asked softly.

"Totally up to you," said Alex. "The tape is yours to keep."

Jonathan looked uncomfortably at the floor. "Thank you."

"Would you mind saying a few things for Nigel?" Alex asked with a glance toward Sean as he added, "Senior."

Jonathan stared nervously into the camera Sean was pointing at him. "Ummm, yes," he sputtered. "Of course... but could I have a few moments to think about what I want to say?"

"Certainly," Alex agreed, nodding toward Jonathan before turning to Sean. "You can shut it off for awhile, Nigel."

"Did you want the tea in here," called Caitlin from the doorway, "or in the kitchen?"

"Let's move it to the dining room, dear," Michelle directed as she stood and crossed to her daughter.

Jonathan guided Alex and Sean to the dining room and invited them to sit at the table. Michelle brought out cups and saucers and carefully sat them before each person around the table. Caitlin held a tray with a white ceramic teapot, matching sugar bowl and creamer, and a plate of lemon slices, waiting impatiently until her mother finished setting the table. There were strings with tags hanging out from under the lid of the teapot. Michelle took the tray and set it next to Jonathan before sitting beside him. Caitlin sat across from Alex, and young Sean immediately plopped onto her lap.

"I'm sorry," apologized Michelle, "all we have is Lipton, I'm afraid."

"I am sure it will be wonderful," Alex graciously assured her.

Michelle stood. "Well, then I guess I'll pour." She picked up the tray and took it behind Alex, leaning around his left shoulder, she poured tea into his cup. "Lemon, sugar, or milk?"

No one but Sean noticed the little twitch Alex made as he queried his computer about tea. "Lemon, thank you."

With little tongs, Michelle placed a slice of lemon on Alex's saucer then moved to Sean's left and poured tea into his cup. "Lemon, sugar, or milk?" she asked.

"Milk and sugar, please," Sean replied. "That's the way my grandma makes it."

"My mom always had milk and sugar for our tea, too," commented Jonathan.

Wouldn't he be surprised to know we are talking about the same person, thought Sean. *And pretty much the only place I've ever drunk hot tea.*

Michelle finished pouring for the rest of the table, then sat down.

"Caitlin said Brits like tea and crumpets," young Sean blurted.

"*Sean!*" hissed Caitlin, her cheeks suddenly redder.

"What're crumpets?" asked the unabashed youngster.

Alex quickly twitched again before answering, "They are a type of griddle cake sometimes served with tea in England."

"Do you put maple syrup on them?" interrogated young Sean.

"No," smiled Alex, "butter and marmalade or perhaps jam. They are thicker than your pancakes."

"My mother took me to a little Tea Shop in Des Moines once," said Michelle. "They *said* they did an authentic British Tea. We had cucumber sandwiches and then scones with clotted cream and raspberry jam... and tea of course. It was really fun. Caitlin, maybe we can go into Des Moines sometime and see if that place is still there."

Caitlin rolled her eyes.

"Most families now simply have tea and biscuits," Alex added.

"Biscuits?" spouted young Sean, crinkling his nose. "We only have biscuits with fried chicken."

"A different type of biscuit, dear," Michelle explained to her young son. "They're more like what we call cookies."

"Why would you call a cookie a biscuit?" sneered Sean, boldly expressing how ridiculous he thought that was.

"Sean," threatened Caitlin, "I'm going to have to muzzle you!"

"They just have different words than we do," Michelle answered patiently. "Like what we call an elevator, they call a lift. What we call an apartment, they call a flat. We say 'truck', they say 'lorry'."

The youngster crinkled his nose again. "That's dumb," he proclaimed with regal omniscience.

There was an awkward silence around the table.

"Good one, mate," the elder Sean said, then laughed. Everyone else joined in the laughter.

"England and America are two countries separated by a common language," quoted Michelle mirthfully. When all eyes turned to her, her own eyes shifted to her cup as she softly added, "George Bernard Shaw."

"An Irishman," Jonathan announced proudly with a lifted cup.

"I noticed you named your children familiar Irish names," Alex commented.

"I can't take full credit for that. The beautiful elder redhead sitting at this table was born Margaret Michelle O'Malley."

"My grandfather was born in County Mayo," Michelle added.

"M. M. O. M.," sang young Sean. "My Mom!" Everyone laughed and the boy looked pleased with himself.

"Sean seems to be getting over his shyness," Jonathan declared wryly. He shifted his attention to Alex. "So, Peter... you made it big in advertising, did you?"

"My cousin exaggerates a bit," said Alex modestly. "I am not the 'wealthy old sod' he seems to think I am." He smiled, then added. "I do all right for myself, though."

The elder Sean noticed that Sean, the younger, seemed to be staring at him. He gave the seven-year-old a little smile.

"Are you a cousin?" posed the youngster as he continued to stare.

"Not that I know of," Sean answered nervously. He considered the question. *Half-brother?*

"Why do you say that, dear," Michelle asked her son.

"He looks like our cousins," he declared simply. "Look at his nose. It's like Christian's."

Sean had heard other Kelly family members comment about how he and Christian had similar features... but that was in some other world that now seemed impossibly far away.

The precocious child had stopped staring at Sean and had turned his full attention to Caitlin, then back to Sean again. "Him and Caitlin have the same eyes," he proclaimed.

Sean looked closer at the girl across the table. When he focused on her eyes, it *was* like looking in the mirror. It was a little unsettling. When he realized she was staring back, he looked away.

"Sean," asserted Jonathan, "why don't you drink your milk and let some other people talk?"

"I don't want any milk," the youngster huffed.

Michelle stood. "Let me see if I can find something to change your mind," she said as she disappeared into the kitchen.

"You," declared Caitlin as she poked her little brother's ribs, "are spoiled rotten." He giggled.

Michelle breezed back into the dining room and set down a platter of hastily scattered cookies. "They're from the store," she confessed. "I don't get to bake as often as I'd like to." She looked sheepishly at Alex. "Biscuit?"

Young Sean immediately snagged a cookie and plunged it into his cup of milk.

"Right, Mom," said Caitlin sarcastically, "in your 'spare time'." She marked the air with invisible quotes.

The elder Sean turned to Michelle. "That sounds like you must be a busy woman. What do you do?"

"Well, I..." started Michelle.

"No, let me," interrupted Caitlin. She cleared her throat and announced formally, "May I introduce to you my parents, Dr. and Dr. Kelly, DVM."

"A veterinarian?" said a surprised Sean as he turned to his Dad.

"Yes," he confirmed, puzzled by Sean's reaction, "we both are. I bought the practice where I'd been working about nine years ago. Fiona and Caitlin were in school, my boss was looking to retire, so it was an excellent opportunity for Michelle to come back into practice... for a couple of years."

"And now that Sean is in school, I'm back," Michelle said frostily as she glared at her husband.

"Ask me about my wonderful summer vacations," grumbled Caitlin.

"Caitlin!" snapped Michelle, "You *love* your little brother!"

"I know, Mom," replied Caitlin, giving the seven year old a squeeze, "and I'll love him just as much when I'm away at college next year." She kissed his cheek. "Maybe more."

The elder Sean was amused by the family dynamics. It seemed so... normal. Maybe it would be nice to have a sassy half-sister.

"We'll see how you feel after you've gone away for a few weeks," Michelle stated confidently. She smiled at her young son. "You'll miss his cute little face."

"No, I won't. I'll hang his picture on my dorm room wall," Caitlin blurted. "My own private poster-boy for safe sex."

Michelle gasped.

"Kidding..." Caitlin added quickly and with obvious regret.

"Caitlin!" barked Jonathan.

The girl shrunk back, head down, cheeks flushed. She cautiously lifted her eyes to glance between her parents who were both glaring at her. "Sorry..." she said softly, "I didn't mean...." She dropped her head back down without continuing.

"We'll discuss it later," said Michelle in measured tones.

"Both of you are animal doctors, then?" asked Alex, attempting to break the tension in the air.

The doctors Kelly glanced at each other, non-verbally determining who would field the question, then Michelle spoke. "Yes, Jonathan specializes in livestock, and since I've come back, I try to keep up with the small animals... pets."

Young Sean grabbed another cookie and happily dunked it in his milk.

"That was how we met," added Jonathan. "We kept having biology and chemistry classes together, and before long we discovered we had a little chemistry of our own."

Caitlin rolled her eyes. Sean's stomach flipped over. He didn't feel comfortable hearing his Dad talk about falling in love with another woman.

"You met at University, then?" asked Alex.

"Yes," Jonathan confirmed, "right here at Iowa State. As you can see, we didn't stray too far after graduating. Or maybe you don't know. Iowa State is in Ames."

"How did you determine where you wanted to attend University?" Alex inquired.

"Because of a friend, actually, and maybe you'll track her down for a video," said Jonathan. "Jimbo and I were planning on going to Golden Valley State in Missouri. We'd even gone there for a spring visit... but then Jane came back over the summer and she kept telling me how great Iowa State was. She said she thought I'd fit right in, and looking back, I think she also kind of wanted me to help her deal with Micky."

"Jane?" asked Alex, now keenly interested. "Jane Carmichael?" He glanced at Sean.

"Yes," replied Jonathan, "I'll bet Nigel, Sr. would love to hear from her. I think they kind of hit it off... even if it was only a couple of days." He turned to Sean. "Your dad was kind of smitten with Jane, I think, and *she* talked about *him* for weeks after he left."

"I understood that Jane Carmichael was killed in an auto-mobile accident," remarked Alex.

Jonathan was perplexed for a moment, then shook his head. "No, that was one of the other girls you met. You must have gotten your information crossed up. That was Louise Rimmer."

"Louise?" gasped Sean.

Jonathan turned back to him. "Yes, did your dad tell you about Louise? Oh, she was a sweet little girl. So peppy... just all-the-time happy, I don't think you could hardly catch her having a bad day." He paused as sadness crept into his face. "That was just tragic."

"Louise died in the car wreck?" Sean breathed. The color drained from his face.

"Yes," reaffirmed Jonathan, "that was a sad October at Mercer High School. One other person was killed and Tony Caparelli got a leg mangled so badly that he still limps after I don't know how many surgeries." He looked at Sean. "Are you all right?" Sean nodded, but it was a lie. "I think Tony felt guilty about Louise getting killed. Maybe even blamed himself. He said it was his fault she was in the car. It was just a crazy turn of events. There was a school dance that night, it was senior night for the football team... last home game of the year. Louise and Micky got into a big fight at the dance, and Louise gave him back his class ring and told him it was 'over for good this time'. Unfortunately, she was right about that." Jonathan paused and closed his eyes, there was still some pain tied to that night. "Sometimes you just have to wonder how different a person's life would be if you could only stop a particular thing from happening." He paused again.

"How do you mean," prompted Alex.

"Just so many things that led up to Louise being in that car that night," Jonathan said, shaking his head slowly. "If she and Micky hadn't had that fight. If she hadn't left the dance when she did. Willie Brighton and Randy Hunter and Tony Caparelli were all seniors. Randy got his hands on a case of beer and they were going to go out and drive around the countryside and drink it. They were in the parking lot making their plans when Louise stormed out. Tony asked her what was wrong, they got to talking and then pretty soon she'd agreed to go with them. Louise didn't ever drink. If it weren't for Tony, she wouldn't have gotten in the car with them. I guess I can see why Tony blamed himself... but you know... if Louise had just stayed at the dance for another ten minutes..." His voice trailed off.

Sean felt sicker as he heard the story unfold. Jonathan stared off into space as he resumed, "I saw the car... morbid teenage curiosity, I guess... we just had to go to the junkyard to see the car. It was a 55 Chevy hardtop. They rolled it. Roof collapsed. Not sure if Louise was crushed, or what happened. Someone said Randy got thrown out and rolled on. I don't know. Closed casket at both funerals, though. Some of us even went out there to see where it happened. You could see the skid marks in the gravel. It looked like they probably crested a little hill and left the ground. When they came back down the car started sliding. You could see where it finally left the road, just missed a telephone pole, or they probably would have all four been killed."

"Why were they going so fast on gravel?" asked Caitlin, having never heard the story.

"Another bad timing thing. Someone tossed an empty beer can at an intersection, and a sheriff's deputy just happened to be coming down the cross road and saw them. He hit his lights and started after them. I guess Willie thought he could outrun him." Jonathan shook his head again. "A different road, or even just five minutes one way or the other where they were. It could have *all* been different."

Michelle patted her husband's hand. "I think that's enough, dear." She looked at the elder Sean and wondered about his pained expression and pale color. The younger Sean happily dunked his third cookie, oblivious to the story his dad had related.

"Was Jane Carmichael at the dance?" asked Alex.

Jonathan looked in Alex's general direction and blinked a couple of times as he thought. "No," he said, "I don't think she was." He sighed. "That's another thing that might have changed things. If Louise had Jane to talk to, she might not have left the dance."

Guilt consumed Sean.

"You know, it was kind of strange," said Jonathan. "I went to see Jane the next day. I knew she'd be a mess. Jane and Louise were so close." He looked toward the person he believed was Nigel Davies, Jr. "That was the last time I think I heard Jane mention your dad. She had kind of stopped talking about him. At first, I think she had hoped he was going to come back. Eventually, she gave that up, but she did mention his name that Saturday. Not that it made any sense. Oh, she was a complete mess emotionally, but I remember her saying several times, 'why wouldn't Nigel save her?' Didn't make any sense to me. Still doesn't."

"Did you think it unusual that Jane was *not* at the dance?" asked Alex.

"Kind of hard to say with Jane," said Jonathan thoughtfully. "She didn't have a boyfriend, but she'd usually go to things like that, just to hang out and talk with people. Maybe she just didn't feel like it that night. I never asked her about it. I don't think I ever even thought about it before today. I mean, it didn't seem important."

"You said that Jane was instrumental in your decision to attend university at Iowa State?" inquired Alex, now sounding more like an investigative reporter.

"That's right," confirmed Jonathan. "And like I mentioned, I think she wanted me to be around to help her keep an eye on Micky."

"How do you mean," asked Alex.

Jonathan mulled the question over, trying to decide where to begin. "Micky was never a very good student. I don't think it was because he wasn't smart enough, he just didn't care about school... even from the very beginning. His parents had him repeat first grade. That's why he was in my grade instead of Jane's. You knew they were twins, right?" When Alex nodded, Jonathan resumed. "Micky was a guy that totally embraced the 60s philosophy of 'if it feels good, do it.' Looking back, I'm surprised that Louise stayed with him as long as she did. Her family was as straight-laced as they come, and Louise was a lot of fun, but she pretty much stuck with her parents' morals. I don't know, maybe Micky was just her attempt at being rebellious." Jonathan paused to gather his thoughts.

"Anyway," he continued, "Micky was pretty messed up after Louise died. For awhile he'd get drunk or stoned every weekend, then he went through a Jesus Freak phase, then it was Buddhism, Hari Krishna, Baha'i, and I don't know what else. Jane made it her mission to get him back on track. I guess with Louise gone, Jane kind of turned to me as her main confidant. I kind of became better friends with Micky because of her. Summer of seventy, they built a new Hy-Vee in Mercer, and Micky and I got jobs as laborers... grunt stuff, but it was three-fifty an hour. That was pretty good pay in 1970. I guess that probably did more to build our friendship than anything, and by then he'd run out of new religions to try." He paused to recompile old memories.

"Senior year, Micky was hanging around with me and Jimbo quite a bit. Scott had turned into a real stoner. That Karen... you met Karen, didn't you? I mean, I'm not saying Scott and I are on par with Lennon and McCartney, but Karen was definitely Yoko Ono."

Alex queried his computer to find out what Jonathan meant.

"She eventually got pregnant, they got married... it was a mess... but never mind that, it's an entirely different story. Anyway, I'm hanging around with Micky more, and Jane asks me about him whenever she comes home for weekends. Like I said, Micky's not the academic type, so he wasn't ever planning to go to college. Jimbo had some kind of friend of a friend or something that went to Golden Valley State in Missouri, and he wanted me to go there with him. I didn't have any solid plans, so it sounded like a good idea. But then Jane was back in Mercer for the summer of '71 and she sells Micky on going to college to 'get away from home.' I guess at the same time she started selling me on Iowa State. So, fall of '71, Micky and I were roommates in the dorm at Iowa State." He looked at Michelle and gave her a warm smile. "Of course the best part of college was finding Michelle." She leaned into him and gave him a quick kiss.

"Oh barf," mumbled Caitlin. She slapped her brother's hand as he reached for a fourth cookie.

"Don't 'oh barf,' little girl," teased Jonathan, "If I hadn't met your mother, where do you think *you'd* be?"

Sean stood abruptly. "I need some air," he wheezed as he fled the room. Everyone watched with concern as the pale teenager fled.

Michelle looked from her husband to Alex and quickly determined they weren't going to act. "Caitlin, will you go check on him?"

"*Muh-thur!*" whined the girl.

"Please?" requested Michelle kindly, "just make sure he's all right. He looked kind of pale."

Caitlin rolled her eyes and sighed melodramatically as she stood. As soon as she was away from the table, Sean snagged his fourth cookie.

Outside, the older Sean was sitting on the steps by the front door, miserable. *It was all my fault!* he thought. *Saving Jane had changed my Dad's life and ended Louise's. How could saving someone's life mess everything else up? It should have been just a little splash in the big river of time. Maybe there really is a good reason for the 'first law' thing that Alex is so programmed to believe.*

The door opened behind him, brushing against his back. Caitlin slid through the constricted opening. "They wanted me to make sure you're OK," she announced.

"Fine," croaked Sean.

"That didn't sound too convincing," Caitlin replied. "Want me to get you some water?"

"No," muttered Sean.

Caitlin stepped around him and sat down beside him. "Was the tea that bad? I mean, you didn't eat any of the cookies... or biscuits or whatever."

"No, it was fine," Sean said, a wisp of a smile returning.

"I wasn't sure," teased Caitlin, "I don't drink much tea. I thought maybe if you Brits got a bad cup, it messed you up... although I guess technically you're not a Brit, are you?"

"No," said Sean, his color returning with his smile. "Technically I'm not."

"So it wasn't the tea?"

"No, not the tea."

They sat quietly for awhile.

"My friends say I'm a good listener," Caitlin suggested, "if you want to talk about something."

Sean turned, somewhat surprised to see the sincerity on her face. He gave her a weak smile. "That's very kind of you, but no thanks." He returned to staring ahead. They sat together silently for several minutes.

"I'm sorry about your dad," she ventured. He turned to look at her again, said nothing, and returned to his vigil of the sidewalk. "I overheard the tape from the kitchen." She waited a bit in silence again before continuing. "I don't know what I'd do if I were going to lose my dad."

That's the absurdity of this whole thing, thought Sean. *My dad is within reach and completely beyond my grasp, both at the same time.*

He wished he could tell her about it... but it was much too strange to believe. He barely believed it himself. He glanced at her again and she smiled. He wondered what it would have been like if she really *were* his sister.

"Sean's right," she declared.

"About?"

"Your eyes. Look at me." Sean turned to look deeper into her frighteningly familiar eyes. "It's kind of bizarre," she continued. "When I focus on just your eyes, it's like looking in the mirror."

"I know," said Sean through a grin, "You have the most amazingly beautiful eyes!"

"Wow," she laughed, punching his shoulder, "Mr. Vanity, here."

"Ow!" complained Sean, grabbing his shoulder in mock pain.

Caitlin flexed her bicep. "Farm-girl power!" They both laughed. "I'm sorry I gave you the evil eye earlier. I thought you were some kind of salesman or Jehovah's Witness or something."

"That's OK," said Sean, "I shouldn't have called you 'girly'... that was kind of rude."

"Yeah," replied Caitlin, nodding as she considered it, "It kinda was." They both briefly laughed, then sat quietly for awhile. The silence made Sean edgy.

"I got the impression that you may not be too pleased to be the live-in babysitter."

"Yeah," she shrugged. "It sucks... but I understand. Dad really needs Mom to help keep the practice afloat. And don't get me wrong... I love Sean to death." She paused. "It just kind of... I don't know... takes over my life?" Sean nodded. "Sometimes it's hard not to blame them. Their lives would have obviously been less complicated without Sean... mine, too."

"Are you suggesting he was a 'surprise'?"

"Let's see," started Caitlin, putting a finger to her chin and pulling her lower lip as if just figuring it out. "Fiona and I are two years apart, and then a ten year gap to Sean. Dad puts the family in huge debt buying out the practice he's been working in. Mom comes in to help run it, because it really does need two people, but two years later, she's back to mostly being a mom. I don't think it takes a rocket scientist to figure out Sean was an 'oops' baby."

"I see what you mean."

"Fiona took the main brunt of it until she escaped to college."

"Is that what you want to do?"

"Sure... but then I feel guilty about it," she confessed. Sean nodded. They sat quietly, side by side, staring straight ahead. "What about your family?" asked Caitlin.

"I'm an only child," replied Sean without thinking.

"I thought you were the youngest of five," said Caitlin, eying him suspiciously.

Crap! "Ummm, yeah," stalled Sean. "You must have good ears." He'd forgotten himself for a moment. At least, forgotten he was supposed to be Nigel Davies, Jr.

"Really?" Caitlin said, "You don't get super-hearing when *you* get sent from the room?"

"Good point."

"So which is it?"

"Which is what?"

"Only child, or baby of five?"

Time to get the character back on track. "Youngest of five," Sean lied. "Wasn't the sweetest spot, I'll tell you. Getting picked on and beat on by four older brothers and sisters. I guess 'only child' was just a wishful dream."

"How many of each?" asked Caitlin conversationally.

I don't know! We didn't prep that part of a back-story! "Ummm... two and two."

Caitlin looked at him expectantly. After a short pause she prompted, "And do they have *names*, or do you really *not* like to talk about them?"

Names? Crap and double crap! I hope no one cross checks names with Alex. "Sure they have names. The two oldest are my brothers.... umm.... Roger and Kevin!" Caitlin raised her eyebrows, signaling him to continue. *Girls' names, girls' names, girls' names!* "Umm and my sisters are... umm... Jane and.... umm... Nicole!"

Caitlin decided it was a little odd that he struggled just telling her his siblings' names. "Are you messing with me for some reason?"

"Nope!" said Sean nervously, "Why do you ask?"

"I dunno... maybe because it seemed like you were just making names up?"

"Nope! Roger, Kevin, Jane and Nicole! That's them! That's my brothers and sisters."

Caitlin continued to eye him suspiciously. "OK, if you say so," she finally said in the same tone one would use to say, 'liar, liar, pants on fire.' "So is Jane named after the Jane my dad knew? The one he said *your* dad had a crush on?"

I've really got to put a stop to this before I dig a hole I can't get out of! "I never really thought about it. I don't remember my dad talking about a Jane from his younger days." That was true no matter which dad he meant, his real one or the phantom Nigel Davies, Sr.

Sean stood abruptly. "Shall we go back in?"

Caitlin also stood, but grabbed Sean's shoulders before he could start up the steps. "Look me in the eye again," she requested. He turned to face her, looking into those strangely familiar eyes. "You have the most amazingly beautiful eyes!" she deadpanned.

"Wow," he mimicked, tapping her shoulder lightly with a fist, "Ms. Vanity, here."

She returned the punch with much more force, even harder than the first time. She followed it with another bicep flex. "Farm-girl power!" Caitlin winked at him as Sean opened the door and they went in.

They hadn't even made it all the way back to the dining room when Alex called out, "Nigel, if you care to get set up in the living room, Mr. Kelly is ready to record a short video for your dad."

Sean went into the living room and got the camera out of the carrying bag. There wasn't much to 'set up' since they didn't even have a tripod for the camera. Caitlin had followed him in. He wondered if it was just a natural continuation of walking in together, or if she felt some kind of connection to him now? A connection like he felt for her.

Alex came in with Jonathan and positioned him in a chair, coached him about talking naturally and just telling his story however he wanted. Michelle had coaxed her son to help her clear the table, and he managed to stuff another cookie into his pocket in the process.

"I am going to go outside for a smoke," announced Alex. "I will call the crew and see if they are returning to collect us."

Sean wondered what Alex was really going to do, but couldn't join him since he was committed to holding the video-camera.

Jonathan told the camera about his wife and children, his work as a veterinarian, and some of the things he considered high points of his life. It took several minutes and a few "can we stop and do that part over" breaks, but he finished up by wishing Nigel the best and hoping that his health improved. Alex quietly slipped back in just before Jonathan finished. Sean rewound the tape and let them both watch it on the camera's small screen. Alex assured Jonathan that it was perfect and that the crew would take care of smoothing out the edits.

"You should get packed up, Nigel," Alex suggested. "The crew was already on their way back, so they should be here soon."

Sean put the camera in the bag and zipped it. *Not much to packing up,* he thought.

Michelle came into the room and asked if the crew would want to come in for some 'tea and biscuits'. Alex assured her they would not, and that there was a tight schedule to keep. The group shuffled toward the front door, with Caitlin and Sean bringing up the rear. Little Sean was right in front of them, so Sean reached out and ruffled his hair.

"Owwww!" he whined.

"What?"

"You pulled my hair!" he squealed.

Sean looked at his wrist and realized that his watch must have caught in the little boy's hair. "Sorry, mate, it was an accident." He looked closer at his watch and pulled a hair from it. He nearly discarded it, but on a whim, he slipped the hair into his shirt pocket.

"So where are you headed now?" Caitlin asked him.

"Umm, someplace in Illinois, I think," Sean replied. "Peter said they worked their way from California to New York."

"Who are you going to see in Illinois?"

"I don't really know the names of everyone. Peter has it all mapped out," he claimed as he passed through the front door and onto the first step.

"Safe travels," Caitlin said, standing in the door frame.

Sean turned back to her. "It was really nice meeting you."

"Yeah," she replied, "A little rocky start, but I guess you turned out OK." She punched him in the shoulder, then flexed a bicep and winked at him again.

To Sean's surprise, a van pulled up to the end of the long gravel driveway. It looked like they actually *did* have a crew. *How had Alex managed this?*

"Come along, Nigel," Alex called as he walked briskly toward the van. "No dawdling." Sean caught up with him. "It is a hologram, of course," whispered Alex. "You will need to follow me all the way around the front. Do *not* touch the vehicle, your hand would pass through it. When we reach the far side, I will open the door to the S.T.E. The cloaking should make it appear as if we have walked around the vehicle and entered it from the far side."

Sean followed his instructions, and they soon were back inside Steffi. Alex moved the ship along the road, continuing the projection of a van on the road for about a mile, then he shut the image off and raised them above the tree line.

"Hey," Sean said as he pulled the hair from his pocket. "Can you run the DNA on this? It's this timeline's version of Sean. Can you compare it to mine?"

Alex took the hair sample from Sean and also plucked another longer red hair from his shoulder. "Caitlin's I believe. You were in closer proximity to her than Michelle. I will run them both, if you wish, but it will simply reveal them to be half-siblings to you."

"I just want to be certain that little Sean is *not* me."

"Impossible," scoffed Alex, "Without the genetic input of your mother, it is a biological impossibility for this Sean to 'be you'. There is no need to map DNA to prove that."

"Just humor me, OK?" Sean finally said.

Alex pulled up a screen of controls and deposited the hairs into a small tray that appeared from the front panel. It retracted and disappeared, as if never there. He punched a few more icons, then turned his attention to Sean.

"Jonathan last saw Jane Carmichael at something called a 'twenty-year reunion' in 1991," said Alex.

"You want to shut off the Brit-speak... and lose that disguise," urged Sean, ignoring Alex's comment.

"Sorry," said Alex, clicking out of his accent and dropping the Peter Lindsey appearance before he continued, "At that time, she was living in Washington, D.C., working as a lobbyist. He does not know if that is her current residence." He paused to glance at Sean, who said nothing. "He said she had separated from her third husband." He looked expectantly at Sean again. "And that she did not have any children."

"Why are you telling me this?" Sean crabbed irritably.

"I thought perhaps it would make it easier."

"Make it easier? Make *what* easier?"

"To know that she did not have children, and perhaps had not been pleased with her attempts at finding a life-mate."

"*What* does knowing that make easier?" Sean's voice was getting edgier.

Alex considered his words carefully before replying. "I assumed it would be more difficult if you knew that Jane was happily married and had children. I thought perhaps letting you know the additional information I received while you were outside with Caitlin would make it easier."

"*What. Are. You. Making. Easier!*" Sean gruffly enunciated each word.

Alex cringed from his outburst. He nervously glanced toward Sean and considered the possibility of rendering him unconscious. He steeled himself.

"Her death."

Sean's fist flew without conscious effort and slammed against the screen in front of him. Sparks flashed and he drew his fist back in pain.

"It has a protective force field," Alex offered timidly.

"Land this thing," Sean growled softly through clenched teeth.

"I do not..."

"*Land it! Now!*" Sean demanded.

"We are currently over a cornfield..."

"*Now!*"

"It will crush the vegetation. It will leave an outline of the ship."

"I don't give a damn if you make crop circles that hit the front page of every major newspaper in the country!" roared Sean. "*Land. This. Ship.*"

Alex quickly manipulated some icons on the forward screen. He turned meekly toward Sean when he had finished.

"Are we down?" Sean whispered throatily. Alex nodded. "Open it," Sean commanded as he banged on the door. Alex complied.

Sean flung himself from the time-craft. He randomly stomped down several stalks of corn, then grabbed one and uprooted it. He swung it around, madly at all of the other stalks within reach. He turned back toward Steffi and with a guttural scream smashed the cornstalk against the roof. Sparks flew.

A timid voice spoke from inside, "Protective f..."

"Force Field!" Sean howled. "I got that! I'm not *stupid* you know." He slammed the cornstalk against the roof and sparks flew again. "Or maybe I am," he snarled, "if we use *your* standards." He repeatedly beat on the roof until the cornstalk was nearly disintegrated. He stopped and stared briefly in bewilderment at the stub in his hand and then let it fall to the ground.

He looked up at the cloudless blue sky, closed his eyes and fell to his knees. Alex warily peered out in time to see Sean fall forward as he began slamming the dirt with his right fist, a primordial wail erupted from his throat. Alex recoiled in fear and waited a few seconds before peeking out again.

Sean's body shuddered as he heaved silent sobs, occasionally broken with a sharp intake of breath like a drowning man's desperate gasp for air.

Alex was frightened, bewildered by this intense show of emotion, but he was also touched. He felt an empathetic ache in his own heart as he observed his ancestor's spasms of pain. He silently watched and waited, feeling more helpless with each passing minute.

Eventually, Sean's retching subsided. He shifted his body around until he was leaning against the S.T.E. with his legs sprawled before him. He looked as limp as a rag doll thoughtlessly tossed against a wall. He stared toward the sky, which from his angle, was mostly blocked by the tops of rows and rows of cornstalks. Alex maintained his silent vigil for several more minutes. Sean did not move except for the rise and fall of regular breathing, his eyes open, staring but not seeing. Alex retrieved a liter of water from the front console.

"Ten degrees," he said softly to the container. "Open three centimeters."

He offered the bottle to Sean. At first Sean didn't react, then he slowly turned his head and stared blankly at the bottle. Alex waited silently, trying to not move, though the weight of the bottle pulled on his outstretched arm.

Alex was querying the computer about catatonia when Sean finally blinked. He had blinked twice more before he lifted a hand to take the bottle. When Alex released the bottle, the bottle and Sean's arm dropped to the ground. Sean gripped it tight enough that it didn't tip over. He sat for several minutes staring at the bottle, as if he didn't know what it was. At last he raised it to his lips and drank. Alex fought back tears.

"Should have been just a tiny ripple," Sean croaked. He took another drink. "Just a little pebble in the big river of time. One little thing," he rambled, "Should have been a tiny ripple."

Alex waited to see if Sean was going to continue before he spoke. "It *was* a tiny ripple, when you consider all the billions of people on the planet. An insignificantly small percentage were affected."

Sean let his head flop to the right, so that his face was mostly pointed toward Alex. He blinked but did not speak.

"Less than 99.99999% of the world's population has seen any change from the original timeline," Alex stated softly. "Most people were far enough away from the event that they were unaware of even the tiniest ripple." He paused, trying to decide if Sean was absorbing any of this information. "It just happens that you and I were right next to where the pebble hit. The shockwave near ground zero was substantial for us."

Sean continued to stare in the same direction. Alex was within his peripheral vision, but he made no attempt to change his focus. "So you're just going to go back and kill her?" he mumbled in an emotionless monotone.

The statement took Alex completely by surprise. It had taken him several seconds of measured contemplation before he responded. "I will attempt to catch the pebble before it hits the water," he said almost cryptically, "and return the timeline to its original path."

Sean continued to stare. "I guess that makes it easier on the conscience than to admit that you're going to murder Jane."

"It is *not* murder," protested Alex.

Sean turned his head and focused his eyes on Alex, suddenly lucid. "Right now, while we are sitting in this cornfield in Iowa, Jane is *alive* in Washington, D.C. I don't care if she *is* childless and been through three husbands... she is *alive*. You intend to go back in time and change things so that she is killed in a car wreck. She is *alive* now, actions that *you* are going to take will make her *dead*. How in your screwed up logical brain is that *not* murder?"

Alex's face flared red. "Let us use *your* terminology, then," he retorted hotly, "and apply your emotional rant to your choices. By *your* actions, *you* changed the events of history that then caused the death of Louise Rimmer. *You*, therefore, *murdered* Louise!"

The mental image of the bubbly, continuously happy Louise being violently crushed in a car crashed painfully through Sean's brain. He took a deep breath, shook off the stabbing guilt and leaned forward, no longer limp against the S.T.E. "What happens to Caitlin?" he fired, "And Fiona? And little Sean Kelly?"

Alex was confused by his question but answered him, "They will not exist, as they did not exist in the original timeline."

"But they exist right now. I talked with two of them. So did you."

"That does not mean..."

"But *your* plan," interrupted Sean, "to *murder* Jane will also get rid of *them*. You effectively *murder* Fiona, Caitlin, and Sean!"

"Your argument is totally irrational!" Alex huffed, "But if you insist on this line of reasoning and this terminology, let me point out that Louise and Charles Jones were *supposed* to have *four* children. *Your* actions that *murdered* Louise, by extension, also *murdered* her four children!"

Sean lifted a hand to point an accusing finger at Alex, but no words came out. Alex continued passionately, "*Your* actions remove all of my lineage back to Jack Kelly. *You* are responsible for the *murder* of *my father! You* are responsible for the murder of my *grandfather! You* are responsible for the murder of *his* father and grandfather. *Your* actions, which removed your own self from the timeline as a son of Jack Kelly has disqualified you from marrying Katherine. Therefore, you have murdered your *own children!*"

Alex's face was beet red. His computer sent him a triggered warning, "Heart rate unnaturally elevated. Blood pressure also elevated. Sedative recommended. Accept sedative?" The information shocked him, but he rejected the sedative. He was acting as irrationally as Sean... and nearly as emotional. It was a very odd sensation.

Sean stared at him, his hand still pointed, ready to accuse... but there were no more accusations... no more confrontations. He let his arm drop, followed by his head.

"Please don't kill her," he whimpered. He collapsed forward, his face in the dirt. "Please," he sobbed. "Please don't kill her. Please. There has to be another way." He lay in the dirt, crying and pleading.

Alex was terrified by what he witnessed. It was far worse than any of the extreme anger Sean had ever shown him. The ancestor was crushed, helpless, spilling all but his very life on the ground. Alex felt like his *own* inner being was collapsing in on itself. It was more than he could tolerate. He mentally issued the command that rendered Sean unconscious.

Chapter Thirteen

"It's too late to fight / It's too late to change me..."

HE FELT LIKE he was floating. On a river? On a cloud? In outer space? It was warm. There was something warm. Something warm flowing over him. Warm.

"Sean?"

There was a voice from far away... far, far away.

"Sean?"

It kind of echoed. Not like a cave... more like a movie special effect, when the sound keeps repeating, but is out of sync and fades away... that kind of echo.

"Do you hear me?"

Kind of annoying, too. Much nicer just floating in the quiet.

"I do not believe I have your brain chemistry correct."

Very annoying. Someone... someone annoying. Quiet is better.

There was a bright flash in one of his eyes and a shadowy figure behind it. "I am *not* a physician... even by your primitive standards."

Very annoying. Very, very annoying. He knew that voice. Someone annoying. He'd heard it before. Water running... the sound of water running. *Alex!*

"This would be considerably easier if you had the correct number of nanites in your system."

Alex! Please go away. Let me float in the quiet. Go away!

"The computer reports cognitive brain function. Sean! Sean! Focus on my voice."

"Go way" Sean slurred.

"We need to discuss some specific information."

"No," slurred Sean, "Floating! Go way!"

"What is my name?"

"L X... fie, fie, fie, one-two, one-two."

"Close. Let us try again," Alex declared, "What is my name?"

"Future Boy! Dum ta da dummmmmmm!" sang Sean, "An' his sigh kick, Nigh jll!"

"Again, close," replied Alex clinically. "Let me reduce the number of endorphins."

"Nooo," complained Sean. "Floating good!"

Alex waited a few minutes as the nanites executed his instructions. "All right, let us try again. What is my name?"

"Alex!" snapped Sean.

"Very good, now can you tell..."

"Peter!" Sean continued louder. "Nicole! Alexis! Katherine! Jogging blonde with no-name!" He shouted each name.

"All right, very good," Alex reassured him. "We can simply stop with Alex."

"Can see why you ask," Sean slurred happily, "You prolly can't keep track."

"Do you have any idea where you are?"

Sean's head wobbled as he looked around. He squinted to try to focus on the mist that enveloped them. "Clouds!"

"No, that is water vapor produced by the water temperature being higher than the surrounding atmosphere. Look beyond the vapor."

"Look beyond the vapor," Sean giggled. "Darth vapor?"

"Concentrate, please," Alex sighed, "Do you see the walls beyond the vapor?"

Sean looked again. "Beyond th' vapor... yup! Walls!"

"What do you deduce from their appearance?"

Sean looked again. "Walls!"

"This is not working," muttered Alex, in frustration. "They are concrete walls. You are sitting on a concrete floor. Notice the water falling on you."

Sean put his hand out and watched water drops splash on his cupped palm. It was very pretty, the way it splashed. It was almost like drops of water were leaping from his hand.

"Concentrate. Why is there water falling?" asked Alex.

Sean studied the drops hopping around on his hand. Eventually, the question sunk in. "Rain?"

"No," whimpered Alex. "I do not even know if the brain chemistry of a twentieth-century boy is similar to my own."

"Shower?" asked Sean.

"Yes!" whooped Alex. "Now look around again. Can you piece together where you are? You have been here before."

Sean looked around. Concrete walls. Concrete floor. Drains. A doorway. There were wooden benches in the next room. At the edge of the doorway a towel... with kittens on it. No! It couldn't be. He pointed up at the shower and shook his head. "Warm. Not warm."

"That actually took some effort," Alex explained. "I was able to remove the spigot section from the shower pipes above you, then open a water container from Steffi and resealed it, but with that piece stuck in the opening. Next, I inverted it, reopened it and placed that opening around the protruding pipe and resealed the opposite side. In a sense, it is merely a pass-through extension between the two original parts. It was more difficult to calibrate the heat needed to bring the water to a comfortable temperature before it exits."

"No," Sean moaned as he struggled to regain control of his mind. "1969. No. High school."

"That is correct. You had gotten quite dirty in that cornfield. It seemed logical to return here. Although I did not believe cold water would be conducive for your condition."

"No," Sean struggled, "1969. No. Don't kill."

Remorse pricked at Alex's heart. "Sean," he said softly, "we must return the timeline to its original state. Neither of us will have a home if we do not."

Sean pointed to the shower head. "Cold."

"I attempted to explain, I modified it to heat the water before it came out."

Sean shook his head and pointed again. "No," he demanded, "Cold!"

Alex was confused. "You want it cold?"

Sean nodded. "Not float. Need cold."

"I believe it is the raised level of dopamine that creates your euphoria, or floating, as you describe it."

"Stop... please?"

"I thought it was the best course of action to pursue with regard to correcting the emotional distress that had debilitated you."

Sean rocked his head side to side. "Not think straight."

"That would be the negative side-effect of the overabundance of dopamine."

"Please... stop... need to talk."

"I must confess that I am also concerned for my own well-being, should you become violent again."

"Promise... not hit...you."

Alex studied Sean's face. He was certainly sincere, but also under the influence of his own spiked brain chemistry. At least there was always the fail-safe of unconsciousness. "Very well," he said as he issued a command to his computer to relay to Sean's nanites. "It will take a few minutes for your levels to return to normal."

Sean pointed up again. "Cold."

Alex looked up at his cobbled shower head. "If you insist." He stood. "I finally set it at 79 degrees to get a comfortable output of 35 degrees. Wait, I forget that you are more familiar with the antiquated Fahrenheit scale." He ran a quick calculation. "Roughly 175 and 95 degrees, respectively."

"Cold," repeated Sean.

"Since I am unsure of the input temperature, this is merely an attempt," he said to Sean, then addressed the container, "15 degrees."

"Aughhhhh!" Sean yelped as the water chilled.

"I will assume by that reaction that you would consider the water cold."

The icy blast of cold water accelerated the process of normalizing Sean's brain chemistry. He no longer felt like he was floating in a fog bank. In less than a minute, he decided he could stand, and did so. The initial shock of the cold water had passed. It still felt cold, but he was adjusting to it. He tried to also adjust to his surroundings. It was definitely the locker-room shower he had used just hours before.

Hours? Days? Years? Decades? Measurement of time had become more and more difficult as he was passed from one time to another. He looked down at himself and found that he was wearing only his underwear.

"How did you manage getting me in here?" asked Sean.

"It was not a simple task," replied Alex. "Mainly, I had to resort to dragging you."

"So, super-strength isn't built into your super-suit?"

"The pseudo-body suit does nothing to enhance the musculature," Alex responded peevishly, "That would require a design with exoskeletal enhancements." He paused to consider his own suggestion. "I do not believe that the two purposes would even be compatible."

Sean pictured being dragged unconscious from Steffi, into the shower and undressed. He gave his head a brisk shake to try to dismiss the embarrassing image. "Where are my clothes?" he demanded.

"I have them laid out on a bench in the next room. It is the Nigel Davies ensemble."

"Ensemble?" Sean snorted. "Thinking of a career in fashion when you return to your own time?"

Alex frowned. "It appears your brain has returned to normal. You have resumed insulting me."

"Why don't you go play a game of chess with Steffi or something while I get dressed?"

"You still have..." Alex mumbled as he rubbed his hand on his own cheek.

"Cornfield on my face? Fine. Crank the heat back up on the water on your way out. Never mind. I'll do it. What did you say? 175 degrees?"

"No! You must use Celsius! 79 degrees!" he shrieked, then considered the container's capabilities, and continued in a calm voice. "Since it is a water container, it would logically only be equipped for a range from zero to one hundred. Still, that would be dangerously hot."

"Got it," Sean acknowledged as he turned to face the jerry-rigged shower. "79 degrees." The water immediately warmed. He turned back to Alex and waved him off. "I'll be out in a few minutes."

Minutes later, Sean pushed through the locker room door out to the basketball court. He wore the bell bottomed jeans with brightly colored patches and a tie-dyed t-shirt. "I assume you're out here somewhere," he shouted, the sound reverberating off the walls and high ceiling.

245

Light spilled onto the floor as the door of the time-ship opened as if in thin air.

"What day is this?" Sean asked.

"July 14, 1969," replied Alex from inside the S.T.E.

"What time?"

"Approximately 5:30 a.m.," came the response.

Sean spotted three rows of basketballs sitting on a long cart against the wall. *Those would be locked down in my school,* he mused as he picked one up and started to bounce it. The echoes from the bouncing ball felt comforting. "Come on out," he invited Alex. "Let's talk." He strolled closer to the hoop as he slowly bounced the ball. The sound thundered in the empty gym. He launched the ball. It hit the backboard, bounced up from the front of the rim and careened back toward Sean. Sean blamed the miss on the dim light. "I don't suppose you've ever played 'horse'?" he asked as he fired a second shot. It also went off the backboard but bobbled a few times between the front and back of the rim before falling through the net.

"Pretended to be a large equine animal?" asked Alex as he slid out.

Sean had to think a moment to translate what Alex had said. "Not that kind of horse, you psycho," he said with disgust. "Basketball. Look up basketball on your computer, if you don't know what that is."

"I am aware of the sporting event called basketball," Alex huffed. "However, I do not understand how it could involve a horse. Is it a hybrid of Polo?"

"Never mind," Sean surrendered, "Let's just shoot some hoops and talk." He tossed the ball in a gentle arch toward Alex. Alex defensively put up his arms and the ball bounced off a forearm. "You're supposed to catch it," Sean complained. He retrieved the ball and handed it to Alex. "You can go first."

Alex looked from the ball to the hoop several times, then looked to Sean. Sean raised his eyebrows expectantly. Alex held the ball at waist level in both hands, then launched it underhand toward the hoop. It fell short by several feet.

"You've got to be kidding me," Sean groaned as he ran under the basket to retrieve the ball that was slowly bouncing toward the wall.

"It will take me several attempts to calculate the required force of thrust and trajectory," announced Alex unabashedly.

"I'd say you shoot like a girl, but even girls don't toss it underhand." Sean dribbled several times as he broke for the basket, going up for a layup. The ball fell through the net. "Why did you pick this day and time?" he asked as he retrieved the ball.

"It is my assumption that the only avenue you had available to warn Jane Carmichael was the brief contact with Louise Rimmer," Alex replied.

Sean fired a jump shot from the top of the key. It just missed. "Go on."

"Since I witnessed the entire time you spoke with Louise and heard no audible exchange, the message passed must have been written. I had even anticipated such a move when you handed her the flashlight, but found it contained no concealed message."

Sean retrieved the rebound near the baseline and put up another shot that went in. "For the sake of argument, let's assume you're correct. What are your intentions?"

"To retrieve the note and return to your time, resetting the timeline to its original course."

Sean bounced the ball as he considered his words, then held the ball as he spoke. "Would you consider listening to my alternate proposal?"

"Proposal?"

"Yes," retorted Sean, "Believe or not, the old caveman ancestor is capable of organized thought."

"Somehow, though your words belittle yourself, it seems they are intended to insult me."

Sean nodded. "You're right. Sorry. No more jabs." He took a deep breath. "Do you agree that the main cause of the alternate timeline is when Jane persuaded... persuades... Time out. Are we going to talk about this from the perspective of 1969 or 1995?"

"Since your argument appears to initially reference the changed events in 1995, let us assume that perspective."

"OK... Let me start over," said Sean. "Do you agree that the main cause of the alternate timeline was when Jane persuaded my dad to attend college at Iowa State?"

Alex considered Sean's opening statement. "With regard to the outcome as it effects your birth... yes, I can accept that statement."

"Then if we can convince Jane to *not* persuade him to go to Iowa State, it will put things back without having to kill her."

"What would motivate her to change?"

Sean hadn't gotten to details in his plan yet. He tried to think quickly. "We could send her a letter telling her a bunch of things that will happen in the near future. Then warn her that if she tries to get my dad to go to Iowa State, it will start World War III."

"That is not true," Alex protested.

"*She* doesn't know that! If all the other predictions come true, she'd believe the warning."

"Is that the method you used to remove her from the automobile accident?"

Sean stared at the ball as he rotated it with little flips. "Maybe," he grudgingly admitted.

Alex checked with his computer. "There is still a 17.3% chance that your father will choose to go to Iowa State if Jane is there, even without an invitation from her, based solely on their friendship."

"That's not very high," Sean argued.

"We need certainty," replied Alex. "But at this juncture, let me also point out that Louise becomes the fatality rather than Jane."

"We stop Louise from getting into that car."

"Do you have specifics for this intervention?"

Sean wished he was better at details. "OK," he said, stalling as he tried to think. "How about if you go to the dance that night disguised as Jane, and drag Louise into the bathroom and make her talk about breaking up with Micky. Like even for ten minutes would be enough."

"There is a 94.4% chance that ploy would be successful," Alex reported.

Sean was pretty happy with that number. Maybe he *could* do details on the fly.

Alex quickly burst Sean's bubble. "Have you considered that with neither Jane nor Louise in the car, another, as yet unknown, person could occupy that fourth seat and lose their life? Or if there is not a fourth person, the dynamics of the car's impact could be changed and Tony Caparelli would become a fatality?"

"Or maybe they wouldn't get into a wreck at all," countered Sean.

"Speculation, with no real data," dismissed Alex.

"So's your fourth 'unknown' person suggestion!" argued Sean.

"Agreed," Alex nodded, "It is all speculation. The only facts we have are those that have been observed after the incident. In the original occurrence, the outcome is what was historically recorded. In the altered event, Louise dies, and you are never born. All other outcomes from potential solutions are speculative."

"So... why don't we just try it, and go back to 1995 and see if it worked?" Sean proposed.

"Your measurement for determining success?"

"Louise and Jane live, and I get born."

"Those are the only factors?"

"What else is there?" shrugged Sean.

Alex was quick to reply, "If the speculation of a different person becoming a fatality in that wreck comes to fruition, how will we examine the outcome of that life prematurely extinguished?"

"OK," Sean drawled as he tried to think of a new approach. "How 'bout we stop the wreck from happening? We could find the deputy ahead of time and slash his tires or something."

"How would you then measure the impact of Randy Hunter living a longer life?"

Sean threw his hands up. "Who?"

"The second fatality... in both scenarios."

"Why does that even matter?"

"It may not have a direct impact on *your* life," Alex took a deep breath, "but is that the *only* measure? What if Randy Hunter's survival makes an impact on someone else's life similar to what Jane's survival did to your father?"

"But we don't know that!" shouted Sean.

"Agreed. It is unknown," Alex replied. "Let me introduce yet another known factor. Your father said Jane had married three times. That is three lives that would have been changed in a substantial way."

"Maybe for the better!"

"Perhaps, or perhaps not," said Alex. He struggled with his decision to release other information, but decided it was necessary to convince Sean. "I did not reveal to you another outcome, unveiled during your father's narrative while you were outside with Caitlin." He paused to take a breath. "Micky falls in with a bad crowd at university, eventually leading to his death from an overdose of heroin."

"What?" breathed Sean, stunned by this information. "I mean, I didn't particularly like him, but I'd never wish that kind of death on anyone."

"In the original timeline, he does not attend college and begins to work for his Uncle Carl. Although I cannot locate any significant accomplishments in his life, I do have an obituary from 2036. That would make his age at death 84."

Sean shifted his gaze to the steel beam rafters above them. "So we tell Jane to not try to get my dad *or* her brother to go to Iowa State."

Alex struggled with his feelings for his ancestor in his desperation to resolve each added problem. He sighed before replying. "You really are not grasping the magnitude of altering events of history. You could monopolize both of our entire lifetimes attempting to patch all the changes that occur. Each solution you propose creates new potential problems."

"OK," Sean breathed, desperation creeping into his voice, "Jane has to take the fourth seat in the car, and Jane has to not be around after the accident." He suddenly sprang to life again. "So we let her get into the car, and then at the last second before the wreck, we swoop in with Steffi and pull her out before the crash. We take her to someplace in the future, so she doesn't go to Iowa State or convince my dad or Micky to go. Why wouldn't that solve all the problems?"

Alex tried to give serious consideration to the proposal. "It is very complex, and does seem to remove most of the variables we are concerned with... however, you have introduced a new complexity. How do the survivors of the wreck explain the total disappearance of Jane Carmichael?"

"I don't know," Sean shouted, hurling the ball toward the hoop, "Alien abduction?" The ball careened off the backboard, completely missing the rim, and bounced toward the far side of the gym.

Both boys watched as the height of each bounce diminished until the ball was rolling on the floor. It finally rebounded off the far wall and inched back toward them.

"Do you not believe that a teen-aged girl simply vanishing would create a disruption that would affect the entire town?" asked Alex firmly but gently.

Sean stared at the ball that had stopped rolling just short of half court.

"Have you *ever* followed your heart instead of your brain?" exploded Sean. Alex was silent. "I didn't think so," he continued as he turned to face Alex. "I feel in my gut that I *have* to save Jane." He paused long enough to blink tears from his eyes, and his voice cracked when he continued, "I *love* her!"

The final reverberation from Sean's confession made the ensuing silence of the huge empty room seem eerie.

Alex was conflicted. The simple solution – the *correct* solution – was to return the timeline to its original state. It was *his* responsibility. He had foolishly taken his ancestor from his own time into the past, completely unprepared and untrained. *He* had to rectify the anomaly. Yet he felt conflicted. Conflicted because he understood. He understood Sean's desire to save Jane because he also felt the same desire to protect someone he loved. He desperately wanted to save Sean from the pain and anguish that his ancient ancestor had already experienced. His only solace was that once the historical timeline had been restored, he could remove Sean's links to those painful memories.

He wished he also had that option for himself.

"Sean," Alex said gently, "I believe that nearly every human being who has ever lived on this planet has felt that way at some time during their life. Husbands, wives, parents, children... faced with losing someone they love. Wanting with all their heart to change the circumstances that create that loss. In some instances, they may succeed, but in most cases, it cannot be. Life is a precious gift, but it is finite. The heroes in movies and fictional stories are successful in their attempts to save their loved ones because that is the innate desire of the audience of the story to *want* them to succeed. It is far more rare in real life."

Sean stared blankly at the floor. He glanced briefly at Alex, then slowly started walking toward the basketball. He picked it up and walked zombie-like to the rack and set it back in the spot he had taken it from. He slowly walked toward the S.T.E. and slumped against its cloaked surface. Alex cautiously joined him.

"If it was just me," Sean said expressionlessly, "I'd let it ride. I'd just have you drop me somewhere in time and I'd try to start a whole new life. But it's not just me. I can't take your life away from you. I can't let Louise die. I can't think of a way to fix it all." He stared at nothing. "I give up."

Alex had never felt so defeated in winning an argument. "Whether you choose to believe me or not, I *am* truly sorry," Alex said somberly.

"Too bad you're not sorry enough to use your super brain to fix things without killing Jane."

"I do not have a 'super brain'," Alex wailed, "I was merely born in a later century than you were. I am accustomed to technologies that you consider advanced, but I am still a mere human being."

Sean let his head lag back and he stared at the skylights above the support girders over the basketball court. They rosily reflected the early stages of dawn. Maybe he did expect too much of Alex. "It's hard for me to remember that sometimes," he said. "You can do all these amazing things. Then when you toss Steffi into the mix, you seem invincible."

"I assure you, I am not."

Sean turned his head toward Alex. "Maybe I wish you were." He took in a deep breath, then let it out slowly. "So what's your plan for getting the note?"

"It is a simplistic plan," Alex admitted as he reached into Steffi, opened one of the lower panels, and withdrew a box. "We will go back into the diner and you will request that Louise return the note to you." He handed the box to Sean.

"What's this?"

"Your hair."

"Hmph," grunted Sean, "I'd forgotten about that already. I suppose I have to stick my head in here and let the hair crawl onto me again?"

"Yes."

"It's really a pretty disgusting feeling, you know."

"I do not doubt your observation."

Sean leaned over, dipping his head into the box. He fought the urge to jerk it right back out when he felt the wispy hairs crawling onto his scalp. He tried very hard to not think about spiders. When he didn't feel any more movement, he lifted his head out. The attached hair hung down into his face and he scooped it back with his hand.

"You will need to arrange it to look the way it did before we left," Alex said as he slid inside the time-machine. Sean followed him in.

"Put me on screen," said Sean. He pulled a comb from his pocket, then stared at it. "You even transferred stuff from my other pants?" Alex nodded. Sean worked a part down the middle of his head, splitting the long locks to either side. "Did I wear that bandana thing?"

"No, not when we last saw Louise."

That seemed so long ago to Sean, and so many things had happened in a short time. He stopped working with his comb. "Good enough?"

"Yes," agreed Alex, "I believe that is how you had it before."

"And we have to do a time-jump?"

"Yes, a very short one. I believe if I arrive at the same spot behind the building five minutes post our last departure, it will appear as if we walked down the street. Then you changed your mind about the note and walked back up the street. Louise will experience your absence as approximately twenty minutes."

"OK," Sean sighed, "Let's do this and get it over. Then get me back to my life and wipe all this away."

Alex closed the door, tapped a few icons on the front screen, and then reopened the door. They were again behind the building in the same spot they'd been twice before. Sean swung his legs out and felt like they were too weak to stand on. They felt rubbery, like after running 'suicide' drills in basketball when the coach was mad at them. He had to command his body to do something his brain really didn't want to do. He took a deep breath and heaved himself up. When Alex joined him, he had already shifted into his sixties disguise.

They maneuvered their way around to the front of the building, halting at the curb to wait for a car to pass. Sean looked both ways before stepping out into the street. At the bottom of the street, he saw a flash of yellow turning left. 'Lemon Drop' flitted through his mind.

"Are you all right?" Alex asked as they approached the door to Ritchie's.

"No," Sean breathed as he pushed through the door.

Ritchie was scraping his grill, and Sean assumed the main breakfast rush was over. He saw Louise back near a booth by the pool table. They started across the room toward her and at the same time she started toward the front with a tray of dirty dishes.

"Oh my gosh! What are *you* doin' back here?" chirped Louise as she set the tray up on the counter and hurried toward Sean and Alex. "Did you see Jane?"

"No," said Sean, "But I've decided I need to retrieve my note, luv."

"This is just the craziest thing!" Louise burbled. "You two hadn't much more'n got out the door when Jane came in. I can't believe you didn't run into her."

"Jane was here? Now?" asked Sean.

"Yes!" continued Louise with characteristic enthusiasm, "She came in to tell me about last night. She was all excited. I told her you were just here, but had to leave town early. She flew right out the door and then just a few minutes later here you come back in again. And you still didn't run into her?"

"No," replied Sean, "Did she say where she was going?"

"To look for you! She was going to drive out to the highway and see if she could catch you. It's just crazy that you missed each other twice in just a few minutes."

Sean remembered the flash of yellow at the bottom of the street. It *was* Lemon Drop! He had been so close to seeing Jane one last time. His heart ached as he continued, "You still have my note, then."

Louise's eyes darted back and forth between Sean and Alex. She chewed her lower lip. It took Sean a few seconds to understand her reluctance.

"It's OK. Peter knows about the note."

"Oh," she said, still glancing back and forth between the two. "I wasn't sure. It seemed like you were bein' real secret-like when you gave it to me."

"I was," confessed Sean, "but things have changed. May I have it back, please?"

"I'm sorry, Nigel," Louise sputtered, "I thought you'd wanted me to give it to Jane."

"I thought you said that she rushed out."

"She did," Louise confirmed. "But I yelled after her and told her you left a note. She came runnin' back and snatched it out of my hand and then ran back out without so much as a thank you."

"Jane Carmichael has already retrieved the note?" Alex pressed. His perfect British accent made him sound formal.

"She has indeed," replied Louise, trying to also be more formal.

"In the few minutes we were gone, Jane Carmichael came in and retrieved the note?"

"Yes, sir, she did," replied Louise, again speaking formally before blurting out, "That's what I was sayin'! It must have been near impossible for you to not have seen each other."

"You two going to order something," came a gruff voice from behind the counter.

Sean turned to see Ritchie glaring at them. "No," he said, then added, "Thank you."

"Then stop wasting my waitress's time!" Ritchie growled.

"I've gotta go," Louise loudly whispered as she picked up her tray and retreated behind the counter.

Sean glared back at Ritchie but decided not to say anything, in case he took it out on Louise. As they walked out the door, he heard Ritchie again, "Louise, if any more of your friends come in today, I'm going to dock you. You hear me?"

Outside, Sean looked up and down the street. "Now what?" he asked.

"I am quite chagrined by this turn of events. As Louise said, it is astounding that we did not cross paths with Jane Carmichael."

"She said, 'near impossible', not astounding."

"Nonetheless, I do not believe we would be able to return to a preemptive position without locating a closer place to materialize."

"Maybe it's an omen," declared Sean.

"An omen?" questioned Alex. "Do people of the late twentieth century still believe in omens and auguries?"

"I don't even know what an augury is."

"The two words are similar in meaning, both are prescient warnings of an event yet to take place. Generally, an omen expects an adverse outcome, while an augury is more positive."

"Fine! Maybe it's an *augury*, then," huffed Sean. "Whoever loaded your dictionary for words people actually use, messed up. Let's just call it a 'sign' that we need to rethink how to fix the timeline glitch."

"I ran several scenarios before returning to 1969. This one had the highest chance of success, with the least amount of effort. The secondary scenario is October 10th."

"The day of the accident?" asked Sean.

"Yes."

"So what's the plan? We just pop in on Jane and say, 'just kidding about the note, go ahead and get into the death car' or something?"

"I will 'suggest' that she forget ever getting your note," said Alex.

Sean looked at him quizzically before it dawned on him. "Oh," he said, "the Jedi mind control thing."

"I do not understand why you use that reference."

"Well, now that you've downloaded all of *Star Trek*, maybe you should download all of the *Star Wars* data, too."

"My ability to 'suggest' is more closely related to your hypnotism than some mystical force like those movies."

"Eh, tomato, tomahto," Sean said flippantly.

"I fail to find the relevance of your variant pronunciation of the large edible berry of the nightshade family."

"See," Sean declared as they started across the street, "that's more proof that you know the wrong things about this century."

Sean had regained a little spring in his step. If he could see Jane again, maybe he could still figure out a way to get her out of this mess alive and still not change his future.

Chapter Fourteen

"If I could reach the stars / I'd give them all to you"

S EAN shivered as he stepped out of the time-machine and reflexively began to rub his hands briskly over his forearms. The October air was considerably cooler than the summer air they had just left, especially since the sun had already set.

"Where did you put that Army jacket you got me?" asked Sean. Alex pulled the jacket from the small space behind the seat and handed it to Sean. Sean shrugged into it. "What time of day is it?"

"The local time is approximately 7:00 pm," Alex reported.

"And how far is it to Jane's house?"

"Less than half a kilometer."

"That's really the closest you could get?"

"It seemed prudent to find a large uninhabited place. The S.T.E. will be safer from discovery."

"Kind of creepy to be walking through a cemetery after dark," complained Sean as he tried to get his bearings. "Do you still have cemeteries in the future?"

"No."

"So what do you do with... oh please tell me you didn't go *Soylent Green*!"

Alex twitched a query. "No," he replied, "assuming I am referencing the correct meaning of your outburst. Why do you make such a macabre statement?"

"I don't know, maybe walking through a cemetery in the dark? And how do I know what you do with dead bodies in the future?"

"I am beginning to believe you are more superstitious than I had initially assumed."

"Ridiculous," scoffed Sean. "Now let's get out of here before some zombie grabs us."

They found their way to the main gate and out onto the street.

"This street," Alex explained, "intersects the street where Jane Carmichael resides at the next juncture."

"Just for future reference, a typical teenager would say, 'take a left at the next block'."

"I would have to refute that."

"Refute all you want, I'm the one who knows how people of the twentieth-century talk."

"Still, you would be incorrect. We will turn right at the next block."

They walked wordlessly to the intersection. Sean was unhappy that he couldn't come up with some snappy comment as they turned right. Before they had gone half a block, Sean caught a glimpse of yellow against the curb toward the middle of the next block – Jane's VW. His heart leapt as he thought of seeing her smile, and just as quickly sunk as he thought about her dying... in just a few hours.

"What do you think I should say?" asked Sean.

"I would prefer that you say nothing."

"Nothing?"

"I require that she be focused on me to enable me to 'suggest' that she forget the note. It would potentially be distracting if you were to speak."

"At *all*?"

"Correct."

"But she's bound to speak to me first, I can't just ignore her."

Alex didn't respond.

They crossed the street when they were even with Jane's house. Sean affectionately patted Lemon Drop as they walked past the Volkswagen. The Carmichael house had a driveway that angled up slightly. It was an older house, with a formal front porch that had a wooden porch-swing hanging at the end farthest from the front door. The five wooden steps popped a little as they climbed them. Sean pressed the lighted bar by the door and a faint short melody could be heard from inside. It was only a few moments before an ornate light by the side of the door came on. Sean involuntarily held his breath. His stomach was a churning icy pit.

A middle-aged woman opened the inner door and peered out through the glass of the storm door. She spoke loudly through the glass which muffled her voice a little. "May I help you?"

"Hullo, Mrs. Carmichael," announced Sean, "We're old friends of Jane, just popped into town. Is she about?"

"Yes," the woman replied, "We were all just watching that new show, The Bradly Bunch. You're lucky Jane didn't feel like going to the football game, or you would have missed her."

"Would we be able to speak with her, please," asked Alex.

"My goodness, you both have accents," she declared, "You're not the boys who were here this summer, are you?"

"Yes, mum, that'd be us," replied Sean.

She pushed the storm door open and held it as she shifted toward the hinge side to allow passage. "Well, please come in, won't you? I'll tell her that you're here." They stepped into the warm entryway of the house. "What were your names again?"

"Peter Lindsey," said Alex, "And Nigel Davies."

"If you could wait here, I'll go tell her she has guests."

Seconds after the woman disappeared through a doorway, Jane stood framed by it. Her mouth dropped open and she put a hand up to cover it. "Nigel?" she chirped, still frozen to the spot. She wore blue jeans and a purple sweatshirt with 'Vikings' across the front in white. Her hair was about the same length as it had been in the Summer, but the brown seemed lighter, and at the scalp, her own sandy blonde hair had grown out a couple of inches. "Nigel!" she said louder as she rushed across the room and swept Sean into a hug. "Oh my God, Nigel! I didn't think I would ever see you again."

It's good to see you, Jane, thought Sean as he tried to say it, but found he had lost control of his voice. He gave a surprised glance toward Alex that then turned cold as he realized what had happened.

"Nigel, unfortunately, has laryngitis," Alex explained, "traveling in the cold, sleeping outside too many nights."

"Oh, no!" sympathized Jane, as she stepped back from the hug to survey Sean's face. "That's terrible. You can't talk at all?"

Sean stared daggers at Alex as he held his right hand to his throat.

"Not a word," affirmed Alex, staring right back at Sean.

"Oh, poor Nigel," Jane said as she pulled into another hug. "I really didn't think I would see you again. I thought you would have gone back home by now, and just didn't come back this way." Suddenly she stepped back, her smile faded, her eyes flitted between Alex and Sean. "Why are you here *today?*" she demanded.

"We just got into town," Alex replied, "After Woodstock, we decided to continue to tour the country. We saw Boston and Washington, D.C., then started back west through the southern states. When we reached the Mississippi River, Nigel wanted to head back north to see you again."

Jane crossed her arms and glared suspiciously at Alex. "It's just coincidence that you arrived *today?*"

Alex noticed a shadow in the doorway to the living room. "Could we step outside?" he whispered, nodding toward the door behind Jane. She turned toward the living room.

"Mom, we're going out onto the porch for awhile," Jane called.

The floor creaked slightly as they heard footsteps move quickly away from the door. "All right, dear," the voice called from the other room, "put on a jacket."

Jane rolled her eyes then opened the coat closet by the front door and pulled out a tan jacket. She pulled one sleeve on as she reached for the doorknob, sliding into the second one as she moved out the front door. Sean and Alex followed her. Jane zipped her jacket as she turned to them.

"Why are you *really* here?" she demanded.

Alex pointed to the swing. "Could we sit and discuss this?"

Jane glanced at the swing, then back to Alex. She looked briefly over her shoulder to the front door, then decided to cross to the swing and sit. Sean followed and sat beside her. Alex sat directly in front of Jane on the low wall that surrounded the porch.

Jane studied Sean. His arms were crossed and he stared blankly at the wall next to Alex. "Are you feeling OK, Nigel? Should you even be out here?"

"He is fine, Jane," assured Alex, "If you could look at me, please? I will tell you what you need to know." She turned back to face him. "We have had a very pleasant journey all around your wonderful country," Alex narrated with a warm voice, resonant and carefully modulated. "Nigel thought of you often." Jane smiled. "He especially missed you when we were on the beach in Florida. Have you ever been to Florida, Jane?" She indicated that she hadn't with a brief head-shake. "It is exquisite," Alex continued, almost melodically. "Try to imagine it. Picture yourself on a warm sunny beach, a soft breeze in your face, blowing off the ocean. The waves are crashing rhythmically." Jane's face softened, her shoulders relaxed and she smiled. "Can you picture it, Jane?" She nodded sluggishly. "It is very relaxing and warm. You feel very comfortable and warm. The sound of the waves is very soothing. You are completely relaxed. You feel as though you are drifting now, floating in warmth. Relaxed. Happy." Jane's eyes closed, her smile grew wider.

"Happy," she purred dreamily.

"Nigel and I came to see you. He wanted to see you again," Alex continued in soothing cadence.

"I love him," Jane sighed.

"Nigel cares deeply for you, also."

"He loves me," Jane lilted melodically, "He wants to protect me."

Tears began to stream down Sean's cheeks as he turned his head away from her.

"Yes, he does," Alex agreed cautiously, "He wants to protect you. The best way he can protect you is for you to forget the note he left you this summer."

Jane's smile faded. "No," she protested, "He gave me that note to protect me."

"Jane, focus on my voice," Alex commanded, "You can hear nothing but my voice. Listen to my voice. I can protect you with my voice. As you listen to my voice, think about the note. Picture it as you listen to me. Now, as you look at the note, the writing is all fading away. The words are disappearing, and you are still protected."

Jane's frowned. Something inside her told her to fight against the voice. "No!" she forced, "Blood! It was written in *blood!* Nigel *loves* me! I trust *him!*"

"You need to relax again, Jane," Alex said, tension creeping into his calm voice. "You are on the beach. It is warm. You..."

"No!" she exploded as she suddenly rose. "It's October, it is *not* warm!"

She threw her head back as if breaking free from chains. "I am on my own porch, I am *not* on the beach!" she argued to the porch ceiling. She looked back to Alex, coldly, as adrenaline rushed to her brain, charged from fear. "You're trying to hypnotize me!" She accused him as she stumbled away from the swing toward the door. "Nigel! Come inside with me!" She tugged on his arm and he stood.

"Jane, wait!" Alex pleaded desperately.

"No," Jane snarled as she tugged Sean toward the door, "I don't trust you!"

"But you trust Nigel?" Alex asked quickly.

Jane stopped tugging. She looked deeply into Sean's eyes. "Yes," she replied.

"If he calmly came back to the swing, would you come with him?"

Her frosty glare showed her distrust of Alex. She gave a quick glance to Sean, then back to Alex. "Are you controlling him?" She put her hands on Sean's shoulders and looked directly at him. "Is he controlling you?"

Sean put his hand to his throat and looked toward Alex. Jane followed his gaze.

"What did you do to his voice?" Jane demanded.

Alex's mind raced. This scenario was not going well. He was both astounded and intrigued by Jane's mental strength, but he had to keep her from going into the house. That was first. Beyond that was as yet unknown. "Will you come back if Nigel *asks* you to?" Alex asked her.

"Not if you've got him hypnotized," she retorted.

"Ask him again if I am controlling him."

Jane looked into Sean's eyes. "Is he?" she asked. "Is he controlling you?"

Sean coughed. "Just my voice," he croaked, then coughed again.

"Are you sure?" she questioned, glancing at Alex.

"Yes," replied Sean. "He can shut off my voice or knock me unconscious, but he doesn't control my mind."

"What *is* he?" asked Jane, "and why are you with him?"

"That's... complicated," said Sean. "Maybe we should sit back down."

"I'm not sitting across from *him!*" exclaimed Jane with a finger pointed at Alex. "*You* sit across from him."

"OK," agreed Sean as he took her hand and led her back to the swing. "He won't actually *hurt* you."

"He tried to *hypnotize* me!" protested Jane. Sean nodded. "And you're OK with that?"

"No...yes...I...Jane... it's really complicated," Sean babbled.

"Nigel, why did you come here *today?*"

"There is a logical ex..." began Alex.

"I didn't ask you!" Jane snapped, silencing Alex with a pointed finger. She turned back to Sean. "Nigel, why did you come to see me *today?*"

Sean's gaze flickered between Jane and Alex. "Some unexpected things happened," he began, "It's really, *really* complicated."

Jane gave Alex an icy glance. "Is it related to the note you left me?"

Sean nodded as he considered what he was going to say. "Yes," he started, "It's safe to say we wouldn't be here if not for the note."

"I would like to know the contents of this note," requested Alex. Jane had leveled a finger at him again and was about to say something when Sean gently took her hand.

"He doesn't exactly know much about the note," he confessed. "I did that without his knowledge."

Jane's eyes flitted between Sean and Alex. "I'm guessing," she said, "that what he *does* know about it, he's not too happy about."

"Yes," agreed Sean, again bobbing his head in a slow repetitive nod, "I think we can safely say that."

"May I see the note, please, Miss Carmichael?" Alex asked politely.

"It's upstairs in my room," she replied, "but you don't need to see it. I've read it so many times I've memorized it. *Today is July 13th, 1969. July 18 – T. Kennedy drowning. July 20 – Moon: 'Houston, Tranquility Base here. The Eagle has landed.' and 'That's one small step for man, one giant leap for mankind.'*" She shook her head in disbelief. "Exact words. I heard them on the news. I even double checked later in the *Des Moines Register*. *Exact words!*" Jane checked for reactions from Sean or Alex before continuing; there were none. "OK, then, *August 8 – Sharon Tate +3 brutally murdered.* Three things pretty close together, then one more. *October 10 – DO NOT GET INTO ANY CARS! Nigel.* In capital letters. Like a warning, or something." She paused again. No one else spoke. "I walked to school today. Almost a mile. I'm skipping the last home football game and Senior Dance because I'm afraid to go out." She turned to Sean. "Why did you write it in blood? I still haven't figured that out. When I first brought it home, our cat kept sniffing at the note. When school started again, I took it to the Biology lab and put it under a microscope to confirm that it was blood." Sean still didn't speak. "For awhile, I thought maybe it was some kind of witchcraft or Satanism thing. The Tate murders and Mary Jo Kopechne kinda fit that... but not the moon landing. So what is the significance of writing in blood?"

Sean sighed. "It was... all I had."

"When you wrote it," Jane reasoned, "you didn't know you were going to be here tonight, did you?"

"No," said Sean softly.

"Then I'll ask you again." Jane locked eyes with Sean and demanded, "Why are you here... on October 10th... the last date listed on your note. The one that seemed to be specifically to me – *stay out of cars*."

Sean looked at Alex. "There were some unexpected..." he started.

"Things that happened," finished Jane, "I got that part. *When* did these things happen?"

Sean rubbed his right eye, then trailed his hand across his mouth and rubbed his chin. "Jane, it's really, really..."

"Complicated!" she jumped in. "You've already said that. Would it make it any less complicated if I guessed that the *when* is actually tonight?"

"I...I don't know what you mean," stammered Sean.

"Yes you do. Somehow, you can jump around through time," she declared. Alex audibly gasped. "I'll take that as a confirmation," she said with a coldly smug look at Alex. "As crazy as it sounds, it was the only thing that I could get to make sense." She turned to Sean. "That night at the drive-in, you weren't pretending to be surprised when Peter said he was from the future. You couldn't believe that he would give you away. You were genuinely shocked." She paused as new thoughts hit her. "Alex! You called him Alex. His name isn't even Peter, is it?" She smacked her own forehead. "And Marcia Brady. I just got that. From the *Brady Bunch*. Why would you let something stupid like that slip?"

"I really didn't know you hadn't seen it. When I watched the reruns, it seemed like it was a 60s show that I thought you would have already seen it."

"Sixties show," repeated Jane. "So *when* are you from?"

"Miss Carmichael," interrupted Alex, "This conjecture has become somewhat ludicrous. Surely time-travel is merely a fanciful theme in science fiction stories."

"I'm not talking to you," Jane snarled. She turned back to Sean. "Is he a robot or android or something? Or what was that thing Juan mentioned? A cyborg?"

"No, he's human," Sean replied. "At least he told me he was. Although with all the nanites in his body, maybe he does count as a cyborg."

"That is ridiculous," protested Alex. "I am no more a cyborg than she is. She uses a mechanical device to enhance her vision." Sean gave him a confused look. "You refer to them as eyeglasses," he explained.

"Let's not get sidetracked," insisted Jane. "The question was *when* are you from?" Sean turned a pleading look to Alex. "Are you *sure* he doesn't control you?" she grumbled.

"No... I mean, yes. No, I'm... yes, I'm sure he doesn't control me."

"Then why can't you answer the question without looking at him?"

"1995!" Sean exploded. Both Alex and Jane drew a loud breath.

"Wow," murmured Jane, somewhat in awe. "We invent time-travel in less than thirty years? Far out!"

"No!" corrected Sean. "We don't have time-travel in 1995! That's crazy."

Jane shrugged with palms up. "Then how did you get here?"

Sean nodded toward Alex. "*He's* from the future... I mean, yeah, I know, to you *I'm* from the future, but I'm not really. Well, not like he is," rambled Sean. "Anyway! He has a time-machine. He's from the 22nd Century."

"23rd," corrected Alex, "2217 if you require specifics." He turned to

Sean. "This situation is becoming hopelessly irreparable."

Jane blinked several times. "So," she finally said with a dubious look to Sean, "he's from 2217, swings by 1995 to randomly pick you up for a joyride to 1969. Or were you abducted?"

"No, it wasn't random," refuted Sean. "I'm his great-great-great-great-great grandfather." He counted each finger on one hand to ensure he got the correct number of 'greats'.

"Wow," said Jane sarcastically, "you look so young."

"I am!" huffed Sean, "I'm 16... but so is he."

"OK," said Jane nodding slowly, "why the family outing to 1969, then?"

"That was actually kind of my idea," Sean admitted. He turned to Alex. "I'm going to tell her everything."

"It cannot make the situation any *more* irreparable," sighed Alex.

Sean turned back to Jane. "My real name is Sean... Sean Kelly. I convinced my 5G grandson that it would make a great experiment for him to observe me and my dad at the same age."

Jane put her hand to her mouth, her eyes widened. "Oh my God!" she gasped. "Juan Kelly is your *dad?*" Sean nodded. "I guess that could explain why you were here this summer... but what about now? Why are you here now?"

"Because of the note," Sean sighed, "it... changed some things."

"What would have happened if you didn't warn me to stay out of cars?" asked Jane solemnly.

Sean took a deep breath, let it out, and closed his eyes. "You would be killed in a car wreck tonight."

The color drained from Jane's face. She glanced back and forth from Sean to Alex. "So," she said slowly to Sean, "you wanted to save me..." Sean nodded. Jane shifted her glance to Alex. "And you want..." her voice cracked, "...to change it back?" She stared at him, still in shock. "Why?" Alex was silent. She turned to Sean. "Why?" she breathed.

"I didn't think anything would happen, other than you not dying. I *swear* that is all I thought I was changing," Sean said to Alex as much as to Jane.

"But there is something," Jane continued slowly, "...something else... that happens?"

"Louise got in the car... gets in the car," said Sean. "She was killed... will be killed in the car wreck instead of you."

"No," gasped Jane, her hand suddenly over her mouth. "We've got to warn her!" She looked tensely between Sean and Alex, expecting them to join her in action. "Aren't you going to save her?"

"Yes," Sean whispered.

"How can you two look so calm? You know someone is going to die and you're not even moving to do anything to stop it."

"There is a larger involvement than merely saving Miss Rimmer," Alex advised.

Jane hit him with another icy glare before turning back to Sean. "What does he mean?" she asked.

"I believe I can explain it more concisely than Sean," said Alex.

"I don't want to hear *you* explain anything," shouted Jane, "you futuristic... *thing!*" She turned to Sean. "What does he mean? What else happens?"

"My dad marries someone else," blurted Sean, "and I'm never born."

Jane scrunched up her face as she tried to come to grips with what Sean said. "I think you lost me," she finally admitted, "If you're not born, how can you be here?"

"I know," agreed Sean, "It doesn't make sense." He pointed to Alex. "He wasn't lying when he said he could explain it better."

"It is a simple matter of positioning in the time-stream," said Alex. "Sean existed in 1995. We traveled to 1969. He gives you a note that changes your actions. When we left 1969 – last summer, to you – and returned to 1995, the time-stream had changed. In the new altered reality, Sean is not born."

Jane nodded slowly as she listened. When Alex finished, she reassessed all she had heard, then turned back to Sean. "I don't think he explains it better," she said flatly. Sean almost laughed, in spite of the tense situation. "So what does the car wreck have to do with Juan and who he marries? Oh my gosh! Juan would have married Louise if she didn't get killed? Is Louise your mom? You've got to be kidding!"

"No," said Sean, "He's not supposed to marry Louise."

"Then what?" asked Jane. "Oh, you *don't* mean that he marries *me* since I survived..."

"No!" yelled Sean in frustration. "He doesn't marry *you!* It's some redhead he meets in college named Michelle O'Malley."

"I'm still not following," declared Jane, equally frustrated. "How does that have anything to do with this car wreck?"

"He goes to the *wrong* college!" shouted Sean. "Because of *you*, he goes to the wrong college!"

"What?" complained Jane, throwing her hands up to accent her bewilderment.

"In the timeline created when you survive the car wreck, you attend Iowa State," explained Alex. "During the summer after your freshman year, you convince Juan Kelly to also attend Iowa State. In the original timeline, he attends Golden Valley State University. When Sean and I originally departed 1969 to return to 1995, we found that Jonathan Kelly was living near Ames, Iowa, married to a woman who is not Sean's mother. Therefore, Sean could not be born in Grover's Corners, Missouri as he was in the original timeline."

"So, *Nigel*," sneered Jane, "you're *not* from New Zealand. I thought some of the stuff you said was a little too far out." She turned to Alex. "What about *you*, future thing, are you even British?"

"No," admitted Alex, "I am not British. I do, however, take umbrage at your suggestions that I am not human."

"You certainly sound British," said Jane.

"Especially when he gets snooty like that," added Sean.

"So," said Jane, facing Sean, "you send me a note..." She turned to point to Alex. "that he didn't know about..." She turned back to Sean. "I stay home. Louise dies. I lure your dad to 'the wrong college' and you are never born... except you already exist." Sean nodded. "Why did you send me the note? Why didn't you just leave?"

"I couldn't stand the thought of letting you die," confessed Sean. "I... I thought... I could change it."

"Oh, Nigel," Jane sobbed as she hugged Sean.

"...Sean," said Sean halfheartedly as he returned the hug.

Jane whispered into his ear, "Is he going to kill me?" Jane pulled back from her hug to check Sean's face. Though it seemed sad, it told her nothing.

"So, you, future thing," Jane addressed Alex, "come here to hypnotize me, so I'll get in that car and be killed... but it didn't work."

"It certainly would have been less complicated," Alex expressed, "...and more humane."

Jane gave a fleeting glance toward Sean. Her muscles tensed as she carefully eyed Alex and considered her options. She abruptly shot from the swing. "Mom! Dad!" she shrieked as she bolted for the door.

Alex reached her just as she was pulling the storm door open. He gripped her shoulder near her neck and her eyes met Sean's just before they rolled back in her head. Alex caught her with both arms under her armpits as her legs buckled. Sean looked on in horror.

"I believe I was premature in suggesting the situation could not become any *more* irreparable," Alex moaned while backing down the stairs with Jane in tow. Her feet clunked against each step as they went down.

Sean did a double-take when moments later, Jane came rushing back up the steps.

"If you have any helpful suggestions," she said, "now will probably be your only opportunity to express them.

Sean stared at her dumbfoundedly as his brain eventually concluded that he was looking at Alex. "Glasses!" he managed.

Alex dashed back down the steps then returned with Jane's glasses. He put them on just as the door opened.

"What's going on out here?" demanded Mrs. Carmichael. "Jane, are you all right?"

"Yes, mother," replied Alex matching Jane's voice as accurately as he matched her appearance. "I am perfectly fine."

Mrs. Carmichael eyed 'Jane' suspiciously. "I thought I heard you scream. Have these boys been up to something they shouldn't? Where's the other one?"

Alex stared blankly, his brain whirring. "Peter decided to visit someone else... Karen... she kissed him last summer. I believe he found it to be an enjoyable experience."

Mrs. Carmichael raised her eyebrows.

"The...er...scream..." started Alex, "...was one of excitement. Nigel wishes to attend a football game, and I found the prospect exciting."

"I thought you'd decided to stay home tonight," countered Mrs. Carmichael.

"Yes...well..." Alex struggled, "er... Nigel has never seen an American football game."

Mrs. Carmichael gave Sean a withering look. Sean smiled weakly back. "I don't know..." she said.

"Please, mother?" pleaded Alex, "Nigel would very much enjoy it. In addition, it is the final game of the year."

Mrs. Carmichael looked past 'Jane' toward Sean again. He tried to brighten his smile. "How long will you be staying in Mercer?" she demanded of him.

"Just the evening, I'm afraid," returned Sean, trying to punch up his New Zealand accent. "Then off we go like a 'roo spooked by dingos! Back out on the road."

She paused to attempt to understand what he'd said, then asked, "You think hitchhiking is safe?"

"Has been so far. Most Americans seem on the friendly side."

She turned back to 'Jane', pursed her lips as she thought. "I suppose..." she drawled.

"Excellent," said Alex. "I will need to collect a few items from my room."

"Are you sure you're all right, dear?" queried Mrs. Carmichael. "You sound a little strange."

"Yes," assured Alex, as he stepped through the doorway. "Everything is... groovy."

Mrs. Carmichael didn't notice the little twitch of her daughter's head as Alex tied into his computer to find a floor plan. He compared several images in the database to what he had seen of the outside of the house and found three that seemed to be a close match. He visualized wire-frame images of each and searched for stairs. Fortunately, each of the three floor-plans had stairs in the center of the house.

"Something wrong, dear?"

He opened his eyes and saw that Mrs. Carmichael was watching him, her brow knit with concern.

"No," he replied, "just thinking."

He turned down a hallway, glancing each way. He almost opened a door but then spied the stairs going up on the opposite wall. They were dark. He checked in the shadows of one wall, assuming there would be a light switch, but couldn't find one. He leaned against that wall to inspect the other side and felt something brush across his face. Startled, he reflexively threw his arms up, tangling in a cord. He jerked back, surprised to suddenly be bathed in light. In his escape from whatever had touched his face, he'd backed to the other wall. Now in the light, he could see a multi-strand cord made up of several bright colors dangling against the wall, ending with a large yellow plastic piece symbol. His gaze followed the string up to see it was connected to a bare light fixture in the second-floor ceiling. He reached out to the cord and tugged it. The light went off. He pulled it again. The light came on. *Very primitive mechanism,* he thought as he started up the stairs.

The stairs reached a landing halfway up, where they turned back in the opposite direction to finish the ascent to the second floor. At the top was a double wide accordion door. To the left and right were regular doors, the one on the right was wide open, the one on the left was slightly ajar. Alex checked the open one first. The room was dark except for the light that spilled through the doorway, but that was enough to see that there were clothes strewn on the floor and an unmade bed. He spotted some shoes that were obviously larger than Jane's feet.

Turning and crossing back to the opposite door, he pushed it gently open. Just before he stepped in, he felt a familiar uneasiness. He paused for a moment, then gave a hint of a smile as he thought, *At least we seem to progress beyond my current dilemma.*

The room was also mostly dark, but there was a colorful pink glow at the dressing table. The lamp was tall and slender, narrower at the top than at the base. Alex watched for a few moments as amorphous opaque red shapes would erupt from the base and rise to the top of the thinner translucent pink liquid. Eventually, the blobs at the top would begin to slide back down, often colliding with one of the rising shapes.

Very distracting, thought Alex as he broke his gaze to do a quick scan of the room. The second room was immaculate compared to the first one. Not only was the bed made, but there was also throw pillows and stuffed animals stacked at the end nearest the wall. Sitting on a night-table next to the bed was a small lamp. Alex reached to turn on the light, but jumped back when a hissing sound came from the pile of stuffed animals. He backed away from the bed and edged slowly around the room, clinging to the wall until he reached the night-table, his eyes never leaving the stuffed animals.

When he turned on the lamp, he saw one of the animals take a step toward him and issue another hiss. "Felis Catus," he said softly, "and you are not fooled by my disguise." The cat replied with a warning growl that ended in another hiss. Alex took a measured step toward it. "I apologize for my intrusion." The cat arched its back and spit loudly, glancing toward the door in mid-hiss. Alex took another half step and the cat sprang from the bed and disappeared out the door. *It must be very interesting to cohabit with domesticated animals,* he thought to himself.

The lamplight didn't adequately illuminate the room, but enough for Alex to see that there was a light in the ceiling with a cord, similar to, though shorter than, the one in the stairway. He pulled the cord and was rewarded with a brightly lit room. He checked the dressing table first. It was covered with neatly arranged cosmetics and grooming aids. There was a large mirror centered on the wall behind it.

Alex looked at the reflection of Jane Carmichael in the mirror. He pulled the glasses off, touched his neck with his left hand and shifted his face to Alexis. He changed from Alexis to Jane and back several times and decided that Sean was correct. The resemblance was uncanny. He made a final shift to Jane and put her glasses back on. Nanites in his corneas realigned slightly so he could again see clearly with the glasses on. He scanned more of the room.

Closer to the bed stood a five-drawer dresser. Alex opened each of the drawers sequentially from bottom to top and carefully shuffled through clothing. Not finding what he was looking for, he sat on the bed to think, when he suddenly noticed the night stand had a small flat drawer in the front. He pulled it out to reveal a little book and a pen. The book cover was a series of red and yellow checkerboard boxes of varying sizes, none of them exactly square. The design appeared to almost vibrate. "An optical illusion," Alex said softly before opening it. He flipped a few pages, scanning the handwritten words without actually reading them.

Jane is keeping a brief chronicle of her life, he realized as he admired the gently flowing script. It was a good thing that there was a session on deciphering ancient cursive handwriting as part of his Twentieth Century English lessons. He quickly identified a pattern of various segments divided by dates. He flipped until he reached July, then paused to read the entry for July 13th.

"I had the most amazing time at the drive in! Nigel is SOOO groovy. He's smart, funny, cute, and a fantastic kisser. At least he seems fantastic to me. My first kiss! And it was so far out! Even more amazing than I ever imagined. I know it sounds crazy, but I think he is my soul-mate! He called me 'ladybug', that's what New Zealand guys call their girlfriends. It's really late, so I should get some sleep. I can't wait to tell Louise! I'm in love, I'm in love, I'm in LOVE!!!!!"

An unfamiliar sadness crept over Alex as he read the words. He felt as if he was intruding... not only by reading Jane's diary, but also by bringing Sean into her life in July. The more he learned about Jane Carmichael, the harder it was going to be to set the timeline back to its original course. He read the next entry.

"July 14, 1969. I'm heartbroken... Nigel left town today without even seeing me to say goodbye. I tried to catch him, but he and Peter just seemed to vanish. He left a note for me with Louise, but it wasn't to say goodbye, it was a list of dates with things. Weird things... and it's weird looking. The

writing is kind of like what we did in Jr. High art class when they were teaching us calligraphy. The ink is uneven, like it was dipped into. Not to mention it's a strange color. I left it laying on the bed and Misty was sniffing at it and trying to lick it. Silly cat! None of it makes any sense. The first date on it is this Friday, maybe it will make sense then."

Alex scanned ahead to the 18th.

"I swear Mom waits until the weekend to pounce on me with housework. We did laundry like all day! It's bad enough I have to iron my own clothes, but now she makes me iron Micky's crap, too. Complete bummer! She says I need to know how to iron men's shirts because it will be important one day. Geez, Mom, it's the sixties! I'm not going to be some man's slave like she is. At least Louise and I had some fun tonight. We drove around in Lemon Drop for a couple of hours, then we hung out at the Dairy Duchess until it closed. Jeannie Singer works there, and she snuck Louise and me a couple of ice cream cones while the manager was in the back. Yum!"

No mention of the note. Alex skimmed through the entry for the 19th looking for reference to Sean's warning but didn't find any. Then he saw the entry for the 20th.

"What the HELL!!! It was in the Sunday paper today that Ted Kennedy was in a car accident and some woman drowned... and it happened on the 18th! Is this what Nigel meant by T. Kennedy drowning? And if that wasn't freaky enough, the moon landing was all over the TV. Nigel had written the EXACT words they said when they landed and when the guy got out of the space ship and walked on the moon. How was that possible? Can Nigel like see into the future? The next one listed is August 8th. Someone getting murdered!?!?! I don't think I even know who Sharon Tate is. Should I try to find out and warn her?"

Alex decided to skip ahead to find the last entry and found Sean's note tucked into that page. He read the entry for October 9th.

"Janet Williamson is such a bitch! She thinks she is soooooo cool. I hate her! I can't believe Louise wants to be on the basketball cheer-leading squad. How could she stand to be around Janet Williamson?!?! I just want to get out of this stupid little town. I can't wait to go to college next year. Tomorrow is the last date from Nigel's note. 'Do not get into any cars'! So freaky! He knew about the other things before they happened, though... so what does he know about tomorrow? I guess if I stay out of cars I won't ever know Oh, Nigel... I wish you had come back to see me. Are you back in New Zealand now? Or were you ever even from New Zealand? Can you magically move through time? Will you ever come see me again? I still love you. If you can travel through time, come back and take me with you!"

Alex took the note and started to put the book back in the drawer. He stopped and held it as he thought. There were too many things that should not have been said. He tucked the note back in the book and started out of the room. Hanging on the inside doorknob was the large bag Jane had when they went to the drive in. Alex picked it up, shut off lights and pulled the door part way closed. He tucked the book into the bag. He felt like he knew Jane better now, having read a few entries that she had written. She was an intelligent girl. It made it all the more difficult to think about putting her back into that car that was going to end her life. He sighed deeply as he walked down the stairs and turned off the stairway light.

"I am departing now, Mom," he yelled as he headed for the front door.

"Jane," Mrs. Carmichael called as she hurried after her daughter. Alex stopped and turned. "Don't go anywhere alone with that boy. You don't really know him. Find your friends and stay with them."

"That is good advice."

"I know, but will you follow it?"

"Yes, I will stay with people I know."

"Are you going to the dance after the game?"

"Yes."

"Dressed in a purple sweatshirt and jeans?"

"Yes."

Mrs. Carmichael shook her head sadly. "When I was a girl, we dressed up to go to a dance," she sighed. "Do NOT stay out late!" she added sternly. "Home by midnight!"

"I will not stay out late."

"Who are you," chuckled Mrs. Carmichael, "and what have you done with my daughter?"

Alex froze with fear. *What had she discerned?*

"I suppose I should be grateful that you're not rolling your eyes at me for a change," she said with a smile. "All right. Have fun, but follow your instincts. I know you have good instincts."

Alex released the breath he was holding. "We will have fun. I am sure Nigel will enjoy watching football." He opened the door but turned back before stepping out. "I love you, Mom," he said softly.

Mrs. Carmichael looked puzzled but smiled. "I love you, too, dear."

Will that help? Alex wondered as he stepped outside and closed the door. *Will it help her when she thinks back to the last time she thought she saw her daughter that she said 'I love you'?* He wiped a tear from his cheek before looking up to Sean.

"You were just here," Sean told him. "The other you, I mean... in Steffi."

"I know," said Alex, "I could feel my other presence while I was in the house. Did I tell you anything?"

"You said to release the emergency brake before trying to let the clutch out."

"Interesting... that would be recursive knowledge," Alex mused.

"I think you said something about re-cursing... but you kind of mumbled."

"Anything else?"

269

"I asked what the plan was and you said to ask you because you'd already told me," reported Sean. "That sounds really stupid when I say it out loud. This crossing your own time-stream gets a little confusing."

"Anything else?"

"Nope, you dragged Jane into Steffi and popped out."

"Then I believe we are to leave here using Jane's automobile."

"Can I ask you something first?" requested Sean, who continued without response from Alex. "Did you know how to do the Vulcan Nerve Pinch thingy before you downloaded all the *Star Trek* stuff?"

"If you are referring to my rendering Jane unconscious, you are mistaken in your assumption," Alex replied. "What I did more closely resembles the device you know as a Taser."

"Huh?"

"The pseudo-body suit has limited defensive capabilities. You are aware of the low-level force-field it can emit. It is also capable of discharging electrical impulses. A directed charge crossing a nerve cluster can cause rapid unconsciousness."

"You keep coming up with new things that suit can do," marveled Sean, "Can you fly?"

"No."

"OK, just thought I'd ask before I saw you fly off and you yell back to me, 'oh, by the way, I didn't tell you before, but I can fly.'"

"You have a vivid imagination."

"You've got a force-field and you can shock someone unconscious... I don't see why asking you to fly is any weirder."

"Perhaps we should continue this conversation as we depart."

"OK... but you'd better let me drive."

"I believe it would be more in character for Jane to operate her own vehicle," Alex insisted.

"You could barely drive an automatic," laughed Sean, "There's no way you could handle a stick."

"Locomotion of this vehicle requires a small tree branch?"

"Trust me," Sean boasted, "if you don't even know what a stick is, you can't drive one."

Sean got into the driver's side of the VW and Alex reluctantly got in on the passenger side. Sean pointed to a long rod protruding from the floor of the vehicle. It had a black knob with a diagram of white numbers on the top surface. "This is a manual gear shift, also known as a stick shift," Sean instructed. "Over here," he pointed to the floor under the steering wheel, "is your old friends Mr. Brake and Mr. Accelerator. But they have another friend called Mr. Clutch. Mr. Clutch is needed to coordinate the manual shifting of gears."

"Do I detect a condescending tone?" asked Alex indignantly.

"Maybe a little," Sean grinned, "I get so few opportunities to know about something that you don't."

"Simply operate this vehicle and I will observe your technique."

Sean held out his hand. "I hope you've got the keys."

"I did not consider that," admitted Alex.

"Check in the bag," Sean suggested, "I think most girls keep their keys in their purse."

Alex opened the bag and rummaged the contents, eventually pulling out a ring with two keys that were part of a cluster of decorative metal, wood, and plastic. He handed them to Sean.

Sean started the engine, depressed the clutch, and made sure the car was in first gear. "The trick is to coordinate releasing the clutch and easing into the accelerator," he instructed as he revved the engine a little. The car hiccupped forward, then died. "Well, crap," he groaned, "I forgot to let the brake off. I guess that was where the re-cursing happened." He released the brake and they rolled smoothly up the street.

"So," Sean questioned, "are we going to go with Alien Abduction as a Plan B?"

"I do not understand."

"We need a Plan B, since you couldn't hypnotize her, and since you've already abducted her... or will have abducted her a few minutes ago... sometime in the future..." His voice trailed off as he tried to figure out the best way to refer to an incident that he'd already witnessed, but had not yet happened to Alex. He decided the hardest part of time-travel was talking about it.

"If you are attempting to clarify your former statement, you have not achieved your goal."

"OK, look..." Sean tried again. "Jane *has* already been abducted, and you *will be* the one who does the abducting. So is the plan to go back to 1995 and see what happens... happened... will happen? Then if my mom and dad are back, you can find someplace for Jane to assume a new identity. Kind of like a witness protection program... for time-travelers."

"That suggestion does not change Louise's fate."

"OK, right, right, right... we have to keep Louise from getting into the car."

"And if some other person were to take her place and become the second fatality?"

"What if no one does?" huffed Sean. "Why not just try it and see what happens? I don't know... go a couple weeks into the future and read the paper and see what happened."

"In this scenario, Jane completely vanishes?"

"Why not?"

"She was last seen with you. The logical assumption people will make is that *you* are the one who abducted her."

"I don't care *what* they think," Sean growled.

"They will initiate a search for Jane," Alex predicted, "It will involve local and national, perhaps international law officials investigating the disappearance."

"So what?"

"The 'so what' is, to use our familiar river metaphor, you are suggesting tossing a stone into the time-stream that could cause even larger ripples than your original meddling."

"*Meddling?*" objected Sean. He fired ice daggers from his eyes at Alex before returning his attention to the road.

"I apologize for the terminology sounding judgmental," Alex granted his ancestor. "However, that should not detract from the point I made regarding the greater time disruption."

"I don't get that," Sean disagreed, "Why is it greater?"

"Mrs. Carmichael does not seem like the type of person who will accept her daughter's disappearance without taking every investigative action possible. I believe she will alter the course of many people's lives in her fruitless attempt to locate her daughter. Once the investigation reveals that Nigel Davies from New Zealand does not really exist, it will be assumed that you are a predator who stalked Jane maliciously, and will perhaps repeat the crime elsewhere."

"Well," Sean said unsteadily, "so... even if they think I'm a serial killer, it won't matter. I'll be gone where they can't find me."

"You do not mind that your image is historically associated with a young girl's abduction and assumed murder?"

"What image? No one took a picture of me."

"I believe it was a common practice in this time for witnesses to describe a suspect for a police artist. Louise, Micky, Scott, Karen, Jimbo, your father, and now Jane's mother have all spent enough time with you to attempt a description. A composite from that many people may be a rather close likeness. Perhaps in this altered timeline your father keeps a newspaper and one day realizes that the suspect in Jane's disappearance looks strangely like his own son."

"OK! OK!" Sean shouted. "Big ripples. Fine! I give up! So what's your plan?"

"I do not yet have one formulated."

Sean took a deep breath and counted to ten before continuing through clenched teeth. "You told me that you *told* me the plan... will tell me the plan... dammit, I hate this jumping around in time stuff. *Future* you... who in the recent past told me that his *past* you... which is currently a *future* you to you... already told me the plan... means that *you* are going to tell me the plan."

"I do not doubt the validity of that statement," Alex calmly assured him. "However, I do not, at this moment, have a completed plan. Perhaps if I have some time of quiet contemplation, I will finish formulating a plan."

Sean pulled the VW to the side of the street near the entrance to the cemetery.

"So, are you going to try to hypnotize her again?"

"It would be futile," Alex reasoned, "She already has knowledge of the fatal car crash. I cannot suggest that someone do something that is truly against their will. The will to live is instinctively very strong."

"So what now?"

"I recommend that you wait five minutes here, then walk down to where Steffi is. Do you remember the location?"

"Yeah, I think so," Sean said with little conviction. "What's going to happen in five minutes?"

"That will give me enough time to remove the craft and return before you reach it."

"Huh?"

"It will not matter if it takes me twenty minutes or twenty hours to fully formulate a plan, I will return to the same spot that will be only five minutes difference to you."

Sean shook his head briskly, trying to shake off the frustration and confusion of time-travel. "I'm not even going to try to follow that. I'll just do what you say. I'll wait five minutes then walk down to where Steffi is parked."

After only a couple of minutes, Sean began to fidget. He felt conspicuous sitting in Jane's car at the entrance to the cemetery, so he started the car and did a three-point turn and then drove slowly through the open gates. "I kind of look like Shaggy, and I'm driving into a dark cemetery," he mumbled to himself mostly to prevent his imagination from conjuring strange graveyard apparitions. "All I need is a big dog as a sidekick." He thought of his own dog. "Maggie would be a great sidekick. Maggie and Shaggy... to the rescue." Once he felt he was out of sight from the main road, he turned off the car, gave his surroundings a quick look, and then reluctantly clicked off the headlights.

"What do you think, Maggie, old girl?" he asked the empty seat on his right. "Close enough to five minutes? I agree, let's head out."

He got out, then tried to quietly close the door. In the silence of the cemetery, the soft click was like a gunshot. "Shhhhh," he said to his imaginary companion, finger to his lips. "We have to be very quiet."

He headed down a row of graves. "I think it was this way. Come on, Maggie, if you figure out who did it, I'll give you a Maggie snack." Fairly certain he was in the wrong row, he gingerly stepped around a large headstone to get to the next row. "I wish we would get to the part where we pull the mask off the bad guy. *Jinkies! It's Mr. Creepwalker, the caretaker!*" He turned his head to the left, as he replied to himself in a gravelly voice, "*And I would have gotten away with it, too, if it weren't for you meddling kids!* That's always the best part, Maggie."

He stopped to look around. His eyes had adjusted to the dim light, but everything was still shadowy tones of gray. A glance up at the moon revealed that only half was shining. "So, at least no werewolves, right Maggie?"

It still didn't feel like he was in the right row, so he crossed over two more before continuing to walk parallel to that row of stones. "Come on, Mags, use your nose!" he coaxed the imaginary dog, "Find Steffi!" In frustration, he muttered, "I wish you really *were* here. I'll bet you could find it."

He stopped again, turned around to look toward the gate, comparing what he saw to what he remembered seeing as they first walked out. It still wasn't the right row. He crossed over three more before again turning to his left and continuing down the new row. None of it looked familiar in the dim light.

Silently cursing Alex for what amounted to hide and seek in the cemetery, he randomly passed through several more rows. As he stepped between two headstones in the third row he'd crossed, a bright light flashed behind him, slapping his shadow against the large stone in the next row.

"Auauaughghgh," he screamed as he bolted to his right almost immediately tripping over a shorter headstone and sprawling onto the grass. "There are no werewolves. There are no werewolves," he chanted to the grass.

"Where are you going?" called a familiar voice.

Sean rolled over and turned his head toward the light. Although he could only see a shadowy silhouette in the bright light, he knew that it was Alex.

"And of course he pops up when I'm lying in the grass talking about werewolves," he mumbled to himself, realizing there was no reasonable lie he could tell to cover that. "I, umm," he started, "I was... um... surprised when you opened the door. The bright flash and all."

"I was favorably impressed," Alex began, "that you found the S.T.E. However, you walked past, so I realized that you did not remember the exact coordinates."

Sean stood and pointed an accusing finger at Steffi. "That's not where you were parked earlier."

"It most certainly is the *precise* spot," countered Alex. "I registered a space/time locator to ensure the exact geographic area plus five minutes time."

"Well, it looks different in moonlight," Sean groused.

"The moon only shifts one-half degree per hour, or roughly the distance of its own diameter. The change in angle is so minute that it could not visually effect lighting on the earth's surface in the length of time which we were away."

"OK, *fine!* I missed where you were parked," Sean growled, "I don't need a science lesson, just give me the plan."

He crossed over to Alex, who cowered slightly. "I do not believe you will immediately appreciate the design of this plan," he said meekly, "I need you to be open-minded."

"I can be open minded," Sean shrugged, "So tell me the plan."

"Some of it may be easier to show you than to fully explain."

Sean rolled his eyes. "OK, so *show* me the plan."

"You will need to remove your clothes," Alex said reluctantly.

"Exactly *what* am I being open-minded about?"

"Do not be concerned," Alex continued quickly, "I will also be removing mine."

Sean squinted his left eye. "This is *not* getting any better. I think I want to know your intentions before this goes any further."

Alex was perplexed by Sean's attitude. "We need to exchange clothing. It is integral to the plan."

Sean stared blankly at Alex, blinking several times as he processed what was said. "*I* get to wear the super suit?"

"Yes."

"*I* get to wear the super suit?" he repeated louder.

"It is actually called a pseudo-body suit... but yes. You will be wearing it."

Sean shucked out of his jacket and enthusiastically pulled his t-shirt over his head. "Dude! This is freakin' *awesome!*" He kicked off his shoes and unbuttoned his pants and slid them off.

"Perhaps you will be more receptive to this plan than I anticipated," Alex commented as he deactivated his hippie guise returning to his silvery, shiny suit. He tugged the head piece off and handed it to Sean, then touched a spot on the right side of his neck and closed his eyes in concentration. His silvery suit collapsed away from his body and fell to the ground.

Wide-eyed, Sean quickly looked away.

"Dude! Don't you have underwear in the future?"

"Unnecessary with the pseudo-body suit," Alex said, adding, "It certainly is cold without it."

"Yeah, I don't feel so hot myself; so let's get this switch over with." He tossed his pants blindly in Alex's direction. "I'm not putting those jeans back on if you don't wear underwear."

"It should not be necessary once the plan is fully implemented," Alex assured him.

"And putting on the super suit is getting less appealing when I think about your junk exposed against the inside."

Alex was perplexed. "The pseudo-body suit continuously sanitizes itself. The forensic scientists of this century would be unable to locate a single particle of my DNA from the interior of the suit. I am the one who should be concerned about wearing contaminated clothing."

"Contaminated? Really?" Sean complained, "You had to say contaminated?"

"Fortunately Steffi's sonic cleaner will remove 98% of all contaminates."

Alex placed Sean's clothes into one of Steffi's nearly invisible drawers under the seat area. In a few seconds, he took them out and put them on. The t-shirt was baggy, but the jeans were ridiculous. Alex was about five inches shorter than Sean and had a smaller waistline. He cinched up the waist by pulling the belt to its last hole and futilely attempted to roll the bell-bottoms up. Having no success, he decided to deal with them later. Pulling on the army jacket, he nearly stumbled over the excess denim that swaddled his feet as he moved toward Sean.

"You really should remove your underwear," he said to Sean. "I cannot predict the reaction of the pseudo-body suit to foreign material inside."

"I'll take my chances," Sean replied firmly.

"I suppose the worst case scenario is that the cotton fibers of your underwear could become fused with the top layers of your epidermis. It would eventually slough off as your skin cells naturally exfoliate."

Sean stared at Alex for a few moments, decided he was not kidding, and slid his underwear down and stepped out of them.

"Now what?" yelped Sean. "I'm freezing!"

"Step over here and place your feet into the center. It should feel similar to sliding into a pair of shoes that are too big."

Sean did as he was told and had to admit that the feeling did remind him of trying on his Dad's boots when he was still a toddler. "Now what?"

Alex bent down and fumbled around with the nearly fluid silvery suit. He found what he was looking for and stood, handing one section to Sean. "Hold onto this while I locate the opposite side." He again bent down and found another section and lifted it up. "Now hold this in your other hand." The material now surrounded Sean to the waist. It rippled in the slight breeze and both looked and behaved like a plastic grocery store bag... but it felt... soft... warm where he held it in his hands. The material fluttered like a plastic bag, but also had a fluidity like water rippling in a stream.

Alex stepped back a half step. "I need you to now place your hands on your shoulders near your neck as you continue to hold the edges of the suit."

"I'm taller than you," Sean pointed out. "It won't be able to reach that far."

"I believe you will find that it does," answered Alex, "If you were ten feet tall, the elasticity of the suit would accommodate you."

Sean pulled the suit up and to his surprise found it did indeed stretch up to his neck. Oddly, it still seemed as billowy as it had at waist level. It was almost hypnotic to watch the ripples.

"Do not move as I attempt to locate the activation switch," Alex said as he started searching Sean's right side. "I have located it." He held his hand in place as he stepped around to face Sean. "I need your complete attention," he demanded. "You cannot joke around or distract me in any way. The suit is linked to my neural network and reacts from my brainwaves, enhanced by my internal nanites."

"More nanite magic," Sean commented.

"I am serious," Alex warned. "I have never attempted this. It will require my complete concentration."

"OK... sorry."

"Perhaps if you look straight ahead and clear your mind."

Sean nodded and did as instructed. Alex closed his eyes in concentration. As he visualized the suit conforming to Sean's body, it began to move, to shimmer, to shift. It began contracting its billowy shape to Sean's body. Sean gasped. Alex refocused his mental image, ignoring the gasp. The suit was now around Sean like a second skin. Alex opened his eyes. "How does it feel?"

Sean stared at him wide-eyed. He held out his hands and looked at his silvery fingers as he wiggled them. He shifted his gaze back to Alex. "Wow!" he said with breathy enthusiasm. "That was awesome... or far out... or groovy... or freaky... or I don't know what!"

Alex nodded approval. "If the fit feels comfortable, I will adjust the aesthetics."

"What needs adjusted? It feels fantastic. Perfectly comfortable. Soft. Warm." He stopped to think, then corrected himself, "Not really warm. More like, completely perfect temperature."

"Yes. I must admit, your own clothing leaves much to be desired for thermal retention. With regard to the adjustments, even in the 23rd century, we do not openly put our genitalia on display."

Sean glanced down and saw that there was nothing left to the imagination. "Whoa! That's pretty weird. It feels like I'm dressed."

"You are," Alex confirmed as he closed his eyes and visualized attire that looked like silvery trousers with a shiny jacket. The suit altered to his specifications.

"Oh, I *soooo* want one of these!" Sean gushed.

"I wish I had a second one," Alex said through chattering teeth, "Your clothing only partially blocks the chill of the atmosphere."

"If it weren't for my face," Sean marveled, "I wouldn't have any idea what the temperature was. This is like totally beyond awesome to the third power!"

Alex stooped to pick up the headpiece that Sean had dropped and handed it to him. "And with this, you will completely block the effects of the external environment."

Sean took it and pulled it over his head and partly over his nose. "How do you breathe with this on?"

"It is so automatic for me," Alex said, "that I barely am consciously aware while putting it on. However, as I will have to make adjustments while we put it on you, you should probably hold your breath."

"Wait... what?"

"When I put it on myself, it is reflexive for me to open the nasal and oral airways. Since you are putting it on and I am activating it, it may take a few seconds to properly adjust."

"You know," Sean protested, "kids in *this* century are taught to *not* put dry-cleaning bags over their heads."

"I assure you, it is not in my own self-interest to asphyxiate you."

"I'm just sayin'... so, like, don't take a coffee break while you're doing the open-the-airways thing, huh?"

"I will complete the task as rapidly as I can," Alex vowed. "As long as you do not attempt to inhale before it is completed, you will not even know that your face was temporarily hermetically sealed." Alex placed his hand on the neck control. "Ready?"

"I guess," sighed Sean reluctantly, "On three. One. Two. Three." He took a deep breath and pulled the headpiece down around his neck. It attached itself to the rest of the suit and Alex mentally signaled it to open the airways for Sean's mouth and nose.

"Auaughghgh!" screamed Sean. "Ick. Ick. Yuck!"

"Can you not breathe?" demanded Alex.

"Yuck!" Sean said again. "I can breathe OK, but you didn't tell me this thing was going to crawl into my nose and mouth!"

"Only about a centimeter inside your nose."

"And practically down my throat!" Sean ranted.

"It is necessary to cover the oral area to affect change. People have different shapes and colors of teeth."

"Well, it's OK now," grumbled Sean, "but when it was sliding in it felt pretty weird."

"I confess that was the most interesting sensation when initially donning the suit, but I believe I am no longer even aware of the transition."

"Right. Interesting sensation." Sean rolled his eyes. "Remind me to put an ice cube down your pants before we swap back."

"I cannot imagine how that would seem comparable."

"Never mind," said Sean as he shook his head in disbelief. "So does it automatically leave eye holes?"

"No. It turns transparent over the corneas... and of course can alter the color over your irises, if you need to change the pigment of your eyes. Once you put Jane's corrective lenses on, it will also adapt your vision."

"It went over my eyes?" exclaimed Sean. "I didn't feel it."

"Your nose and lips are much more sensitive to touch than your eyes. I would suggest that your attention was diverted and you did not notice."

"Eyes are a lot more sensitive," Sean argued, "Haven't you ever got just a little bit of shampoo in your eyes? Man that hurts."

"That is because of the chemical reaction. I am referring to pressure sensitivity. Since the area of the suit that covers your eyes is pH balanced, it matches the saline of your tears on contact. You might compare it to your era's vision-correcting devices you refer to as 'contact lenses'."

"I wouldn't know," Sean shrugged. "Hey, the bottom half of the suit was all silvery and shiny, what's the headpiece look like?"

"Similar."

"I wanna see it. Put the mirror-cam on in Steffi."

Alex and Sean slid into the time-machine and Alex adjusted the front view-screen to display Sean's reflection.

"Cool!" exclaimed Sean. "I kinda look like the Silver Surfer." He looked at his hands. "So why don't you ever look like you have silver gloves on?"

"I automatically change everything when it is on. Let me adjust your hands and face." Alex found the tiny control nub on the left side of Sean's neck and closed his eyes to concentrate on the changes.

"Really?" Sean sneered. "You make my face look like yours?"

Alex opened his eyes and saw that Sean was correct, he was looking at his own face. "Sorry," he apologized, "that was an automatic response." He closed his eyes and concentrated on Sean's features.

"Much better," Sean announced, checking both profiles. "What about the hair? What if we wanted to go back to hippie Nigel's hair?"

Alex closed his eyes again, then opened them to see that Sean's 'hair' had grown out to the same length as his extended hair.

"Awesome! Man, I wish I could do the changes myself. That would be so cool. I'd do Tom Cruise and go to a bar or something and just sit there and watch people stare at me and wonder if I really was Tom Cruise."

Alex twitched a query to identify Tom Cruise. "However, in 1969 no one would make visual identification of Tom Cruise."

"Hmmm... good point," Sean agreed. "OK, so what part of the plan needs me to be the one wearing the super suit?"

"Pseudo-body suit," corrected Alex. "Let me simply show you. I need to reach around again to the control on the left side of your neck. There. Now, quiet as I concentrate on the change."

The blood-curdling scream that filled the cabin started in Sean's voice, but ended in a much higher register as the unconscious form of Jane Carmichael slumped against a wide-eyed Alex.

Chapter Fifteen

"Buy me a drink, sing me a song / Take me as I come 'cause I can't stay long"

"**S**EAN? Sean can you hear me?"

"Mmmhmmm," Sean slurred, "wuh happent?"

"I do not know," said Alex. "You screamed as I activated the suit. Then you were unconscious."

"Jane here?" murmured Sean. "Heard her voice."

Alex gently slapped Sean's face. "Concentrate. You need to focus. Fight your way back to full consciousness. Are you currently in pain?"

"Mmmm don't think so," mumbled Sean, "keep hearing Jane, though. She repeats what I say."

"Sean, open your eyes wide and look at the view-screen."

"K," he said, opening his eyes. "There's Jane... and there's you..." he squinted. Jane squinted back at him. "Where am I?"

"What is the last thing you remember?"

Sean paused as he pondered the question. "I was looking at you and Jane and wondering where I was."

"No. Before you blacked out! You were sitting here admiring your profiles, then I said I was going to activate the pseudo-body suit. Then you screamed during the transformation and became unconscious. What else do you remember?"

Sean struggled to think, tried to review what Alex just said and remember it as it happened. His eyes flew open. "My legs!" he exclaimed, "It felt like someone was ripping my legs off. And kinda pressure all over, but my legs hurt the most." He studied the view-screen as he moved his head from side to side. "You turned me into Jane?" It dawned on him that he heard her voice as he spoke. "Test. Test. Testing one, two, three." He watched Jane's lips carefully as he enunciated each word. "How much wood would a woodchuck chuck? If a woodchuck could chuck wood? Peter Piper picked a peck of pickled peppers. Oh, man, this is beyond insane." He pinched his nose and pushed it left and right as he watched Jane doing the same. He crossed his eyes to try to stare at the tip of his new nose. "OK, now I see why this thing bothers her so much."

"You had extreme pain in your legs?" prompted Alex.

"Hmmm?" muttered Sean as he watched Jane open her mouth, move her jaw from side to side, stick out her tongue, pull her hair around and tie it in a slip knot under her chin.

"Your legs!"

Sean broke away from his fascination of making the image of Jane move as he wished. "Oh. Yeah, legs. Hurt like hell. And I kinda felt like I was being crushed all over, but that was nothing compared to my legs."

"Where on your legs?"

Sean felt phantom pains as he reviewed his memory. "It almost seemed like in the bone. And it wasn't that someone was pulling them off, it was like they were being crushed."

"Any residual pain?"

"No," Sean said absently as he regained his fascination with Jane's reflection. He cupped his hands over his newly found breasts. "Whoa. That is really really weird."

"Can you please focus on our conversation?"

Sean looked back at Alex. "What? I'm fine now. So I guess you don't feel any pain when *you* shift?"

"No," Alex replied, thoughtfully adding, "but perhaps the neural net blocks the pain sensation when I change myself. I know nothing about the details of the design of the pseudo-body suit. I only received information related to its operation. It makes rational sense."

"What makes sense?"

"Both the pain and the pain reception blocking."

"Care to explain it in a way that a caveman..." Sean glanced at his reflection. "Make that cave *woman*... can understand?"

"Remember when I explained the properties of molecular passing with regard to Steffi moving through a supposedly solid wall?" He put his hands together interlocking his fingers through each other.

"Vaguely... and to tell the truth, I decided just to go with 'magic' for that one."

Alex rolled his eyes. "There are similar properties we could apply."

"That was good," interrupted Sean. "The eye roll. It looked natural."

Alex winced. "It was natural," he said gruffly, "I am picking up bad habits from you."

Sean laughed but immediately stopped to stare at the Jane reflection. "Wow," he mouthed, starry eyed, "She has such a beautiful laugh."

"Do you wish an explanation or not?" demanded Alex testily.

"Sure," Sean shrugged.

"Do you remember the part of the explanation about the amount of free space at the molecular level?"

"I think so. That was the orange, pea, sand, water thing, right?"

"Yes. It is similar when you activate a change in the pseudo-body suit that involves a significant body *size* change," Alex lectured, "You do not gain nor lose any mass. Even when your body becomes smaller, you retain your original mass. If you were to step on a scale, you would weigh your standard Sean Kelly weight." Sean scrunched Jane's face up as he tried to comprehend. He nodded unenthusiastically.

Alex continued, "The only way to physically reduce your size for your smaller appearance is to compact space at the molecular level. The bones in Jane's legs are considerably shorter than yours. Apparently, compressing them to the degree required, activated your natural pain receptors."

"But it doesn't do that to you?"

"Not that I am *aware*. However, it is reasonable that it *would*. Therefore, it is a logical assumption that something in the interface between the pseudo-body suit and my neural net blocks the pain signal from reaching my brain. Since there is no residual pain once the compression has completed, there is no reason for the brain to be troubled by temporary pain. External control of a shape shift is *not* a normal condition."

"So you are saying that once the shift is over, no more pain?"

"It appears so."

Sean nodded thoughtfully. "What about when I change back?"

"Unknown. I would hypothesize that expansion would be less painful than compression, but we will ascertain the validity of that hypothesis when we actually attempt it."

"Looking forward to being the test subject," Sean said sarcastically. He stared at the Jane reflection again. "Why do you need *me* to be Jane, instead of you?"

"I will be making critical course corrections for interfacing Steffi with the automobile that is destined to crash," Alex explained. "I've spent several hours on the mathematics and run the simulation dozens of times. I believe I am satisfied with the time factor, but the space factor might need ad hoc corrections at the moments of materialization."

Sean's eyes narrowed. "And where will *I* be during these 'corrections' you're talking about?"

"In the automobile."

Sean raised his eyebrows. "*In* the automobile?"

"Yes."

Sean crossed his arms. "The one that is going to crash and kill two people and maim two others?"

"Yes."

He stared at Alex in disbelief. "You're crazy!"

"It is an implementation of one of *your* ideas."

"*My* ideas?" Sean exclaimed, "I don't remember volunteering to get into a death car."

"Not that part," Alex clarified, "The rescue part. When you were suggesting desperate measures to spare Jane's life, one was to 'swoop in and pull her from the car' just before the crash takes place."

"So you're saying the 'swoop in and grab her' thing will actually work?"

"Yes. As I have already stated, I have spent several hours on the mathematics and modeling simulations. The initial difficulty was the computations required for semi-materialization, which took most of the five hours. In effect, rapid materialization and dematerialization between dimensions will establish a pocket of nearly null time. Not completely null, of course, but my calculations will create a rate of 600 seconds inside Steffi per second to you in the automobile. It should be unseen to anyone in the vehicle."

Sean closed his eyes to concentrate. "OK... so how does going 600 times faster help?"

"I will have ten minutes to fully adjust the spatial coordinates and complete the rescue during what you will perceive as one second. I am relatively confident that the event can be completed in less than five minutes, thus not even one-half second to you."

Sean squeezed his eyes tighter, then finally shook his head and opened them. "OK, I think I almost can visualize this." He rubbed a hand over the length of his face. "I think I'll file it in the mostly 'magic' category again, though. Wait. When did you have 'hours' to do all this mathematics stuff?"

"While you were walking from Jane's vehicle to here."

"So, five minutes to me, and you were gone five hours?"

"Actually closer to eight."

"Eight? What did you do with the other three hours?"

Alex returned to lecture mode. "Some of it was spent studying the velocity of the automobile, seconds before the crash. Other data was obtained by examining the scene tomorrow. Physical evidence remains where the vehicle crested the hill, temporarily attained zero-gravity and achieved a degree of elevation. The disturbance in the gravel reveals where it returned to earth and began sliding. Finally, it is evident where the undercarriage of the vehicle sheers off some of the earth from the edge of the road as it plunges off. From that data, I extrapolated both the speed and path of the vehicle."

"So you didn't actually watch the wreck?"

"No. I needed to avoid that window of time to insure that there is no temporal interference with the semi-materialization process that will create the bubble of nearly null time. That is also why I may need to make minimal corrections in the spatial coordinate. The simulation models project the rescue window to be as much as three meters apart when comparing the extremes."

"Three meters? That's like, what... ten feet? You might be off by *ten feet?*"

"Only 1.5 meters at maximum," Alex corrected, "The initial materialization will be at the midpoint of the extreme models. "

"Oh, only five feet off! Much better!" groaned Sean.

"I have already pre-written 30 unique course corrections of one-tenth meter each. It will be nearly instantaneous for me to recognize the actual variance of the spatial coordinate and execute any needed compensation."

Sean put his hands over his eyes and pleaded, "Tell me you were really good at math in school."

"Good?" asked Alex, "In comparison to what?"

"The other kids."

"Oh. I see," Alex nodded, "I forgot that learning was only partial in the twentieth century. Everyone in the 23rd century is 'good at math', we all achieve 100% proficiency of the curriculum."

"Wow. So even the jocks are math nerds in the 23rd century?"

"I do not understand."

"Never mind. OK... back to the other three hours. What else did you do?"

"Much of the remainder of the time was spent securing Jane Carmichael in a hospital room in Omaha, Nebraska, and getting her fully sedated."

Sean's eyes went wide. "What?"

"The effect of the electrical charge that rendered her unconscious was temporary. I required a longer term of unconsciousness, thus, medical sedation."

"What?" Sean repeated louder, shaking his head. "How did you manage that?"

"Research. I cross-referenced the level of safe sedation that I required with the drugs used in this era and chose sodium thiopental."

"Which anyone can buy at their local drug store," Sean commented facetiously.

"No, it is a controlled substance," Alex refuted, then paused to check Sean's expression. "But you already know that. I had to gain access to the sedative at a hospital."

"Why all the way to Omaha?"

"In these closer small rural communities, there is a greater chance of the employees of the hospital personally knowing all of the patients in their care. A larger hospital was required for greater anonymity. Omaha was Mercer's closest population center of optimal size."

"So you just walked in and said, 'hi, I need some sodium tri-potimal for my friend' and they just let you have it?"

"Sodium thiopental," Alex corrected.

"Whatever."

"As you are fully aware, it was not that simple," Alex explained, "After selecting the hospital and locating an internal room large enough to materialize Steffi, I moved forward to three a.m. My rational was that there would be fewer people moving about, and those who were, possibly were at a relatively high level of fatigue. I assumed the appearance of a medical doctor and accosted a fatigued nurse who was very susceptible to my 'suggestions.' She helped me attain the drug and set up a vacant room with a bed and IV to place Miss Carmichael. I then 'suggested' that she forget any awareness of Miss Carmichael or myself."

"OK, back up a minute... you've already taken Jane to this hospital?"

"Yes."

"But when you picked her up, you said to me that you had already told me the plan."

"That seemed the most efficient way to stifle your curiosity for the moment."

"You *lied* to me?" exclaimed Sean.

"Prevarication seemed the expedient option to minimize our interaction."

"Oh, no. Not this time, buddy," Sean countered, "No big words to make it sound better. You *lied* to me."

"Are you quibbling over semantics?"

"No, I'm calling you on using big words instead of just admitting you lied."

Alex's face noticeably reddened. "That term carries a connotation of premeditated malice. I had no such intentions."

"Yeah, right! That explains why your pants are on fire."

Panic gripped Alex as he started examining his unfamiliar jeans. "Where?"

"Never mind," chuckled Sean, "OK, back to the plan that you *said* you had already told me about."

"Where is the fire?" squeaked Alex.

"There isn't one, it's an idiom you apparently don't know. Forget about it," Sean declared. "So you've got Jane doped up in some hospital in Omaha..."

"Not yet."

"Huh?"

"Not at this time," Alex clarified, "Not until approximately three a.m."

Sean was confused. "So where is she now?"

Alex shared his confusion. "Now?"

"Yes, now."

"At this exact point in time, Jane Carmichael does not physically exist on this planet."

Sean squeezed his eyes shut tightly and spoke through clenched teeth, "I am really getting tired of this short hop time-travel stuff. Let's just go with Jane's perspective. You grabbed her from her front yard a few minutes ago, and took her to Omaha, but also went forward in time to three a.m."

"Correct."

Sean put his hands over his eyes, then rubbed them down his face. "So right now, she is in the future."

Alex considered the statement. "I believe the terms 'right now' and 'in the future' are mutually exclusive."

"OK, I give up," Sean yelled as he tossed up his hands in surrender. "Jane magically is hidden away somewhere! Now... why am *I* Jane?"

"There are two critical tasks that you must accomplish. You must prevent Louise from getting into the automobile destined to crash, and *you, yourself* must get into that vehicle, thus preventing an as yet unknown person from possibly taking that position when Louise is detoured. Anyone observing would be convinced that they saw Jane Carmichael get into the vehicle."

"So, *I* have the super suit to look and sound like Jane... which I gotta say is a little weird, but I'm actually getting used to hearing her voice when I speak... anyway... I look like Jane so that I can take her place in the death car. The reason you aren't doing it is because you have to do some fancy flying to swoop in and pull off the alien abduction idea I came up with."

"Other than your annoying insistence to refer to the pseudo-body suit as 'super', your summation of the planned events is a reasonable approximation."

"Well then," shrugged Sean, "Let's get me to the dance."

"That event does not begin until nine o'clock, which is sixty-seven minutes from now. Do you wish to wait, or take a short time-jump?"

"You're sure all these short hops don't drain Steffi's batteries?"

"There are no batteries," replied Alex. "Though you do not have a proper frame of reference to understand the principles behind Steffi's power plant; I will again assure you that by your standards, the power is all but limitless."

"OK, if you say so," sighed Sean. "Let's hop."

In only a few seconds, Alex reopened Steffi's door. "Do you know how to get to the high school from here?"

"Can't you just drop me off close?"

"I believe it would be more in character for you to arrive at the dance in Jane's automobile."

"Ah... good point," Sean agreed, then added. "Eh, it's a small town... I should be able to find it."

Alex activated the map function on the forward screen. "We are currently here." He pointed to a red flashing dot. "Jane's house is here." He touched a spot and a yellow square appeared. "And the high school is here." He touched another spot and it formed a red triangle.

"OK, so over, down, over, then back this way," Sean said as he traced a path. "Got it."

"I will not see you again until I extract you from the automobile. You will need to have your window down, sit behind the driver, and have your left arm outside of the vehicle."

"Behind the driver, window down, arm out. Got it. So what are you going to do until then? Or are you jumping straight there?"

"I believe it would be prudent for me to sleep for four hours. That will ensure that I will be more mentally alert and have better reflexes."

"You're going to take a nap?" complained Sean.

"That may be how you would phrase it, yes."

"Wait... for four hours? That's after the time of the wreck."

"Indeed. However, I will simply go back in time to make the rendezvous point."

"But you won't leave until after the wreck?"

"Correct."

"So, the wreck will take place before you leave."

"In linear time, yes."

"Then technically, I would be dead before you leave."

"No, I will intervene."

Sean shook his head. "I don't really like the way that feels. Maybe your way I actually have to die once before you come back and save me."

"That is not logical."

"Logical or not, I don't like the idea of you sleeping through the crash the first time, then coming back."

"Linear time is irrelevant for this outcome."

"No," Sean loudly disagreed, "I was born, then things changed, and then I wasn't born. But I still exist because I was here while I wasn't being born in the new timeline. So how do you know that I won't die before you change it? Maybe in some timeline, I get killed in this car wreck. Blam! Dead!" He took a deep breath and exhaled loudly. "I don't like it. Why don't you go back in time to take your nap, then you won't have to cross back over the wreck. I don't want to experience getting killed even if it isn't permanent."

A strange smile crossed Alex's face as he stared off into space to absorb Sean's words. "That is a fascinating theory," he said absently. "It could merit further study. In the original timeline, Jane was the fatality, but because of your interference, that event changed and Louise became the fatality. We have been to the future to verify the two separate events did indeed occur. What you are suggesting is that at this point, the plan is to put you in that vehicle, thus without interference, you would become the fatality. You further suggest that by my initiating the rescue from a point in time *after* the event, that you would indeed be killed in yet another creation of an alternate timeline."

"No," Sean corrected forcefully, "I'm suggesting we *don't* find out! You go back in time, take your nap and be ready to get me out of the car from *this* side of the crash!"

"I suppose that would be a more prudent approach," Alex agreed.

"And make sure you set an alarm clock," Sean demanded as he slid out of the time-machine.

"Review the objectives once more?" Alex called after him.

Sean held out a hand and counted fingers as he regurgitated the steps, "Go to dance. Keep Louise out of car. Get in car, behind driver. Have window down. Stick arm out." He held up his thumb on his other hand for the sixth step, "You swoop in and pull me out."

Alex nodded. He watched for a few moments as Sean walked away, then closed the door. He felt anxious. Although he had run the simulations over and over, no matter how much he practiced, the best probability of success achieved was 98%. What if the unthinkable 2% became the new reality?

He set the controls, second guessed himself, and then reset them to go an entire day into the past. He wasn't sure how long it would take to force himself into the sleep that he needed to function his best.

Sean turned back toward the spot where Steffi had been sitting and heard the soft pop the air made as it rushed to fill the temporary vacuum from the time-machine's exit. He was alone in a time where he didn't belong and he looked like someone he wasn't. He knew he would feel even more alone in the death car, even with three other people with him. Two of them he had never met and the third he only knew as someone who defended Louise from a drunken redneck.

He tried to imagine getting into the car and his thoughts plagued him with doubt. How should he act with them? How would Jane have acted with them? How would he have the courage to even get in that car? He had to trust his descendant, and he knew that Alex had as much on the line as himself. After all, getting killed in the car wreck would mean that Alex couldn't have a home to return to either.

"Hello, Lemon Drop," Sean whispered as he reached the Volkswagen. "Ready to go to the dance?" He opened the door and slid in. "Sorry you won't be seeing Jane anymore, but at least be happy that she'll be alive somewhere in the future."

He leaned forward, resting his head on the steering wheel, and shivered. Even wrapped in the warmth of the super suit, it felt like ice water was flowing through his veins. His stomach flipped over so many times it felt like it was on a hamster wheel. He took a deep breath as he raised his head. "OK... let's do this." He adjusted the mirror and slid the seat forward a little. "It is so weird being smaller."

He told himself that he hadn't spent *too* much time driving around aimlessly. After all, it really *was* a small town, and the big parking lot full of cars made it rather obvious that he had found the high school.

Locating an open space, he pulled in and shut the engine off. He dropped the keys into Jane's purse, slid out, and patted the car on the roof. "I hope they sell you to someone nice. I'm really sorry if you become Micky's car." He slung Jane's bag over his shoulder. "Man that feels weird."

"Hey, Jane," someone relatively close shouted, "who you talking to?"

Sean glanced around the lot and spotted a head hanging from an open window of the car to the right of the one just in front of Jane's VW. The guy obviously knew Jane, so Sean tried to imagine what Jane would do. He took a step toward the car. "No one, just thinking out loud to myself. Ummm, what are you up to?" He moved closer.

"About five seven," the voice called, then laughed. "Get it? Five seven...

you asked what I was up to."

"Yep, got it. That was a good one." *Really? That passes for funny in 1969?*

"We're just having a little toke before going in. Want one?" he said, holding out a hand with something that glowed red.

"Ummm, no... I'm cool," Sean stammered, "er... thanks."

"For sure."

"I'll...umm, see you later," Sean said as he walked past the car, trying to get a closer look at who he was talking to.

"That's cool," the voice said. His face glowed a little as he inhaled from whatever it was in his hand. He flashed a peace sign with his left hand as he rolled the window up with his right. *It might be the kid from the grocery store.* Sean held his two fingers in a return salute, then started toward the main door of the school. At least the stoned guy thought he was Jane. *Maybe this would work.*

Near the entrance, a few guys stood around smoking regular cigarettes.

"Jane," one of them called, "what's happening?"

"Not much," Sean smiled back. *What was that term he'd heard? What was the term?* "Just...umm... mellowing out... like groovy, you know?" *Geez, was that right?*

"Far out," the guy nodded, then turned back to his friends.

Sean walked through the door. *OK... they say cool, but not awesome. What else? Far out. Groovy. Mellow. Out of sight. Harsh my mellow.* His thoughts were interrupted.

"Jane, *¿qué pasa?*" someone said.

"*Hola, estoy bien, ¿cómo estás?*" Sean replied automatically with his Spanish class response.

The guy knit his brow in confusion. "Huh?"

"Ummm," Sean recovered, "I'm cool. Everything is... uhhh... far out."

"Oh... I was like doing George Carlin. You know... Hippie Dippy Weatherman? *¿qué pasa?*" the guy replied. "You've heard that, right?"

"Sure... umm, he's cool," Sean affirmed as he hurried on down the hall. He did actually know who George Carlin was.

The music was getting louder, so he obviously was headed in the right direction. The hall ended in an open area just outside the very gym he'd already been in twice. The double doors were open and he could see colored lights and hear loud music.

"Tickets?" said one of the two girls sitting behind a table near the doors. They wore matching red sweaters and skirts that screamed 'cheerleader' to Sean even before he noticed the megaphone with the 'M' on the front of the sweater.

"What?" asked Sean.

"Tickets. Did you buy a ticket in advance?" asked the second girl.

"Ummm... no, I don't think so."

"Then it's a dollar at the door," the first girl announced. "Or couples pay $1.50. Do you have a date?"

The girl next to her started giggling. Sean fought the urge to punch her, but wondered if Jane would have. *Probably not.* He felt totally embarrassed as he dug into Jane's bag hoping there was a dollar somewhere. He found a wallet and opened it. There was a five and two ones inside. He selected a single and handed it to the first girl. She took the money and the second girl grabbed him by the wrist. He instinctively tried to pull away, then saw she was stamping the back of his hand.

"Hey, do either of you know Louise Rimmer?" Sean asked as he looked at the blob on the back of his hand and tried to decipher what it might be.

"Geez, how stoned are you?" sniped the first girl, which prompted the second one to break out laughing.

"Not at all," Sean countered belligerently, "what's *your* problem?"

"What's *your* problem?" parroted the first girl. "Like you could even find *anyone* in the school that *didn't* know Louise."

Oh yeah... small town... small school... everyone knows everyone. "No, I asked if either of you had *seen* her tonight," Sean quickly lied.

"Right, Jane," the first girl said cattily, "I must be going deaf." The second girl laughed out loud again. "She's in there somewhere with your brother."

Sean stretched his mouth into the broadest smile he could muster, trying to show all of Jane's teeth, and hoping it looked a little bit fierce. "Thank you. You've been a great help." He turned from them and started into the gym.

"Hold it," barked the first girl. "Need to look in your bag."

"Oh, come on," Sean complained, "Do I look like someone who'd carry a gun?"

"Gun?" yelped the second girl, "Who said anything about a gun? Freak. We just need to make sure you're not taking any booze inside."

Sean plopped the bag on the table. The two girls pawed through it, eventually pulling out a paperback copy of *1984*.

"Planning on reading at the dance?" the second girl taunted.

"Maybe," Sean sneered back, "Either of you two learned how?"

She snarled as she put the book back and pushed the bag toward 'Jane'.

"Have fun," sneered the first girl.

"Don't break too many hearts," said the second. They high-fived each other and broke into laughter.

Sean's temper boiled. He considered that this might be the only time he could ever feel like it was OK to hit a smug girl and get away with it. Any witnesses would see it as just a girl fight. He took a deep breath. *Not worth it. Maybe if one of them looked more like Megan...*

The smell of popcorn hit him as he entered the large room and pulled his attention to his left where he saw a concession stand; popcorn, candy and Cokes, just like at a basketball game. He scanned the room and saw dozens of couples gyrating strangely to the song that was blasting the room. It was *Honky-Tonk Woman* by the Rolling Stones... and he realized he knew all the lyrics. At least with Alex's programming he really did know the current songs here... even if he didn't feel like he knew much else. He edged over to the concession counter to lean back as he searched the room for Louise.

"Jane!" A voice from behind the counter made him jump. "What can I get you?"

Sean panicked. Everyone here knew Jane by face, by name... and he didn't know any of them! He turned, planning to make something up that would pass for conversation, but breathed a sigh of relief when he saw it was someone he knew. "Jimbo! Good to see you," he said with a genuine smile.

"Tab? Sure, coming right up!" Jimbo said, then turned to pour the drink over some crushed ice.

"No," Sean said to his back, "I didn't..."

Jimbo sat the cup on the counter and leaned forward. "Just put your hand over mine, and I'll act like I'm putting money in the cash box." He winked.

Sean did as asked, watched Jimbo go to the cash box then return. "Hey," he shouted over the loud music. "I thought you were staying home tonight. Juan said you were all freaked about some prophecy that Nigel guy had about today."

So... Jane told my Dad. I wonder who else she confided in? Probably Louise for sure. He took a sip of the Tab and nearly wretched. He wasn't that fond of the taste of diet drinks in 1995, but the stuff he just swallowed was disgusting.

"I decided I wasn't really superstitious," Sean shouted back to him. "Hey, have you seen Louise?"

"Yeah," yelled Jimbo, "she's here somewhere with Micky. They just got drinks about ten minutes ago. Want me to tell her something if I see her again?"

"Yeah, tell her..." Sean shouted, then lowered his voice when the song ended. "Tell her I'm looking for her."

"You got it," Jimbo smiled, pointing a finger gun at Sean and firing it.

"Come on, Jimbo," said a freckled kid with long reddish hair. "You're supposed to be helping out, not rapping with friends."

"Maintain your cool, Mike," Jimbo answered him. "Catch you later, Jane." He slid to Sean's left and pointed at a short kid at the counter. "What can I get you, freshman?"

The music started playing again. *In the Year 2525 by Zager & Evans*, mused Sean. *That would be the future even for Alex.* He watched as the people on the dance floor tried to force jerky motions to the song's slow opening. They settled into their former gyrations as the tempo of the song sped up.

He started walking around the edge of the gym, searching for Louise. There were several small tables and folding chairs near one corner. Sean cruised near an empty table and set his Tab down. He glanced back at the concession stand, hoping Jimbo wasn't watching him. Relieved to see that Jimbo had his back turned, pouring another drink, Sean stepped away from the table. He decided that people in the 1960s must have been desperately counting calories to be willing to swallow that garbage.

"Jane!" called a voice behind Sean. *Now who?* He turned to see the teen-aged version of his Dad walking toward him.

"Juan," Sean said with a smile, "*¿qué pasa?*"

John frowned at him. "Cut it out. You know I don't like Spanish."

"Oh," Sean apologized, "Sorry. I was just doing George Carlin... you know... Hippie Dippy Weatherman?"

"Still not funny," grunted John. Sean glanced abashedly to the floor. "I'm surprised you're here," John continued. "I thought you were all freaked out about something Nigel put in a note about today."

"I decided I wasn't superstitious. I mean, no one can really know about the future, can they?"

"Wow," exclaimed John, "you've changed your tune. Just yesterday you were trying to convince me that Nigel and Peter were actually some kind of 'visitors from the future'. You thought they were telling the truth when we were pulling that gag on Scott this summer."

"Yeah, well, you know," Sean said nervously, "sometimes women just get hysterical and say weird stuff."

John leaned closer to 'Jane' and squinted his eyes. "Are you feeling OK?"

"I'm great!" Sean proclaimed a little too forcefully. "Like the Simon & Garfunkel song... just feelin' groovy!"

John continued to eye 'Jane' closely. "You're acting strange tonight... and talking even stranger. You don't even like Simon & Garfunkel."

Sean's stomach flipped; he needed a quick way out of the conversation. "I was trying to find Louise," he said suddenly. "Have you seen her?"

John turned to scan the crowd, then pointed. "She's dancing with Micky, between the free throw line and center court. See her?"

Sean looked down his Dad's arm to the pointed target. "Yep, got her," he smiled, "thanks." He started out amongst the dancers but stopped when John gripped his wrist. He swung back around.

"Are you *sure* you're OK?" John interrogated.

"I'm fine," laughed Sean. He patted his Dad's hand. "You're a good friend, Juan." John released his grip.

"Everything will be back to normal after tonight," Sean murmured to himself as he turned to walk away.

John's face watched as the familiar form of his friend, Jane, wove her way through couples on the dance floor, heading toward Louise and Micky. He couldn't put his finger on it, but something seemed off about Jane.

Sean decided he had observed the natives long enough to be able to mimic whatever dance moves were reasonable for 1969. He let the beat of the music guide his hips and shoulders as he closed in on Louise.

Louise smiled brightly as her friend, Jane, came dancing up. She slid next to her and did a hip bump with her. "Hey, you!" Louise chirped, "I thought you were stayin' home tonight."

Micky frowned at his twin. "Yeah," he grumbled, "what are *you* doing here?"

"I'm just here to talk to my best friend," said Sean as he smacked Louise back with a hip bump. Louise grinned and bumped back.

The beat of the music suddenly dropped out, leaving only softer, slower vocals.

Now it's been ten thousand years... On a whim, Sean dramatically froze posed like a ballerina. Louise laughed.

...man has cried a billion tears... Louise struck a similar pose.

...For what, he never knew... Sean shifted to a melodramatic wrist-to-forehead pose.

...now man's reign is through... Louise arced a hand to her head and pirouetted once under her fingertip, then froze.

...But through eternal night... Sean introduced them to the clawing move from *Thriller*, then froze.

...the twinkling of starlight... Louise mimed a penguin waddle, then froze.

...So very far away... Sean turned his back to Louise, crossed his arms and leaned back.

...maybe it's only yesterday... Louise mirrored the pose, leaning her shoulders against Jane's.

The beat started up again and Jane and Louise resumed dancing. *In the year 2525, if man is still alive...*

Micky bent his face to Louise's ear. "I'm going out for a smoke. Hopefully, you'll be back to normal when I get back."

She smiled and gave Micky a tiny finger wave as she kept dancing with Jane. Micky shook his head in disgust and walked away.

The song ended and Louise gave Jane a big hug. "That was fun! I'm so glad you came," she gushed, "Are you feelin' better?"

"Better?" inquired Sean.

"You were actin' kinda weird last night when we were talkin' on the phone. Then today, you wouldn't accept a ride home from school... so I didn't know what was goin' on with you."

"I think I was just overreacting. I'm fine now," Sean assured her, "But we need to talk."

Louise grabbed Sean's hand and started toward the exit. "I need to use the little girls' room anyhow." When she saw that Jane was following, Louise dropped her hand.

Jimbo waved at them as they passed the concession stand. Sean turned his head to wave back and almost slammed into Louise when she stopped right outside the door.

"Hey, Janet, hey, Suzie. Still holdin' down the fort?" Louise said with her normal perkiness.

"Hi again, Louise," said Janet or Suzie, Sean didn't know which, but they both smiled brightly at Louise.

"I see your 'friend' found you," the second one said, dropping her smile.

"Sure did," Louise replied brightly, ignoring the sneer from the second girl. "See you two in a bit. We're just headin' to the little girl's room."

"Thanks for the update," said the second girl with obvious sarcasm.

When they had rounded the corner to the hallway, Louise whispered. "That Suzie has a bug up her butt about something tonight."

OK, now I know which one is Suzie and which one is Janet, but hopefully, that's nothing more than useless trivia, thought Sean.

Louise pulled open the door and went in. Sean reluctantly followed.

"Did you make it to the football game, too?" Louise asked as she paused in front of the mirror to check her makeup.

"Umm, no," Sean stammered, nervously looking around.

"Oh my gosh, it was close," Louise said as she headed for the stalls.

"Exciting game, huh?" Sean inquired, his nerves ratcheting higher.

"I don't know about that," Louise commented as she pushed open a stall door and entered. "They went back and forth, up and down the field. It was..."

"I'll be back in a minute, Louise," Sean interrupted as he bolted out the door.

He immediately plastered himself against the wall right outside. *I know, I look like Jane, I sound like Jane, and Louise thinks I'm Jane. It's no big deal to be in there. Everyone uses the bathroom. It's normal. It's no big deal. Who am I kidding? I get embarrassed when Maggie stops to pee during a walk.*

He counted to sixty using the one Mississippi, two Mississippi method, hoping a minute would be long enough. He took a deep breath, closed his eyes and jerked the door open. When he opened his eyes, Louise was back in front of the mirror.

"Where'd you go?" asked Louise.

"Umm," Sean mumbled. *Think. Think. Think.* "I... uh... thought I remembered leaving my lights on and I was going to run out to check, but then I remembered shutting them off."

Louise stared at Jane's reflection, concern in her eyes. "Are you sure you're OK?"

"Yeah," squeaked Sean, "Maybe a little headache."

"I've got some aspirin if you want," Louise offered.

"No that's OK."

Louise pulled a lipstick from her purse and touched up her lips. Sean decided to rummage through Jane's bag to see if there was anything he could find to help him act more like a girl. He grabbed a brush and starting using it on his already perfect hair.

"So anyway," Louise resumed the earlier story. "They just keep going back and forth and nobody even scored before halftime. Then we get the opening kickoff in the second half and run it back for a touchdown... but then miss the extra point! Wouldn't you know it, Greenwood makes a touchdown with only three minutes left in the game and they *do* make their extra point." Louise blotted her lips on a paper towel. "So we lost 7-6."

"That's too bad," Sean said, trying to sound like he really cared. He put his hand on Louise's shoulder. "Louise," he started slowly, "I just want you to know that you can always talk to me about stuff."

Louise smiled at Jane's reflection. "I know that."

"So... like if anything happens... you'll come talk to me, right?"

"Sure," said Louise, her smile faded. "Do you know something?"

"Well... not exactly," Sean hedged.

"Is it about Micky?"

"Well... maybe..."

"What did he say? Was it about me?"

"He didn't actually *say* anything..."

With wide eyes, Louise turned from Jane's reflection and looked Sean in the eye. "You *saw* him with someone else? I knew it. I knew he'd been actin' funny. It was Barb Newland, wasn't it? I've seen the way she looks at him."

Sean wasn't sure what to say. He wondered what Jane would say. "I just don't want to see you get hurt," he finally offered.

"I guess I can't say I'm surprised," Louise sighed. "Micky and me keep gettin' into it about sex. I know that more and more girls are doin' it... but I just don't feel right about it."

"Hey, it's your choice," Sean said supportively, "you shouldn't feel bad about what you think is right."

"You're right, as usual," Louise nodded. "I probably should have done this weeks ago." She burst through the door.

"Wait," Sean called as he put back the brush and gathered up Jane's bag. "Done what? I mean did what?"

"Cut him loose," Louise said over her shoulder.

Did I just cause Micky and Louise to break up? Sean wondered. "Louise," he shouted after her, "wait up."

Sean was only a couple of steps behind Louise as she stormed back into the gym, but was suddenly dragged back by the shoulder. Janet had hooked Jane's bag.

"Where do you think you're going?" Janet growled.

"I need to catch Louise."

"Maybe she doesn't want you to catch her," Suzie jeered.

"Let go," Sean demanded.

"We need to search your bag again," Janet forcefully informed him.

"Oh, come on! You just searched it a few minutes ago!"

"And then you went out," smiled Suzie, obviously enjoying her power. "We don't know that you didn't grab a hidden bottle to take back in."

"You didn't search Louise!" Sean protested.

"Louise doesn't drink," Janet replied smugly.

"Right! And I'm an alcoholic," Sean snarled as he tossed the bag on the table. "Hurry it up!"

He waited impatiently as the two dumped the bag and slowly put items back in, one by one. It was obvious harassment. Suzie found Jane's diary and flipped through it, then feigned a yawn. After what seemed like hours, Janet handed the bag back to Sean.

"There you go," Janet sang with an overly sweet voice, "Enjoy the dance."

"I hope I never meet any of your kids," Sean growled as he grabbed the bag and started for the door.

"Freak!" Suzie shouted at his back.

The music was off and every head in the room was turned to one focal point. Sean briskly trotted in that direction. As he got closer, he found that everyone was packed into a ring with Louise, Micky, and some other girl in the center. He could see that Louise was screaming at both Micky and the girl, but he couldn't hear what was being said above the chant of the crowd. "Fight. Fight. Fight. Fight..."

He moved around the ring, searching for an opening. Each time he tried to move in, someone elbowed him back. He turned ready to punch when an arm grabbed his shoulder, but he relaxed a bit when he saw it was his Dad.

"Jane," he shouted above the crowd, "any idea what set this off?"

Sean hopped up and down to try to get a better look. He wished he had his own body's height to be able to see over most of the crowd.

"Tell me that girl's not Barb Newland," Sean yelled to his Dad.

John frowned. "What's wrong with you tonight, Jane?" he shouted. "Of course that's Barb."

Sean could feel the crowd shift. He hopped up and down again and saw that Louise was pushing out of the other side of the circle. He tried to back out of his side with the intent of circling around but was blocked by his Dad.

"I've got to get to her," he shouted.

John gripped Sean's shoulders and looked into Jane's eyes. "Jane, what's going on? Is it something I can help with?"

"Yeah," Sean said as he pushed against his dad, "get out of my way!"

John held on. "Just tell me what's going on."

"Louise is going to die if I don't get to her," Sean shouted as he pivoted, broke free, and pushed toward the middle of the collapsing circle.

"Jane!" John shouted after her.

Sean barely got a few steps across the opening of the circle when Micky grabbed him by the elbow.

"What the hell did you tell her?" Micky demanded.

"Let go of me, Micky, I don't have time for this," Sean answered as he tried to tug away. He was slightly off balance and Micky pulled him back.

"Louise said she's breaking up with me because you told her you saw me with Barb."

"Yeah, so?"

"Well, that's total bullshit!"

Sean looked from Micky to the girl standing closest to them. "Really?" he pointed at the girl. "Who's that?"

"Barb and I were just talking while I waited for Louise to come back. Then she storms in and goes ballistic on both of us. Said you said I was cheating on her."

"Not my problem, Micky," Sean snarled. "Let go."

Micky tightened his grip. "It's going to be your problem when I tell Mom and Dad that you made up some lie just to break me and Louise up."

Sean glanced toward the door. Louise was already out of sight. He shifted his weight and brought up a right cross that caught Micky under the left side of his jaw. Micky went down like a sack of bricks. *Huh,* thought Sean, *I didn't even feel that. Must be the super suit.*

The crowd made a cacophonous noise that was a mixture of "oh. Wow. Whoa. No way." plus a few shrieks from girls and a few groans. Then the disparate voices settled into a unified chant. "Jane. Jane. Jane. Jane..."

Sean resumed his quest for Louise and the chanting crowd parted for him almost magically. When he reached the door, the cheer-leading twins tried to block him. He pinched down on Suzie's neck and tried to imagine electricity sparking from his hand. Nothing happened. He shrugged and simply pushed through them.

"We're reporting you!" one of them shouted to his back. Sean raised his hands just above shoulder height and flipped them each a bird. "We're reporting *that,* too! You're going to get a month of detention, you freak!"

He trotted briskly down the hall and pushed through the outside door, running into a small group of smokers.

"You guys see Louise?"

One of them pulled a slow drag from his cigarette then pointed lazily to the parking lot.

"Thanks," he said as he turned toward the mass of cars. "I hope you're smart enough to quit before you get cancer," he added over his shoulder.

Sean cursed himself for not asking Alex what kind of car the death car actually was, or at least the color. He peered into the back windows of cars both left and right as he trotted down the first row. He stopped when he noticed heads inside one of them.

He rushed to the back door and jerked it open. "Louise, you can't go with these guys," he yelled before even looking in. A cloud of sweet, acrid smoke rolled out.

The reply was a shrill scream, and Sean saw a dark haired girl pull her blouse closed. "Sorry," he said, "wrong car."

He started to close the door when the girl called out to him. "Jane, wait." He looked back in and realized it was Karen Silver. "You won't tell Scott about this, will you?" Sean glanced at the guy. Not Scott.

"Nope," Sean said as he slammed the door, then mumbled as he walked away, "He's going to have to figure you out all on his own."

Sean resumed trotting down the row of cars, looking right, then left. "Louise," he called out in desperation.

"Jane?" returned a voice from somewhere on his left.

"Louise," Sean called again. "Where are you?"

"Over here," came the answer. Sean scanned the area the sound came from, but saw nothing. He stepped between two cars.

"No time to play Marco Polo," Sean shouted. "How about a visual clue?"

"Over here," Louise called again and Sean saw a hand bobbing up and down over a car roof two rows away.

"Stay right there," Sean commanded as he slid between two more cars. "Don't move until I get there."

He emerged from the next row of cars and found Louise and three guys leaning against a car, four to the right of him. He quickly joined them, puffing slightly, more from adrenaline charge than exertion.

"Louise," he said as he reached them. "You don't want to do this."

"Do what?" Louise asked.

"Go drinking with these guys."

"I'm not," she refuted. "Tony said that Willie would give me a ride home."

"Is that right, Willie?" Sean asked, looking halfway between the two guys he didn't know.

"That's right," said the one of the left. "What's it to you?"

OK, thought Sean, *Now I've got Tony and Willie. What was the other guy's name?* "So, just straight to Louise's house?" he asked.

Willie and the other guy looked at each other and grinned. "Well, maybe not straight to Louise's house. We might ride around a little," said the other guy.

"Maybe drink a few beers while you're driving around?" Sean suggested.

"Maybc," Willie acknowledged.

"Maybe *I* should join you," Sean said.

"The more the merrier," Willie agreed.

"But not Louise," Sean asserted as he pulled keys out of Jane's bag and held them out to Louise. "Take Lemon Drop and go home, Louise."

Louise glanced at the keys then looked to Sean, "Why don't *you* just take me home, Jane?"

Because Alex seems to think I need to keep these idiots from killing some unknown person by getting in this stupid car, Sean thought angrily.

"I've got some other things I have to do, Louise," Sean replied, "Just take the keys and go home."

Louise stared at Sean's outstretched hand. "That just doesn't feel right," she protested.

"We're best friends, right?" Sean coaxed.

"Of course!" Louise agreed.

"And you trust me, right?" Sean continued.

"I guess so, but..."

"Then take the keys and go home, and trust me that I know what I'm doing."

Louise reluctantly took hold of the dangling keys and Sean released them into her hand.

"I don't understand why..." Louise began.

"I'll explain it all tomorrow," Sean lied. "For now, just trust me."

"All right, I guess," Louise said without conviction. "I've got to work eleven to seven tomorrow, so I'll bring you your car around ten."

"That'll be great," Sean said, wondering how Louise will react to Jane's disappearance.

"Are you workin' tomorrow?" Louise asked Tony.

"Yeah," Tony nodded, "Five to close. I'll see you there."

"All right," Louise said, then turned to walk away. She turned back briefly. "Y'all be careful, OK?"

"Goodnight, Louise," Sean said, trying to sound cheerful. Tony and the others also said goodnight.

"All right, boys," Sean addressed them, "shall we party?"

"What kind of party are we talking about?" asked the guy Sean still didn't know.

"What kind of party do you want?" Sean replied, trying to make Jane's voice sound a little coy and a little seductive.

The nameless guy bounced his eyebrows suggestively, "Maybe after a few beers you and me can have a private party."

"Cut it out, Randy," Tony growled, "We're just going to drink a few beers and that's all."

Randy, thought Sean, *OK, that'll be an easy name to remember now.*

"Hey, if she's up for a little action," Randy insisted, "I can give it to her."

Sean took an instant dislike to Randy, then realized that he was the one who gets killed. He didn't like the idea of letting anyone die, but Alex insisted that the timeline be restored, and in both versions of the future, Randy had been killed.

"Shall we?" Willie proposed, opening his door then pulling and tilting the seat forward. The car was a two-door '55 Chevy hardtop, light blue with a white roof. Tony quickly got in.

"Hey," protested Randy, "What if I wanted to sit back there?"

"Snooze, ya lose," Tony declared.

"Jane?" Willie invited, sweeping a hand gallantly toward the door.

Sean struggled to get in since he'd never previously been in a car with a fold forward seat. He had to kind of crouch at the same time as lifting a leg over the edge of the bent seat. He tried to pivot to sit, but lost his balance and flopped down into Tony.

"Have you already been drinking?" Tony asked.

"No," Sean snorted, "I just lost my footing and tripped. Sorry."

Willie pushed the seat back into position and got in. Randy grudgingly went around the car and got in on the passenger side. There were no seat belts, Sean noticed, and he wondered if it would have saved Randy's life if there had been.

Willie backed out of the parking space, then roared the engine and popped the clutch. The tires squealed as they rocketed out of the lot.

Great, thought Sean, *minors in possession of alcohol, and this idiot is just begging for the cops to stop him.*

Tony reached into a small cooler at his feet and pulled out a can. He pulled the tab all the way off and slid it into the opening before handing it to Sean. "Why didn't you just take Louise home," Tony asked as he fished out a second beer and handed it to Randy.

"What, and miss all this?" Sean replied flippantly.

"It just seems a little out of character for you, Jane," Tony said as he handed a beer to Willie.

That was good to know, thought Sean, *seemed odd to me, too. Why did Jane get in this car in the original timeline? Was it to protect Louise, or did something else happen that didn't happen this time around?* "Sometimes a girl just gets in the mood to be a little crazy, I guess," he quipped, taking a small sip of his beer.

"I like to get crazy," Randy leered.

Sean ignored him. "What was your plan if Louise had been here in my place?" he asked Tony.

"Hey, I'd like that little southern girl to go south on me," chortled Randy.

Tony smacked him hard on the back of his head. "Don't you talk about Louise like that!" he scolded menacingly.

"Hey," protested Randy, "What's your hang up, man?"

"Your *mouth*," Tony growled.

"Like *you* don't want to do her," Randy sneered.

Tony swung at Randy again, but Randy ducked forward.

"Just drink your beer," Tony ordered.

"Chill out, man," Randy replied brusquely but continued to lean a safe distance forward.

"I want to know, Tony" Sean demanded, "What were your intentions for getting Louise in the car?"

"I wouldn't let *that* moron touch her," Tony grumbled, aiming his thumb at Randy, "if that's what you mean."

"Louise doesn't even drink," Sean declared.

"I know that."

"So why get her to ride around with you guys if the plan was to be drinking?"

"I just like to talk to her," Tony said, then looked down at the floor before softly adding, "She's nice."

A crush! thought Sean, *You've got a crush on Louise!* "Did she tell you about Micky?" he asked.

"Yeah," Tony said to the floor. "She seemed pretty tore up about it."

"So it looked like an opportunity for you..."

"No," he snapped at Sean, "It's not like that. I wouldn't hurt her for the world!"

"You didn't let me finish," Sean objected firmly. "An opportunity for you to tell her that you like her."

Tony's eyes went back to the floor. "We've worked together for over a year now. She's cute... she's funny... she's just great to be around. I never said anything before because she was dating your brother... although I never knew what she saw in him."

No argument there, thought Sean. "So when she came storming out, you could see something was wrong, and when she stopped to talk, she was comfortable enough with you to tell you about Micky."

Tony shrugged. "I guess."

"And you offered her a ride home, hoping she'd ride around with you guys and talk for awhile."

"I guess."

"Sorry that part got spoiled. Maybe you'll get another chance."

"I get it that you didn't want her to get in the car with us," said Tony. "You were just protecting her. What I don't get is why *you* got in, instead of just leaving with her."

I know, thought Sean, *it seems more stupid all the time.* "Maybe I wanted to find out what your intentions were." *Could that be it? Could that explain why Jane originally got in the car?*

Tony took a long drink from his beer, then turned to Sean. "You're a good friend to her, Jane. She's lucky to have a friend like you."

And maybe you, too, Tony, Sean thought as he took a sip from his own can.

He glanced out the window and saw farmland. "Hey, where are we?" he asked.

"North of town," Willie replied, "Baxter road."

"Gimme another beer," Randy belched. He rolled down his window and tossed his empty can.

Sean's adrenaline spiked. The can hit a cross road. There were car lights a quarter of a mile up that road, and then there were flashing red lights. *This is it!*

"Are you kidding me," roared Tony, "Miles of country ditches and you throw your empty at a cop car?"

"I can lose him," Willie said smugly as he mashed the accelerator to the floor.

Sean was frozen with fear. *How long before the crash? Where's Alex? Is he watching? Is he just going to pop in at the last second?*

"You can't outrun the cop," Tony argued.

"I didn't say I was going to outrun him," Willie sneered, "I said I was going to lose him."

The car went into a slide as Willie jammed on his breaks.

Sean panicked. *This is it! Where's Alex? My window! I don't have my window down.*

The rear of the car swung around as Willie slid onto a crossroad and again floored it. He reached to the dash and clicked the lights off.

"What are you doing?" screamed Randy. "We can't see! Turn the lights back on!"

"Maintain your cool, Hunter," growled Willie. "I know what I'm doing. I know this road. It's as straight as a board. I just need to hold the wheel still until my night vision kicks in."

Sean's heart thudded in his chest. *This has got to be it! Fifty miles an hour on a gravel road at night with no lights!* He rolled his window down.

"What are you doing?" yelled Tony.

"Getting rid of my beer," Sean replied.

"You don't need to do that," Willie said smugly, "I've lost that loser cop."

Randy turned to look out the back window. "You haven't lost him yet," he reported. "He's about a half mile back now."

"How'd he find us with our lights off?" Willie cried in disbelief.

"Maybe the dust trail that's hanging in the air," Tony suggested dryly. "It hasn't rained in a couple of weeks."

"Well, crap," cursed Willie. "I'm going to try to tack back north then. It's kind of hilly up by Mt. Hudson, maybe that'll help hide us."

Hills! Alex said something about leaving the ground cresting a hill.

Willie flicked his lights back on just before reaching another junction. The car slid around again as he jammed his brakes. As he reached the intersection, he floored the accelerator again and the car fishtailed for a quarter of a mile. When he'd straightened it out, he clicked the lights back off. Sean's stomach knotted.

"This is crazy, man," Tony yelled. "You're going to get us all killed!"

"Just hang tight back there," Willie boasted, "I know what I'm doing."

"Do you have to keep shutting off the lights?" Randy whined.

"Quit bitching," Willie snapped, "There's moonlight. Haven't you ever

302

driven on a moonlit night with your lights off?"

"It's not even a full moon," complained Randy, "and no... I haven't."

"The gravel is white. There's enough light for me to see that," insisted Willie. "And anyway, I know these roads."

"If you don't lose that cop pretty soon," said Tony, "I think we should toss the beer out and take our chances with the cop stopping us."

"Yeah, well he's not going to take your license since you're not the one driving," countered Willie. "I'm not stopping. Jane! Roll that damn window back up!"

"I like the fresh air," Sean claimed.

"Fresh? It's freezing! Roll it up!"

I guess with the super suit on, I can't tell the temperature. "How close are we to the hills?"

"Three miles north of here and we're still going west."

"You'll tell me when we get to the hills?"

"Ha," Willie snorted, "you'll know!"

Sean reluctantly rolled the window up. His heart was in his throat as the rear of the car slid around again. This time Willie turned right at the intersection without turning his headlights on.

"I think he's falling back a little," Willie bragged, "He's not making the turns as fast as I do."

"Neither's my stomach," grumbled Tony.

Willie sped up again when he got the car straightened out. "Maybe I should take up race-car driving for a living," he crowed.

"I'll bet you won't think that tomorrow," said Sean.

"What's that supposed to mean?" Willie sneered.

"I just hope we make it to tomorrow," whined Randy.

"Are you sure you know this road?" asked Tony.

"Like the back of my hand. For instance, there's a bridge over a small creek coming up. It's a bit higher than the road, so it ramps up a little. We'll catch some air in just a few seconds."

"Catch some air?" gasped Sean.

"Yep... hang on to something."

Everyone's head but Willie's thumped against the ceiling as the momentum of the car leaving the ground caused an instant of Zero-G.

"I thought you said you were going to warn me when we got into the hills," shrieked Sean as he hurriedly rolled the window back down.

"That was just a bridge," Willie said, "Still a couple of miles before we hit any real hills. Put that window back up."

"No!" screamed Sean, "I... I'm going to be sick."

"You better not puke in my car!" warned Willie.

"Then shut up about having the window up," retorted Sean.

"Fine!" shouted Willie just as he slammed the breaks and slid around to the left at the next intersection. "He's falling back a little more. A couple more turns and I'll lose him in the hills."

Sean glanced to his right, Tony's face was grim. He looked up at Randy. Randy looked terrified, white as a sheet. With the thought of Randy's fate, Sean suddenly felt sick. The guy was in a state of panic and would be dead in a few minutes. He decided he couldn't just sit there and allow it to happen without saying something.

"Willie, you've got to stop," Sean ordered, mustering as much authority as Jane's voice could manage. "Randy is going to die if you don't stop... and you and Tony will be seriously injured."

"Getting scared back there, sweet cheeks?" Willie taunted, "I'm in control. Nothing is going to happen to anyone."

"You're wrong, Willie," Sean stated gravely. "Randy is going to be killed. Do you want to live with that on your conscience the rest of your life? Just stop the car!"

"Why are you singling me out?" Randy wailed, near tears. "What about you? Aren't *you* afraid of getting killed?"

"Cut it out, Hunter," Willie ordered gruffly. "You're acting more like a girl than Jane."

"I'm serious, Willie," Sean shouted. "You can change things. If you stop now, you can save Randy's life."

"Why do you keep *saying* that?" Randy shrieked, "Stop saying *my* name!"

Willie slammed the brakes and power-slid the car to the right at another intersection.

"Come on, Willie," Randy begged. "She's right. This is crazy!"

"We're almost to the hills," Willie stated coolly. "We'll lose him in just a few more minutes, then we can go back to drinking a little beer."

Almost the hills, thought Sean. *It's almost over. Willie's not going to change his mind. This car is doomed! Alex, I hope you're out there.* He stuck his left arm out of the window and hugged the car as tightly as he could. His heartbeat pounded in his ears.

"Hang on," advised Willie mirthfully, "this is where it gets fun!"

The car crested a small hill and briefly left the ground. Sean's heart was in his throat.

This is it! Alex! Where are you?

"Woohoo!" shouted Willie triumphantly as they bumped back down. "There's three more like that one, then a *really* good one!"

"Come on, man," pleaded Tony. "You're freaking everyone out. Slow down a little."

"Don't be such a chicken, Tony," Willie mocked, "I've topped these hills millions of times, just for the fun of it. Now they're going to help me get away from that stupid cop." The car crested the next hill and again briefly left the ground. "Woohoo! Come on! This is fun!"

"At least turn your lights back on," sobbed Randy.

"I can see just fine! Don't wuss out on me, man." They crested another hill. "Woohoo! Better than a roller coaster!"

"Willie, I'm going to throw up," Randy whimpered.

"Not in my car!" barked Willie. "Hang your head out the window if you're going to puke." They crested the third small hill. "Woohoo! I can't believe you pantywaists aren't loving this. You don't know how to live."

Randy hung out the window retching. Fear had Sean nearly hyperventilating.

"That better not take any paint off, either," Willie warned Randy. "OK, here comes the really good one. We go down this big hill, build up momentum, and then we really lift off at the top of the next hill."

Randy retched again. Sean clung tightly to the outside of the car. He held his breath.

Come on, Alex! Be there! Don't miss! Come on, Alex!

Sean felt pushed into the seat and heard the undercarriage drag as they hit the bottom of the hill, the next second he felt like he was flying. *This is it! This is it!*

"Woohoo!" shouted Willie as the car left the ground.

From that point, everything became chaos. The car seemed to hang in the air forever, then it came down hard. The undercarriage groaned against the gravel as the car started sliding sideways. Willie tried to bring it back, but over-corrected and the car started twisting the other way. He panicked and jammed the brakes. The locked tires dredged furrows into the gravel with a deafening roar.

"Hang on! Hang on!" screamed Willie.

Randy just screamed.

As the car slid to the edge of the road, Sean heard Jane's voice screaming above the cacophony, "Alex! Alex!"

Suddenly, everything became a blur; the shrieks of everyone's panicked screaming, the roar as the car's locked tires plowed through gravel, and then Sean felt the car start to roll. "Alex!" he again heard Jane scream.

And then... everything was black. He tumbled. Felt pain in his shoulder. Then a crushing impact, and then silence. He tried to take a breath, but couldn't. There was a smothering weight, and he felt tangled up with another body.

His brain tried to process the blackness, the complete silence. The chaos was gone; no crunch, no roar, no screams... just absolute silence. Only one answer made sense.

He didn't make it, thought Sean in disbelief. Alex *didn't make it... and I'm dying.*

Chapter Sixteen

"And the children are the only ones who blush / 'Cause life is just to die."

S EAN HAD never given much thought to death, he assumed he had decades before it would ever be an issue. It was strange how peaceful it was, especially in contrast to the chaos that surrounded him only minutes earlier. It had been so loud. The roar of the car skidding on the gravel, everyone screaming as the car left the road. So incredibly, chaotically loud... replaced instantly with silence. Silence and complete darkness.

A memory from some movie or TV show popped into his head. There was something about moving toward the light when you die. Maybe he wasn't quite dead yet... there was no light, just crushing silent blackness. His shoulder still hurt, and he struggled to breathe. Breathe. He wouldn't need to breathe if he were dead. He decided he was still on the ledge between life and death.

Then miraculously the crushing feeling lifted, followed by a blinding burst of light. It was so painfully bright that he could see no better than he did in the darkness. He shielded his squinted eyes with his forearm and realized he had the sensation of floating. Floating? Was he drifting toward the light?

When he bumped lightly against something, he realized he could still feel... and his shoulder still hurt... like someone had almost jerked his arm out of its socket. That didn't seem right. Why would he still feel pain if he were dead?

As his eyes adjusted to the light, he discovered it wasn't just an ambient glow, and it wasn't coming from a single source that he should move toward. He began to see shapes, and they seemed familiar.

He was definitely floating! Nothing made sense. Why was he floating? Being dead made no sense, and he wished there was someone to tell him what to do next. As his eyes adjusted to the light, he discovered that there *was* someone else there. Someone floating beneath him... beside him... or maybe above him; he couldn't be sure, since nothing felt like up or down.

Everything came into focus several seconds before anything he saw made sense. He was in Steffi! Why had it been so dark and quiet? Where was Alex?

Almost as quickly as he'd asked himself the question, he realized that the person floating beside him *was* Alex! Another item on the growing list of things that made no sense. Why would Alex also be dead? A second Alex popped up on his right, but that Alex was on screen and perpendicular.

"I had hoped you would not have the opportunity to view this," the sideways Alex said. "Unfortunately, since you are, that means I am currently unconscious. Although this scenario was indeed the highest probability, I had hoped it could be avoided, particularly whatever damage you have inflicted on my body."

The appearance of on-screen Alex was more than Sean's brain could process, but he was beginning to think that he just might not be dead. Surely if there were an afterlife, it wouldn't have his descendant droning instructions... unless he was in hell!

"Sean, you will need to orient yourself. If I am not directly in front of you, with the screen in the proper viewing position, you will need to adjust your position. Since you are not experienced with maneuvering in Zero G, I will pause until you have righted yourself. To continue this narration, tap the screen."

Sean attempted to right himself, but overcompensated and bounced lightly off the wall and ceiling before getting into a sitting position slightly above the actual seat. He pushed against the roof and forced himself to sit, then reached out and touched the screen.

"Very good," the image of Alex said. "Now, please maneuver my unconscious body into a similar position beside you. Again, I will pause."

Floating Alex reminded Sean of someone doing the dead-man's float in water. The first attempt to straighten him out caused Sean to tumble out of his own corrected position.

"Every action has an opposite and equal reaction," he murmured to himself as he worked back into his original position.

He braced one arm against the ceiling and his legs against the floor and tried to move his descendant again. Even with only one arm, it was relatively easy to shift Alex around into a sitting position just slightly above the actual seat. He touched the screen.

"Very good," screen Alex said. "Now, please examine my body for any significant trauma, such as bleeding, protruding broken bones or any other abnormalities. Once you have completed an initial triage, please press one of the numbers on the screen. Zero would indicate no visible damage, ten would indicate serious trauma that would require you to engage emergency medical technicians. I will pause until you select a number." The numbers one through ten appeared at the bottom of the screen.

Sean braced himself again as he attempted to check Alex for broken bones, and quickly decided there weren't any. The only visible problem was a little blood around Alex's nose. He looked at the numbers on the screen. *What score does a bloody nose get,* wondered Sean, *a one? Nah, Alex will probably be all freaked out about it and call it a five... so maybe a three?* He pressed the three.

"Very good," said screen Alex. "No severe damage, but perhaps some minor damage. My nanites will repair all minor damage shortly if they have not already done so. Please verify that my body is in an approximate sitting position and then touch the screen."

He pushed the screen and immediately felt himself slowly sink onto the seat. Alex's body also settled onto the seat and slumped toward Sean like a passed-out drunk.

"You are now experiencing one-eighth standard gravity. Gravity will slowly return to Earth normal over the next five minutes." A drawer containing a test-tube sized clear vial slid out from beneath the screen. "Please place one end of the container under my nose and issue the command to open it one-half centimeter."

Sean placed the tube as instructed. "Open point five centimeters." A small hole dilated open and Alex immediately jerked his head away from it. Sean could smell something like ammonia in the air.

"Augh," grunted Alex followed by, "oww" as he put his hand to his nose. "Close" was the first actual word he spoke, followed by, "End program." The on-screen Alex disappeared.

"What happened to you?" asked Sean.

"I rescued you," Alex said simply.

"And that gave you a bloody nose and knocked you out?"

"Yes," replied Alex, "and also four fractured ribs."

"Do you need to go to the emergency room?" Sean asked urgently.

"No, they are repairing. It is already in the fibrocartilaginous callus phase."

Sean winced. "And as bad as that sounds... that must be a good thing?"

"It is a *normal* thing," replied Alex. "I should say, a standard process sped up by nanites."

"Good old nanites," groaned Sean, rolling his eyes, "what would a boy do without 'em?"

"In this instance, spend weeks healing rather than minutes."

"So you said 'normal thing'... this fiber cardigan analogous thing. Did I have that when I broke my arm when I was eight?"

"Fibrocartilaginous callus," corrected Alex. "Yes, it is part of the bone healing process." Alex twitched a query. "Under twentieth-century medical conditions it would take place several days post-fracture."

"But, lucky you, you've got nanites."

"I sense an edge of agitation in your voice," Alex pointed out.

"Must just be the way it sounds with Jane's voice," Sean lied. "So, can I switch back to me, now? If your nanites are done fixing you up, that is."

"Certainly," said Alex. He grabbed 'Jane's hair' in one hand and touched the control switch on the left side of Sean's neck. He tugged the headpiece off

308

as he envisioned Sean's likeness, including t-shirt and jeans. "Since you are still conscious, I assume expansion is less painful than compression."

"It kind of tingles, I guess. Like when your arm falls asleep when you lay on it wrong."

"Do you suppose one of your ancestors would begrudge your use of antibiotics?"

"What are you talking about? Do I need antibiotics?"

"Not at all, I was merely suggesting a comparison for you to consider," Alex said. "You seem to find fault with the advanced medical remedies that I employ. My hypothetical question poses that perhaps one of your ancestors would think the same thing of your use of antibiotics."

"That's not the same thing," argued Sean.

"Microscopic 'magic' entities that promote the healing process that would take longer without them. The difference is simply that yours are organic while mine are robo-organic tech."

Sean glared at him. "Why do I bother arguing with you?"

"I must admit, at times I wonder that very same thing," returned Alex smugly.

"OK, fine," huffed Sean in exasperation, "you've got 'normal' magic things that make you recover faster. So let's get back to why you *need* to heal... fast or otherwise. What happened to you?"

"I am surprised you did not ask about it during the planning stage."

"Ask about what?"

"How I could physically muster enough strength to pull you from the automobile."

Sean tried to imagine the smaller, relatively non-muscular Alex lifting Sean out of the car before it crashed. "I guess I was so focused on you even getting there that I didn't care about the lifting part."

"Fortunately, I did," Alex reported with what Sean considered a bit of smugness. "First of all, the initial materialization was off by less than half a meter, so that adjustment was minimal and quick. I, obviously, do not have the upper body strength required to pull you from the automobile even if it were level. You were at a negative thirty-degree angle from the road at the time of connection." He paused.

Sean waited a beat, decided Alex was looking for a response, "OK, even *harder* to pull me out."

"Therefore," Alex smiled, "I needed an assist from Steffi. At the moment I grasped your arm, I had Steffi activate gravitons in the opposite wall at 3G. I 'fell' against the opposite wall with three times my normal weight, which was enough force to pull you from the automobile, which was nearly motionless from my perspective. The drawback, of course, is that once you were within the confines of the S.T.E., you also tripled your weight as you plummeted toward that wall. Although I had hopes of being able to maneuver to the side of the impact zone, in the cramped space, it was nearly impossible. Thus, your more-than 230 kilograms of weight came crashing onto me."

"How much is that in pounds?"

"Just over 500 pounds."

"Ouch."

"Indeed. The impact rendered me unconscious and also inflicted minor injuries."

Sean lifted a questioning finger. "So how did you start up the screen if you were out?"

"A timer, set from the point of impact. It ran automatically at impact plus five seconds, first closing the door and materializing at a pre-programmed isolated location, next activating null gravity and then lights, followed by the prerecorded instructions."

Sean nodded as it pieced together in his mind. "So the tumbling I thought was the car going over, was me falling into Steffi, which was blacked out."

"That blackout was necessary. Even for the split second that a lit interior would have been visible, it would have appeared as a noticeable flash of light to anyone in the automobile."

Sean considered telling Alex that he'd made the assumption that he was dead, but decided no one really needed to know about that. "So now what?"

"First," said Alex as he tapped the front screen, "standard gravity. Then I get my pseudo-body suit back." Alex handed Sean his 1995 clothes.

The gravity returned to normal and the door slid open. Sean and Alex stepped out onto a deserted pasture. Sean rubbed his shoulder. "I think I almost dislocated my shoulder from you jerking me out of the car... better than the alternative, though."

Alex touched the right side of Sean's neck and the pseudo-body suit all-but melted from him.

"Yow! It's cold out here. Man, I can see why you want this thing back. Just for the warmth if nothing else."

Alex began unfastening and sliding out of Sean's sixties clothes. "While the moderated temperature certainly is appealing, it is also necessary to impersonate a doctor to be able to retrieve Jane Carmichael."

Sean put on his shirt and khakis from 1995 as Alex quickly enveloped himself in the pseudo-body suit and changed his appearance to a generic approximation of a late twentieth-century doctor.

Alex handed Sean the army jacket. "This will help block the cold, although I will not be gone long," he advised. "It will only seem like seconds to you."

"Wait," questioned Sean, "Gone?"

"Yes, to retrieve Miss Carmichael."

"Why don't I just go with you?"

"There would not be enough maneuvering room in the S.T.E. if you were along."

"Maneuvering? What's to maneuver?"

"To get Miss Carmichael into position for insertion."

"Insertion? What the hell are you talking about?" The pitch and volume of Sean's voice went up. "Inserted into what?"

"The automobile," Alex related in monotone.

Sean's face morphed from confused to outraged. He grabbed two fistfuls of lab coat and tugged Alex closer. "*What* automobile?" he threatened through clenched teeth.

Alex's 'doctor' face lost color as the pseudo-body suit detected his fear. "The one you just evacuated," he squeaked.

"Are you crazy?" screamed Sean. "Why would you do that?"

"To reestablish the correct timeline," Alex gasped.

"You said the alien abduction thing would work," Sean growled menacingly, "and it did!"

"Only the rescue part," Alex timidly clarified, "I thought you understood it was only to rescue you since we could no longer convince Jane Carmichael to voluntarily get into the automobile."

"So all along, you planned to stuff her into the death car after you pulled me out?" Sean roared.

"Yes... I thought you understood," Alex whimpered, "To return the timeline to its correct path."

"You are *not* going to *kill* her!" Sean raged, punctuating each word with a shake of Alex's body.

Then Sean's eyes rolled back in his head and he collapsed.

Alex stood over his unconscious ancestor, wringing his hands. "I thought you understood," he whined. "I truly thought you understood."

He regretted using the fail-safe again, but had no time for any thought other than self-preservation. Sean was irrational... possibly, *probably* violent. He connected to his computer to review every word of the conversations they had earlier. It was true that he never specifically mentioned Jane being placed back into the automobile just before it rolled over. It wasn't an omission designed to hide the fact, but to be sympathetic to Sean's feelings. He really had thought his ancestor fully understood the entire plan. He knew Sean didn't like the part about Jane dying, but thought he had accepted the necessity of returning everything to the way it had historically been.

Now what was he to do? Leave the ancestor laying in the field until he returned from the completed mission? No. He had to speak with him again. Explain again. Sean needed to understand and accept that what he was doing was the right thing... the *necessary* thing.

He slid into the time-machine and closed the door. He activated the dual projection system so that it appeared as if the top half was clear glass, then he waited for Sean to come around.

Sean first saw a half-moon floating in a starry sky as he swam back to consciousness. When he realized that he was flat on his back, he snapped up

311

to a sitting position. Steffi was directly in front of him, though the appearance of the time-ship was almost like a convertible with the top down.

When he saw 'Doctor' Alex, he sprung to his feet and rushed him, surprised that he couldn't grab hold of him, even though he looked to be sitting in the open air. His arms slammed against the solid upper half of the S.T.E.

"Are you always going to cheat when you can't handle a fight?" Sean challenged.

"Perhaps the 'fair' thing to do," Alex answered, "would be to allow you to pummel me with your superior strength and size. Would that be your interpretation of a 'fair' fight?"

"I should know by now that there's nothing fair about you. *You* always win. *You* are always right."

"It is simply human nature to use any skills or tactics that give one an advantage over an opponent."

"How would *you* know anything about that?" Sean spat, "Obviously mankind stopped being human somewhere between me and you."

"I will ignore that ridiculous statement since it is irrationally spurred from your anger."

"Humans don't callously murder people," Sean roared. "Have you already done it?"

"If you are speaking of Miss Carmichael, no, I have not."

Sean's face softened slightly as his voice changed from threatening to pleading. "Then don't. Don't do it. Please don't do it. We can figure this out."

Alex studied Sean's face and could see that the anger had melted away to be replaced with pain. "I still do not understand," he started as he looked into Sean's pleading eyes. A moment of silence passed as Alex felt Sean pouring his heart through his eyes. He could feel his ancestor's pain flowing into his own heart.

Alex closed his eyes as he continued, "When we came to this October 1969 date, I thought you understood and were accepting of Jane's fate."

"I... I went along with it," Sean confessed, "but I kept hoping something would change. And it has! Look what happened! We couldn't get the note back, then you couldn't hypnotize her. It seems to me that fate doesn't want us to change it back."

"I will grant you that it has been difficult to return all things to their original path, but at this point, we have overcome all of the challenges. All that remains is to place Jane Carmichael into the automobile a half second after pulling you out."

"But why?" Sean ranted, "*Why?* We saved Louise! I risked my life when I got in that damned car so that no one else could get in and be killed. If we just take Jane out of here, she can't convince my Dad to go to Iowa State. Everything gets put back like it was!"

Alex looked deeply into Sean's desperate eyes. It was so difficult to attempt to sway an emotional argument with logic. Alex closed his eyes again, took a deep breath and exhaled slowly. "We have already discussed this," he said with little enthusiasm for his own point of view. "If Jane Carmichael simply disappeared it would potentially have an even larger impact on the future than her survival. This small community could become completely disrupted."

"Potentially! Could become! We don't know!" Sean argued in desperation.

Alex sighed again. The discussion weighed heavily on his own emotions. "Sean, if your friend Raj just mysteriously vanished, how would you react? How would his family react? What kind of upheaval would you expect at your school? … in your town?"

All hope crumbled from Sean's face as his rational side had to admit that Alex was right. "We could try it," he sobbed. "Try it and see what happened. It might not be so bad. After a few weeks or months... maybe everyone would get back to normal."

A tear slid sympathetically from Alex's eye. "You know it would not be normal."

"We could try it," Sean cried desperately, "Just *try* it."

The doctor face that Alex wore became placidly firm. "She will not even be aware of what happens," he uttered stoically. "She will not feel the terror of the automobile crashing as she would have experienced in the original timeline."

"No!" Sean sobbed as he collapsed onto the invisible barrier that kept him from Alex.

"She will remain unconscious," Alex continued. "I promise I will handle her gently and respectfully."

"Please..." Sean cried. He spread his hands out and smashed his face against the S.T.E.

"We will be in zero-gravity," Alex droned, "I will float her out of Steffi and into the automobile."

"Why are you telling me this?" Sean sobbed. He raised a hand and slapped against the time-craft.

"Then it will all be over in seconds," Alex assured Sean as if dispassionately explaining a medical procedure

"You said the alien abduction would work!" Sean shrieked.

"I am... sorry," Alex choked, then turned his head away.

"You said the alien abduction would work!" Sean screamed as he hammered his fists against the S.T.E. "You said..." His fists passed through thin air. He heard a soft pop as he fell forward to the ground where the time-machine no longer sat.

He lay on the cold grass, sobbing. "You said the alien abduction would work," he bawled once more before collapsing into spasmodic wails.

"Sean?"

He barely heard the voice behind him the first time.

"Sean?" it repeated.

It was Alex. Had he changed his mind? Sean pushed himself up and whirled around. It *was* Alex. Not Doctor Alex, who had just left, but Alex... sitting in the invisible-topped time-machine. A tiny spark of hope quickly flickered and died. He sunk back to his knees.

"Did you do it?" Sean asked in a flat, emotionless voice. He already knew the answer.

"Yes," Alex replied softly.

Sean closed his eyes. He felt empty. Numb. All hope of saving Jane was finally crushed.

"But there was... an anomaly," Alex continued in a soft, unsure voice. Sean didn't move from his silent kneeling. "When I was moving Miss Carmichael into the S.T.E. I received a message." He paused, but Sean said nothing. "It was relayed through Steffi's computer." He paused again. "No one in this century would know how to accomplish that... or have the technology." Alex searched for some reaction from Sean, but he remained motionless, head tilted down, arms limp. "Just a single word." He took a deep breath and exhaled slowly. "I have a theory, but I require your assistance."

He watched Sean for a moment, hoping to see a sign of compliance or even recognition. When there was none, he pressed on. "I need you to tell me a place. When I say the name 'Jane Carmichael,' what *place* do you think of?" He waited. No reply. He waited several seconds more.

"Flying saucer," Sean mumbled.

"Flying saucer?" repeated Alex, but without comprehension.

"Drive-in," Sean mumbled.

"Flying saucer... drive-in?" Alex asked, still mystified.

"Playground," mumbled Sean.

Alex pieced the three phrases together. "The playground at the drive-in movie?" he asked.

Sean nodded blankly.

"Sean, I need you to trust me," Alex proposed gingerly. "Can you do that?"

Sean didn't move or even acknowledge Alex in any way. The door slid open to the S.T.E.

"Sean, I need you to trust me," Alex repeated.

In a flash, Sean had sprung on Alex and had his arms around his throat. "No!" he raged through clinched teeth. "I will *never, ever* trust you again!" Sean could see the panic in Alex's eyes... briefly... before everything went black.

Alex gently put a hand to where Sean had been choking him. "We must find another way to end these conversations," Alex rasped as he tried to settle his jangled nerves.

He struggled to pull Sean's limp body the rest of the way into the S.T.E., closed the door and lifted off. He cloaked, then sped toward Colgate, Iowa.

Sean could see stars and the moon again as he lay flat on his back, but also looming to his left was a huge dark rectangular shape. He sat up. Alex was again sitting in the S.T.E., the top half transparent to the eye. "Stop messing with me," he groaned, his voice wrapped in defeat. "Just knock me out and take me home."

"I believe you will change your mind if you simply turn around," Alex replied.

Sean slowly rotated around. In the dim light, he could see a small saucer shaped object with a shadowy form laid out on top of it. He glanced up to his right. The huge rectangle was a movie screen. His peripheral vision recognized the swing set on his left as he slowly walked toward the playground UFO.

The shape on the saucer wore a jacket open over a purple sweatshirt. He could see the white letters 'ikin' peeking out. He turned back in disbelief to look at Alex. Alex nodded and beamed brightly.

Sean dropped to his knees next to the saucer. He ran his fingers through the blonde rooted straight brown hair. "Jane?" he whispered so softly that he could barely hear himself. He gently jostled her. "Jane?" he said a little louder.

"It may require a little more to wake her," Alex suggested from behind him.

Sean looked over his shoulder to Alex, then bent closer to Jane and kissed her.

"That would have been interesting if the fairy tale method actually worked," Alex remarked as he stepped closer and knelt beside Sean. "However..." He held a small tube under Jane's nose. "Open point five."

Jane's nose twitched. Alex waved the tube back and forth under her nose. She turned her head away.

"It may help to place her more upright," Alex suggested.

Sean put his arms behind Jane's shoulders and lifted her as he sat beside her. Her head lolled on his shoulder. Alex applied the vial again.

"Mmmph," Jane sputtered as she jerked her head away.

"Open point nine," Alex said, then slipped the tube under the new position of Jane's nose.

"Stop it," Jane mumbled. This time a hand came up.

"This may take awhile," Alex commented.

Suddenly, Jane's eyes flew open. "Mom! Dad!" she shrieked as she pushed away from Alex.

"Jane, it's OK," Sean assured with a soothing voice, "It's OK. You're safe."

"Mom! Dad!" she screamed again, then pushed against Sean and tried to stand up. She tumbled to her knees and started to desperately crawl away. "Mom! Dad!"

Sean leapt to her side and put an arm around her to stop her from crawling. "It's OK! It's OK!"

Jane pivoted and scrambled to crab-walk away. She flailed blindly at her assailant, then her eyes fell on Alex. "He's trying to kill me! Mom! Dad!"

Sean slid around behind her to stop her retreat. He fell to a sitting position behind her and gathered her in. "Shhhh. It's OK. You're safe. Shhhh."

Jane struggled against him and he tightened his arms around her. She tried to pull at his hands. Her eyes were still fixed on Alex. "Let me go!" she screamed. "He wants to kill me! Mom! Dad!" She struggled fruitlessly against Sean's enveloping grip, then suddenly went limp in surrender.

"Where are we?" she asked softly as her wide eyes took in the strange surroundings.

Sean joined her in assessing their location. "Ummm... seems to be the drive-in."

She continued to gaze around in wonder. "In Colgate? How did I get here?"

Sean turned a questioning eye to Alex. "That I don't know myself," he admitted.

"Did he bring me here to kill me?" she asked with even tones, her eyes fixed defiantly on Alex.

"No," Sean reassured her but realized with a glance at Alex that he was unsure of his current intentions. "But even if he were to try, I won't let him. Even if I get trapped in 1969 forever, I won't let him hurt you."

"Nigel, I..." she started, then turned her head toward Sean. She touched his short hair.

"Sean," he said softly.

"Sean," she repeated, "Sean... Kelly... Juan's... son. That is so freaky." Sean nodded. "I was running. Trying to get back in the house. How? Why are we here?"

Sean's thoughts rolled back to Jane's porch, then rushed through the emotional roller coaster that led them to the current moment. "I really don't know," he sighed.

She nodded toward Alex. "He wanted to kill me."

"He told me that he already had killed you," said Sean. Jane looked mystified. "I really don't understand either," he continued.

"If everyone is calm now," Alex began, "perhaps I can shed some light on this puzzle."

Jane stiffened.

"It's OK, Jane," Sean whispered into her ear, "I promise I won't let him hurt you. We just need to let him talk." Jane relaxed a little, then nodded.

"OK, Alex," Sean signaled, "shed away."

"I do not claim to have everything fully deciphered," Alex admitted.

"Just tell us what you know... like why did you bring Jane here?"

"I did not," Alex replied. "At least not yet."

Sean squeezed his eyes tightly shut. "Is this going to be another cross time-stream thing-a-ma-bob?"

Alex shrugged. "That would be my current hypothesis."

Sean kept his eyes clamped shut. "OK. Let's take it from where you knocked me out. Not this last time, but the time before."

Jane turned her head to Sean, her brow furrowed. "How many ti..."

"Too many," Sean interrupted, "We can get back to that." He addressed Alex, "OK, you knocked me out, I woke up, and you said you were going to get Jane from the hospital and stuff her in the death car."

"Hospital?" Jane demanded, "What hospital?"

"Let's get to that part later," he said to her, then turned back to Alex. "You were popping out to get Jane to put her in the car so it would kill her when it rolled."

"What!?!" Jane exclaimed.

"Please, this is way too complicated even without you interrupting," Sean groaned.

"That is correct," Alex replied. "As I left you, your words echoed in my mind, 'the alien abduction should work' you said." Sean nodded. "Something about your inflection caused me to remember the story you fabricated about the woman murdered in Detroit."

"What woman in Detroit?" Jane again interrupted.

"Jane," Sean whispered in her ear, "I'm sorry... but if you keep asking questions, we'll be here all night."

"What woman murdered in Detroit?" Jane demanded more forcefully.

"Later!"

Alex continued, "You suggested that aliens could have abducted her and left the remains of a clone for the authorities to find."

"Yeah," Sean nodded, "I was just kind of grasping at straws for another explanation."

"But when I thought of your story, it caused me to realize that it presented a viable alternative!" Alex gushed, smiling broadly.

"What?" Sean and Jane asked simultaneously.

"A clone!" Alex declared gleefully, "human cloning was briefly popular for the rich in the mid-22nd Century."

Sean and Jane looked at each other, then back to Alex, thoroughly confused.

Alex could see they weren't understanding. "Remember I told you that I received a message when I placed Miss Carmichael in Steffi? A one word message? It was 'Clone'!" Sean and Jane stared blankly at him, so Alex continued his narrative. "It is impossible for anyone in this century to send a message in that manner. It seemed to have been triggered solely by the proximity of Miss Carmichael... or more accurately, Miss Carmichael's clone... to Steffi."

"Steffi? His girlfriend?" Jane asked.

"Jane, please," Sean pleaded, "don't distract him."

Jane frowned and poked an elbow into Sean's ribs.

"From that point," Alex expressed enthusiastically, "I was convinced that I placed a clone of Miss Carmichael into the automobile milliseconds before the crash. Miss Carmichael had been replaced!"

"But *who* replaced her?" asked Sean.

"Someone older and wiser," Alex grinned. Jane and Sean again stared at him. "I am 99% certain that it was *me!* Will be me. Will have been me." Sean's mouth dropped open. "But I had no idea where the *real* Jane Carmichael would be. Then I realized that I would key that to you. *You* knew where she would be."

"*I* knew?" Sean pointed to himself.

"Yes," Alex replied, "More correctly, you told me where I will have placed her."

"Will have placed?" questioned Jane.

"You *really* don't want him to try to explain that," Sean sighed.

"And that completes the circle," Alex shrugged with a smile.

Sean sighed dramatically and clamped his eyes shut to steel himself. "Let's make sure I've got this. So, past-you remembers my story about a clone, and by the time you get to Jane, future-you has already replaced her with a clone."

"Correct," Alex nodded.

"You know it's a clone because future-you left you a secret message that no one else could have possibly left."

"Yes."

"You stuff the clone into the death car, so that when the cop gets to the scene of the accident, he'll find a dead clone that everyone will assume is Jane."

"Correct."

"You come back to tell me about it, but you don't know where the real Jane is, so you ask me."

"Yes."

"And because no matter what I tell you, future-you will take her where I say, so that's why she's here?"

"Very good!" Alex clapped his hands with excitement. "You followed it completely!"

"And now Jane doesn't have to die because, as far as anyone knows, she's already dead?"

"Correct."

Sean cradled his chin over Jane's shoulder and hugged her. Tears dripped from his eyes. "I *did* save you," he breathed.

Jane tilted her head back and gently rubbed her check against Sean's and stared at the stars as she attempted to process everything she'd heard. Everyone was quiet for a few moments before she leaned forward to stare coolly at Alex. "Do you feel even a little guilty for creating my twin just to murder her?"

"Clone," corrected Alex, "not your twin."

Jane shook her head ruefully. "Is that how you justify it? Hide behind words? Twin. Clone. What difference does it make? You created an exact copy of me just to kill her!"

"For the timeline to be properly reset, the body of Jane Carmichael, or a reasonable facsimile is recovered from that automobile accident. The clone seemed to be the only substitute for your own body," Alex insisted.

"Why is she any less deserving of a life than I am?" Jane demanded.

"It was a clone!" Alex protested, "Clones do not have lives. That is to say, technically it is possible, but that is not the way it works. They are maintained only for body replacement parts."

Jane's jaw dropped. "That's monstrous," she breathed.

"Do they know that's why they exist?" Sean asked, equally shocked.

"No!" Alex was exasperated. "They do not know anything. They are..." He paused as he realized what they were protesting. "I am sorry. You know nothing of cloning history. Let me give you a limited outline of events. Even before the Dark..." He stopped himself and cleared his throat. "By 2055, fringe groups had experimented with cloning and had successfully created human clones. They were denounced and then outlawed by most governments. The process I have been referring to took place nearly a century after that, off-world in a private satellite. It was a sovereign state with no ties to any Earth government. These clones that were set up for replacement parts had portions of their brains disconnected during early development. I believe you would use the term 'vegetative state' to describe their existence. Because of the expense to maintain them, they were available only to the very wealthy."

"That's barbaric!" Jane exploded.

"Many people of that era agree with your assessment," Alex shrugged. "The service was rather violently terminated."

"You believe that's where the Jane clone you stuff in the car comes from, right?" asked Sean.

"That is the only logical conclusion I can draw, based on observed facts," Alex replied.

"So how will that work?" Sean asked, "You take Jane to the future and pay to build a vegetable clone?"

"Again, that is the most logical conclusion."

"No!" Jane protested vehemently.

Sean and Alex turned to her.

"No," she repeated. "I'm not going to have any part in this!"

Alex recoiled slightly from the force of her declaration but recovered and looked her in the eye. "If you will not comply with this solution, the only remaining option is to render you unconscious and place you back in the hospital. Thus, the Jane Carmichael I put in the car was you... and will be you."

"No!" barked Sean, "That is *not* going to happen!"

Jane turned on Sean. "It's *my* life, *I* get to choose my own fate!"

"Like hell you do!" Sean spat. "I've been through one nightmare after another trying to save you, and we made it. You're safe, the timeline is back to whatever it's supposed to be, and I didn't go through all that just to end up killing you again!"

Alex stepped between them before the argument could escalate further. "If you could indulge me long enough to answer a few questions, it might help me to understand your reluctance to accept this solution."

Jane's eyes were slits, and her mouth was puckered into an angry pout. She crossed her arms over her chest and gave Alex a curt nod.

Alex forced a timid smile. "Thank you. Let me first refresh my memory with regard to 20th Century medical techniques." He twitched a connection to his computer, then continued. "It appears that historically, with each new advancement such as blood transfusions, kidney transplants, heart transplants, there are detractors who find the practice an abomination. Do you, Jane Carmichael, find those procedures to be in any way repugnant?"

"No," Jane replied thoughtfully, "Heart transplants are pretty new, and I guess the first one might have freaked me a little, but I guess I'm cool with it now."

"May I then pose a hypothetical question? I believe there are casualties that return from the Vietnam War missing appendages... arms, legs, both. If you could remove some cells from their bodies, and regrow an arm or leg for them in a laboratory and then attach it to return the person to a more normal life, would you object to that procedure?"

"You mean, like, grow a new arm in a fish tank? Just an arm?"

"For the sake of this hypothesis, let us say the answer is yes."

Jane thought again, trying to picture an arm growing in a fish tank. "I guess that would be OK."

"Thank you," Alex said softly. "Let us now propose that a person is terminally ill with multiple organ failures. If a procedure were developed that could regenerate healthy replacement organs, grown from the person's own cells, would you find that acceptable?"

Jane was hesitant. "I don't know..."

"Allow me to personalize my previous supposition: your brother, Micky lies dying of multiple organ failures. It is your choice to save him with the procedure I described, or allow him to die."

"That's not fair," Jane snapped.

"Come on, Jane," Sean prompted, "Do you let Micky die, or save him?"

Her jaw tightened. She bit her lower lip and closed her eyes. "I couldn't just let him die," she admitted.

Sean put a hand to her cheek to gently turn her so that their eyes were level. "And I can't just let you die, either."

"But you're not just growing parts," Jane countered, "You're growing a person."

Alex's head slowly bobbed as he considered her argument. "Then it appears your objection is not in growing replacement body parts, as long as they are not all connected."

Jane crinkled her nose. "That's kind of a messed up way to say it."

"Another question, please. Do you realize that you already grow your own replacement parts?"

"Are you nuts?" Jane exclaimed, "Do not!"

"But you do, Miss Carmichael," Alex insisted, "systematically. Whether you realize it or not, at your age, 90% of the cells you were born with have terminated and been replaced."

"That's just mumbo-jumbo. Obviously as babies grow up, they grow new cells."

"However, in another 17 years, you will again have replaced approximately 90% of your current cells."

"What does that have to do with making a clone?"

"I am merely demonstrating that it is a normal systemic function of the body to replace itself."

"So? Assuming you're not making it up that's still just me replacing me. It's not somebody else."

"But in essence," Alex argued, "cloning is merely an external extension of that very process."

Jane plopped down on the edge of the flying saucer with her elbows on her knees and head in her hands. "You're making my head hurt."

Sean sat beside her and looped an arm around her waist. "He does that to me a lot."

Jane looked up at Alex. "So this time-travel thing and putting either a clone or me in the car... that can happen anytime, right? I don't have to decide right now?"

"That is correct," Alex agreed.

"Then let's just cool it for now and I'll think about it."

"As you wish," Alex nodded.

The feisty determination on Jane's face gradually dissolved into a haunted, sad expression. Tears welled up in her eyes.

"So you got what *you* wanted," she said to Alex, "Jane Carmichael is historically dead in a car wreck."

She put her hands over Sean's and tilted her head back slightly. "And you got what *you* wanted... to save me." Sean squeezed her and kissed her cheek. "But now what happens to me?"

"What do you mean?" asked Sean.

"Do I get what *I* want?" She turned a chilled stare back to Alex. "Now that you boys are both happy, do I get what *I* want?" She turned back to Sean. Her breath hitched. "I want to go home," she sobbed, "I just want to go home." Tears slid down her cheeks and collected on the rims of her glasses.

She pulled off her glasses and sopped up her tears with her right sleeve. She stared at the cuff. "This isn't my jacket. I tore my sleeve last week at Louise's farm. Louise's mom sewed it up. 'A stitch in time, saves nine,' she said. This can't be my jacket; this sleeve is perfect."

"Jane," Sean said softly. "You can't go home."

"So what *are* you going to do with me?" she shouted angrily. "Take me home to *your* time? How would that work out? 'Hey, Mom, I was in 1969 and this girl followed me home... can I keep her?' Think your dad would still recognize me?"

"Jane... I..."

"Why did you guys have to mess with my life?" she wailed.

Sean's temper flared. "Because if we didn't, your life would be *over* now!" he shouted back.

Silence again hung briefly in the crisp autumn air.

"Isn't it anyway?" Jane said quietly, staring at the ground. "As far as anyone knows?" She started to sob again, "My life *is* over."

Sean pulled her into a hug. "It's *not* over," he whispered, "You're alive!"

"Not to my mom!" she choked, "Not to my dad!" Her voice cracked completely as her face twisted in pain. "How long has it been?" she sobbed. "Have the cops already come to my house?" She gasped in a ragged breath. "Have they already told my mom *I'm dead?*"

She fell completely into Sean's embrace as she melted in grief. He held her tightly, feeling helpless as her body spasmed against his, her wailing was broken only as she gasped for breath. "Jane," he said repeatedly, softly, as he stroked her hair. He held her... ached from the pain she poured out. They fell into a rocking motion as they sat on the edge of the saucer, Jane collapsed like a rag doll. He rubbed her back... patted it... stroked her hair. "It'll be OK," he whispered over and over as he rocked her.

Minutes slipped painfully by. Alex stood silently over them; both fascinated and terrified by the emotional outpouring he witnessed.

The wailing eventually turned to sobs, the sobs finally to silent tears punctuated with little sharp hiccup breaths. Jane finally lifted her head from Sean's shoulder and mopped her face with her coat sleeve.

"I'm sorry about your jacket," she mumbled absently, staring at the huge damp spot on his shoulder.

"It doesn't matter," Sean replied.

"Why didn't you just let me die?" she asked, her voice devoid of emotion.

Sean scooped her back into a crushing embrace, his heart ached. "I couldn't! I just couldn't!"

"Why?"

He released her and held her shoulders at arm's length, staring into her damp reddened eyes, his head rocked slightly side-to-side as he searched for words. "Because..." he began haltingly, "because I... love you." His eyes flicked around her face, desperate for any clue of her reaction. Her face remained unchanged and Sean's heart dropped into his stomach.

Jane slowly slid her glasses back on. She stoically watched his eyes dart around and could see the edge of panic creeping into his face. "I fell in love, too," she said and paused as her lips curled into a brief rueful smile, "...Nigel."

The name stabbed at Sean like a dagger. Perhaps not intentionally, but the pain was no less sharp. Nothing was going the way he'd imagined it. He was so relieved to have saved her life, thought she would be grateful, and imagined they would somehow live happily ever after.

Hearing her call him Nigel, slapped reality in his face. He'd deceived her. The feelings he'd hoped Jane would have for him were, in reality, for someone he'd only pretended to be. He'd both saved, and at the same time, destroyed her life. He'd taken her away from everything she knew, everyone she loved. Just as a kiss didn't wake her, there would be no fairy tale ending.

Jane felt the pain that crept into Sean's face and quickly turned away to address Alex. "So, Alex... thing from the far future. If you're not going to kill me, what *are* you going to do with me?"

"I do not have a plan," Alex said levelly, "My goal in returning to 1969 was to reset the timeline to its original state. It appears that has now been accomplished since, as you put it, 'Jane Carmichael is historically dead in a car wreck'."

"I thought maybe Alex could..." Sean started but stumbled as Jane turned her cold eyes back to him. "...could... maybe... just kind of... I don't know... take you somewhere in the future."

She stared at him in disbelief. "Did you think I would happily just go along with that?"

"I thought you'd prefer that over being dead! Yes!" Sean snapped.

"When you went to this 'changed' future where I was still alive and had somehow dragged your dad to the 'wrong college'... how did you feel? How did *that* feel to have no family or friends? Bad enough to come back to change it?" She sadly shook her head. "Don't you see that now you've put me in the same spot? No family. No friends. No identity."

"I was willing to accept that changed future!" Sean shouted. "When Alex said the only way to fix it was to come back and make sure *you* died, I was willing to be some kind of... I don't know... time orphan!"

"But you didn't."

"I *would* have if it was just me!" Sean insisted, "I would have given up my life to save you... if it was *only* my life... but Alex started stacking up the bodies. If I don't go back to my regular life, I change everything between me and him. I'd be killing his dad and grandfather and both their grandfathers and however many other people are in between... I can't keep track... but Alex knows them all by name... and they'd all be gone. And Louise and all her kids... and Micky..."

"Micky?" Jane interrupted. "What happens to Micky?"

"In the original timeline," Alex stated, "he goes to work with your Uncle Carl and lives a relatively successful life to the age of 84. In the altered timeline, you convince him to go to university, he falls in with a bad crowd and is dead before age 20 of a drug overdose."

Jane reflexively put her hand to her mouth. "Micky?" She gasped. She covered her face with her hands. "Just because I lived, Micky and Louise both died?"

"That is the way the events fell," Alex stated with his clinically objective voice.

"But now you think they'll be OK?" Jane asked.

"We know that Miss Rimmer was not killed in the car wreck," Alex confirmed, "Without your guidance, it is unlikely that your brother will attend university."

Sean leaned toward Jane, started to put his arm around her again, but decided it might not yet be the right time. "I'm sorry, Jane," he said sincerely, "I am so sorry that I've hurt you with this. I only wanted you to live and be happy. I didn't think about how it would pull you away from everything you love."

Jane turned to him, the bitterness that had flashed in her eyes was fading. "Would you really have walked away from your own life to save mine, if nothing else were changed?"

"Yes," Sean said without hesitation.

She smiled at him weakly, pulled her glasses off again and dragged her sleeve across her eyes before the tears that were forming could slide down her checks.

"What kind of material is this?" she asked as she put her glasses back on. "I can wipe my eyes and nose on it and it's just immediately dry." She glanced at the damp spot still on the shoulder of Sean's coat, then back at her own dry sleeve. "This *isn't* my jacket." She looked from Sean to Alex and back. Sean shrugged.

"It would be logical that the clone was dressed in the clothes you had on earlier tonight," Alex suggested.

"So what do I have on?"

"I have a theory," Alex posed, "Are your cheeks cold?"

"Sure," Jane replied, "It's October... and I've been crying."

"Are your hands cold?"

Jane held up her hands and stared at them as she wiggled her fingers and rotated them at the wrist. Her face reflected a concerned curiosity. "No. No, they're not."

"How about your ears?"

"Yeah, they're cold... a little, not like my cheeks."

"Do you feel any chill at all below your neck?"

Jane's eyes flitted around her body as she thought about it. "No. Not at all," she said. "What does that mean?"

"I can confirm my hypothesis by touching your neck," Alex proposed as he took a couple of steps toward her. She stopped him with a look. He raised his hands, palms toward her. "I guarantee it will not harm you."

"Says the guy who tried to hypnotize me and kill me," Jane spat sourly.

"What are you getting at, Alex?" asked Sean.

"I believe Miss Carmichael is wearing a pseudo-body suit," Alex replied. "Currently mimicking her apparel from this evening."

"Where would she get that?" asked Sean.

"From me," answered Alex. "Eventually."

"What kind of suit?" asked Jane.

Alex closed the distance between them. "Please, allow me to show you. All I need do is touch your neck briefly."

Jane winced at his touch but then bolted upright when she saw the change. Alex hopped defensively backward.

"What did you do?" Jane yelped. She was now in the t-shirt and fringed blue-jean shorts and flip-flops that she wore the day they all met in July. She stared at her legs and nearly bare feet. "How did you do that?"

A frightening thought suddenly struck Sean. "Wait a minute, if she's got a super-suit, she could be anyone!" He turned his suspicion angrily to Jane. "Alex, so help me, if that's you in there I'll kill you on the spot and live stuck in 1969 with no regrets."

"Have you gone psycho?" Jane snapped back at Sean. She turned to Alex. "Put my fall clothes back," she commanded.

"Why?" asked Alex. "Are you cold?"

"Are you nuts?" she fired back at him. "I'm in shorts and flip-flops and it's October!"

"Are you cold?" Alex asked again calmly enunciating each word.

Jane blinked a few times as she thought about it. "Umm... no. Actually I'm not."

"That could be anyone in there!" Sean yelled at Alex.

"I do not think so," Alex replied calmly. "She is not wearing a headpiece. Remember, I asked if her cheeks were cold? Also, when I instigated the change, I envisioned how Jane Carmichael appeared at our first meeting. Notice the hair. It is not in braids and the blonde roots are longer."

Alex knelt down onto the saucer and started running his hands over the surface. He stood, holding a gossamer silvery shape in his right hand. "*Et voilà!* The headpiece."

"This is freaked out!" Jane exclaimed as she rubbed her legs with her hands. "I can feel my legs with my hands, but my legs can't feel my hands, they feel like I have pants on. I mean, to my hands, I feel skin when I touch my legs. But my legs don't feel skin from my hands."

"The pseudo-body suit mimics appearance and texture exactly," Alex explained. "But regardless of how you look, you are fully covered... with the exception of your head at this point. There is also total tactile pass-through of the portion that covers your hands, but not the rest of the suit."

"I don't get it," said Jane.

"Perhaps it will be more apparent if I were to display the suit completely in its natural format."

Alex touched the control spot on Jane's neck and closed his eyes. Jane looked down at her now silvery skin-tight suit. She gasped, then immediately draped her right arm across her chest and splayed the sterling fingers of her left hand as a make-shift loincloth.

"Put my clothes back on, you perv!" she shrieked.

Sean's heart skipped a beat and his jaw dropped, but he managed to force himself to reluctantly look away. Alex returned Jane's appearance to the jacket, purple sweatshirt, and jeans she had on earlier.

"What the hell?" Jane screamed. "You mean in reality, I'm running around naked, covered with silver spray paint?"

"The pseudo-body suit clings snugly to your body, following every curve, but when activated with a clothing design, it mimics that shape. Although you currently appear to be wearing a jacket, you cannot actually remove it."

"How did I get this thing on?" Jane demanded. "And not only that... who took my *real* clothes off me?"

"Although that is an event still in my future, I assume that I will have," Alex shrugged.

Jane slapped him across his cheek. "Perv!"

"I assure you," Alex snorted, "it will not be a lascivious encounter."

Jane turned to Sean. "A what?"

"Someone screwed up when they loaded his 20th Century dictionary in his head," Sean explained.

She smiled at him. "You mean even without the British accent he still talks weird?"

"Would you have preferred I used the term 'prurient' or 'lecherous'?" Alex asked gruffly.

"I'm afraid so," Sean said to Jane, "I sometimes try to figure it out from context."

"Something more simple, perhaps monosyllabic, like 'lewd'?" Alex interjected.

"So what do you get from 'lascivious encounter'?" Jane asked Sean.

"I think he means he won't get any kicks out of seeing you naked," Sean smiled with a shrug.

"Very gallant of him," Jane said with a pink-cheeked grin back to Sean.

"All of them are perfectly acceptable and very descriptive words!" Alex bellowed.

"Yeah, he's basically an OK guy," Sean shrugged, "You get used to him."

"It *is* rude to discuss someone as if they were not standing right next to you!" Alex scolded.

"Does he always get so uptight this easily?" Jane asked.

"He's got kind of a superiority complex," Sean explained, "so he really doesn't like being ignored."

"I do *not!*" Alex exploded.

"And no sense of humor," Sean winked.

Jane smiled... almost laughed. "I can see that."

"You are both..." Alex puffed and blustered as he tried to decide what to say, "Twentieth-century ruffians!"

Jane and Sean broke into laughter as Alex continued to rant. Sean slid his arm around Jane and pulled her into a hug. "Are you going to be OK?" he asked when the laughing subsided.

She looked into his eyes, tried to smile. "I don't know, Nij..." She turned away, embarrassed. "...Sean."

He gently lifted her chin and coaxed her eyes back to his. "It's OK," he gently assured her, "I don't mind if you call me Nigel, if it makes you more comfortable."

"No... I need to try to accept things as they really are... no matter how *insane* that reality may be."

Alex turned and stomped away. "If anyone should ever wish to speak to me again, I will be in the S.T.E."

They watched as he dramatically got into the time-machine, closed the door and set the top part back to opaque.

"He won't get mad and take off for the future without you, will he?" Jane asked.

"No... he still needs me. If I don't get back to my 'regular' life, he can't go home either... won't have a home to go to, I mean."

Jane took Sean's hand and looked soulfully into his eyes. "Would it be so terrible, though, if he did? I mean, if he left us here, both adrift in time with no connections to anyone? No identities? We could just... start over. Would that be so bad?"

He gazed deeply back into Jane's eyes. "Not for me."

"We could go to New Zealand," she teased.

"How would we get there?" Sean asked skeptically.

"We've got this flying saucer," she quipped as she patted the playground piece they sat on.

His eyes flicked to her lips. She smiled and leaned closer. "I think I remember how to make it fly," he said, leaning into her.

"Mmmhmmm," she agreed as their lips joined.

After a sweet lingering kiss, Jane slid her head onto Sean's shoulder. "Can we?" she asked. "Can we somehow be together?"

Sean stroked her hair as he tilted his head back to gaze at the stars and let them tug at his imagination. "It seems like we should," he said wistfully. "After all we've been through, it seems like we should."

Steffi's door slid open. "This is astounding!" Alex shouted. "You need to observe this phenomenon!"

"I told you he doesn't like to be ignored," Sean moaned.

"I don't know," Jane replied, "He sounds more freaked out than uptight. Maybe we should check it out?"

Sean stood, then helped Jane to her feet. "You might be right. He doesn't get astounded by much."

They walked arm in arm to the S.T.E. Sean slid in. "It's kind of a two-seater," he advised her, "so this will be snug, but I think there's room if you kind of sit on my lap."

"Wow," Jane taunted dryly, "You boys from the future really have some great pickup lines."

Sean blushed as she squeezed in and slipped onto his lap.

"Look at the screen!" Alex demanded.

The front view-screen flashed a series of pictures that jumped around the screen like a screen-saver on steroids. Each was on the screen so briefly, it was difficult to see what they were.

"So what is this?" Sean asked.

"I do not know!" Alex admitted, his voice tense. "It simply started on its own!"

"What do you mean, 'on its own'?" Sean asked, "What started it?"

"I do not know! It originates from Steffi's computer," Alex clarified, "But it cannot! It is impossible!"

"Kind of hard for me to accept something I'm seeing with my own eyes as impossible," Sean responded. "Can you slow it down?"

"I have tried!" Alex yelled, "It will not respond to my commands!"

"OK, OK, calm down," Sean said, "If that first 'impossible' message was from future-you, then I'd say this one is, too."

"Then why do I have no control over the display?" Alex fired back.

"Maybe future-you put another key in it that needs me," Sean theorized. "Try this. Place your right palm on the screen at the same time I do." They both put their hands on the screen, but there was no change. Sean switched hands. "Maybe right and left?" No change. "I was sure that would work," Sean muttered, pulling his hand back to rub his chin.

"Both of you put your right hand back," Jane ordered. As they obeyed, Jane touched the screen with her right hand, and images began tiling across the screen. When the screen had completely filled with thumbnail pictures, one of them slung to the center and expanded to fill most of the screen.

"Jane was the key!" Sean exclaimed.

"But what is that?" asked Jane.

"It looks kind of grainy like an old newspaper photo," Sean guessed.

A red rectangle drew itself around a section of the photo, then that box popped out and expanded. The faces in the enlarged picture displayed as a clump of various sized dots.

"Enhancing," said a disembodied voice.

"Whoa!" Sean marveled, "Steffi can talk?"

The dots on-screen shifted several times to become a solid gray-scale photo. A red circle arced around one of the faces.

"Facial recognition engaged," said the voice. "Probability face in the picture is Jane Carmichael, 37%."

The process repeated for a second face in the image. "Probability face in the picture is Sean Kelly, 54%."

A third face was circled. "Probability face in the picture is KLE1752-NI28-949-LX, 32%."

"What?" asked Jane. "What's the letters and numbers for that one?"

"That's Alex's real name," Sean explained.

"Proximity of three faces in same picture increases identification probability to 41%," said the voice.

Jane looked at Alex incredulously. "Your real name is a series of letters and numbers?"

"That is my formal designation," Alex huffed. "My friends refer to me as LX."

"Which I kind of changed to Alex," Sean added.

"That part makes sense," Jane agreed.

"Yeah... you should hear about the NI28 part," Sean chuckled.

Alex shushed them as he pointed to the changing screen. A second grainy picture went through the same process, with slightly different percentages.

"Why would *we* be in old newspaper photos?" Jane asked.

"Shhhh!" hissed Alex as a third picture started the same routine.

As the pictures progressed, the resolution became markedly clearer until the final image jumped out to form a 3-D representation in full color. As facial recognition scanned one of the faces, it rotated a full 360 degrees. Sean was 100% sure it was him, even though the computer placed the probability at only 93%. The girl in the picture had her hand to her mouth and eyes closed as if caught in mid-sneeze. But even the partially obscured face scored a 74% probability that it was Jane. Alex did not seem to be in the image.

Suddenly, the screen went blank.

"Far out!" exclaimed Jane. "That last one was, like, out of sight! It was like we could almost touch it!"

"But what's it mean?" asked Sean. "Where'd these pictures come from, and why does the computer think that it's us?" He looked to Alex for an answer. Alex stared at the blank screen. "Alex? What do you think?" Some of the color had left Alex's cheeks as he continued to stare. Sean snapped his fingers in front of Alex's face. "Hello? Are you still here?"

"I recognized the place of the last picture," Alex mumbled in disbelief.

"Groovy!" Jane enthused, "Where was it?"

Alex began to manipulate the screen and eventually was able to redisplay the tiled view of the pictures. He touched one of the thumbnails and the 3-D image popped out again. Alex 'grabbed' a corner of the holograph and rotated it, then reached in with both hands and cupped something. He then pulled his hands back and pulled on the object he'd removed from the main picture and it grew in size.

"Awesome!" whooped Sean.

"Far out! You're blowing my mind!" Jane said almost simultaneously.

The object appeared to be setting on tripod legs. The upper part was mostly boxy with twin shock-absorber shaped cylinders in the front area. A small satellite dish stood tallest in the back. It was all a rust-brown color.

"What is it?" asked Sean.

"The Viking Monument," breathed Alex, though his voice sounded like he didn't believe it.

"Groovy," nodded Jane. "Like in Minneapolis or something?"

"Bradbury City," Alex corrected, still sounding unconvinced as he stared at the object.

"I don't know that place," Jane admitted.

"Of course not," Alex replied absently as he stuck in a finger to slowly rotate the object. "It has not been built yet."

"Wait a minute," Sean murmured as the gears in his head whirred. "Viking. Orangish brown. Bradbury. Are you kidding me?"

"One of the Mars Colonies," Alex confirmed, still staring.

"For real?" Sean gushed. "Mars? We're on Mars? Is that the *real* Viking Probe?"

"Yes," Alex said absently, his eyes still unfocused, "the first one, I believe."

"You don't seem excited," Sean chided, "Come on! How can you not be excited about going to Mars?"

"I have already been," Alex stated blandly, "Mother took me to Bradbury City when I once visited her."

Sean's jaw dropped. "Your mom lives on Mars?"

Alex ignored Sean's comment and flipped the picture away and brought up the second to last one that they had seen. After some manipulation, he had pulled the focus away from the people and onto the object in the background. "Analyze," he said softly.

"Object is Picasso Sculpture, Chicago, Illinois. Probability, 99.3%," droned the computer.

"What year?" queried Alex.

"Insufficient data. Sculpture unveiled 1967. First restoration, 2117. Second restoration, 2192"

"I've seen that one," Sean realized, "but what's with all the different colored paint and graffiti?"

"Use the building in the background to estimate the date," Alex ordered.

The picture shifted around to various views and close-ups. Partial areas were enhanced in a series.

"Some of those windows look broken," Sean commented.

"Daley Plaza," said the computer, "2082 plus or minus fifteen years."

"The Dark Decades," whispered Alex.

"Dude, you're starting to freak me out," said Sean, "What's the deal?"

"You should not *be* there!" gasped Alex. "Something must be terribly wrong for you to be in your own future."

The cabin was silent as Jane and Sean watched Alex put all the pictures away.

"What kind of wrong?" Jane finally ventured.

"I cannot begin to imagine," Alex whispered, then silence fell on them again.

Sean had never seen Alex this bleak. "Come on," he eventually prompted, "how bad can it be? Future-you sent you pictures, so you must get through it all."

"But why?" asked Alex, "What does it mean?"

"I don't know," said Sean with a shrug, "Maybe if you figured out where and when all of these pictures are, it would make sense."

"That seems as logical as any for a starting point," Alex agreed. "We should return to 1995. I have more resources there, and we have a great deal of planning to do."

Jane shuddered.

"What's wrong?" Sean asked her.

"1995," she replied, "That's like almost the next century. Do you, like, have flying cars?"

"I wish," joked Sean.

"Does anyone, you know, live on the moon?" she asked.

"You'd think," he replied, "especially since you know that we already landed there... but no. Not even a moon-base."

"So what *is* it like?" she asked, "...the future, I mean."

"Kinda boring," Sean shrugged, "It's not all that different. Well... everything costs a lot more than what you're used to."

"I am sorry to interrupt your uninspired attempt at a history lesson, but I need to somehow prepare Miss Carmichael for the unpleasant experience of her first jump," announced Alex.

"Too bad you can't just knock her out, like you do me," Sean commented.

One of the many small drawers that seem to appear from nowhere suddenly slid open from beneath the front view screen. It contained a small hypodermic needle.

"This is very distressing," Alex moaned, "It is as if Steffi has a mind of its own and I'm not in control."

"Looks like future-you did some serious messing with the S.T.E.," said Sean, "will do some messing... will have done some messing." He looked into Jane's wide eyes. "I really hate these time crossovers!"

Chapter Seventeen

"And then we'll move on / But we will remember long after Saturday's gone"

THE DOOR slammed in Sean's face. He stood dazed for a moment, then slowly walked away from his house. He crossed the street at a run and started ringing the doorbell at the Wilson's. He waited impatiently. "Come on, come on," he muttered as he rang the bell a second time. To his relief a light came on. The door cracked open enough for Sean to see Mr. Wilson dressed in a robe over his pajamas. He adjusted his glasses but said nothing to Sean.

"Mr. Wilson," Sean said, "something is going on over at my house, and I don't know what it is."

Wilson looked him up and down, a frown on his face. "Who are you?" he grunted.

Sean couldn't believe his ears. "Mr. Wilson... I'm Sean Kelly. I've lived across the street since I was seven years old. You know who I am."

Wilson's frown deepened. "I don't know where you think you are, or if you're out of your mind on drugs; but there's no one by the name of Kelly in this whole neighborhood." He slammed the door.

Sean was stunned. Nothing made any sense. There were strangers in his home, and a neighbor he'd known for almost ten years claimed that he didn't know him. Sean's throat tightened as he felt panic well up.

"Nicole," his dry throat croaked. He started running down the street to her house but then somehow was already at her door. He started hammering on the door with his fist. There was no response. "Come on, come on," he said as he continued to slam against the door. "Nicole," he cried, "Alexis, Katherine... anyone!"

It was completely insane... nightmarish... and all seemed so impossible. Tears started to cross his cheeks when the door opened and he saw Nicole.

"What is it, Sean?" she asked calmly. "What is wrong?"

"You know me?" he sobbed. "You know who I am?"

"Of course I do."

"Were we just on a date?" he cried hysterically. "Did we just get back from a date? Did we see *Hackers* at the movies?"

"Yes," she slowly agreed, drawing the word out.

He grabbed her shirt with both hands, popping the top button open. "Where do I live?" he demanded maniacally, *"Where do I live? WHERE. DO. I. LIVE?"*

"You seem distressed, Sean," Nicole said soothingly as she somehow was free of his grip, "Why don't we step inside?" She opened the door wider and Sean stepped in. "What has caused you to be so upset?" she asked as she closed the door.

"No one knows who I am," he shrieked, "there's this strange girl in my house and she says she's the babysitter, and she slams the door in my face. Then I go across the street to the Wilson's and he says he doesn't know me. What is going on?"

"You should not worry about that," Nicole said with nonchalance.

"Don't worry about it?" Sean screamed, "Don't worry about no one knowing me?"

"No," Nicole smiled, "It is all going exactly as planned."

"Planned? What are you talking about? What plan?"

"To erase you from everyone's memory," she said simply.

"What?" he gasped.

"That is *so* much easier than leaving behind a dead clone."

"Clone? Nicole, what are you talking about?"

"I thought you had almost figured out who I really was," she said as she grabbed a handful of her hair.

"What? I... I don't..." He stopped in mid-sentence as Nicole tugged on her hair and pulled her whole face off. Sean gasped as he tried to make sense of the gray almond-shaped face with large bulging black pools for eyes that now sprung from Nicole's shoulders. He glanced down to see that there was some type of weapon in her... its... hand. He saw the flash as he felt a jolt like electricity, and then he couldn't move a muscle.

"You will make a wonderful exhibit for the intergalactic zoo," the thing said, "My spaceship is just below. Time for us to leave."

The floor below Sean suddenly dissolved and he could feel himself falling. Falling into a deep, dark, black nothingness.

"Nooooooo," he managed to scream.

"Nooo," Sean gasped as his eyes flew open. He tossed his covers back and sat bolt upright, his heart pounding in his chest. He gasped for breath, then took one long deep breath and let it out slowly as he took in his surroundings. His room.

He stumbled across the hall to the bathroom and splashed cold water on his face. He stared at his reflection, almost expecting to see someone else in the mirror. He'd had some crazy dreams before, but nothing so incredibly vivid.

"Sean?" his mother called from down the hall. "Are you finally up?"

"Yeah, Mom, I'm up," he replied, splashing his face one last time.

He wanted to see her. Weirdly enough, he felt like he wanted to hug her. What was wrong with his head? He quickly tossed on some clothes and went back to her office. She was still wearing a robe and pink fuzzy slippers, sitting at her computer.

"Were you out late?" she asked, "We didn't hear you come in."

"Um... no," he said, thinking about it. "After the movie we..." he paused as he had a flash of searching the parking lot for Kevin's car. "...drove back to her house and..." Another flash. Riding in a cab. "...we just sat there in the driveway and talked for awhile..."

"Are you all right?" she asked.

"Yeah... sure... I just had this crazy dream."

"You should get some breakfast. Your father made pancakes and we saved you some. If you put them in the microwave for about 20 seconds, they'll be just like fresh off the griddle."

"Sure, pancakes," he mumbled.

"I think he wants you to mow today. Check with him to be sure. He's probably still reading the paper. We slept in a little late, too... well, late for us."

"Sure... great... pancakes and mow the lawn."

"Are you sure you're all right?" she asked, shifting to her concerned-Mom voice.

"Yeah, I'm fine. I'm just glad to be home."

"What?"

Sean felt as surprised as his mother looked. "I have no idea why I said that."

Michelle stood and crossed to her son, her hand went immediately to his forehead. "You don't feel feverish." Her face turned stern and her voice serious. "You weren't drinking last night, were you?"

"No!" Sean protested. "We just went to the movie."

"Be honest with me... does Nicole use drugs?"

"Moooom!" Sean pulled the word into at least two syllables.

"I have to ask, Sean. You're acting peculiar this morning and I'm just checking."

"None of my friends use drugs. We weren't out drinking, we went to a movie... that's it," Sean reported, trying to hold his temper in check. "I had a weird dream and I'm still thinking about it, but I'm fine."

"What was your dream about?" Michelle asked, suddenly in her counselor's voice.

"Oh no," Sean said, shaking his head. "We're not going to do dream analysis. It was weird, it's over, and there's no deep hidden meaning. You don't need to try to get inside my head. Save that for the classroom."

"Oh, Sean," she said almost playfully, "I'm not going to psychoanalyze you." She finished with an unconvincing laugh.

"Mom," he said earnestly, "I love you... but you are always trying to psychoanalyze me."

"Want to tell me about your date, then?" she asked with a smile.

"No!"

"All right, dear," Michelle shrugged, "Get some breakfast."

He went down the hall, shaking his head, wondering what it would be like to *not* have a mom with a Ph.D. in psychology.

He cruised into the kitchen, found the pancakes and popped them into the microwave. As he waited, he went to the window that looked out over the driveway. Kevin's car sat there, right where he'd left it. Why did he think it wouldn't be there? Why did he keep picturing himself in a cab with Nicole? Was that in the dream?

The microwave interrupted his thoughts with an insistent beeping. He pulled the plate of pancakes out and set them on the table. The butter and syrup were still sitting out, so he collected a knife, fork, and glass to set on the table with his pancakes. He poured a glass of milk and sat down. The pat of butter he slapped on top of the pile quickly melted and he slowly drizzled syrup in a spiral from the edge to the center. He watched it run to the edges and drip down the side of the stack.

"Didn't hear you come in last night," his dad said as he walked into the kitchen, folding his newspaper. "Want the sports page?"

Sean waved off the paper. "Yeah," he replied, "Mom said you guys didn't hear me."

"How late were you?"

"I don't know," Sean shrugged. "I don't remember looking at the clock."

"Sean?" his dad coaxed, voice rising as he drew out his name.

"I don't know, Dad!" He turned to face him. "It wasn't that late, but I don't know what time."

When he looked at his dad's face, he felt the urge to hug him, like he'd been away a long time. What was going on? Why would he want to hug his parents? Maybe he *was* sick.

"Well... I was up at 12:30 and checked on you, so I guess you weren't out too late."

"Just went to the show, came back to her place, sat in the driveway and talked..."

"You have a good time?" his dad asked more cordially.

"Umm... yeah... I guess. It was a good movie."

"You like this girl?"

"Yeah... but I'm not sure how she feels about me."

"No goodnight kiss, huh?"

Had he kissed her? No. It seemed foggy, but when he tried, he vaguely remembered her turning to offer him a cheek.

"Come on, Dad... It was our *first* date!"

"OK," Jack said, putting his hands up in mock surrender. "Just checking.

336

I was your age once, you know. You can always come to me if you've got questions about girls."

"Not gonna happen," Sean assured him as he stuffed a wedge of pancake in his mouth.

Jack playfully swatted his son with the newspaper. "Hey, the lawn needs mowed this weekend, and there's a chance of rain tomorrow... so maybe you can get to that today?"

"Sure," Sean said between bites. "I need to get Kevin's car back to him this morning. Nothing else planned." He wolfed the rest of his pancakes and chugged his milk, then quickly popped the dishes into the dishwasher. He headed for the front door.

"Taking Kevin's car back," he shouted loudly over his shoulder. "Back in a few."

He slid into the convertible and reached under the seat for the keys. As he backed out of the driveway, he noticed that Mr. Wilson was out raking the few early leaves that had fallen.

Waste of time, Sean thought, *Retired people must be bored. It's stupid to rake leaves before they all come down.*

"Nice looking car, Sean," Mr. Wilson called.

He knows me! He knows my name! Sean gave his head a quick shake. *Of course he knows me... stupid dream.*

"I wish it was mine," Sean yelled back to him, "I just borrowed it from my friend, Kevin."

They waved to each other as Sean started down the street.

He could have turned at the first intersection... but it wasn't really *that* much farther to go on down the street before turning. He slowed as he came to Nicole's house, craning his neck for any sign of her. At the last second before passing it, he impulsively pulled into her driveway.

"What am I doing?" he moaned to himself. "I'm such an idiot." He opened the car door. "Nicole is going to go back to thinking I'm a stalker." He walked to her door. "I don't even know what I'm going to say to her... I am *such* an idiot." He knocked.

When the door opened, he felt embarrassed. Nicole stood barefoot, in blue jeans and an overly large floppy peach t-shirt. Her hair was pulled back into a pony tail and she wasn't wearing any makeup.

"I shouldn't have come over this early," Sean apologized, "and I should have called first. I'm sorry." He couldn't make eye contact.

Nicole stepped out and closed the door behind her. "I do not mind," she said quietly. "Are you returning Kevin's car?"

Sean looked over at the car. "Um... yeah... and I was just driving by and..." He paused as he tried to figure out what to say. He still didn't really know what he was doing there. "... I guess I just wanted to see you," he finished, cheeks flushing.

"That is very sweet," she responded, pausing in the awkwardness. "Did

337

you sleep well?" she suddenly said.

"Umm, yeah," he answered automatically, then looked into her eyes. "Actually... I had this weird dream."

"Oh?" she said timidly, "What was it about?"

"I don't know... just completely bizarre," he said. "No one knew who I was... strangers lived in my house... and then I came to talk to you and...." He stopped.

"And then..." she coaxed.

"You were really an alien," he blurted, "and that sounds really stupid when I say it out loud."

"An alien?" she laughed.

"I know, right? But... you kind of pulled your face off... well, I guess it was like a mask, and you had this alien head. One of those standard little grays, like in movies when the aliens are harmless. Big black bugged-out eyes... you know."

"That is a *very* unusual dream," affirmed Nicole.

"Yeah," Sean nodded, "But the weirdest part was how real it seemed. Especially the part about people not knowing who I am."

Sean looked away, shaking his head in disbelief that he was telling her his stupid dream, then saw a figure at the living room window. He waved when he noticed the blonde hair. Nicole turned quickly to see where Sean was waving. The blonde smiled at Sean and waved back, then stepped back from the window.

"Dreams can sometimes seem very real," Nicole said hurriedly. Sean continued to stare at the window. "Our subconscious mind can invent some very strange images."

"I thought I was waving at Alexis," Sean mentioned, still looking toward the window. "But that wasn't her. Kind of looked like her, but it wasn't her." He looked to Nicole for an answer.

"Oh," she responded, overly dramatic, "That was my cousin. She came for a visit. Just passing through."

"She looks a lot like Alexis," said Sean.

"Yes, there are some strong..." she began, then froze as she heard the door open behind her. Sean looked past her at the girl framed in the doorway.

"Hi," the girl said shyly.

"We should all go inside," Nicole said abruptly as she pushed the blonde back into the house. Sean followed. Nicole steered them toward the living room.

Sean and the girl stared at each other as Nicole closed the door. She somehow seemed familiar, but he decided it was because she looked so much like Alexis. She smiled warmly; a comfortable smile, almost like she already knew him.

"Sean, this is my cousin... Jane," Nicole said undiplomatically.

"Carmichael," added the girl, "Jane Carmichael."

"Nice to meet you, Jane," Sean returned politely.

Jane's smile melted and she turned a disappointed face to Nicole. "He really doesn't..." Jane started.

"Plan on staying long?" Nicole interjected quickly. "I do not think so. Do not worry, we will have ample time to discuss our families before you must depart."

"No... I..." Jane looked from Nicole to Sean and back again.

"Jane," Nicole said forcefully, "could you go into the kitchen and get Sean a glass of water? I think he looks thirsty."

"But, I..."

"Please!" Nicole nearly barked.

Jane frowned, then left the room and headed toward the kitchen.

"Sean," said Nicole, suddenly gracious, "Would you sit down for a minute?" She hooked his arm and pulled him toward the couch. Confused by her strange behavior, Sean obediently sat.

"Mobo Gerga retrieve LX seventeen nine," Nicole rattled off quickly.

Sean's head recoiled back. "Uhhhh," he grunted, "Oh man, that one was a doozy."

"Are you all right?" asked Nicole as she checked his eyes.

"Yeah," Sean replied, then gave his head a quick shake. "Hit hard. Really complex now." He massaged his temples. "I think it actually worked, though... I'm pretty sure I believe it was all a dream, even though it still seems so real. It's the only explanation for those memories of the 'other' time."

Jane came back into the room carrying a glass of water. Sean sprang up. "Jane!"

She spilled the water as she hurriedly sat it on the end table. He scooped her into a hug and she wrapped her arms tightly around his waist.

"You know me now?" she breathed as a tear dripped onto his shoulder.

"Yeah, that must have seemed kind of weird, huh? I guess I'm starting to get used to it, although it still seems to be kind of a shock that first instant when he opens my whole memory up."

"So Lex controls what you remember?" she said darkly, stepping back from their hug.

"Wow... sounds so sinister when you say it that way. Did you call him 'Lex'?"

"Yeah, you know, like Lex Luthor, evil scientist enemy of Superman? You still have Superman in the future, don't you?"

"Sure, but this isn't really the future," Sean parried.

"That is merely a matter of perspective," said Alex.

Sean turned to see that his descendant had dropped the Nicole disguise. "So, Jane," he said as he turned back to her, "how do you like your 'cousin' Nicole? Did you meet the rest of the family, too?"

Alex stepped around Sean to insert himself into the conversation. "I have been explaining many things to Jane Carmichael, including her likeness to

Alexis Townsend, however, I have not yet broached Katherine Tuttle."

"Aw," mocked Sean, "Aunt Katherine is the *best*. How could you leave that part out? What else have you been 'explaining' since I last saw you?"

Jane lightly tapped Sean's arm to get his attention. She flipped her head to the left and right to get her hair to swirl. "Check it out, Nij... sorry, Sean... I promise I'll stop calling you Nigel. Isn't it groovy? I mean, the style looks kind of fifties to me, with the curls and all, but look! It's all the same color! He got my hair all back to the right color!"

"It looks good," nodded Sean. He noticed that the style was similar to what Alex used as Alexis, although longer.

"And check this out!" Jane said excitedly, making her thumbs and fingers form circles as she put them up to her eyes. "No glasses! Is that far out or what?"

"That's pretty amazing," Sean agreed as he eyed Alex suspiciously. "How did he manage that?"

"I'm not exactly sure. He gave me some magic futuristic drink with something in it. Tasted like water, though."

Sean narrowed his eyes at Alex.

"It *was* water," said Alex, then added "With nanites, of course."

"Did you explain to her what the nanites are?" Sean challenged.

"I attempted to explain, but she seemed disinterested. I think she prefers 'magic' as an explanation."

"Yeah," interjected Jane, "he said they were like some little invisible robots or some trippy thing." She shrugged. "I guess as long as he's not going to kill me, and since he fixed my hair and eyes..." She stopped suddenly and grabbed Sean's wrist, her face lit up and she put her other hand briefly over her mouth. "And guess what?" she gushed. "He said these little invisible robots can be set up to fix my nose! No surgery! And for free! It'll take him a while to set it up, but isn't that the grooviest?"

"Sure. I doubt if you could get even one more tiny groove on it," Sean deadpanned.

"What?"

"No one says 'groovy' anymore, Jane," Sean explained.

"Well, whatever you say then." She stepped back and twirled around. "How do you like the threads? I think the color is kind of boring and the skirt's a little long, but Lex says this is what people in the future wear."

Sean hadn't yet realized she was wearing his favorite green outfit that Alex wore as Nicole. He looked questioningly to Alex for a second, then turned his attention back to Jane. "It looks nice. You look like you'd fit right in at my school... and it's *not* the future."

"This 'thing' that I've really got on is, like, out of sight! It's a million different outfits! All you have to do is think what you want to look like... well... Lex has to think it right now, but he said if I drink some more futuristic invisible robots he can teach me how to change it myself. People in the future... well, his time, I guess... can look like anything!"

"I don't know if loading up on nanites is such a good idea," warned Sean, again narrowing his eyes as he glared at Alex.

"If it fixes my nose for free without surgery," Jane shrugged, "it's a *great* idea."

"Jane, there's nothing wrong with your nose."

"Right. I saw you staring at it when you were all brain-controlled and didn't know me."

"That was only because, as a *stranger*, you looked a lot like Alexis to me. The biggest difference is your nose."

"And what a *huge* difference that is," Jane complained.

"That's not what I meant!"

"It doesn't matter. I've always planned on getting it fixed anyway. This way looks like a pretty cool option. Or do you not say 'cool' in the future, either?"

"No, cool is still cool," Sean said, then laughed at the redundancy.

"We also have taken some short time-hops, to acclimate Miss Carmichael to the sensory explosion experienced when shifting dimensions," Alex said.

"How was that?" Sean asked Jane sympathetically, thinking of his own first experience and the aftermath.

"Oh, man!" Jane enthused, "Wasn't that a trip? I mean, like blow my mind! Psychedelic!"

Sean turned questioning eyes to Alex.

"She seemed to find the experience exhilarating," Alex shrugged.

"For sure! I mean, I've never actually dropped acid, but that's *got* to be what it's like!"

Sean lifted an eyebrow.

"I believe she is referring to ingesting lysergic acid diethylamide, commonly abbreviated LSD," Alex explained.

"Yeah, I got that part," Sean said. "I'm just not sure what to think about her thinking it was fun."

"What? Did you have a bad trip?" Jane asked Sean. "You didn't like, see snakes and spiders and stuff, did you?"

"While it is amusing to listen to you compare experiences," Alex interrupted, "I am afraid we cannot leave Sean in extended memory mode much longer. The time lapse will become noticeable."

"What do you mean? What's 'extended memory mode' mean?" asked Jane.

"He means it's time for me to go back to being the Sean who knows nothing about time-travel," Sean explained, "or Jane Carmichael."

"I still don't get that," said Jane. "How can you just forget about all that?"

"Alex's little 'magic invisible robots' handle it," Sean grumbled. "I suspect you'll know about it firsthand before long." He gave Alex a dark look.

Alex glanced away.

Alex cleared his throat. "We all need to resume the positions we were in when Sean's extended memory was opened. Sean, you are sitting on the couch. Jane, you are in the kitchen getting a glass of water... you need to take this one out with you." He picked up the glass from the end table and handed it to her. "And I need to resume my appearance as Nicole," he finished, touching his neck and shifting his appearance.

"And we're still going to get rid of Nicole?" Sean asked rather forcefully.

"Yes," replied Nicole. "I will attempt to be firm but gentle."

"Firm but gentle?" snorted Jane. "You make it sound like you're breaking up with him."

Sean glanced sheepishly toward Jane, then turned his gaze back to Nicole's feet.

"Wait. What?" Jane said incredulously. "Lex is like your girlfriend when you're mind controlled?"

"It's not mind control!" insisted Sean. "But, yeah... when I forget about the whole time-travel thing, I don't know that Alex is Nicole... and I... kind of... have a crush on Nicole."

Jane wrinkled her nose. "Isn't that a little creepy?"

"It was the most efficient way to become close to Sean in a short time," Nicole said petulantly.

"Wow, Lex," Jane exclaimed. "You're drifting a little more toward evil again."

"It was a simple matter of assisting my research," fumed Nicole.

"And won't matter after today," concluded Sean. "We're getting Nicole out of my life."

"Now, Miss Carmichael," Nicole commanded, "If you would be so kind as to return to the kitchen?"

"What if I don't want to play along?" Jane challenged.

"Then I believe I will not be able to find the time to program the nanites to alter your nose," Nicole countered, chin slightly elevated.

Jane stared open mouthed at Nicole, left hand on her hip. Nicole glared defiantly back. Jane held her stare a few moments, then, in capitulation, looked away and took a sip of the water. She turned toward the kitchen. "Evil, Lex," she muttered, "definitely drifting more toward evil."

Nicole waited until Jane was gone, examined the room, then positioned herself. "Mobo Gerga store LX seventeen ten." Sean blinked a few times. "I need to tell you something, Sean."

"That sounds a little ominous," Sean ventured.

"I have very much enjoyed the time that we have had together..."

Sean put up a hand. "OK, got it! No need to continue with the 'let's just be friends' speech. I know how it goes from here."

"That is not what I need to tell you," Nicole protested. "I was going to add that I will miss you very much."

"Miss me?"

"Yes," Nicole said, looked away, then looked back into Sean's eyes. "I have decided to return to New York."

"What?"

"My mother is going to be released from the institution. My Aunt Louise... Jane's mother... has agreed to take her in and help her get re-established. We have also decided that it will be beneficial for me to be part of the process. For now, Alexis will remain here with our Aunt Katherine."

Jane came back into the room and handed the water to Sean.

"Thanks," he said numbly as he accepted the glass and drank. "That's, um, good news," he added with false bravado. "About your mother, I mean. I'm happy that she has someplace to... umm... recuperate." He took another swallow of water.

"Cousin Jane came to help me pack some things, then we will leave tomorrow."

"Tomorrow?" Sean asked weakly.

"I am sorry," Nicole nodded. "I should have told you last night. But I wanted to have one more fun night here... with you."

"Oh, Lex," moaned Jane as she rolled her eyes.

Sean looked at her, slightly puzzled. "You mean Nikki," he said, attempting to smile at Jane.

"What?"

"Yes, Jane," said Nicole, "even though we are not identical twins, you seem to get our names mixed at times."

"What?"

"Cute names," said Sean, "I tried to call her Nikki, but she wouldn't let me. She said it was just a family thing. I'll bet they called you 'Janie' when you were all younger."

Jane furrowed her brow. "Umm, yeah... sure... sorry, *Nikki.*"

Sean rose to his feet. "I guess I, um, should get the car back to Kevin." He handed the glass back to Jane. "It was nice meeting you, Jane."

She took the glass reluctantly and looked at him with glistening eyes. It was a haunting look that made him feel even more uncomfortable. He turned and gazed hopefully into Nicole's eyes, then glanced to her feet. "I guess this is goodbye, then," he said uncomfortably. He looked back to her eyes again, then awkwardly put his arms around her. She didn't immediately respond, but then did manage to gently put her arms around him. "I'll get your email address from Alexis," he said to the top of her head. "And phone number, if that's all right."

"Of course," replied Nicole. Alex set Steffi to the task of trying to devise a way to set up and intercept the New York phone number he would give to Sean.

"Maybe you'll come back to visit?" Sean suggested hopefully. "Christmas? Spring break? Maybe next summer?"

343

"I do not know," Nicole responded tentatively. "It would depend upon how well my mother recuperates."

Sean stepped back from their hug. He slid his hands along her arms as they parted, taking up her hands in his. "Sure," he said. "If...*when* she gets better."

"We will see how it progresses," she said softly.

Sean tried to lean in for a goodbye kiss. Nicole tilted her head down slightly. He kissed her on the forehead. "I'll miss you," he said, just above a whisper. She didn't respond. He released her hands, glanced toward Jane. "Drive carefully," he said to her. She nodded. There was a sparkle in her eyes. *Is she on the verge of crying?* Sean wondered. *She seems more emotional about this than Nicole.*

He walked toward the door, the two girls trailing him. He glanced over his shoulder as he went out, lifting his hand in an almost wave. He didn't look back again but heard the door click shut.

"Great breakup, Lex," Jane cooed sarcastically.

"It was his request," Nicole said defensively as she reached up to the left side of her neck and shifted to Alex. "And I concur that it was better for his psyche to not have to deal with Nicole any longer."

"I can see that it could be a real bummer to find out that the girl you hoped to make out with is really your great-great-grandson."

"Great-great-great-great-great-grandson," corrected Alex.

"Sure, Lex," Jane taunted, "like tossing in a few more 'greats' makes it less twisted."

"It was merely a logical means to an end," snapped Alex. "I resent your insinuation that it was of a prurient nature."

"Hey, whatever floats your futuristic boat," shrugged Jane. "So will I see him again? I mean if he comes over to see Alexis, or whoever your other little girl-guise is, can you let his mind loose so he'll know me?"

"At this point, I have not yet calculated what type of relationship Alexis will pursue with Sean."

"And what about me?" Jane asked. "Have you calculated what your long term plan is for me?"

"The initial step will be to begin the reconstruction of your nose, which will involve a molecular disassembly of the cartilage and reshaping of the bone and epidermal layers. It will not be entirely painless."

"That's cool. It's not as if living with this nose has been entirely painless."

"Although initially, it will not involve you," Alex continued, "I will need to plan some investment strategies that will allow me to accumulate three billion dollars by 2160. At that point, we will get an appointment to have your clone made."

"Three *billion* dollars?" gasped Jane, her mouth remaining open along

344

with her wide eyes.

"I believe that is sufficient remuneration for cloning. I will need to verify my assumption before we go."

"Three *billion!*" Jane repeated, "And you can get your hands on three *billion?*"

"Yes," Alex said offhandedly, "It will take considerable calculations, a historical overview of stock prices... perhaps a few sporting events, and I will need to assemble thousands of independent bank accounts to divert any unwanted attention. You do realize that is one hundred sixty-five years? A substantial portion of the money can simply be earned as interest. The most difficult task is bridging accumulated investments over the Dark Decades."

"If you say so," Jane said, not hiding the disbelief in her voice. "So then what? Where are you going to drop me off for my 'new life'?"

"That is something I find quite confounding."

"Figuring out where I should go?"

"Not exactly. Do you recall the screens that popped up at the end of our test excursion in the S.T.E.?"

"Screens?"

"Particularly the three rows of three columns."

"Oh," Jane nodded, "The Brady Bunch tic-tac-toe with the different pictures like we saw the first time."

"Two in particular were highlighted."

"Right. Alice and let's see, the other one was lower left... is that Cindy or Bobby? I can't remember if the boys or girls are on the left."

"Your references to the television program are irrelevant," Alex snapped.

"Wow, Lex... don't lose your cool."

"You did not notice the DNA files linked to each picture?"

"Vaguely... but after that far out ride, I wasn't paying that much attention."

"You did not notice that I became distressed as I viewed them?"

"I guess not... sorry, but it all looked like squiggly lines anyway."

"I have reviewed those files multiple times, but cannot justify the conclusions that I am forced to consider."

Alex stared off into space, lost in his own thoughts. Jane waited a beat before responding. "If you're trying to build suspense, Lex, you're not doing a very good job."

"The first file had initially displayed when we were in 1969. I had gathered DNA samples from the camper at the lake." Alex paused again.

"Still not feeling the suspense."

"Besides locating the DNA of Sean's grandfather, which I needed for navigation to be able to travel deeper into the past, there was another match. I was uninterested in examining the secondary results at that time."

Jane waited, then rolled her eyes. "OK, I'll *fake* it," she said flatly, then added with great enthusiasm, "Wow! What did it match?"

345

"My great-great-great-great-great-grandmother, Katherine!"

"Wowie zowie!" Jane exclaimed, throwing her hands enthusiastically into the air. She then dropped into a shrug as she blandly added, "So?"

"Katherine could not have been in that camper," Alex insisted.

"Why not?"

"Because she had not been born yet!" he exclaimed.

Jane raised an eyebrow. "OK, that's a little bit freaky."

"With total disregard for logic, I followed an intuitive compulsion. I tested *your* DNA!"

Jane crinkled her nose. "OK, *more* than a little bit freaky. You're not going to go creepy evil on me, are you?"

"It is a perfect match!"

"To your multi-great grandmother, Katherine?" Jane squawked.

"I ran the tests redundantly until there was *no* possible doubt."

Jane shuddered. "So what are you saying?" she whispered.

"That *you* somehow are Katherine."

"*What?*" she bellowed.

"It is logically impossible, and yet the data are irrefutable," Alex insisted.

"*I* am Katherine?" Jane laughed, "Me? *I* am your umpty great grandmother?"

"Impossible, yet undeniable at the same time," marveled Alex, "A complete paradox."

"Lex, I think you've tipped from evil scientist to evil *mad* scientist." Jane twirled her index finger in circles near her temple. "That is like *crazy!*"

Alex sadly nodded, as if he wished he could agree with her. "It is not yet the most unbelievable part."

"There's *more?*" Jane said with raised eyebrows.

"Not about you," Alex assured her, "The data for the second DNA sample on the screen was *also* a match to one of my ancestors."

"Someone else that was in the camper is another relative?"

"No! This sample was collected from the alternate 1995. Caitlin Kelly's DNA matches another of my ancestors!"

"Alternate 1995?" Jane's brow furrowed. "Who's Caitlin Kelly?"

"Sean's half-sister!" Alex cried.

"I didn't know he had a half-sister."

"Nor should you, since he does *not!* She does not *exist!* And she cannot exist since we repaired the timeline!"

Jane eyed him with careful skepticism. His face was a cross between excited and confused. "OK, Lex," she said in a soothing voice that accompanied a placating smile, "are there any futuristic meds around that you haven't been taking lately?"

"Come with me to the S.T.E.," Alex insisted.

Jane followed him into the garage and slid into the time-machine. Alex was already deeply involved in the manipulation of icons floating in front of the forward view-screen. Jane watched silently for a few moments.

"So, Lex... you brought me out here to watch you play some futuristic game of chess?" Jane chided.

"I am going to show you the detailed DNA samples, proving how your DNA matches that of one of my Great-great-great-great-great-grandmothers. First I have to remove some of the details that you cannot know about your future. It will only be..." Alex stopped and drew a sharp breath as everything he had been working with vanished.

The forward screen divided into three rows of three columns. Pictures filled into each of the boxes, then flashed as they jumped from square to square.

"That's kind of psychedelic, Lex, but what does it have to do with DNA?"

"I did not request that data," Alex breathed. "Computer. Why are you showing..." He stopped as nine faces each filled one of the squares.

"OK," Jane nodded, "*Brady Bunch* again. Hey! One of them's me!"

Each of the faces expanded sequentially to fill the screen while uttering a single   word   that   together   created   a   sentence: "Without...Jane...Carmichael's...help...you...will...not...find...me."

"Wow," Jane commented, "Freak out!"

Alex turned to her, his face drained of color. "You saw that? You saw those faces? Heard those words?"

"Yeah... and I think one of them was me."

"I concur," Alex nodded, then turned his attention to the screen. "Computer. Replay series of nine faces as displayed on screen."

The words "Insufficient Data" appeared on the screen.

"Computer. Jane and I both saw a series of faces on the screen. Each face spoke one word of the sentence: 'Without Jane Carmichael's help you will not find me.' Please redisplay."

"Information does not exist." filled the screen.

Alex silently stared at the screen.

"Problems, Lex?" Jane finally asked.

"This has happened before," he mumbled, "but I eventually decided I was hallucinating."

"So, besides me, who were those people?"

"Previously I did not recognize any of them. It happened before I met you. One of them may have been you, even then."

"So you don't know who they are? Besides me?"

"I recognized one other face," Alex said in monotone, "Caitlin Kelly."

Jane quietly studied Alex as he blankly stared toward the forward screen. She waved a hand in front of his face, but he didn't react.

"OK, then," she nodded, "Back to that question about the futuristic meds..."

* * * * *

Mowing the lawn had given Sean a lot of time to think. Although he had a heavy place in his heart for Nicole, the initial pain had already begun to level out. He decided the semester may have been a little too crazy in the girl department. Alexis had seemed to be after him, then suddenly there was Nicole and he had been smitten with her. Then just when it seemed like something good was going to happen between them, she said she was leaving.

"What's that old movie plot, Mages?" he said as he tossed the tennis ball across the freshly mowed grass. "Boy meets girl, boy loses girl, boy gets girl back in the end?" Maggie wasn't listening since she was happily dashing after the ball. "Think I'll eventually get the girl back?"

The setter returned, dropped the ball at his feet and tensed her muscles, ready to spring the moment the ball was in the air again. Sean scooped up the ball and tossed it in a lazy arch toward the back of the yard. Maggie mouthed it on the second hop and contentedly trotted back.

He threw the ball over and over until his arm ached. Although Maggie was panting heavily, he knew she would keep going, so he finally stopped throwing. He knelt down to ruffle her ears. "I think that's enough, girl." She licked his arm, intensely watching the ball in his other hand. "No, we need to take it easy now. Settle down a little. Come on, let's get you some water, and me a Coke."

They started walking together back to the house, Maggie's eyes were still glued to the tennis ball. "You know, Mags, I thought maybe I was going to have an exciting year this year, but turns out that, as usual, I just lead a pretty boring life."

#   #   #

348

Epilogue

Mumbai, India, November 2058

I STILL FEEL inadequate for the task, even though it is nearly completed. My negotiations for the various pieces of artwork and significant artefacts have served to occupy my mind and consume nervous energy. Without this focus, I fear I would spiral into madness. I force myself to not think about Jane and what she will become because there are elements of her metamorphosis that seem cruel, but primarily because it is all impossible.

If I had not taken Sean Kelly to 1969, Jane Carmichael would be dead. If she were dead, she could not possibly be one of my great-great-great-great-great-grandmothers. If she were not one of my great-great-great-great-great-grandmothers, then I could not genetically be who I am. Therefore, I would not have travelled into the past to become not only the means for her survival, but also the vessel for her temporal relocation.

Recursion.

Logic defying recursion.

I force myself to concentrate on the task at hand and break free from my troubling thoughts. I activate the next pre-programmed jump which takes me to a dark loading dock in Mumbai. The merchant's insistence that I arrive specifically between three and three-thirty a.m. leads me to suspect that his wares may have been obtained unscrupulously. I take the thin plastic card that validates my transaction to the scanner by the large door.

A light flashes green and the door rises to reveal a large servo-loader. From the worn tread on its tires and flaking paint on its bulky frame, I would surmise that it has been in service for twenty –if not thirty– years. It moves toward the S.T.E. and lowers a small pallet near the opening of my ship. I give the command for it to proceed loading, but it remains motionless. With great frustration, I realize it is not equipped to redistribute the pieces on the pallet individually into the cabin of the S.T.E.

For a moment, I stare at the tiny pool that accumulates from the slow drip of processed petroleum near the rear of the motionless robot. I do not believe I have enough energy to complete the task manually, but by the time I off-load the fifth package from the pallet, I realize that the exhaustion I feel is more mental than physical and the cabin fills quickly.

When I remove the final parcel from the loading pallet, the robot begins to slowly trundle back into the darkness of the warehouse. Shadows consume it well before the door lowers and locks down. I stand there staring, marveling at the surrealism of the entire transaction. Breaking my mesmeric state, I fit the final package and squeeze myself into the limited space that remains.

I have nearly depleted the $795 million that has accumulated since 1995. Knowledge of future events made it simple to capitalize on every investment put into motion over the sixty-year span, popping in and out at the optimal times to buy and sell. It will be equally simple to make such investments after the Neo-Renaissance. The struggle is to bridge something of value across the Dark Decades. Historically, wine and art appreciate in value over long periods of time, as long as there is affluence in a society. Recovery in the early part of the twenty-second century will sufficiently supply affluence. The unique item of value in this particular instance is electronics. Traditionally, decades-old technology would be relegated to museums, if not castoff as refuse. However, it would also be normal for technology to make appreciative advancements, not decline to a state of near nothingness.

With each purchase made, I struggle to override the criminal feelings I ascribe to myself for looting the art of Indian and Chinese cultures. Justification is a simple, logical argument. If the pieces remained, *they* would become vaporized instead of the eCurrency I traded for them. Somehow the logic does not completely quell my dark feelings.

I activate all of the upper view-screens as the cloaked S.T.E. rises above the densely populated metropolis. As I drift above the city, I look out in a horrific wonder as it teams with life that will all too soon become ashes. A sigh is too trivial, but all that I offer as I enable the short jump forward in time.

The brief dimensional shift is also the quickest way to cover the geographical distance to nearly the other side of the globe where Jane awaits my arrival high in the Sierra Madras between Durango and Monterrey. She has embraced the role of supervising the shelving robots and insisted on giving each a name. I wonder if the optimal number of units had been something other than seven if she would have given them entirely different designations. They have almost completed shelving the last load I dropped off hours ago... or minutes ago from Jane's perspective.

"Are you getting close to the last load?" she asks the nanosecond I step from the S.T.E.

"Nearly."

"And everything's going to be from India now, right? No more surprises from China?"

"I believe that is true," I say as I connect to the computer to verify. "Yes. Three more selections to collect, all from India."

"Good, 'cause I had to pull Bashful and Grumpy off the main job to rearrange stuff."

"It is not a requirement to keep the two cultures segregated," I tell her.

"Look, Lex," she says, "You don't want your secret lair to be a cluttered mess. 'A place for everything, and everything in its place'." She punctuates her remark with a curt nod.

"It is not a 'lair'," I tell her. "It is a storage facility. It is remote and has been sealed to preserve the artefacts securely."

"Don't be so uptight, Lex. Every evil genius has a secret lair."

"It is a secure, climate-controlled storage facility. Its sole function is to preserve the value of the items stored here. It is not a lair and I am not an evil genius."

"Well, it's definitely not as cool as Dr. No's secret lair, but I guess it would have cost a few more million bucks to build swimming pools and stuff." She pauses and puts a finger to her chin. "Of course then I'd probably have to be the girl-toy in a bikini, and that is just not my bag."

She places a hand on my shoulder. I have actually become accustomed to the way people of the twentieth century will touch when they shift to a more serious level of conversation. "You're sure nobody's going to find this place in the forty-whatever years you've got it sealed up?"

"I can assure you, no one will be mounting expeditions or, for that matter, doing anything other than basic survival during the Dark Decades."

"You keep saying 'Dark Decades' like it's this super-terrible thing, but you won't give me any details. What's going to happen that's so awful?"

I admire her bright inquisitiveness and have already related information that I would never have entrusted to Sean Kelly. Perhaps it is because she is an enigma herself, plucked out of time, evidently photographed in three distinct centuries.

"Over two-thirds of the world's 10 Billion people are terminated during the Dark Decades," I tell her before my Chrono-Historian training overrides my response. She stares at me dumbfounded and I regret speaking.

"OK," she finally says softly, "I guess that's reason enough for the Doom and Gloom name. Looks like it really is Doom and Gloom."

I attempt to reverse her sudden dismal mood with a distraction, "I have purchased a selection of Indian cuisine. You have labored long enough without sustenance." Unsure of the actual duration of Jane's time at the storage unit I quickly check with the computer—four hours and twenty-three minutes.

She lifts her shoulders in her nonverbal twentieth-century expression of indifference. "I'm cool. A little hungry, though, now that you mention it." Her brow briefly furrows, "Hey, how long have *you* been at this? I mean, you know, how long are you actually gone between the few minutes of popping in and out?"

"Ninety-one days," I reply.

"That's so freaky," she says and slowly shakes her head, "Months for you, hours for me."

"It has been an exhausting task," I confess. "I am indebted to you for your supervision of the storage phase of this project."

She smiles at me. I believe I am beginning to comprehend Sean Kelly's attraction to her. I return the smile as I retrieve the packaged foodstuff.

"You know, now that I think about it," she says. "Uncle Carl visited New York a couple years ago and came back with stories about eating different international foods. Let me think a minute. Is there something called chicken vinganew?"

I twitch a connection. "Perhaps chicken vindaloo?"

Her eyebrows, as well as her shoulders, rise. "Maybe."

I check the ingredients. "It may contain flavor accents that your Western palate finds undesirable."

"Well, I know that your Formula Ten goo you let me taste contains no flavor at all, and my Western palate finds that undesirable, so let's give the vingaloo a try." She turns her attention to the nearest shelving robot and shouts to it, "Happy, you're in charge while I take a lunch break. I've been watching you and I think you might be management material."

I have explained to her that the robots are programmed to ignore all speech that does not contain words that can be interpreted as a task-oriented command, but she persists in her irrelevant comments. I theorize that it is similar to Sean Kelly's anthropomorphic treatment of his canine.

My involuntary urge to smile is allowed to go unsuppressed. Spending time in the environments of my ancient ancestors has altered my perspectives, and Father would, in all likelihood, find my adapted behavior inappropriate. I may need to give serious consideration to relocating to Mars and habitation with Mother when I return to my own time. My smile fades. *If* I am able to return to my own time.

Jane takes the package from me and looks around, scanning all corners of the room. "I guess there was never a plan for a lunch room," she remarks. She walks over to the closest portion of empty shelving and puts the take-out down, then moves to the nearest robot. "Grumpy, stop shelving and go unload the new shipment," she commands. The robot immediately changes course and begins its new assignment. I step out of its way.

"Sneezy," Jane calls, "Stop shelving and come to me." She walks back to the shelf where she placed her food. The robot follows her. "Legs, fully compressed, body, ninety degrees, arms, extend to match legs," she commands. The robot assumes the position she requested and Jane sits on its back surface. "Move six inches toward the shelf." She puts her hands on the shelf in front of her. "Move two more inches toward the shelf and extend arms and legs four inches."

Satisfied with the position of her makeshift bench, she turns her attention to the package of food. After studying it for a moment, she turns to me. "Little help, Lex?" she says. "How do I get into this?"

"It is a rather efficient packaging design," I tell her as I walk toward her. "The components lock firmly together for ease of transport, yet come apart with a simple twist." I grasp one of the top corners and twist as I pull. It comes free from the remaining mass. "I believe you will find eating utensils in this one." I twist the top off and she reaches in to extract the cutlery. She scrutinizes the fork.

"What's this made of?"

I twitch a connection to the computer for the answer as she begins to test the tinsel strength of the tines. "Given the year we are in there is a ninety-seven percent probability it is a soy-based plastic polymer."

She grips the points of the tines and applies pressure. "Plastic? Really? If I did this to a plastic fork from my time, it'd snap like a toothpick." She looked thoughtfully at the fork then at me. "Or maybe toothpicks don't snap anymore, either."

"Many of the people of your era and beyond were compelled to make improvements to ordinary objects as well as invent new ones," I tell her.

She taps the empty container against the shelf. "Isn't this plastic kind of overkill for takeout? I mean, this looks better than my mom's Tupperware."

"Actually, it is biodegradable. It has a six-month shelf life, then a chemical reaction turns it brown as a warning. Within another week, it will become compost."

"So tell me how far in the future we are again?" Jane asks.

"Currently, we are in 2059."

Jane closes her eyes in a manner I recognize as computation. "So in... ninety... years. We invent hard plastic containers that self-destruct into dirt? That freaks me out."

"It is less than seventy years from the first successful powered flight until man walks on the moon," I point out, "Does that freak you out?"

She looks away and her eyes track slightly upward as she is ponders the question. She looks back at me. "No, I guess not," she says, also gesturing with her shoulders, "Not sure why." She again looks contemplative. "Just seventy years, huh?"

"Actually sixty-five years, seven months, and three days," I state more accurately.

She laughs. "Oh, Lex," she says, "Sometimes I think you've got more in common with these robots than you do me."

Initially, I feel insulted, but I determine that Jane did not make her statement maliciously. I suddenly realize that she has attitudes similar to Sean Kelly with regard to factual data and logic.

"Well, anyway, freaky or not," she says, "I guess I should eat this before it gets cold."

"I believe you will find that there will be no significant change in internal temperature for several hours," I say. I notice her eyes are wider and her mouth is slightly ajar. I have learned to interpret this non-verbal expression as

353

either amazement or disbelief. She slowly shakes her head. "I guess DuPont was right. 'Better living through chemistry.' Far out."

She begins to look into several of the containers. "So is one of these chicken vingaloo?"

"As you twist off each individual container, the package will name its contents."

"Far out," she says and twists off the first container.

"Mango Lassi," the package says.

Jane turns to me. I interpret her facial expression as annoyance. "Not real helpful, Lex," she complains, "I still don't know what this stuff is!"

I connect to the computer for information. "Mango Lassi is a tropical fruit blended with a thin yogurt and served as a beverage."

She samples the Mango Lassi then makes popping sounds with her tongue and hard pallet and lips. "Kind of like..." She makes three more popping sounds. "... a melted Dreamsicle, but not exactly orangey. Good though. I like it."

Jane twists the remaining containers apart and is told the contents of each vessel. She eventually discovers the chicken vindaloo, as well as tandoori chicken, lamb korma, lamb tikka masala, samosa, naan, mango chutney, basmati rice, mulligatawny soup, and eggplant pakora. I relay descriptive information from the computer and she tastes each of the components.

"Pull up a robot, Lex," she says to me. "I can't eat all this stuff by myself, even if I only take the ones I like."

My initial thought is to reject her invitation. Obviously this collection of foodstuffs is nutritionally inferior to Formula Ten, but I find myself nodding acceptance as I consider the twentieth-century ritual of daily communal nourishment. Perhaps a conversation with Jane will also serve to reverse the mental fatigue that I experience.

I retrieve a liter of water and a spoon from Steffi and return to sit next to Jane. I take small portions from the eight containers that contain no animal flesh onto the plate fashioned from the bottom of the food parcel. Jane has already filled her own plate with samples from nearly all of the containers.

Lost in my own thoughts of nutritional value comparisons, as well as my novice experimentation with the various levels of stimulation of the flavor receptors in my mouth; I do not immediately recognize that Jane has halted her consumption and is staring at me.

"Your facial expression suggests you wish to ask me a question," I say to her.

She nods. "Yeah, I was just thinking. So, like, except for all the French wine you stowed in the extra-special climate controlled section of the lair, all this art stuff is, like, from either China or India."

"That is correct," I confirm.

"And I kind of get the idea that this year that we're in right now, is like, the start of Doom and Gloom?"

"Also correct."

"So..." She pauses and absently stirs her soup. "So... do we nuke them? I mean, I guess I can see how we'd get into it with Red China, but I don't get it with India. Do they, like, become communists, too?"

I find it difficult to reconcile the components of her question. "Who do you reference with the term 'we'?" I ask her and she initially appears puzzled.

"The country... our country," she says, "You know... the United States."

I am somewhat surprised by her response, given my own observations of Jane in her native environment. My only hypothesis is that an intrinsic Nationalism overrides other political views when the topic is global interaction of nations. "Thank you," I say, "I was confused by your suppositions. To answer your initial question: no, the United States does not 'nuke' them."

"Oh..." She pauses to think. "Then... the Russians?"

"No." I determine that she is going to continue to guess and decide to proactively intercede. "Political climates continually shift, Miss Carmichael. Your 1969 reference points are irrelevant in 2059. The conflict is between India and China. There is a long-term buildup of political friction between the two countries over many years. Scarce resources, burgeoning populations, and disputed borders all contribute to tensions between India and China that are not unlike what you experienced as the 'Cold War' between the U.S.S.R. and the United States. From the onset of the initial incident, it was only a matter of minutes before both countries depleted their arsenals and vaporized more than two billion human beings in the brief sortie."

Jane's face becomes one of quiet contemplation. I remain silent alongside her. She picks up her fork and pushes rice and lamb korma together. I assume she means to combine them for consumption, but she seems distracted and drags the fork repeatedly through the mixture.

"Lay it on me straight, future-man," she says without raising her eyes from the food she manipulates, "Does it bum you out at all that you guys from the future know all about what's going to happen and just let it go without lifting a finger to stop it?"

"It is a complex issue, Jane Carmichael," I attempt to explain, "I do personally feel remorse for the loss of innocent lives, but I also embrace the wisdom of nonintervention. Any effort to reverse such a cataclysmic event might result in a greater disaster that eliminates the human race entirely. The First Law of nonintervention is to be followed."

"Then what about me?" Jane asks in a tone that leads me to believe she assumes she has entered the definitive question to sway the argument to her favor.

"That strikes me as a rather broad, open-ended question which is totally unrelated to our current topic," I tell her.

"Come on, Lex," she states forcefully, "If you follow your rules, I should be dead. But since you found out that I'm somehow one of your ancient grandmas, suddenly you're not so keen on making me dead. So why's it OK to change the rules for me?"

Admiration of her debating tactics does little to appease how much I am disturbed by her argued point. "I have no acceptable answer to that question," I admit. She smiles in a manner I interpret as triumphant. "There is no logical explanation for you," I add, "You are an enigma."

Jane takes two bites of rice and lamb korma, then says, "I guess nothing should-be-dead-girl says is going to change your mind about blowing up the world, so let's get those last loads of trinkets in and get out of here."

I consider telling her that my inaction is not the catalyst which brings the events to bear, but decide a potential re-escalation of the argument is not prudent. I rise to make the departure she has suggested. I am half way to the S.T.E. when I hear her shout, "Hey, Lex!" I turn back to her. "Thanks for lunch. It was... interesting. Some of it was pretty good. Maybe I'll try it again sometime."

I smile and nod, then turn back to my original path. "Lex!" she calls again. I turn again. "Safe travels," she says, then holds one hand in the symbolic gesture her generation uses for the word 'peace'. I have to look at my own hand to assure myself that I have properly mimicked the configuration, then return the salute.

Jane has already resumed supervising the shelving robots as I slide into the S.T.E. and begin the process for another dimensional shift.

* * * * *

High in the Sierra Madras, Mexico, March 2121

It has been thirteen months since I last saw Jane Carmichael, although it has only been minutes since she last saw me.

"Did you get a good price for those last five cases of wine?" she asks as I slide out of the S.T.E. I actually cannot recall. Though it appeared to Jane as the final transaction, it was actually the first that I sold.

"I did," I reply, assuming that I speak the truth.

"So now do you have time to tell me what the heck happened here?"

"Could you rephrase the question with specifics, please?"

"One minute we're shutting down the dwarfs after the Lair is packed full of goodies, then after a little psychedelic ride in Steffi, you drop me here in the mostly empty Lair. You load up what looks like the last of the goodies, and pop out. Five minutes later, you pop back in." She looks down at my feet. "Are you wearing lifts? You seem a little taller." Throughout her narrative, Jane has been animated with a series of wild gestures. I smile. It is good to see her again. "Something funny?" she asks.

"No," I reply, "I am pleased to see you again." One of her eyebrows lifts as I continue, "Do you recall our conversation when you asked how long I was gone between trips?"

356

"You mean the one we had forty-five minutes ago?"

"Perhaps from your perspective. It has been more than a year for me." Her eyes widen. "I did not need your assistance for the dispersal phase, so the logical choice was to place you at the end of the process first. I then began the task of converting the various artefacts back to eCredits. I needed to complete small transactions over more than a decade. I have also made all of the financial investments necessary to accumulate the required fee for your cloning."

"So in the last five minutes, you've been gone a year?"

I have to resist the urge to report the exact chronology. "Yes."

"OK. So what year is it right now?"

"We are currently in the year 2121."

"So you jump me ahead from 2059 to 2121, then hop back to 2111 and start selling all the stuff?"

"Actually, I made my first transaction with the wine in this same year, but then I went back to 2107 to begin depleting the other items."

"And then for a year you've been hopping around from 2107 to 2121 selling stuff and then making big money on the stock market?"

I choose not to explain the complicated business modules that replace the concept she recognizes as the stock market. I also forgo relating the time spent in 1995 and 1996 finishing Alexis' junior year of high school. The simplicity of that time was actually a refreshing contrast to the stressful ventures of capitalism. I decide the best response is, "Yes."

"Man, that makes me exhausted just thinking about it." She looks around at the empty shelving. "So now what happens to the Lair?"

"It will remain as it is, other than natural entropy. Perhaps a future geologist will stumble upon it and speculate as to what civilization it belonged."

"What about the dwarfs?" she asks.

"They have been shut down."

"You're just going to leave them here?" I believe her tone indicates she does not approve of that outcome.

"Yes," I say, wondering if she is about to explode as Sean Kelly would.

"Can't you at least sell them to someone? Or even give them away, since you've got all the money you need."

"They are obsolete in 2121."

She stares at me but says nothing. I believe her facial expression is an odd mix of anger and sorrow. She steps wordlessly away from me and walks to each immobile robot and touches it. She speaks to the last one she touches. "Well, Sleepy, I guess you're going to get plenty of rest now."

Her eyes seem to glisten when she comes back to me. "So now what?" she asks me.

"We move to 2152 to initiate the creation of your clone."

"And then what?"

"Then we prepare you for integration into your new life."

"2152... I just realized that's like 200 years after I was born. I'm not going to live there, am I?"

"No."

"Then when?"

I slide into the S.T.E. and beckon Jane to join me. She reluctantly slides in. "We can discuss that in length as we travel," I tell her.

She sits quietly as I prepare the calculations for the jump forward. I feel sorrow that we are about to complete the final chapter of Jane Carmichael's life. More than that, though, I feel inept and frightened by the prospect of opening the chapter that will be Katherine Llygoden.

A note from the Author: Thanks for reading ... *Saves Nine*. If you enjoyed this book, I would greatly appreciate it if you could write a review and help spread the word. Feel free to Friend me on Facebook at https://www.facebook.com/llouis.lynam

Also please visit my Author pages and leave comments:

https://www.goodreads.com/author/show/8771851.Les_Lynam

http://www.amazon.com/-/e/B00O5GYROU

About the Author: Les Lynam (1954-) was born in Creston, Iowa, into a farming family which also included an older brother and two older sisters. The family farm was near the tiny community of Corning, Iowa, (birthplace of Johnny Carson). After graduating from Corning High School, he attended Central Missouri State University (renamed University of Central Missouri in 2006), graduating in 1976 with a Bachelor's degree in Mass Communications. After a short, mostly unsuccessful, attempt at running a print shop, he refocused and returned to a life of studies at the University of Missouri. He received an M.A./M.L.S in 1986 and began a new career as a librarian at Ward Edwards / James C. Kirkpatrick libraries at UCM. He took an early retirement on December 31, 2012 to pursue his lifelong dream of writing Science Fiction. His premier novel, "...Before You Leap", was first published in 2014 with hopes and dreams of many more to come. His favorite sub-genre of Science Fiction is Time-Travel, with Martian Colonies a close second. He has one son and three grandchildren.